"COMPUTER, PLAY MESSAGE," RICHARD ORDERED.

The voice that came over the bridge speakers was female, and as clear as if the woman speaking were standing there with them.

"*MSS Victor Hansen*, this is Captain Leora McFadden of the heavy freighter *Bearer of Burdens*, outbound for Stableford. You'll forgive me if I'm suspicious you're who you say you are: your ship IDs as *BPS Sanctification*. The few of us left alive in Earth space have been wondering when a Body warship would come back.

"But whoever you really are, there's no reason you shouldn't know the situation in Earth system before you do something foolish like taking someone aboard.

"Earth system is dead. A plague has killed the vast majority of the planet's population. Not all, apparently: someone calling himself the Avatar still broadcasts orders occasionally, but I haven't heard anybody responding to them. There have been a few bursts of communication that indicate groups of survivors are hanging on in various remote locations, but for the most part . . . Earth is one giant ball of corpses.

"So whoever you really are, *MSS Victor Hansen*, you've pretty much got the system to yourselves . . . and you're welcome to it. Just don't drink the water and don't breathe the air. . . ."

DAW Science Fiction Titles by
EDWARD WILLETT:

TERRA INSEGURA

MARSEGURO

LOST IN TRANSLATION

TERRA INSEGURA

Edward Willett

DAW BOOKS, INC.
DONALD A. WOLLHEIM, FOUNDER
375 Hudson Street, New York, NY 10014

**ELIZABETH R. WOLLHEIM
SHEILA E. GILBERT
PUBLISHERS**
www.dawbooks.com

First Printing, May 2009
1 2 3 4 5 6 7 8 9

DAW TRADEMARK REGISTERED
U.S. PAT. AND TM. OFF. AND FOREIGN COUNTRIES
—MARCA REGISTRADA
HECHO EN U.S.A.

PRINTED IN THE U.S.A.

This one is for my best friend in high school, John "Scrawney" Smith. All those after-school writing sessions together finally paid off!

Acknowledgements

My sincere thanks to my perspicacious and patient editor, Sheila Gilbert, whose insight makes every book better; to my hardworking agent, Ethan Ellenberg; and to Stephan Martiniere, whose gorgeous cover art delighted me the moment I saw it.

My heartfelt gratitude to my long-suffering (not to mention radiantly beautiful) wife, Margaret Anne, and my practically-perfect-in-every-way daughter, Alice, for sharing me with my computer.

A grateful tip of the hat to Dr. Robert Runte, who read this before anyone else did and offered sagacious advice.

And finally, effusive thanks to all those who read and enjoyed *Marseguro*. May you enjoy this one even more!

Chapter 1

*B*UMP.

Emily Wood jerked awake in the pilot's chair of the tiny sub, heart pounding. Her eyes flicked over the control panel, searching for red lights that would indicate they'd hit something.

But nothing had changed. All the indicators still glowed green. The sub continued to purr along on autopilot, and the Marseguroite ocean outside the transparent canopy remained as black and impenetrable as always, with dawn still hours away on the surface, a hundred meters above.

Emily glanced at the woman in the chair beside her, but her mother still slept, her graying hair an unruly halo around her head, the gill slits on the side of her neck showing the slightest trace of pink.

It was a sign that her sleep had been helped along by drugs: relaxed like that, gills dried out faster, so normally a Selkie's gills remained as tightly closed in air when the Selkie slept as when she was awake.

But it was also a sign Dr. Carla Christianson-Wood, formerly the foremost genetic engineer of Marseguro and a member of the Planetary Council, really was asleep, not just keeping her eyes closed because she couldn't be bothered to take an interest in anything around her.

These days, that was just as likely.

Not even the news of the impending marriage of Emily's sister Amy to her old school friend John Duval had stirred much response. But least she had boarded the sub under her own power, even if she hadn't said a word since they'd left Newhome Station five hours ago.

Emily sighed and settled back against the soft black pseudoleather. *Something in my dream,* she thought, though the dream remained clear in her mind and nothing had happened within it that should have jolted her out of it.

Richard had been in it, of course. He often showed up in her dreams now, more than a week after he had left Marseguro aboard *MSS Victor Hansen,* bound for Earth. She both missed him and worried about him. No one knew what the *Victor Hansen* would find on the home planet. If the Body Purified remained in power ...

She didn't like to think about that possibility. If the Body Purified remained in power, Richard faced imprisonment or death.

But the other possibility was maybe even more horrific: that the crew of the *Victor Hansen* would find Earth devastated by the plague the Marseguroites had created to kill the Holy Warriors who had attacked and occupied their world six months ago.

The *Victor Hansen* carried vaccine, and the knowledge of how to make more ... but would there be anyone left alive on Earth to save?

The crew, in other words, faced a mission fraught with uncertainty and danger ...

... rather like her relationship with Richard.

With a finger, she traced the stitching of the pseudoleather covering the arm of the chair. She and Richard had fought together. They'd become friends ... more than friends. She'd thought—fantasized—about their becoming lovers ... but it hadn't happened. Not yet.

Once, she'd thought ... but the moment had passed.

She hadn't been ready. She'd told him so. He'd taken it well ... but another moment hadn't come.

His fault, or hers? She wasn't sure. They'd been working apart for much of the past few months, Richard focused on bringing the former *BPS Sanctification* back to life as *MSS Victor Hansen*, while she'd had her mother to worry about, and her sister Amy, and the job she'd taken on coordinating construction of the new deep-sea habitats the Planetary Council had started to build as insurance against further attacks or natural disasters. They'd hardly had a moment together since they'd ridden the crippled *Sanctification* down from orbit.

And now he was gone. Maybe for good.

She shook her head. *No*, she thought fiercely. *He'll be back. He promised.*

As if *that* guaranteed anything.

She checked the board one more time, then settled back in the chair and closed her eyes, hoping to recapture the dream. She and Richard had been walking along the shore of ...

Bump. Bump.

She jerked upright again. No denying it this time!

She scanned her controls. Nothing, but the little sub didn't have the greatest suite of sensors, and those it had were all focused in front of it, to guard against collisions with other vessels or one of Marseguro's sea predators.

Could it be a daggertooth? Emily had never heard of one of the killer whale-sized creatures trying to attack a sub, but ...

Of course, it could be something entirely new. Except for one island continent, the whole world was ocean, almost completely unexplored. Emily felt a surge of excitement. *Here there be monsters? If I could get a photo of a new species ...*

She still wasn't worried. A predator might check out the sub, but since it obviously wasn't edible, the creature would lose interest in a moment. Maybe as it swam away, she could . . .

And then Emily was thrown forward hard, only the pilot's harness she kept fastened by habit keeping her from smashing her nose into the control panel.

Her mother opened her eyes at last. "Emily? What's happening?" She almost sounded scared, which perversely pleased Emily. Any real emotion from her mother was so rare these days she leaped at it like a drowning landling lunging at a twig, hoping it was a harbinger of recovery.

"I don't know," Emily said. "Something has grabbed us, I think. We're at a dead stop." She peered uselessly through the canopy. The sub's headlights showed only plankton, swirling in twin cylinders of light that faded away into darkness within a dozen meters. And still nothing showed on the sensors. "It's under us, whatever it is. It must be a predator, something bigger than we've ever . . ."

She stopped. Her mother's eyes had closed again, the drugs pushing her back into sleep. Emily was talking to herself.

The floor canted. They were descending. Emily glanced at the depth gauge. Pressurized, the sub was good to three hundred meters. She had no idea how deep the ocean was at this point, but she'd bet it was deeper than that. If this thing pulled them far enough down . . .

She could flood the sub. Flooded, it might survive all the way to the bottom. But she and her mother would not, not unless they put on deep-water suits. Even before the pressure crushed them, they'd asphyxiate, their gills, though far more efficient than any fish's, unable to draw enough oxygen.

Getting her mother into a deep-water suit would have been a nightmare under ideal conditions. Now . . . she looked at the older Selkie woman, once more asleep, gills once more over-relaxed. *How many pills did she take?*

A strange vibration rolled through the sub. It felt mechanical, not biological, and it was followed by a series of clanks that were most definitely mechanical: metal against metal. Then came a high-pitched whine that set Emily's teeth on edge. *Drilling,* she thought. *It must be another sub. We've been grabbed by another sub, and someone is trying to get in.*

But that made no sense. If someone needed them, they could wait until their next radio check-in, due in an hour. No one would send a sub to grab them in the middle of the ocean. No one would have any reason to.

Unless . . .

Emily's already oversized eyes widened even further. "Shit!" She scrabbled at the buckles of her harness, got free, then scrambled out of her chair and plunged through the cockpit's after hatch into the hold.

Like the rest of the sub, the hold was full of air on this trip, because they were carrying all the food for the upcoming wedding reception, including a magnificent wedding cake, five tiers high, with Amy and John re-created in colored sugar atop the highest layer. The cake resided in a large box placed safely on the floor. As Emily burst into the hold, she saw the box rise on one side, then tip over. It crashed to the floor, breaking open and spilling pink icing and yellow cake across the decking. The spun-sugar Amy and John skittered across the floor but somehow remained intact.

A metal tube protruded into the hold from where the box had been, shiny silver shavings of metal scattered around it and clinging to its tip.

Something hissed. White mist spewed from the tube. Emily took one abortive step toward the deep-water suits racked at the back of the hold before the floor somehow rose up and smacked her on the cheek. She found herself staring at the sugar figures of Amy and John, lying in a welter of crumbs. They seemed to whirl around Emily in a bizarre wedding dance, and then everything went black.

"Impressive, isn't it?"

Richard Hansen just barely managed not to jump as the voice sounded in his left ear. It wouldn't do for the captain of the *Marseguro Star Ship Victor Hansen* to appear anything less than perfectly calm at all times. It particularly wouldn't do to flinch violently in zero gravity, which could send him on an unintended journey down the cylindrical corridor, bouncing off the padded walls as he went . . . and given his stomach's usual reaction to violent maneuvers in zero-G, possibly throwing up as well. And it *particularly*, particularly wouldn't do for Richard to give the owner of the voice the satisfaction of knowing he'd been startled.

"Isn't it," Richard said mildly, without looking around. "Hello, Andy."

An amused snort, and Andy King drifted across the corridor to cling to the webbing next to Richard, and look out with him into the main equipment hold of the *Victor Hansen*. Assault vehicles, cargo shuttles, boats, submarines, ground vehicles—some armed and armored, some not—small airplanes (ditto), racks of personal weapons and body armor: there was enough matériel in the hold to equip a small army: a lot more of an army than they had, for sure, since their entire ship's company numbered seventy-eight souls, fifty-two Selkies and twenty-six nonmods. But then, if it came to fighting—if, against all their best estimates, the Body Purified still held sway over Earth and refused to even talk to them—they didn't stand the proverbial snowball's chance in hell.

Or, as they used to say on Marseguro, a landling's chance in deep water, though the term "landling" was no longer considered polite when talking about a nongenetically modified human. ("Normal" was even worse, since it implied Selkies *weren't*.)

Richard realized Andy was looking at *him*, not at the equipment ranged around the hold, and turned to face his first officer.

"You're thinking again," Andy said, as though accusing him of a misdemeanor, if not a capital crime. He was a bald-headed, round-faced, brown-skinned, short-but-muscular Selkie. He wore a black landsuit: one hold of the *Victor Hansen* had been flooded, lit and equipped with oxygenators to provide the Selkies with a swimming area, but most Selkies still wore landsuits while on duty to enable them to remain at their stations as long as necessary in the event of an emergency.

Like the rest of the crew, Andy King had no space experience. But he had captained the largest ocean-going vessels, surface and sub, that Marseguro boasted, and he knew how to gain a crew's respect and keep it disciplined. He'd also become, in the few months that Richard had known him, a good friend.

"Does it show?" Richard said wryly.

Andy made a circular gesture near his vestigial ears. "Smoke," he said. "Burning smells."

Richard laughed. "Well, I promise not to do it again."

Andy's smile faded. "I didn't just come to insult you—respectfully, of course," he said. "I've got news. Planetary Communications forwarded it just before we entered branespace."

"Nothing good, I take it."

Andy shook his head. "No. O'Sullivan's been murdered."

"*What?*" O'Sullivan, the former Holy Warrior who had thrown in his lot with Richard and Emily aboard this very ship and done more than anyone else to help her return to space under her new name, had sent good wishes to the crew just two days before, as they broke orbit. Richard couldn't believe he'd been killed. And murder? Crimes of any sort were rare on Marseguro; murder almost unknown. Richard didn't even know when the last had been committed.

Unless you counted all the people killed by Holy Warriors in the attack he had facilitated on the planet.

He shoved that thought away, as he did a dozen times a day. "Do they have a suspect?"

"They have the killer himself," Andy said. "A Selkie. I didn't recognize the name. He shot O'Sullivan dead in the street, then slung his body over his shoulders, walked to Peaceforcer headquarters, dumped the body on the doorstep, and turned himself in. Said he was avenging his daughter. No Holy Warrior could be allowed to breathe the air of Marseguro after what they'd done, that kind of thing." Andy shook his head. "There's a lot of anger, a lot of tension between land . . . nonmods and Selkies. O'Sullivan was a hero to a lot of nonmods. I'd say the tension just got worse."

"Which is why this mission is so important," Richard said. "We're Selkies and nonmods—Marseguroites, all—working together for the good of people we haven't met, in the name of our common humanity." He couldn't help smiling a little. "It's a team-building exercise."

Andy winced. "I've always hated those."

Richard changed the subject. "Well, you claim you didn't come down here just to insult me, and as it happens, I didn't come down here just to be insulted. I'm looking for Smith. He's supposed to be in there," he indicated the hold, "somewhere, but I don't . . ."

"Here I am, Captain."

This time Richard did jump. So did Andy. Neither let go of the webbing, though, and so were at least spared the embarrassment of floating away.

Smith, the *Victor Hansen*'s quartermaster, was a stolid nonmod with a uniform air of grayness about him: short gray hair, short gray beard, gray eyes. His skin had a grayish tint. Even his pale-green standard-issue jumpsuit looked a little gray around the edges, Richard thought.

His first name, of course, was John.

"You wanted to see me?" Richard said—a little too quickly, to cover his startlement.

"Yes, Captain," Smith said. "I found something you should see . . ."

Ten minutes later Richard, Andy, and Smith floated inside the quartermaster's cube-shaped zero-G office. Most of the senior staff operated in the ship's rotating habitat ring, where something approaching normal gravity existed. The quartermaster needed to be close to his stores though, like the rest of them, his sleeping quarters were in gravity.

The room's walls were, naturally, gray. (Richard had sometimes wondered—though not enough to actually ask the computer—if the *Sanctification*'s quartermaster had also been named Smith; he couldn't remember a thing about the man, though he must have met him sometime during the two-week-long flight from Earth.) Glowstrips broke up the plain metal walls at meter intervals, and almost-invisible seams marked the various panels that could be opened to access storage compartments—and a vidscreen, which Smith now activated.

"As you know, Captain—"

Richard sighed. "Please don't start your explanation like that, Smith. It makes me feel like I'm trapped in a bad adventure novel."

Smith blinked, which was as close as he ever came to looking flustered. "Very well, Captain. Well . . . um . . . as you . . . um . . . that is, we've been having difficulty penetrating the quartermaster's personal security to access his records, which for some reason are segregated from the main ship's data store. As a result, we've been uncertain how much of the ship's original supplies remain aboard. Thanks to our own manual inventory we know what we have, but we haven't known what we're missing." Smith's thin lips curled up in a tight smile. "Until now. Computer, display file Smith 23A."

The vidscreen lit up with a series of text entries, accompanied by small pictures of various items. "I've gained access," Smith said, entirely unnecessarily.

Andy whooped. Richard didn't go that far, but he gave the quartermaster a huge grin. "Fabulous! How'd you do it?"

Smith snorted. "The quartermaster's software encryption was unbreakable. However . . ." He reached into the right breast pocket of his jumpsuit and drew out a small rod that glittered like a jewel in the light from the glowstrips. "I found this taped to the underside of his bed. It's a data crystal, and it unlocks the files."

Hanging on to the webbing with one hand, Richard shook Smith's hand with the other. "Great work, John."

Smith shook his head. "I should have looked for something like that sooner. But thank you, Captain."

"So what have you found out?" Andy said. He gestured at the display, still flicking automatically through page after page of records. "This kind of thing makes my eyes glaze over."

"As near as I can tell, we're primarily missing only what you would expect—some small arms, ammo, personal armor, that sort of thing. However, there are two major items which remain unaccounted for." Smith turned back to the vidscreen. "Computer, display items UWV108 and ASV03."

The screen blanked, then showed two images side by side. Andy and Richard leaned in. "A sub," Richard said.

"Pretty big one, by the look of it," Andy agreed.

"And a shuttle?" Richard looked closer. "It doesn't look like any of the others, though . . . it's huge!"

"The sub is a Jonah-class attack submarine," Smith said. "Crew of eight. Designed to sneak up on other subs and either sink them or board them. A nice toy, if we're ever able to retrieve it. The shuttle, though . . ." Smith paused. The thin smile broadened; for a moment Richard thought the quartermaster was actually going to show his teeth in a grin. "It's something special. It's a GDPSS." He looked at them expectantly.

Richard glanced at Andy. Andy shrugged. They both looked back at Smith, who sighed.

"A Grand Deacon Personal Star Shuttle. It's twice the size of any other shuttle aboard, and that's not all: it has Cornwall engines."

"It's a mini-starship?" Richard took another look. "A second ship for our navy?"

"If we can find it," Smith said. "According to these records, it was off-loaded the day after the attack. Presumably, it was intended to take Grand Deacon Ellers back to Earth once Marseguro was pacified, so he could move on to other things while *Sanctification* remained on station."

"But we've seen no sign of it," Andy said. "Wouldn't we have noticed . . . ?"

"Computer," Richard said.

"Yes, Captain," the computer replied instantly.

"Computer, whereabouts of shuttle . . ." he looked at Smith.

"*Divine Will*," Smith supplied.

". . . *Divine Will*."

"*Divine Will* is not on board," the computer said.

"I know that, you . . ." Richard stopped himself. He was pretty sure arguing with the computer was not a captainly thing to do. He tried again. "Computer, State the last known whereabouts of the shuttle *Divine Will*."

"*Divine Will* is on Marseguro."

Richard sighed. "Computer, *where* on Marseguro is the shuttle *Divine Will*?"

"Precise coordinates unknown."

"Why?" No answer. It's just a machine, Richard reminded himself for the umpteenth time that day. "Computer, *why* are precise coordinates of shuttle *Divine Will* unknown?"

"Shuttle *Divine Will* launched without proper authorization on Day 22 of current mission. Shuttle descended erratically. Shuttle disappeared from ship's sensors beneath ocean surface at coordinates . . ." It reeled off a string of letters and numbers.

They meant nothing to Richard. "Computer, display those coordinates on a map of Marseguro."

The screen obligingly shifted to a map. Richard recognized the northern tip of the island continent at the bottom of the screen. A red spot glowed in the waters offshore. Andy pointed at it. "It went down a good fifteen kilometers offshore. And way north of any settlements or habitats. No wonder we had no idea."

"Day 22," Richard said thoughtfully. "That's when the plague hit the ship. Whoever took the shuttle must have realized what was happening and tried to escape. Probably collapsed or died during the descent, and the ship hit the water and sank. Computer," he said, raising his voice, "was impact of shuttle *Divine Will* sufficient to destroy it?"

"Negative," the computer said.

"Computer, what is the maximum depth of water shuttle can withstand?"

"Two thousand meters," the computer replied.

Richard whooped. "Another starship, waiting for us!"

"If we get back," Andy said.

Randy waved him off. "We'll send a null-brane pulse as soon as we emerge from branespace." He turned to Smith. "Great work, John," he said. "Congratulations. If this were a proper military, I'd promote you."

"Thank you, Captain," Smith said. His face actually colored a little.

Richard and Andy took their leave, pulling themselves along the webbing toward one of the transport platforms that would whisk them along the ship's giant central shaft to the habitat ring. "So tell me, Captain," Andy said as they went, "which are you looking forward to more when we emerge from branespace in two weeks: letting Marseguro know where to look for a second starship, or talking to a certain Selkie girl?"

Richard resisted the temptation to kick him. "I doubt I'll get to talk to Emily," he said. "I'm sure she's busy. Amy's wedding."

"Uh-huh." Andy was quiet for a moment. "I envy you," he said at last. "I don't have anybody waiting for me on Marseguro."

Richard said nothing. Most of the crew didn't: it had been planned that way. It was one reason he'd kept his distance from Emily over the past few months. There had been that one night, after the victory celebration, they'd kissed, and they'd almost . . .

. . . but she'd pulled away, said she wasn't ready. And afterward he had kicked himself for even letting things progress that far, knowing he would soon be off on this dangerous adventure. If anything happened to him . . . well, she was young. She was Selkie. He didn't want her pining after him instead of getting on with her life.

If he made it back, then maybe . . .

"Emily is her own woman," Richard said. "She may not be waiting at all."

Now why did I say that? he wondered. The possibility stung.

Well, whether she's waiting for me or not, I'm glad she's safe back there on Marseguro. "Hurry up, Number One," Richard said over his shoulder. "We're going to be late for the staff meeting."

"Race you to the platform," Andy said, and after that, they were working too hard to talk.

For the moment, that suited Richard just fine.

Chapter 2

EMILY WOKE IN THE DARK to confusion and a pounding headache, wrists bound behind her back so tightly her hands felt numb. Where was she? What had happened to the sub's cockpit?

Where's Mom?

She blinked. It wasn't completely dark. Maybe it would have been to a nonmod, but her Selkie eyes saw a faint, indirect glow, and as her vision cleared and the headache receded slightly, she could see enough to get a sense of the space she lay in. Small, but . . . living quarters of some kind? Certainly she lay on a bed, not on a bare floor. And that looked like a tiny sink and counter over there. *Submarine quarters,* she thought. *But not our sub. And not any sub I've ever been in on Marseguro.*

That really left only one other possibility, and so when the door suddenly opened and flooded the tiny space with light so bright it made her wince and turn her head away, she wasn't surprised to glimpse a man in the powder-blue uniform of the Holy Warriors.

She'd hoped to never see that uniform again. She'd seen enough of them, generally splattered with blood, during the battle to free Marseguro from the Body Purified's occupation, and the long cleanup afterward.

Why was this Holy Warrior still alive, when the plague had taken all of his comrades?

"She's awake," the man said. Emily turned her head back to see a different Holy Warrior take the first one's place. Both men were bearded, something she'd never seen in the original force. *Makes sense if they've been hiding in a sub all this time . . . but they're doomed now. Mom and I are carriers of the plague. Everyone on Marseguro carries it. It's only a matter of . . .*

"Bring her out," the second man said. "I want to talk to her." He stepped out again, and the first man bulled into the room, grabbed her by the arms, and hauled her to her feet. She tried to kick him, but he spun her around and propelled her headfirst into the narrow corridor outside the door. Then he marched her down it to what was probably one of the largest spaces in the sub, since its curved walls suggested it extended the full width of the hull. Some sort of wardroom, furnished with four unpainted metal tables bolted to the walls, two on each side, each with four attached, red-painted chairs.

Three more Holy Warriors stood at the far end of the wardroom. Her mother sat in one of the chairs, arms tied like hers, face cheek-down on the metal table, eyes closed.

"Mom!" Emily tried to pull free. The second man she'd seen said, "Let her go," and a moment later she fell to her knees at her mother's side.

Dr. Christianson-Wood's eyes were open just a slit, but only the whites showed, glittering in the light. Her skin looked waxy. But she was breathing. Emily gulped a sigh of relief. For a moment she'd thought . . .

"What's wrong with her?" said the Holy Warrior who seemed to be in charge.

Emily struggled to her feet and turned to face him. "Who are you?" she demanded.

"Don't tell me you don't recognize the uniform," the man growled.

"I know you're Holy Warriors. I want to know your name. I want to know who I'm talking to."

The man cocked his head. "Fair enough. After all, I know who you are, Emily Wood. I'm Alister Stone, commander of the Body Purified submarine *Promise of God*."

"What do you want, Commander Stone?"

"We've got what we want, Emily Wood," Stone said. "We've got your mother."

"And me?"

He shrugged. "You're incidental. Bit of a nuisance, really. Unless you can help us talk to your mother, I might decide to just put you out the air lock. At depth."

Emily ignored the threat. "Why do you want my mother? Why do you need to talk to her?"

Stone's lip curled. "Because she designed the filthy plague that murdered every other Holy Warrior on this planet."

Emily felt as if he'd slapped her. "How—"

"How do I know? Because we've been down here since it started, listening. We know what happened to all of our comrades. We know what happened to *BPS Retribution*. We know about the vaccine—and we stole some for ourselves, so don't start listening for a cough."

"You've been hiding out—underwater—for six months?"

"Lots of rations on board these subs, Miss Wood. Enough to keep us going this long."

"But ... why? What do you hope to accomplish?" Emily looked down at her unconscious mother. "What do you want with my mother?"

"Retribution," the Holy Warrior said. "Like the name of our former ship."

"But that won't get you anything in the long run," Emily said. "When we don't show up at our destination, there'll be a search. Subs, surface ships ... they'll find you. And then you'll have to deal with a whole planet full of people who'll know what you've done. How long do you think you'll last then?"

"Oh, there'll be a search," Stone said. "And they'll find exactly what we left them to find: debris—wedding presents, that sort of thing—" he showed his teeth in a wolfish grin,"—floating on the surface, and in the deep-sea trench you were crossing when we grabbed you, the flattened remnants of your sub, five hundred meters below its crush depth."

John ... Amy ... Emily imagined them getting the news, their grief, the wedding postponed ... "You can't hide forever," she snarled. "Your rations will run out. Your recycling equipment will foul. You'll have to surface ..."

Stone's grin widened. "Will we?"

"No sub remains underwater forever," Emily said.

"We're not going to be remaining on the sub." Stone moved closer, uncomfortably so, until his face was only centimeters from hers. "Listen to me, Emily Wood, and listen well. We are going to board the shuttle *Divine Will*, lying sunken but intact in relatively shallow water just fifty kilometers from our current position. We are going to take that shuttle, and your mother, back to Earth. And then we will hand her over to the Body Purified for trial and punishment, and accept our reward from the Avatar with all due humility."

"But the plague—" Emily said. "You must know—"

"That it returned to Earth with *Retribution*?" Stone shook his head. "Ridiculous. Do you really think something your mother cooked up in a lab on this water-soaked rock could overwhelm the Body Purified on Earth itself? It may have sickened a few people, but it won't have swept the planet as you naively hope. The Body Purified still rules Earth, Miss Wood. Count on it." He leaned in even closer, until she could smell his slightly sour breath and feel its heat on her face, and lowered his voice to an intense, vicious whisper. She forced herself not to flinch away. "You'd *better* count on it. Because if we get to Earth and find no authorities for us to answer to, we will use you two Selkie bitches as God Itself intended men to use women, and discard the broken bloody remains without a moment's regret. Because never forget, Miss Wood . . . you . . . are . . . not . . . human!"

Emily felt an old familiar rage building inside her, the rage that had driven her during the battle for Marseguro, when she had watched men die horribly—at her own hand, from the plague, and at the hands of others—without pity or regret. "You try," she snarled, "and I'll snap your spine like a twig. Because I'm stronger than you, Alister Stone. Stronger, and faster, and smarter. Not human? Maybe not in your eyes. But if I'm not human, it's because I'm better, not worse." She showed her teeth. "New and improved. Humanity 2.0."

Stone's lips tightened and his eyes narrowed. "Blasphemy!" he spat—literally; she felt the spittle hit her cheek, but she forced herself to ignore it. For a moment she was sure he would slap her, but instead he stepped back. His mouth curved in a cold smile. "You may indeed be stronger than me," he said. "But your mother . . ." He glanced at Dr. Christianson-Wood. ". . . is not. Would you prefer we start with her?"

Emily stiffened. "Don't touch her."

"We won't . . . for now." He gestured to the first Holy Warrior Emily had seen. "Release her hands, Abban." He looked back at Emily. "Look after your mother. I want her awake and talking when we present her to the Avatar. But cause any trouble, and I'll reconsider the advantages of presenting her to the Avatar catatonic . . . or dead."

Emily fought the fury inside her, tried to turn it cold instead of hot. *While there's life, there's hope*, she thought. It wouldn't do either of them any good if she got herself killed. Her mother needed her. "I'll behave," she said finally.

"I know you will," said Stone. He looked at Abban

again. "We're only a couple of hours from the *Divine Will*. She can stay in here with her mother. Keep a close eye on her."

"Aye, aye, sir." Abban saluted.

Stone turned to the others. "Pass the word," he said. "I want everything ready to transfer to *Divine Will* the instant we arrive."

A chorus of aye-ayes followed, and the men dispersed fore and aft. Stone gave Emily one more long, hard look, then went forward.

Emily sat beside her mother. "Mom," she said. She glanced at Abban, who stood by the forward hatch. He watched her, his hand resting on the black grip of the sidearm in his belt holster. She looked back at her mother. "Mom, can you hear me?"

Slowly, as though emerging from a fog, her mother's face somehow . . . came into focus. She raised her head from the table, blinked at Emily, and managed a small smile. "Emily," she said. The cheek that had been pressed against the table was bright pink. "Have I been sleeping?"

"Yes, Mom," Emily said carefully. "Don't you remember what happened?"

"We were . . . going somewhere?" Her mother frowned, and looked around the Spartan wardroom. "Have we arrived? Where are we?" Then her eyes drifted over to the Holy Warrior in his distinctive blue uniform. She stared for a moment, her eyes growing wider and wider—and then she screamed, the sound bright and piercing as a laser. Abban whipped the gun from his holster and pointed it at them, holding it in both hands, finger on the trigger.

Running footsteps sounded, and a moment later Stone and four crewmen, whether the same ones as before or others Emily couldn't tell, burst into the room. "What have you done?" Stone shouted above her mother's unending screams. He shoved Abban's gun down; the Holy Warrior lowered it but didn't holster it.

"Shhh, shhh," Emily said, kneeling by her mother, putting her arm around her, but her mother would only look at the Holy Warriors, eyes jumping from one to the next. Emily stood and confronted Stone. "Get them out!" she shouted. "Get them all out!"

Stone hesitated, then nodded. "Everyone out," he said. "Close and bolt the doors. Abban, you stand guard outside the forward hatch. Biccum, stand guard aft. Move."

The Holy Warriors exited, all of them this time, Abban the last to go, looking back over his shoulder at them as he finally holstered his gun.

The hatches closed, leaving Emily alone with her mother. Dr. Christianson-Wood's screams tapered off, but her eyes still darted around the room as though she expected the Holy Warriors to reappear from thin air.

Maybe she does, Emily thought. "It's okay, Mom, they're gone." She knelt and put her arm around her mother once more.

Her mother turned wide, stricken eyes to her. "Ghosts!" she whispered. "Ghosts, Emily. Didn't you see them? They're all dead . . . all the Holy Warriors . . . I killed them . . . I killed them all . . . but they were here! They were here a minute ago!" She grabbed Emily's hand. "They were here!" But then her face softened and her eyelids drooped. She blinked. "Weren't they?"

"They were here, Mom," Emily said. She squeezed her mother's shoulder. "But they're not ghosts. They're survivors. They were in this sub when the plague hit. They figured out what was going on, and they got hold of some hypervaccine somewhere. They're immune." She took a deep breath. "And they don't think Earth is dead, Mom. In fact . . ." She swallowed. "In fact, they're planning to take us there."

But her mother's eyes were almost closed, and Emily didn't know how much she'd really heard and understood. "Don't be silly . . ." Dr. Christianson-Wood murmured. "We don't have a spaceship. Richard took it."

And then she was asleep again, head dropping heavily onto Emily's shoulder.

Emily held her as once her mother had held her. She didn't cry. She wished she could.

In the sudden silence, all she could hear was the steady thrumming of the sub's propellers, the hiss of ventilation . . . and her own thoughts, which were not very comfortable companions.

Her future had suddenly narrowed to only two possibilities. The best: imprisonment on Earth, a life of slave labor. The worst: horrible death or gang rape. Oh, she'd meant what she'd said to Stone, but of course they could tie her down or drug her or in some other way keep her from fighting back. She would struggle, but they'd have her in the end.

So forget about her. Her focus had to be on her mother. She turned her head, studied her mother's slack, waxy face. Dr. Christianson-Wood had always been so vital, so in charge of herself and whatever situation she found herself in. But something had broken inside her when she'd heard that Chris Keating had taken her plague to Earth.

On Marseguro, it had been one hundred percent fatal among nonmodded, unvaccinated humans. Dr. Christianson-Wood's colleagues believed—hoped—it would not be quite as deadly on Earth, because a portion of its effectiveness depended on interaction with Marseguro-native viruses. But only a portion: it seemed likely it would be at least as deadly as Ebola-Zaire, which, before effective treatments and vaccines were developed in the early twenty-first century, had sometimes killed as many as nine out of ten.

And, unlike Ebola, it was easily spread. It could pass from person to person with a breath or a cough or a handshake, or linger in the very air of a building. Worse, most small mammals—rats, mice, cats, dogs—could carry it without themselves being infected. So, probably, could birds.

Dr. Christianson-Wood herself had been unable to provide any input: in her mental breakdown, she seemed to have rejected all the knowledge and experience that had enabled her to make the plague in the first place. She could not or would not draw on it: she wouldn't even make the effort.

Her mental breakdown had been followed by a physical one. She had always been strong, athletic. Now she looked weak and underfed, and her hair, still mostly blonde just months ago, was now almost entirely gray.

In a strange reversal, Emily had become the strong one, the grown-up, the one who had to have all the answers and make everything all right when the world seemed broken.

She took a deep breath. She *would* be strong, whatever the future held. For her mother. For herself.

And one thread of bright hope wove its way through her personal tapestry of darkness, a thread she held in her mental grip like a lifeline: they were going to Earth . . . and so was Richard.

When they reached the home world, *MSS Victor Hansen* would already be there. And if things on Earth were as bleak as the Marseguroites thought, she might be the only ship in orbit, the only ship to greet the shuttle when it arrived.

By Emily's count, Richard still owed her several rescues. She hoped he'd get a chance to even the score.

Chris Keating crouched in an empty garbage bin and listened to wild dogs howling in the streets of the City of God.

More dogs than people inhabited the city these days. Chris hadn't seen a human being now in a month, unless you counted the flotilla of aircraft that had roared low over the burned-out shell and toppled spire of the House of the Body two weeks ago. Chris had stood in the rubble-strewn street outside the Body's central place of worship, torched at some point during the days of violence that followed the outbreak of the plague, and shouted himself hoarse, jumping, waving, begging the Avatar and his surviving followers to take him with them, but of course they hadn't heard him. Even if they had, they probably would have left him behind.

God Itself has some other role in mind for me, Chris had comforted himself. *God wouldn't have gone to such extraordinary lengths to ensure I would be on Earth at this time if I weren't part of Its plan.*

He still wondered how Richard Hansen had done it. For a long time he'd been convinced that the deaths on Marseguro, on board *Sanctification* and, later, *Retribution*, had been a sophisticated chemical attack planned by Hansen. But he'd had to change his mind shortly after he'd reached Earth.

He'd tried to radio Earth Control when *Retribution* arrived in orbit, but though he'd been able to send a final message to Marseguro as the ship had left that system, he no longer had communications control by the time he reached Earth: the computer kept telling him that attempts had been made to compromise its programming and it had therefore initiated Security Protocol something-or-other. He would have told them what had happened on the ship, and they would have taken precautions, even though at that point he still hadn't believed the plague was a plague.

Why should he? He'd worked in a genetics lab. It was impossible—absolutely impossible—for the Marseguroites to have created a plague, specifically targeting normal humans, in the few days that had passed between the Holy Warriors' initial attack and the day the Holy Warriors started dying. Therefore, it *couldn't* be a plague. It had to be something else, most likely a chemical agent of some kind that Richard Hansen had somehow smuggled aboard.

The Holy Warriors who had boarded the ship, and

taken him off of it, and brought him to the City of God, had been looking for armed intruders or mutinous crew, not viruses or poisons. And shortly after they detained him and took him to the Holy Compound in the City of God, they began to die.

"Damn Hansen," Chris muttered, as he did several times a day. He'd obviously been wrong about the deaths being caused by a poison. But he was obviously right about the Selkies having been incapable of creating such a finely tuned plague. The only thing he could figure was that Victor Hansen, creator of the Selkies, had himself designed the disease organism before he died, and that Victor's grandson, Richard, had brought that knowledge to the Selkies as part of his own twisted plan to gain power.

Because if there was one thing Chris was absolutely certain about, it was that every disaster that had befallen him—and the Body Purified, of course, but especially *him*—could be laid squarely at the feet of Richard Hansen.

By the time the Body Purified had realized what was happening, the plague was out of control. Incredibly infectious, incredibly deadly, carried by animals—there had been no controlling it. It had swept the world like a tsunami.

The hospitals filled with the infected, then overflowed with the dead. Few bodies ever made it to the morgues. Mass graves were dug and bodies bulldozed into them by the dozens, but soon enough there was no one to drive the bulldozers. The Holy City's infrastructure continued functioning on automatic. Lights stayed on, water flowed, Body hymns wafted from loudspeakers five times a day. Bots emptied the already-empty garbage bins, like the one he crouched in now, and roamed the streets searching for debris, finding little but the occasional leaf or animal corpse: the human bodies had all been cleared away long since, delivered to the back doors of morgues, where they piled up in rotting, reeking heaps. Chris had gotten downwind of one a few days ago and had retched till he'd thought his stomach would come out his nose.

The howling had faded. Chris poked his head up, then climbed out and brushed dirt from his stylish black pants and tight-fitting red shirt. No point dressing in rags when the city was full of unused clothes, he'd decided. Fresh meat and produce had become impossible to find, but the city contained enough frozen, canned, and irradiated food to last him the rest of his life.

For his lodgings, he'd selected the penthouse of Paradise on Earth, the tallest and swankiest hotel in the city. The smell of decay wasn't so bad fifty floors up: down here on the streets, it hung over everything, fainter than it had been, but not gone.

Not by a long shot.

He'd come out today to pick up some warmer clothes from Splendid Raiment, his favorite clothing store. The leaves were starting to turn, and the nights were cooler than they had been. The City of God, built on the ruins of what had once been known as Kansas City, was a long way from the Arctic, but it was also a long way from the moderating effects of the ocean that had kept the climate of Marseguro's single land mass temperate all year 'round.

He'd been halfway to Splendid Raiment, located about two kilometers from his hotel, when he'd heard the dogs howling. He didn't think they were on his scent, but at the same time he knew that the plentiful supply of food . . . something else that didn't bear thinking about . . . the dogs had enjoyed for days must be approaching inedibility even for them, and that they were increasingly going to be looking for fresh meat. Probably they were hunting the deer that had begun wandering through the deserted streets, but Chris saw no reason to offer them an easier alternative.

Now he emerged from the alley onto the street, and looked both ways.

It was the main boulevard of the city, the one that ran past the ruins of the House of the Body straight to the Holy Compound, the city-within-a-city where the Avatar and all the highest members of the Body hierarchy had dwelt in happier times. Paved in spotless blue ceramic tile, it glittered in the sun. The white stone sidewalks and white stone buildings that lined it were almost too bright for him to look at, and he'd foolishly left his sunglasses back in the hotel.

Well, he'd pick up another pair at the store.

Nothing moved along the boulevard. Directly across from Chris lay Mercy Park, immaculate lawns and manicured flower beds surrounding a cheerfully plashing fountain, whose central, pyramidal spire of golden metal spouted water in glistening streams into bowls held in the outstretched hands of dozens of nude men, women, and children. Chris had wandered over once to read the inscription: apparently it represented God Itself pouring out Its mercy onto the grateful people of Earth.

With no one to tread on the grass, trample the flowers or spread their litter, the park had never looked better. As he watched, a tiny gardenbot trundled into view, carrying a single wilted flower in its manipulator claw.

Chris crossed to the park side of the boulevard and headed away from the Holy Compound toward the commercial district, still four blocks away. The sun shone warm on his shoulders, and birds chirped in the trees. He couldn't help grinning, and tilted his face to the sun to enjoy the warmth even more. Despite everything, he was happy to be on Earth, happy to be far away from Marseguro and its genetically modified monstrosities. The Body had long since cleansed Earth of such things.

Then why has God visited this punishment on Earth? a rebellious voice whispered inside him. *Why did It save the Earth all those years ago, if It intended to destroy it now?*

Chris shook his head. He would not question God's Will. He dared not: only the mercy of God had enabled him to survive this long.

The mercy of God, and the mercy of the Selkies, who had given him their vaccine before the plague was unleashed against the Holy Warriors.

No! He shook his head again. Their mercy had been unintentional. They would certainly have let the plague take him if they had realized it was he who had brought the Holy Warriors down on their blasphemous planet in the first place. No, God's mercy, not that of the Selkies, had been at work in that moment. God wanted Chris Keating alive, and It wanted him where he was right now.

Why else allow him to escape Marseguro to *Sanctification*, escape *Sanctification* for *Retribution*, and come at last safely to Earth? Why else ensure that he was released from detention when it became clear everyone else was dying?

He'd been terrified of being trapped in his cell. He'd banged on the door and screamed until his hands were bloody and his voice gone, and then, when he'd almost given up hope, the door had been opened by a Holy Warrior whose face was mottled and splattered with blood that ran in trickles from his nose and eyes.

"You seem to have escaped it," the Warrior had wheezed. "I won't leave you to starve in there."

Chris had thanked him and run, run as fast as he could, out of that charnel house . . . and into the greater charnel house of the City of God.

He had dreamed of coming to Earth, to the City of God, since he'd first listened to the contraband recordings of the Body's holy book, *The Wisdom of the Avatar of God*, that his grandparents had smuggled to Marseguro decades ago. He'd dreamed of seeing for himself the new order the Body had imposed on the scarred but Purified Earth.

He'd arrived just in time to see that order unravel.

Lost in his thoughts, he'd been watching his feet instead of his path; he looked up to discover he was already across the street from Splendid Raiment. He crossed and climbed in through the shattered front window. One reason he favored it was that it had been locked up before the riots began, and no one had died in it. Finding a space free of the reek of corruption and the buzzing of flies was rare enough to make it his favorite store even without the fact that he thought the clothes in it made him look damn good.

It was too bad no one else seemed to be alive to appreciate it. Not that he hadn't imagined what it would be like to find another survivor: a beautiful young girl, of course, lost and alone and desperate for human company . . . for male company . . .

He shook his head. The hotel had a rich collection of vids he'd begun to explore, with much, if unavoidably lonely, pleasure. He'd have a romantic date with himself that evening. For now . . .

He spent a few minutes browsing through the coat racks, finally settling on a long black overcoat that looked warm and also had enormous pockets he could fill with anything he came across that might be useful. On his way out, he grabbed some multi-shades, dialed them to their second-darkest setting, and stepped out into the sunlight.

A block from the safety of his hotel, he realized he was being stalked.

When he first glimpsed movement out of the corner of his eye, he thought it was the dogs . . . but it had looked too big to be a dog. A human?

Chris' pulse quickened. Unlikely though he knew it to be, his fantasy of the beautiful young girl resurfaced. Certainly he had no reason to think another human survivor would be a threat. With a whole city to loot, what could he possibly have that another survivor would want?

Unless they knew I was on board the Retribution *when it brought the plague back to Earth,* he thought uneasily. *Which they just might, if they're from the Holy Compound.*

Well, it couldn't hurt to pick up the pace just a little—

And then, from the alley on his right, from behind the trees in the park, and from the lobby of his hotel itself, dark figures emerged.

Chris stopped. *What the hell . . . ?*

They weren't human. Not fully. No more so than the Selkies. Maybe less. They wore no clothes except for straps and belts that held tools and weapons, but they weren't naked. Instead, they were covered in thick fur, not like a gorilla's but more like a cat's. Ears larger than a normal human's, pointed and tufted, sat high on their heads and twitched and swiveled like a cat's. Their faces were catlike, too, nose and jaws extended to make a kind of muzzle, though without the harelip of a cat or dog. Just like the Selkies, they had human-looking mouths, the full lips looking incongruous on the animal-like faces—but unlike the Selkies, when those lips were drawn back into a grin . . . or a snarl . . . they revealed sharp fangs. One female, staring at him without blinking, ran her tongue over the tips of those fangs.

After one shocked, frozen moment, Chris dropped the coat he was carrying, turned, and ran the only way open to him, into the park.

They followed instantly, in unnerving silence. And they were fast—incredibly fast. As he dashed headlong toward the fountain, two of the creatures ran past him as if he were strolling, leaped up onto the fountain's lip, and turned to face him.

Chris stopped. He had no choice. He turned slowly, encircled, taking in more details of the creatures as he did so, particularly their hands, shaped the same as his but covered with fur on the backs and black pads of naked skin on the palms. As they came nearer, needle-sharp white claws sprang from the tips of each finger and toe. "What . . . what do you want?" Chris finally managed to squeak out. "Who are you?"

"We are the Kemonomimi," said the biggest, a huge male whose fur did nothing to hide just how male he was. He made Chris feel small in more ways than one, and his voice rumbled like thunder. "You will come with us."

Chris could smell them now, a musty scent, not unpleasant, but . . . feral. Disturbing. They stopped just out of reach, but close enough he had no doubt they could rip him to pieces with their formidable natural armament before he took two steps.

"But . . . where? Why?"

"You will come with us," the male repeated, then nodded. Chris felt his arms suddenly seized from behind. He tried to struggle, but they were strong, so strong . . . stronger than anyone he'd ever met, except for Selkies.

They're moddies, he thought, horrified. *But . . . Earth was Purified. There are no moddies on Earth. This is impossible!*

The Kemonomimi didn't seem to realize that they couldn't exist. He felt his hands being tied together, then someone jerked a black hood down over his head. A moment later he felt himself being lifted; then he was thrown over a furry shoulder like a . . .

. . . well, the image that came to mind was of an animal trussed for butchering.

He remembered his earlier thoughts about the dogs searching for fresh meat in a city where even the plentiful carrion was becoming too gamy, and hoped fervently that he hadn't just become the main course for that evening's Kemonomimi feast.

No, he thought, as the creature carrying him broke into a loping run that caused his head to bounce hard against its back with every step. *No. God Itself has spared*

*me for a purpose. That purpose cannot be to feed moddie
monstrosities. It* can't.

But he couldn't help remembering something the Avatar had always emphasized: God's ways are mysterious. To think you understand them is to verge on blasphemy. And those who blaspheme deserve death.

It's not fair! Chris thought.

But fair or not, it seemed, once more his fate lay in the hands of moddies.

Chapter 3

"**E**MERGING FROM BRANESPACE in five ... four ... three ... two ..."

The blank screens showing the view outside the ship suddenly filled with light: the light of Sol itself. "Computer," Richard snapped. "Tactical situation: *Sanctification* status, other ships in system. Specify sizes and types."

"*Sanctification* has been recognized and approved for Earth approach by System Defense," the computer said. "System Control has provided data for insertion into assigned orbit; executing maneuvers now. Other ships in system: twelve. In orbit around Earth: One commercial freighter. Two forty-person ground-to-orbit shuttles. One hotel ship. One Holy Warrior vessel."

Richard and Andy exchanged glances as the computer continued. "In orbit around Luna: One Earth-Luna transport. In orbit around Mars: Two commercial freighters. Docked at Europa Station: One passenger liner. One government freighter. In solar orbits: One commercial freighter. One vessel of unknown type." A pause. "Correction. Vessel of unknown type has just leaped to branespace. In solar orbit: One commercial freighter."

"Somebody running away from us, or just from Earth in general?" Andy wondered.

"Computer," Richard said. "Why are you unable to identify the type of vessel that just jumped to branespace?"

"Unknown vessel was not within *Sanctification*'s sensor range and was not transmitting standard identification codes to System Central," came the reply.

"I don't like that one bit," said Andy.

"Me neither," Richard said. "But whoever they were, they're gone now. Let's worry about who's left." He cleared his throat. "Computer, size, armament, and current status of military vessel in Earth orbit."

"Vessel is *BPS Vision of Truth*," the computer replied. "Calcutta-class Earth-to-Luna troop transport. Unarmed. Status unknown."

"Computer, establish communications link with *BPS Vision of Truth*," Richard ordered.

A pause. "Unable to comply. *BPS Vision of Truth* does not respond."

"Crew dead? Or lying low?" Andy murmured.

Richard shook his head. "No way to tell. But let's see if anyone else is talking." He raised his voice again, though there was really no need; the computer would hear a whisper as easily as a shout. "Computer. Scan all in-system voice communication channels for conversations related to *Sanctification*'s appearance in the system."

Another pause, then, "No in-system voice communication detected," the computer said.

Richard felt relief, followed immediately by a chill of horror—was no one left alive in the entire system? "Computer, send out general broadcast to all ships in system, null-brane and light speed. Message follows: '*MSS Victor Hansen*, formerly *BPS Sanctification*, to all ships. What is the status of Earth system? Please respond.' End message. Send."

"Message broadcast," the computer said.

"Computer, inform me the moment any response is received."

"Confirmed."

Richard turned to Andy. "So which of our scenarios do you think we've jumped into?"

They'd talked about all the possibilities they could think of long before they'd set out from Marseguro, of course; talked about them, brainstormed them, and drilled the crew in procedures to deal with them. Finding everybody in the system dead had been one of those possibilities, but Richard had never considered it very likely: there was no reason a ship in orbit should be infected if its crew realized in time what was happening on Earth.

Of course, that had brought up the disturbing possibility that they would jump into the system and into the teeth of a fully operational and very angry Body Purified fleet. They seemed to have avoided that one, since no one was either shouting or shooting at them.

That didn't mean there weren't Holy Warriors lurking on *BPS Vision of Truth*, or on the Moon, or on one of the half-dozen stations orbiting the Earth and Mars, staying silent, awaiting their chance to attack the *Victor Hansen*. That possibility seemed so strong that they'd drilled that scenario the most.

As Richard had learned when he'd first come aboard the ship, prior to the Body Purified's attack on Marseguro, she'd been designed with mutable spaces in the habitat ring: walls that could move, folding, unfolding, rotating or withdrawing altogether, blocking off the routes invaders might otherwise follow to the bridge or other crucial locations and at the same time herding them into places where they could be imprisoned or killed. With some careful modification and programming—thanks largely to the late O'Sullivan (Richard felt a pang of mingled grief and anger when he thought of the former Holy Warrior's murder)—they had created hidden spaces that even the computer no longer remembered existed: important, because as far as the computer was concerned, this was still a Body Purified ship, and how it would behave once they were in orbit around Earth had been the greatest uncertainty of their mission.

In the event of an attack, the entire crew could go underground—although, given the aquatic nature of most of the crew, the actual code word was "Submerge"—and make plans to counterattack. During the last drill, they'd gotten everyone under cover in eight minutes and fifty-three seconds.

Five minutes would have been better, Richard thought, but he'd take what he could get.

"Everyone in the system could be dead," Andy answered Richard's query, echoing his own worst fear. "But then again, they could simply be playing it safe. If central authority has broken down, ships and stations are going to be hurting for supplies pretty soon. Piracy might start looking pretty good."

Richard nodded thoughtfully. "And we're the biggest ship in the system, and a warship to boot. Pirates won't want to tangle with us, and everybody else will think we just might *be* pirates, trying to get them to reveal themselves."

"Makes some sort of sense," Andy said.

"Reply received," the computer said. "Null-brane."

"Computer, identify source."

"Heavy Freighter *Bearer of Burdens*."

"Computer, plot location of *Bearer of Burdens* on main tactical display, scaled as needed."

A cylindrical, three-dimensional diagram of the system appeared in midair at the center of the bridge. A spot of light marked their location, with a solid red line marking their path into the system and a dotted green line their projected path, barring course changes. Another spot of light, blinking blue, indicated the source of the transmission.

"The other solar-orbiting ship," Andy said. "Not really orbiting at all. She's outbound clear across the system from us. Figures she has nothing to worry about."

"Computer, play message," Richard ordered.

The voice that came over the bridge speakers was female, and as clear as if the woman speaking were standing there with them: null-brane transmissions weren't afflicted by static. Nor did they suffer from speed-of-light lag. They either made it through instantaneously without change, or were reduced to unintelligible gibberish.

"*MSS Victor Hansen*, this is Captain Leora McFadden of the heavy freighter *Bearer of Burdens*, outbound for Stableford. You'll forgive me if I'm suspicious you're who you say you are: your ship IDs as *BPS Sanctification*. The few of us left alive in Earth space have been wondering when a Body warship would come back. I don't think you'll find anyone very interested in a rendezvous.

"But whoever you really are, there's no reason you shouldn't know the situation in Earth system before you do something foolish like taking someone aboard.

"Earth system is dead. A plague has killed the vast majority of the planet's population. Not all, apparently: someone calling himself the Avatar still broadcasts orders occasionally, but I haven't heard anybody responding to them. There have been a few bursts of communication that indicate groups of survivors are hanging on in various remote locations, but for the most part . . . Earth is one giant ball of corpses.

"Luna Station was infected early on. I think a couple of habitats managed to cut themselves off from the rest of the station and ride out the initial die-off, but they fell silent a week or so ago; I suspect they weren't self-sufficient and eventually had to open up again, and the plague took them.

"Europa Station seemed to be fine for a while, but I haven't heard a peep out of it recently. Don't know if it was the plague or in-system pirates: ships without Cornwall drives had nowhere to go, and Europa didn't want to let them in. They may have tried to take the station, and if something went wrong . . . well, decompression will kill you just as messily as the plague.

"The orbital stations around Earth went silent at the same time as Luna. Somehow the plague got to Mars, too.

"We waited long enough to make sure we weren't infected, and now we're getting the hell out of here. Stableford hasn't welcomed any Body ships for a long time, so it should be clear.

"So whoever you really are, *MSS Victor Hansen*, you've pretty much got the system to yourselves . . . and you're welcome to it. Just don't drink the water and don't breathe the air.

"McFadden out."

"Computer, send following message to *Bearer of Burdens*—" Richard began, but the computer interrupted him.

"*Bearer of Burdens* has entered branespace," it said. "No message can be sent."

In the tactical display, the blue icon winked out. Richard sighed. "Computer, tactical display off."

The system diagram disappeared. Richard walked over to the captain's chair and dropped onto its plush black upholstery. "It's as bad as we thought," he said. "Maybe worse. Earth . . . all those millions of people . . ."

"Most of whom who would have killed everyone on Marseguro if they'd had the chance," Andy said. His eyes weren't really focused on Richard; he seemed to be looking at something Richard couldn't see.

Richard got to his feet. "Let's take a walk, First Officer," he said. "Second Officer Raum, you have the bridge."

Cordelia Raum, a pink-haired Selkie with a scar across her face caused by shrapnel on the day of the Body's attack on Marseguro, nodded and came up to the captain's chair.

Andy looked from her to Richard. He raised his eye-

brows but followed Richard out through the massive
bridge security door, currently locked open. Just outside
the door stood a statue of Victor Hansen, a copy of the
one that had once stood in the courtyard at the center
of Hansen's Harbor. It had been placed there, welded
onto a steel pillar, during the ship's renaming ceremo-
nies three months ago. Richard tried not to look at the
thing. It was unnerving to see an older version of your
own face on a statue.

Richard turned to the right and led the way around
the next corner to the briefing room where he typically
met with the senior staff. He led Andy inside, turned and
closed the door.

Normally, when they were alone, neither stood on
formality, but Andy must have sensed something of
his mood: he stood at what a Holy Warrior would have
called parade rest, and looked straight ahead as Richard
sat on the edge of the glass-topped table and folded his
arms.

"I was disturbed by your comments on the bridge,
Number One," Richard said. "You seemed to be im-
plying that the people of Earth deserved whatever the
plague has done to them."

"They attacked Marseguro," Andy said.

"No," Richard said. "They didn't. The Body Purified
did. The Holy Warriors did. But not the people of Earth.
Most of them are as innocent as Marseguroites killed in
the attack by the Body. Y—" Richard stopped. He'd been
about to say "your," and that sounded like an accusation
he didn't want to make. "*Our* plague was only intended
to defend Marseguro. We never wanted this. At least, I
hope we didn't. But if you *did*—I need to know."

Andy's gaze flicked to Richard, and his eyes, green
like those of every other Selkie, narrowed. "No," he said.
"My apologies, Captain. I misspoke. Of course I didn't
want the innocent to suffer. But don't ask me to mourn
the Holy Warriors or the Body Purified."

"I won't," Richard said. "But we must all remember that this is a mission of mercy. Not one of revenge. Especially now, Andy, because very soon we're going to have to decide how to distribute the vaccine."

"We don't know enough yet," Andy said.

"Not yet," Richard agreed. "But our list of scenarios is narrowing. We know the system has been devastated by the plague. We know, thanks to Captain McFadden, that there are survivors—maybe just in isolated pockets, but survivors nonetheless." He turned his head to look directly at Andy. "And we know something else. The Avatar is still alive—and broadcasting."

"McFadden didn't say anything about anyone responding," Andy said.

"She wouldn't necessarily hear them, would she?" Richard shook his head. "If the Avatar is still alive, then the Body is still alive. Maybe in retreat, but not destroyed. Remember, the Body is *designed* to survive apocalyptic conditions. Whether through luck or divine revelation, the first Avatar built underground shelters all over the planet long before the Fist of God—the killer asteroid—approached. They kept the faithful mostly unharmed during the meteor bombardment that followed the Day of Salvation. Those shelters, hardened, self-sufficient, still exist: it's a holy duty to the Body to keep them operational. Some of the faithful will have fled to those before the plague reached their regions. There are other Body bases and compounds, isolated, secure. And the Body is ruthless enough to do whatever is necessary to prevent the spread of the plague to areas it wants protected."

"If it had time, maybe," Andy said. "You know how fast the plague moves. And all it would have taken was one infected person—hell, one infected *mouse*—to wipe out everyone in even the most secure location."

"Nevertheless, the Avatar probably survives," Richard said. "And the Avatar has access to the planetary computers that control all the resources of the planet. Microfactories, transportation, distribution nodes, surveillance systems. Exactly what we need to find survivors and distribute vaccine to them."

"Shit." Andy glared at Richard, who didn't move. "You're still considering negotiating with the Body! You know how *I* feel about that."

"Yes." They'd argued through this scenario several times already. Even if they hadn't, Andy's comments on the bridge moments before would have made his position clear. "But in the end, the decision will be mine." Richard stood up and stepped close to his First Officer so he could look him squarely in the eye. "So I need to know now, before that moment of decision arrives: will you support me?"

"It may not come to that."

"But it may."

Andy drew himself to full attention. "If it does," he said stiffly, "I will obey any orders you give me ... to the best of my ability. Captain."

What does that mean ... exactly? Richard wondered. He started to ask; then stopped himself. After all, this might all be moot. Until they arrived in orbit themselves, they couldn't be certain what the situation was on Earth. "That's ... enough," he said. He tried a grin, but he didn't get one back.

"Permission to speak, Captain?" Andy said.

"Of course, Andy."

Andy relaxed from attention. "You're worried I'll be blinded by the thirst for revenge," he said. "And maybe you're right to worry. But here's the thing, Richard: you could be just as blinded by your thirst for redemption."

Richard blinked. "I don't—"

"You blame yourself for the attack on Marseguro. And so you blame yourself for the plague being unleashed, and for it making its way back to Earth. You're desperate to make up for all of that. But the fault for what has happened to Earth doesn't lie with you: it lies with the bloody Body Purified. The Body didn't have to attack Marseguro just because you told them where it was. But they did. Their fault, not yours. The plague followed from their aggression. Like it says in the Christian Bible, they sowed the wind and reaped the whirlwind."

Richard's mouth quirked. "I didn't know you were religious."

"I'm not. But Tahirih . . ." Andy's voice broke off and Richard mentally cursed himself for asking the question. Tahirih, Andy's wife, had died in the Body's initial attack on Marseguro. Andy cleared his throat and continued. "The point is, Richard, the Body got what was coming to it. It needs to die, for the good of Earth, for the good of all of humanity, nonmods and moddies alike. Don't let your desire to make up for your perceived sins blind you to that. Use the Body if you have to, but don't trust it."

"Not much chance of that," Richard said. "But I'll take your comments under advisement." He turned away from Andy and raised his voice. "Computer. ETA until Earth orbit."

"Fifty-two hours, thirty-six minutes," the computer replied.

"Computer, general address to the ship."

"Ready," said the computer.

"Attention," Richard said to the ship at large. "Senior officers report to the briefing room in one hour." He paused. "Ladies and gentlemen, it appears the situation on Earth is every bit as grim as we feared. But there are survivors. This is a mission of mercy, ladies and gentlemen, and I expect all of you to do whatever is necessary to ensure that we save as many of our fellow humans on Earth as possible. Captain Hansen, out. Computer, end general address." He glanced at Andy. "You have the bridge. I'll see you back here in an hour."

"Aye, aye, sir," Andy said, once more at attention. Richard nodded once, and went out.

As he walked toward his quarters, Richard replayed the conversation in his head. He hoped like hell he wouldn't end up negotiating with the Body. But he'd made up his mind a long time ago to do whatever was necessary to save the largest number of people. If that meant giving the Body a new lease on life, well, how much of a lease could it be on a plague-ravaged world?

He hoped it wouldn't come to that. He hoped they could find a way to not involve the Body. But if they couldn't . . .

There had already been so much death and destruction, and so much of it could be laid squarely at his feet. He knew that. Decisions made for the wrong reason, decisions made for the right reason that had gone wrong, failing to make a decision when he should have . . . the ways he had failed were myriad. In the end, Marseguro had been saved, and he had contributed to that, he guessed. But he never forgot—could never forget—that Marseguro had only been in jeopardy to begin with because he had helped the Body find it.

Now the tables were turned. Now Earth was in peril. And though he hadn't created the plague devastating the planet, and no one had intended for it to infect Earth, the fact remained that this, too, was the direct result of his determination . . . less than a year ago, though it seemed two lifetimes ago . . . to clear his family name and rise as high as possible within the Body hierarchy. One thing had followed another. Thousands . . . probably millions, by now . . . of people had died, domino falling on domino, all set in motion, at least in part, by his actions.

Yet what could he do but make more decisions, the best decisions he could with the information he had at hand? If he could not stop the dominoes from falling, at least he might be able to divert them into a different direction, one that minimized the suffering and death. And if that meant negotiating with the Body, then he would negotiate with the Body, up to and including the Avatar himself.

And hope that his crew would all, like Andy, obey his orders . . .

"To the best of my ability," Andy added. The phrase niggled at him. It sounded like . . . an out. As if his desire for revenge wouldn't let him commit fully.

And what about your own desire for redemption? he thought. *Is it blinding you to the dangers of the Body, like Andy said?*

He shook his head. No. Far from being blind, he was seeing more clearly than ever the cost of the conflict he had helped instigate. It had to stop.

Andy had quoted the Christian Bible. Richard remembered another part of it, which talked about "A time to kill, and a time to heal."

Surely the time to kill was past. Surely it was time to heal at last.

His cabin door slid open at his approach as the computer recognized him, and he stepped into his spacious-but-Spartan captain's cabin. He'd brought few personal items to Marseguro from Earth, and he hadn't acquired many more in the months since—and he'd stripped the cabin of everything that had belonged to its previous occupant.

The only bit of decoration was a holopic of Emily Wood, standing on the shore in her yellow-and black zebra skinsuit, the Marseguroite ocean stretching out green and glittering to the horizon behind her. Glistening drops beaded her suit and skin, and she smiled at him, the holopic making it seem she turned to watch him cross the cabin floor and sit on the bed.

"You'll" understand if I have to negotiate with the Body, won't you?" he said to her.

She said nothing, of course. And the uncomfortable

thing was, he didn't know what she'd say even if she were there with him. Despite all they had been through . . . he didn't really know.

He hoped she'd have supported him, at least for the sake of her mother, undone by the horror of what she had unleashed on Earth. But she also had her own reasons to hate the Body, which had killed her father and several of her friends.

He couldn't be certain what she'd say, if worse came to worst and he had to treat with their enemies. And that troubled him most of all.

He lay back on his bed and threw an arm over his eyes. "Computer, wake me in thirty minutes," he said.

"Affirmative," the computer said.

But though he did his best, sleep wouldn't come.

Andy King sat in the command chair on the bridge and stared at the tactical hologram without seeing the vector lines and ship ID numbers it displayed. Instead, the images that filled his mind were those from six months before, when the Holy Warrior assault craft had swept down over Hansen's Harbor and shattered his world.

He'd been on deck aboard the *Bel Canto* that morning, preparing for a cargo run up to Firstdip. The sun had just edged over the horizon when he'd heard the scream of jet engines, a sound he'd never heard before except in vids. Marseguro had only a handful of aircraft, and they were all low-speed fanprops.

He'd looked up, puzzled but not yet alarmed, to see the three enormous black delta-winged craft, each almost as big as the *Bel Canto* herself, sweep low over the city. Missiles riding on tails of flame speared the city, blossoming into ugly flowers of orange and black. Fire rippled along the leading edges of the strange crafts' wings, and explosive slugs ripped up streets and shattered walls and windows.

He'd gaped, stunned, horrified, unable to speak or

move: then the trio of craft had banked and turned back toward the city . . . and he'd suddenly realized their second pass would take them right over the harbor.

"Get off!" he'd screamed at his crew, four Selkies, two landlings, all on deck, all staring up at the sky like he was. He'd shoved the nearest man into the water, then leaped in himself. His gills opened as he plunged under and he dove deep—but not deep enough that he didn't feel the awful impact of the explosions above, as missiles tore through the *Bel Canto*'s hull. Chunks of metal ripped through the water all around him, trailing bubbles. One sliced through both skinsuit and skin, laying open his right calf so that he trailed blood as he dove still deeper.

Here in the harbor anchorage there were no underground structures, nowhere to go, so he sat on the muddy bottom of New Botany Bay until the thump of explosions had ceased to make the water shudder. Only then did he resurface, cautiously, barely poking his head into the air.

Beneath a filthy, smoke-streaked sky, Hansen's Harbor lay in ruins, its towers shattered and burning. Some had fallen completely, and he instantly knew that half the underwater city must have been buried in rubble. "Tahirih!" he'd screamed, and dove again, swimming as fast as he could through water that reeked in his gills of oil and explosives and . . .

. . . blood.

He'd reached the floating lights that marked the swimways, had followed them as he had followed them so many times when he'd come back from a voyage, turned at the first intersection, swam toward the shore . . .

. . . and found his way blocked by the ruins of one of the towers, tons of steel and stone and glass forming an impenetrable thicket of wreckage.

Somewhere beneath that, he had left his wife sleeping.

"No!" he had click-screamed in Selkie. He'd pulled at the wreckage, but even as he bloodied his hands on twisted steel and shattered stone, he knew it was hopeless. It would take heavy equipment days just to dig down to the habitats that had lined this street. If anyone still lived down there, could they survive that long? The Selkies could breathe underwater, but the water had to circulate, had to be reoxygenated . . .

He needed help. They all needed help.

Then he had swum to the surface and discovered that no help would be coming.

Rounded up with the other Selkies, locked up first in a cage in the harbor then, after John Duval escaped, in one of the larger surviving underwater habitats, he had waited, helpless, for the Holy Warriors to decide his fate. Cut off from everyone else, none of the prisoners had known what was happening in Hansen's Harbor . . . until one day, their guards fell ill, then disappeared. And the next day, two Selkies had swum into the habitat to free them . . . and tell them the Holy Warriors were all dead.

Then, at last, equipment had been brought in to dig down to the buried habitats, though on shore the ruins were left largely intact to confuse the follow-up force of Holy Warriors everyone knew would be coming.

No survivors were found. Few of the bodies discovered were even whole. Andy had identified Tahirih only by the delicate pattern of winding vines tattooed on her shaven head; her face was . . . gone.

He'd lost other people that were important to him that day: friends, distant relatives. The Selkies who had been aboard the *Bel Canto* all survived. The nonmods, unable to swim deep enough or stay down long enough, had all been killed.

When the Holy Warriors returned, he'd been one of those in the Square with Richard and Emily. He'd felt a fierce joy as he'd pulled the trigger and seen a War-

rior collapse with a bullet in his brain ... but revenge
couldn't bring back Tahirih.

He'd volunteered to join the crew of the *MSS Victor
Hansen*, because, he'd told himself and everyone else, he
didn't want the innocent people of Earth to suffer like
he'd suffered. And he didn't: he would gladly vaccinate
any survivors they found ...

... any survivors, that was, who didn't wear the uniform of the Holy Warriors and hadn't served within the
Body Purified, the fascist death-cult that considered him
and all those like him abominations in the sight of the
bloodthirsty God it served.

But now Richard Hansen—the man he had sworn to
obey as captain of this vessel and commander of this
mission—was hinting he wouldn't hesitate to do exactly
that, if he thought it the best way to get the vaccine to
the maximum number of people quickly. And if the
Body got the vaccine, Andy knew what it would mean,
because he and Richard had discussed it over and over
as they'd mapped out various scenarios for their arrival:
around the world, surviving Holy Warriors would receive the vaccination first. Only then would they spread
out to vaccinate the other survivors, and at the same
time retighten the Body Purified's slipping grip on the
planet.

And if that happened, then instead of destroying the
Body, destroying the Holy Warriors, destroying the evil
that had slaughtered Selkies without mercy on Marseguro, then the crew of the *Victor Hansen* would be helping it, healing it, ensuring it remained alive, like a zombie
from some horror vid.

*So they can come back to Marseguro and Purify it
"properly" next time.*

He was First Officer of the *MSS Victor Hansen*. He had
sworn to serve the ship and obey the captain's orders.

And so he would. *To the best of my ability*.

But Andy King knew one thing: it was *beyond* his

ability to obey any orders that would let the Body rise from the well-deserved grave the Marseguroite plague had shoved it into.

He might be worrying about nothing. The situation might never arise.

But if it did . . . he knew he could find others with like minds among the crew.

He glanced at the chronometer. Time for the staff meeting.

"You have the bridge," he told Second Officer Raum.

"Aye-aye, sir," Raum replied. She reminded him of his dead wife . . . except for the scar on her face. He watched her slender fingers slip fluidly over her control panel for a moment longer than was really necessary, then headed for the briefing room.

Chapter 4

KARL THE FIRST, Third Avatar of the Body Purified, did not claim to talk to God directly. His predecessor, Harold the Second, had made such a claim, but back then Karl Rasmusson had been Right Hand, not Avatar, and as such knew enough of Harold's myriad weaknesses of both personality and intellect to discount out of hand the claim that he had frequent intimate conversations with the Creator and Destroyer.

On the other hand, Karl had no doubt whatsoever that the First Avatar, Harold the First, had indeed had such a hotline to the Wrathful One. The existence of human beings on Earth was proof enough of that. Harold the First had foretold the miracle that had seen a previously undetected asteroid shunt aside the approaching planet-killing asteroid known as the Fist of God at practically the last possible moment. The odds of such a thing happening by chance were, well, astronomical. And the Avatar had positioned himself so perfectly to take over the planet in the wake of the initial panic, the devastating meteor storms, and the ensuing chaos, that he *must* have been telling the truth when he said God Itself had spoken to him and told him what to do.

Harold the First had talked to God. Harold the Second had not. And Karl the First . . . ?

Well, he was listening. He was listening *very hard,* because a little divine whisper in his ear would have been a welcome sign that God still cared about what happened on Earth. Because without such a sign, all the evidence seemed to point to God Itself turning Its back on the planet, its people, and the Body Purified.

Karl stood on the porch of his modest dwelling, which looked exactly like a log cabin even though not a speck of it had ever grown on a tree, and looked out through a carefully maintained clearing in the pine forest to the rocky shore of Paradise Island and the fog-shrouded water of the Pacific Ocean beyond. Somewhere behind him, the sun had risen, but it was still hidden by the mists it had not yet burned away. On a clear day, he would have been able to glimpse the low blue hump of another island, fifteen kilometers away over open water, but so far today his own island sailed alone through swirling clouds of gray.

It seemed appropriate, since that was what Karl felt he had been doing for some time now.

He'd never intended to be Avatar, never *wanted* to be Avatar. He'd liked being the Right Hand, the man who really ran things, no matter who the Council of the Faithful had selected as the current physical representative of God Itself. He'd hoped (and discreetly lobbied for) the ascension of Samuel Cheveldeoff, former Archdeacon of Body Security, when Harold the Second had suffered his unfortunate illness (a stroke brought on by a prodigious drinking binge). Cheveldeoff's success at purifying Marseguro was to have ensured that ascension.

Unfortunately, Cheveldeoff's ship had fallen silent, like *BPS Sanctification* before it. With the Marseguroite mission clearly a failure of monumental proportions, the Council of the Faithful had unanimously raised Ashok Shridhar to the position of Avatar when Harold the Second had finally (with a little judicial medical help) succumbed.

Karl had met with Ashok the First, established, with

the help of certain information he had judiciously collected about Ashok's pre-Ascension activities, who *really* ran things, and had settled in for what he thought would be a few more years of very pleasant (for him, anyway) *status quo*.

And then *BPS Retribution* had returned.

Obviously under AI control, she had arrived silently, except for automated recognition signals. She had placed herself in a standard parking orbit around Earth. No one aboard responded to hails and the computer either didn't know or wouldn't say what had happened. The experts thought the AI had been tampered with in an attempt to subvert the command hierarchy, and had responded (as it was designed to) by becoming unresponsive to anyone. Essentially, it kept saying it would only speak to its captain, but it didn't know where its captain was, or even who he was.

The consensus was that there had been a mutiny. Nobody was thinking of disease. Why should they? Germ warfare had been abolished long before the Body took over, and with its distaste for genetic modification of any kind, even the thought of it was anathema.

So the Holy Warriors had taken no special precautions when they boarded *Retribution*, and no special precautions when they found the lone survivor, Chris Keating, who swore up and down that the dead had been murdered by Richard Hansen via mysterious chemical means.

Chris Keating, Karl thought. The name was burned in his mind. Immune to the plague, but a carrier. *Does he still live? Did he starve in prison? Or did someone figure out what he'd done and put a bullet in his head?*

In a way, Karl hoped he still lived, because then the possibility remained that someday Karl would have an opportunity to personally make him pay an appropriate price.

The Holy Warriors should never have taken Keating

from the ship, of course. But they had. And they were the first to pay the penalty for their foolishness ... but far from the last.

The doctors had never seen a disease like the one that gripped every man who had gone on board the *Retribution*. It started with a cough, proceeded to joint pain and fever and nosebleeds, and killed with alarming rapidity and efficiency, as victims bled to death internally or literally drowned in the blood that flooded their lungs. And "contagious" didn't begin to describe it. Just being in the same room with someone infected, or in a room connected by an air vent to a room containing someone infected, or using a bathroom used by someone infected, or ...

They'd questioned Chris Keating. Why wasn't he infected? He'd told them he'd been given a shot by the Selkies, who had somehow protected the normal humans living on Marseguro from the disease. They'd taken his blood, tried to use its antibodies to formulate their own vaccine ...

But it was too late. The doctors died before their work was half begun.

The Body authorities tried to stop the spread of the disease, but too many people had already been infected before they realized what they were dealing with.

A few—a very few—people seemed to be naturally immune, though no one knew why. Even fewer—maybe one in a hundred thousand—managed to fight off the disease and survive. Almost everyone else, everywhere on the planet, died.

The new Avatar, Ashok the First, briefed by men who had talked to Chris Keating in person before anyone knew about the plague, died in his office, vomiting blood across the diamond-topped desk hewn from one of the meteors that had slammed into the planet after the Day of Salvation. *Appropriate,* Karl thought blackly. The desk was a symbol of how God Itself could choose to destroy or to save. Once before It had chosen to save Earth. This time, It seemed to have chosen to destroy it . . .

And yet, a remnant clung to life. Almost too late, some members of the Body had realized that their only hope lay, not in isolating the victims, but in isolating the survivors.

The Body existed because the first Avatar had had the inspired foresight to build self-contained shelters beneath all of the Body's Meeting Halls. The largest complex of such shelters lay beneath the Holy Compound. The commander of Holy Warrior forces in the Holy Compound made it there first with a handful of his best men, all pressure-suited. They let in other survivors. Anyone could enter through one of the outer air lock doors into the shelter, which was essentially a buried spaceship. But no one came through the inner door until they had spent a full twenty-four hours inside the cramped air lock itself. In the end, one hundred and thirty-seven people had made it through. Another forty-six had fallen ill in the air lock and been expelled, alive or dead, their choice.

Among the other survivors: the forty-seven people, including the Right Hand, Karl Rasmusson, who waited in orbit aboard the Earth-Luna Shuttle *Reflected Glory* while plague felled humanity like a scythe through ripe wheat.

Not a single member of the Council of the Faithful, normally charged with selecting a new Avatar, survived. Fortunately, the inspired laws of the Body provided for that contingency: if the Avatar died without the Council being able to appoint a successor, the Right Hand ascended.

And so Karl Rasmusson, through no wish of his own, had become Avatar Karl the First.

He would have preferred to stay in orbit, but *Reflected Glory* was intended for short hauls only; food and water soon began to run low, and the air grew increasingly foul. And so he'd returned to the Holy Compound. Not everyone aboard the ship had agreed with that decision, but the half-dozen Holy Warriors who formed his personal bodyguard soon convinced them.

Reflected Glory carried enough pressure suits for thirty people. The new Avatar and those who had been part of his entourage each got one. That left eighteen suits to divide among thirty-five people. Six of those went to out-of-uniform Holy Warriors who had been on recreational leave. The remaining suits were handed out through a lottery. Only one of those who didn't get a suit had to be clubbed to death. The others decided to remain on board the landed shuttle, keep it sealed, and hope the plague burned itself out before they had to exit.

They watched as Karl and the rest of his tiny band of followers exited the shuttle and headed across the vast flat expanse of the spaceport toward the looming towers of the City of God, only dimly visible through the thick haze of acrid smoke that hung over everything.

The smoke came from buildings that burned, unattended, all along their route. They stepped over and around the bodies of men, women, and children, bloated and bloodstained. The corpses lay in the streets, huddled in vehicles, sprawled in parks and ornamental pools. Occasionally a large bot would trundle by, corpses stacked like cordwood in the bed of its trailer.

Not everyone was dead yet. A few survivors shrank back against walls when they saw the armed, pressure-suited Warriors coming, and clung there, coughing. A few of the bravest trailed along, begging for help, but the Warriors warned them off—with rifles, if necessary.

Window glass crunched under Karl's boots as they passed another looted store, and he shook his head. The looters must have known they were as doomed as everyone else. What possible use could they have for a holovid or cookbot?

The two-story gates of gleaming copper at the main entrance into the Holy Compound were closed and sealed, but unguarded. Karl went into the gatehouse and ordered the Compound's AI to open the gates: it complied.

Like the city, the Holy Compound was occupied only by the dead or the dying. The Holy Warriors shot two men and a woman who came running toward them, coughing, faces streaked with blood, begging for help. As the woman fell, Karl recognized her as a former secretary of his. After that, the other walking dead kept their distance. Karl's party had no further trouble until it reached the entrance to the shelter. As he ordered the AI to let them in, some of the survivors rushed them. None of them got within ten feet, falling in a hail of automatic weapons fire, but a well-hurled missile smashed the faceplate of one of the Holy Warriors. His comrades shoved him away from them. As the door closed, he was putting his pistol in his mouth.

Stripped, irradiated, sprayed, washed, then irradiated, sprayed and washed again, they emerged four stories underground into an island of normality. One hundred and thirty-seven people were living in the shelter, swelling to one hundred and sixty-six with the Avatar's arrival.

It had been intended to house a hundred at most.

From the smell alone, it was obvious it wouldn't do for long-term residence. But at least it had a communications center that allowed him to contact other Body sanctuaries around the world.

No one had good news.

The plague had spread to every corner of the globe. Only the most remote outposts remained unaffected, and only by way of ruthlessly preventing the arrival, or even the approach, of anyone from the outside world. More: since the virus could be carried by small mammals, every cat and dog had to be slaughtered, every mouse and rat exterminated, and none could be allowed to enter the protected area. Birds, too, might be carrying the plague—though no one was certain—and so also had to be shot on sight.

Difficult measures to enforce: too difficult for some sanctuaries, which fell silent shortly after he contacted them.

He also managed to contact a few sanctuaries outside of the Body's hidden shelters: remote communities, mostly, high in the mountains or in the middle of deserts, where the plague hadn't reached. When he identified himself as the Avatar, they became guarded and unwilling to talk. Most refused further communication from him. It had infuriated him, but until he reestablished control—if he reestablished control—he could do nothing about their rebelliousness.

None of the places he contacted were in any position to take in the large number of survivors still in the Holy Compound shelter. Karl had then turned to the computer, searching the database for a place that could. It had to be remote, free of the plague, and able to maintain the necessary containment measures until ... if ... the disease somehow burned itself out.

He had found ... this place. Paradise Island, formerly a resort for high-level members of the Body hierarchy. Avatars vacationed here. So had Karl, once. Fishing bots and extensive gardens provided some fresh food to complement the thousands of tons of stored supplies. The island boasted recreation facilities, communications facilities, and a full hospital, whose laboratory would enable the few scientists who had survived to continue studying the virus.

There was no need to remind them of what it would mean if their samples escaped containment: an error would carry its own death penalty. For all of them.

The island also boasted its own large population of survivors, including various relatively high-level Body officers who would form the core of his new staff, and a sizable contingent of Holy Warriors, since the island had always been an obviously tempting target for attack by anti-Body terrorists. That contingent had been further enhanced by escorts of some of the officials who had fled to the island even before Karl arrived, and the complete complement of the mainland garrison that watched over the island's ferry port. The total population of survivors on the island, in the end, numbered over 3,000, of which fully seven hundred were Holy Warriors, armed and armored: a small army.

It was a shame, Karl thought, that their enemy could not be defeated by guns.

Staring into the mist, he prayed, not for the first time, that God Itself would tell him what he must do, how he could turn Its wrath away from Earth and once more gain Its favor.

The sound of gunfire interrupted his murmured prayer, as the automated weapons that ringed the island's shore locked onto some unlucky bird and blasted it into bloody feathers. The sound reminded him of the propane "bird-banger" cannon that had frightened birds away from the vineyards surrounding his childhood home in the Niagara Peninsula.

He wondered how his father would have felt about his son becoming Avatar, then snorted. It wouldn't have mattered: Pietr Rasmusson thought only about his vineyard and his wine. It had broken his heart when his eldest had chosen to enter Body service instead of following in his footsteps. Karl's younger brother Gunther had taken over the vineyard instead. The last Karl had heard, Gunther's wines were carrying on the family tradition of winning awards.

Karl winced and closed his eyes. No more. His brother and his brother's wife, along with their four children, were almost surely dead. They and their grapes were probably rotting together in the fields, a feast for the birds at last.

As if on cue, the guns fired again.

As the echoes died, Ilias Atnikov, Karl's former chief of staff, and now the new Right Hand, stepped onto the porch. "Your Holiness," he said softly—Atnikov *always* spoke softly—"we've just received a transmission from AI at System Control. It reports a new starship has just entered the system."

Karl felt a surge of . . . hope or fear, he wasn't sure which. His prayer had barely died on his lips. Could this be an answer, so soon? "Can we identify it?"

"It has identified itself, sir," said Atnikov. "It's *BPS Sanctification*."

"*Sanctification!*"

"Yes, Your Holiness. However, it has broadcast a message to the whole system using a different name."

"What name?" Karl demanded.

Atnikov raised his voice. "Computer, play message broadcast from *BPS Sanctification* at 0635 local time."

"Message follows," said the computer. Its uninflected male voice, apparently coming from thin air, was immediately followed by the voice of a living man: "*MSS Victor Hansen*, formerly *BPS Sanctification*, to all ships. What is the status of Earth system? Please respond."

"*MSS Victor Hansen?*" Karl's heart quickened still more. "It's from Marseguro!"

"It seems a reasonable deduction," Atnikov said.

Karl looked back out at the misty ocean, taking a moment to compose himself. If the Marseguroites were aboard *Sanctification*—he'd be damned if he'd call the vessel by the name of the monster who had birthed the Selkies, the inhuman creatures who had created the plague—then the secret of the vaccine that had kept Chris Keating alive and could save all the survivors of Earth was there, too.

And one way or another, he, Karl the First, Avatar of the Body Purified, the chosen human vessel of God Itself, Creator and Destroyer, would have it.

It was the sign he had been praying for. God had

heard his prayer, and It had, indeed, spoken to him . . . in, as always, Its own way.

Which meant It had a purpose for him, and the means by which salvation had been delivered told him what that purpose was.

Once he had the vaccine, then all the abominations of Victor Hansen would die as horribly as the millions they had murdered.

He looked up at the pearl-white sky. "I swear it, Creator and Destroyer of All Things," he whispered. "I will Purify this world and theirs with fire and the sword. Or I will die in the attempt."

He looked at the sky a moment longer, then turned to Atnikov. "Let's go," he said. "We have plans to make."

"Yes, Avatar," said his Right Hand, and led him inside.

Richard Hansen came onto the bridge of the *Victor Hansen* and, as he had for the past two days, looked first to Second Officer Raum, who had been the officer on duty during the night watch, the third since they had arrived in Earth's system. "Anything?"

"No, sir," she said, then had to cover a yawn with the back of her hand.

Richard had already known that, of course. If there had been any response from the planet below to their endlessly looping message, he would have been awakened immediately. But he still had to ask.

"Very well," he said. "You stand relieved."

"Thank you, sir." She got out of the captain's chair, sketched a salute, and then went out through the bridge door just as Andy King came through.

"I don't think we're going to hear anything, Andy," Richard said.

Andy said nothing. Richard wondered if he were secretly pleased. After all, the most likely people to hear from would be the Body.

"I think we're going to have to send a shuttle down," Richard went on. "Let's call a staff meeting to discuss possible—"

"Signal from Earth," said the computer, its voice as calm as always.

Richard and Andy exchanged a glance. "Computer, map and show location of signal's origin and play message."

The tactical display lit with a globe of Earth, zoomed in, and stopped, displaying the coast of British Columbia, north of Vancouver Island, where a multitude of islands of all sizes nestled off a mountainous shoreline cut with deep inlets. One island, in particular, was highlighted. Some of the other islands had names associated with them; that one did not.

"*MSS Victor Hansen . . .*" The voice that crackled into the bridge sounded strained and worn. "Receiving your transmission. Please respond. *MSS Victor Hansen . . .*"

"Computer, establish two-way link." Richard studied the tactical display. The message had been routed to them by one of the Body's communications satellites: they were currently on the other side of the planet from the source. But that didn't mean the speaker was a Holy Warrior or any other kind of Body official: their own broadcasts had been routed through those satellites, too. It was the only practical way to ensure anyone with an active receiver might hear them.

"Link established," the computer said.

"This is *MSS Victor Hansen*, Captain Richard Hansen speaking," Richard said. "Can you hear me?"

Crackle, then the sound of cheering. "Yes, *Victor Hansen*, we hear you! God, it's so good to know there are still people alive out there . . ."

"Good to hear voices from Earth, too," Richard said. "Who are you? And what's your situation?"

"My name is Jacob," the voice said. "There are a couple of hundred of us on this island . . . we were on vacation when we heard about the plague. We've been stuck here, afraid to go to the mainland. We've got lots of water, but food's running short. We've been patrolling the shore, shooting birds like crazy. So far no one has fallen sick. But we need help." The voice broke. "God, we need help so bad—"

Richard looked at Andy. "Are there any Body officials in your group?"

"A couple of Lesser Deacons who were on vacation," the voice said. "And four Holy Warriors on leave. They're the ones shooting the birds." The voice turned almost frantic. "What difference does that make? Won't you help us? Please!"

"Stand by, Jacob." Richard had moved over to the captain's chair while he talked; now he reached down and touched the manual control that muted his end of the signal. "What do you think, Andy?"

"It sounds legitimate," Andy said. "But that doesn't mean anything. It could be a Body trap."

"Or it could be just what we've been hoping for," Richard said. "A group of survivors without strong Body ties. A beachhead on the ground from which we can launch a planetwide effort to locate and vaccinate survivors."

Andy nodded slowly. "We haven't heard from anyone else," he said. "Things must be getting pretty desperate for all the survivors, wherever they are. I think we have to trust them."

"I think so, too," Richard said, and inwardly felt a huge weight lift from his spirit. He hadn't liked wondering if he could trust Andy to back his decisions. Now he wouldn't have to. He reactivated the bridge microphone. "Jacob, thanks for waiting. Yes, we'll help you." He glanced at Andy, who nodded. "More than you might expect. We have a vaccine."

Silence on the other end, then a new outbreak of relieved shouting and cheers. "We can't tell you ... thank you! Thank you!" Jacob said. "How soon can you join us?"

"Within twelve hours, I would think," Richard said. "Our computer has your location. Is it possible to land a shuttle there?"

"Yes, it's ... it was ... a pretty nice resort. Big landing field. You shouldn't have any trouble."

"Excellent. I'll give you a precise ETA when I can." Richard deliberately didn't look at Andy as he added, "I'll talk to you soon in person. Richard Hansen out. Computer, end transmission."

Only then did he turn to face Andy again. His First Officer was glowering at him, pretty much as he expected.

"You'll talk to him in person? What crap is that ... Captain?"

"I have to go myself, Andy," Richard said. "I know Earth. I know what the political situation was before I left. I have a pretty good idea of where we'll have to go to find the resources we'll need to gear up for planetwide distribution of the vaccine. I have to talk to these people."

"We can't afford to lose you," Andy said. "The ship recognizes you as its captain. Without you—"

"And the ship recognizes you as First Officer," Richard said. That had taken some careful programming by Simon Goodfellow, the computer genius they'd recruited early on in the process of turning *Sanctification* into *Victor Hansen*, but he'd managed to make it happen: the ship's computer, eternally loyal by design to an unbroken chain of command, now thought that Andy King—and all the other ship's officers—had enlisted in the Holy Warriors some six months ago and made the most remarkably quick climbs in rank in the history of military service: battlefield promotion after battlefield promotion, sometimes two or three on the same day. Andy King was now officially recognized by the ship as having the rank of Grand Deacon, Third Class—roughly equivalent to lieutenant commander in one of the old national Earth navies. "If something happens to me, the ship will accept you as the captain."

Andy couldn't argue with that. But he didn't look any happier. "There are other precautions we should take," he said. "An armed bodyguard—"

"Agreed," Richard said. "We'll discuss the makeup of the landing party together." He also readily agreed to take the other precautions they'd already planned to protect the vaccine from simply being seized and handed over to the Body. The doses he would take would be locked inside a high-security container that could only be opened by Richard without destroying its contents. "Okay?" he said at last, when all of Andy's objections—except the big one, against Richard going at all—had been dealt with.

"Okay," Andy said grudgingly.

"Good." Richard glanced at the chronometer. "I need to go talk to the scientists," he said. "Call a staff meeting for one hour from now. In the meantime, you have the bridge."

Andy watched Richard walk out and took a deep breath. He had a bad feeling about the whole situation, but he didn't know why. The voice from the surface had sounded convincing enough. Though it was odd the island this apparent luxury resort was on had no name on the map. "Computer," he said. "Display best satellite imagery available of island from which last transmission originated."

The tactical display blurred, then refocused to show a wooded and rocky island. The scale helpfully included in the image revealed it to be about ten kilometers long and maybe six wide at its widest point. The north end was rounded and mountainous, the southern end flatter and much narrower, petering out into a series of islets and rocks, splashed white with surf. In the middle of the island were several buildings, just nondescript roofs from his vantage point. Boats were tied up to a series of piers along the eastern shore, and not far inland from them there was, indeed, the long flat scar of an airstrip. Half a dozen aircraft were parked next to hangar buildings along the western edge of it.

"So far, so good," Andy muttered. But he still wished Richard weren't going himself. If it was a Body trap, Richard would be a huge prize . . . thought not as big as the vaccine he would be carrying with him.

Well, he thought viciously, *if the Body does capture or kill Richard, then I will be the new captain of* MSS Victor Hansen. *And in full command of its weaponry. Including the very same assault craft that killed Tahirih.*

Your bloody God Itself isn't the only one who can rain down destruction from on high.

He settled back in the chair. The dice were thrown. Now they just had to wait to see what numbers came up.

Karl Rasmusson leaned back in his chair as the transmission ended, and turned to Henry von Eschen, formerly chief of his security detail and now, as ranking officer of the surviving Holy Warriors, the new Archdeacon of Holy Destruction. "That went well," he said.

"I thought so, too . . . Your Holiness 'Jacob.' " Von Eschen grinned. "They fell for it."

"Seems that way." Karl glanced over his shoulder at the half-dozen Holy Warriors who had moments before been cheering the news that *MSS Victor Hansen* was carrying a vaccine against the plague. "Good work, all of you. You're dismissed."

The Holy Warriors filed out of his office. Karl waited until the last one was out and had closed the door behind him before turning back to von Eschen. "You're sure no one else has heard Hansen's messages?"

Von Eschen nodded. "As expected, *Sanctification*'s computer automatically routed its transmissions through Body satellites. It was a simple matter to ensure the only place those messages were relayed was here."

"And Hansen won't suspect?"

"No. At our instruction, the satellite falsely confirmed to *Sanctification* that the broadcast was going out over the whole planet."

Karl nodded. "Good." He pulled a datapad over to him and studied again the text message that had appeared on it while he was pretending to be the grateful civilian survivor Jacob. "And you're sure about this, too?"

"Computer confirms."

"And the shuttle?"

"It checks out."

Karl grinned. "Make sure Hansen gets down here safely first. Then do it."

"Yes, Your Holiness." Von Eschen saluted and went out.

God does *hear prayers*, Karl Rasmusson thought again. "I am the Avatar of the Body Purified, and God Itself is with me and in me," he murmured.

Those were the words of the Ascension Ceremony. When he had said them perfunctorily aboard the *Reflected Glory*, he'd given them little thought. When he had been Right Hand, he had even silently scoffed at them every time they were spoken by Harold the Second at the annual Ceremony of Reaffirmation.

But now . . .

"God Itself is with me and in me," he whispered again; and for the first time since he'd become Avatar, he truly believed it.

Chapter 5

CHRIS KEATING WOKE to find himself bound, blindfolded, and gagged, lying on his side on what felt like bare metal. He tried to roll over and couldn't. He listened, but all he could hear was a deep rushing and roaring. The cold surface beneath his left ear thrummed.

A vehicle? he thought. *Aircraft? Boat? Groundcar?*

He waited, but nothing else happened. He wiggled to attract the attention of whomever might be in the vicinity . . . and to get some blood flowing to his limbs . . . but nothing changed.

Where are they taking me? he wondered.

It appeared he'd have a long wait before he found out.

Emily Wood sat in the wardroom of the sub with her mother for the two hours it took them to travel to where the *Divine Will* lay on the bottom of the ocean. After an hour or so, Dr. Christianson-Wood stirred and opened her eyes, but she sat staring into space, occasionally muttering something to herself that Emily couldn't catch. She paid no attention to Emily or her surroundings at all.

At the end of the second hour, a subtle shift in the vibration of the sub told her the engines were slowing.

A few moments later they stopped. She heard distant shouts and clanking sounds, and after a few minutes the forward door opened and Alister Stone came in, Abban right behind him, sidearm drawn.

"We've reached the *Divine Will*," Stone said without preamble. "Time to get you aboard."

"We can swim," Emily said.

"We can't," Stone said shortly. "We've got a three-man minisub aboard we're going to use to ferry people across. We've told the shuttle's computer to open the cargo hold and let it flood. We'll take the sub into the hold, pump it out, let people out, rinse, and repeat."

"What makes you think that shuttle is still good?" she said. "Salt water is highly corrosive. And it's been down here for months."

"The computer says it's fine," Stone said. "I guess we'll find out when we launch."

"Or when you get into orbit. Or when you jump into branespace. Or on landing. One failure, and—"

"—and we all die." Stone shrugged. "You included."

Emily got to her feet and took a step toward him. Abban lifted his weapon, and she stopped. "Why not give yourself up, Stone? Marseguro could use your expertise. We're not vindictive. The Planetary Council will offer amnesty if I recommend it. You could start a new life—"

"A new life?" Stone's lip twisted. "A new life with the monsters who murdered my friends? A new life with *things* like you? I'd rather die. And I'd rather die doing my duty than die a traitor when the Body comes back to rip this filthy sponge of a planet to shreds."

"How do your men feel about it?" Emily shifted her eyes to Abban.

His pistol didn't waver, but his eyes flicked from her to Stone. Stone glared at him. "The same," he said tightly.

Emily turned back to her mother. "Have it your way," she said. "But I think it's a mistake."

"Then we'll all live—or die—with the consequences," Stone said.

Emily touched her mother's shoulder protectively. "I should—"

"You should shut up and do what I tell you!" Stone snarled.

Emily blinked and very carefully didn't smile, but she couldn't help but think, *I got to you, didn't I?* And the only reason she could think of was that Stone wasn't as sure of his men as he pretended. Some of them might not be as fanatically committed as their commander.

She wasn't sure how that could help her. Maybe it couldn't. But maybe it was worth poking at, like a weak spot in a brick wall. She just might break through to someone. And if she could get any sort of ally among the Holy Warriors, it could make all the difference on the trip to Earth, and maybe even after.

But then her spirits dropped like a rock falling into the Deep. The trip to Earth. God, she couldn't believe it was really going to happen. But here they were, about to board the *Divine Will*. And once they were in space, there would be no chance of escape.

She looked at her mother. *There's no chance* now. If it had just been herself, she might have tried something once she got aboard the minisub. But she couldn't leave her mother to be dragged to Earth alone, as a war criminal at best, as a plaything for Stone and his crew at worst.

"Get her moving," Stone snapped. Without a word, Emily tugged her mother to her feet. She stood willingly enough, and walked when Emily applied a little pressure to her arm, but she still didn't seem to be registering anything around her.

Emily wondered how she'd react when they were separated for the trip to the shuttle, but she took no more notice of Rusk, who accompanied her on the first trip over, than she had of Emily.

Emily waited in the big sub's internal docking bay, guarded by Abban and another Holy Warrior whose breast-pocket name tag proclaimed him to be Biccum. Stone stood a little way off, talking in a low voice with another man whose name she didn't yet know.

Forty-five minutes after they'd watched the minisub submerge, it reemerged into the big sub's bay, water streaming from its transparent canopy. "Biccum and the Selkie," Stone commanded. "Then Abban and me."

"Shouldn't you stay and go down with your ship?" Emily said.

"I'm transferring my flag," Stone said. "Move."

Settled in the smaller sub, Emily couldn't help but think of her own little sub, now lying crushed on the ocean floor. Just a few hours ago she'd been packing it in anticipation of John and Amy's wedding, her happiness tempered only by her constant concern for her mother and the more distant worry for Richard.

Now it was happiness that was distant, so distant she couldn't see how she could ever find her way back to it again.

The journey from sub to shuttle took only a few minutes. Stuck in the windowless passenger compartment, she couldn't see a thing. She could only listen: thumps, clangs, the rhythmic swish of pumps. The sub suddenly listed to the left, then stopped at about a ten-degree angle. And then the hatch undogged and swung open.

Biccum crawled out first, then turned to offer her a hand as she followed. Surprised, she took it. Once on the wet deck plates of the cargo hold, she looked around for her mother, but of course she'd been taken somewhere farther inside the shuttle. Biccum pointed her to a hatch. It opened at his touch on the control plate. Inside was a ladder, leading down into a corridor that, at first glance, appeared to extend almost the entire length of the shuttle. Emily had expected something utilitarian, but the corridor was lit with subtle, hidden lights, and painted in muted tones of blue and green. The netting that covered the walls to provide easy hand- and footholds in zero gravity was cleverly designed to look like intertwining vines, complete with leaves and red, yellow, white, and blue flowers. The air was cool and dry ... and tainted, just faintly, with a hint of decomposing flesh.

The crew, Emily thought.

Rusk stood at the bottom of the ladder with her mother, whose glazed eyes made it clear she was not seeing the corridor at all. "We're supposed to confine them in one of the cabins," Biccum said as he climbed down after Emily. He glanced at her. "We'll be making a couple of final runs with the sub after everyone is aboard to bring over the cargo we're taking back ... including a landsuit for your mother."

Only one? Emily, who could already feel the tingle of dryness along the edges of her gills, felt a sudden chill. *Of course only one. They didn't plan for me.* "What am I supposed to do?" she said.

Biccum looked uncomfortable, but shrugged. "I don't know. You'll have to talk to Stone about that." He pointed toward the rear of the shuttle. "That way."

"How long is the trip to Earth?" Emily asked as she followed Rusk and her mother, Biccum bringing up the rear.

"Two weeks."

Two weeks? She swallowed, mouth—with horrible appropriateness—suddenly dry. "I won't make it."

"Talk to Stone," Biccum said again.

Emily changed the subject. "What kind of shuttle *is* this?" She reached out and ran her fingers through the zero-G webbing. It felt soft as velvet to the touch.

"Interstellar conveyance for Grand Deacons and the like," Biccum said. His tone was almost friendly, at least compared to any other Holy Warrior she'd ever spoken to. She gave him a closer look. About the same height as she was, he had a bald head and bushy black eyebrows, and either the thickest neck she'd ever seen or no neck at all. He smiled, startling her. "I've never been in one myself until now."

Rusk, thin and dark-skinned, shot him a sharp look over his shoulder, brown eyes glittering, but he said nothing. They moved slowly down the corridor at her mother's shuffling pace. "It's even bigger than the sub," Biccum went on. "We could have carried two more attack craft on *Sanctification* if we hadn't brought it, but Grand Deacon Ellers insisted. He figured we'd have Marseguro Purified in no time, but we'd have to stay on station here for a while to keep things quiet . . . and he didn't intend to hang around in person for that. There was supposed to be an Ascension fight shaping up back home and he wanted to be in the thick of it."

Emily didn't know what an Ascension fight was, or particularly care, but she was glad to have found, if not an ally, at least a possible source of information among the Holy Warriors. "Interesting," she said.

"Shut up, Biccum," Rusk snarled at last. "Stone didn't say nothin' about chattin' with the pris'ners." He had a different accent from Biccum's, though Emily didn't know enough about Earth to know what part of the planet he might have come from.

"He didn't say *not* to talk to them either," Biccum retorted, but he fell silent for the rest of the slow trip to their quarters. When the door opened, Emily gasped. Three rooms, tiny, but still; three entire rooms in a shuttle?

Not really a shuttle, she thought. *More like a mini-starship.*

One of the rooms was a dining/sitting room with a small table with low sofas on either side of it and a vidscreen/entertainment unit in the bulkhead next to the door. From it, open sliding doors revealed a bedroom, taken up almost entirely with bed, and a bathroom with very odd-looking fixtures.

In fact, everything looked odd. It took a few seconds for Emily to realize that everything had two configurations: one for when they were in gravity, like now, and one for zero-gravity. That strange collapsed tube pressed up against the ceiling of the bathroom, then, must be a zero-G shower or bath. Emily eyed it doubtfully, all too aware it might be all that stood between her and an agonizing death.

"The Grand Deacon's own quarters," Biccum said. "Commander Stone said you'd need it, with two of you."

"I'm surprised he didn't keep it for himself," Emily said. "I expected something more dungeonlike."

"Naw, Stone doesn't go in for luxuries," Biccum said. "He's one of the men."

"Biccum . . ." Rusk snarled.

"Right. Well, here you are. I'll be outside the door." Biccum turned to Rusk. "Well, go on, Rusk, what are you waiting for? You're supposed to help shift cargo!"

Rusk gave him a blistering look, but turned and went out. Biccum went out, too, but as he closed the door behind him, he . . .

Emily blinked. Had that been a wink?

Holy Warriors are human, too, she thought as she guided her mother to the bed and helped her lie down on it. It had been easy to forget that during the war. It had been easy to celebrate every time she saw one die . . . or every time she killed one. After the first few, she'd felt no more empathy for them than she did for squigglefish.

Or so she had told herself.

But now . . .

Biccum seemed almost kind. She didn't think for a second he'd help her escape, but he wasn't a monster himself, just a man in service to a monstrous ideology. A man she might have been friends with, if he'd been born and raised on Marseguro instead of in the Body Purified.

She watched her mother, lying on one of the couches beside the table, blinking sleepily up at the ceiling. After a moment she closed her eyes and began to breathe deeply.

Mom knew that from the start, she thought.

Her mother had known her plague would kill men who didn't deserve to die, men who served the Body only because they had no other choice, men who might harbor doubts but couldn't act on them, men trapped inside the system.

Richard had escaped that system, had realized . . . on his own, or with the help of the gene-bomb Victor Hansen had left inside his brain . . . that he had to turn against the Body. How many others among the Holy Warriors might have done the same, but were never given the chance? Her mother's plague was no respecter of persons: every nonmod, friend or foe, who didn't receive the vaccine in time, died.

Emily's mother had steeled herself to that knowledge, but when she'd learned the plague was on its way to Earth . . .

She'd retreated, unable to face what she'd done.

Emily went into the bedroom and lay down. Her mother hadn't said anything, but she must be starting to feel the effects of dehydration, as well. She hoped Stone would hurry up with the landsuit.

And after that . . .

She rolled over onto her side and stared at the zero-G bathtube again.

Stone didn't bring the landsuit himself: instead it was Rusk, who handed it over without a word and retreated again at once. Emily woke her mother and helped her pull on the heavy suit, its reservoir tank already filled. A slight frown had settled on Dr. Christianson-Wood's face, and she kept blinking around the cabin as though trying to work out where she was. *The drugs are wearing off,* Emily thought uneasily. *And we don't have any more.*

The drugs kept her mother calm, kept her from hurting herself or someone else when she lost herself in hysteria. Without them, Emily didn't know what would happen. Especially when her mother remembered, as she eventually would, that they were on a shuttle filled with Holy Warriors bound for Earth.

She'd better talk to Stone about it.

She went to the door and knocked. It swung open at once, out into the corridor, revealing Biccum's broad face. "Yes, miss?"

"I need to talk to Stone," she said.

"I'll let him know."

Stone showed up about half an hour later. "What is it?" he said without preamble, standing in the doorway without coming in.

She told him about her mother. "If you have any sedatives on board, I might be able to . . ."

"We don't," Stone said. "The crew of the shuttle used everything in the med station trying to save their lives when they became sick. In the end they killed themselves . . . using the supply of sedatives. We've been disposing of the corpses for the past thirty minutes."

"I don't know how my mother will react when she fully wakes up," Emily said. "She might—"

"I suggest you control her," Stone said. "See to it that she doesn't hurt herself. I want her undamaged when we hand her over for trial. And if anything happens to her . . . I don't need you."

Emily's mouth tightened. "I remember."

"Good. Now don't bother me again. We lift within an hour."

Twenty minutes later, Biccum knocked, then came inside. Rusk, she saw, remained outside on guard. "Beg pardon, ma'am," Biccum said, "but we need to rig your quarters for zero-G." He glanced into the bedroom at her mother, asleep once more. "We'll start in here."

Emily nodded and stood out of the way. With a few

twists and clicks, Biccum turned the ordinary couches into acceleration couches, complete with harnesses for takeoff and landing and single lap belts to enable passengers to "sit" in them without gravity. He helped Emily prod her mother into one of them and strap her in, then went into the bedroom, where, in a few moments, he had transformed the ordinary-looking bed into two tubes like sleeping bags. In the bathroom, the bathtube descended and was sealed and the previously passive toilet came to rather sinister hissing life at the touch of a button, the water in it vanishing away, the seat replaced with an odd kind of flexible seal. It had a seat belt, too.

"All done, miss," Biccum said at last, crossing the sitting room to the door.

"Thank you," she said.

He smiled. "You're welcome." And out he went.

They must have been waiting for his signal on the bridge, because five minutes later an alarm whooped and Stone's voice came from speakers in the ceiling. "Prepare for launch. Five minutes . . . mark."

Emily strapped herself into the couch beside her sleeping mother. Dr. Christianson-Wood's head tossed restlessly, and her mouth formed unheard words, then she subsided, though she continued to frown slightly in her sleep.

"One minute," Stone said.

The seconds crawled by.

"Beginning ascent," he said abruptly.

The actual event was anticlimactic, which in a shuttle that had been submerged in salt water for six months was a very good thing. The shuttle swayed slightly, presumably rising through the water, then the slight vibration shaking the deck plates changed frequency and the ride smoothed out. Acceleration suddenly pressed Emily hard into her couch. It lasted only a few minutes, then eased off. She felt lighter and lighter and . . .

The straps on the couch creaked slightly as she turned

her head and her motion lifted her off the seat. Zero-G. They were in space.

They were going to Earth.

Her mother's eyes fluttered open, and she blinked up blankly at the ceiling (if you could still call it that), then turned to look at Emily. "What's . . . sweetie, what's happening?" she said faintly. "I've had . . . nightmares."

"Go back to sleep, Mom," Emily said. "I'll tell you later."

Her mother blinked at her a few times, then her eyes, still dragged down by the drugs slowly fading from her system, closed once more.

And what will you tell her? Emily thought bleakly. *That the nightmare is real, and just beginning?*

Her gills had moved beyond tingling to burning and itching. She moved her head irritably, then sighed and unstrapped.

She'd better make the acquaintance of the zero-G bathtube.

Richard Hansen hung in the hold of one of the *Victor Hansen*'s cargo shuttles, checking the straps securing the precious security chest full of vaccine—and, even more importantly, the microfactory programming for creating more vaccine. Of course it was secure—it had been checked and double-checked already—but he needed something to occupy him while the minutes dragged by until they launched for the rendezvous with Jacob and the other survivors at the island resort.

Andy King floated in. "Not particularly good management technique, double-checking the crew's work," he said mildly.

"I know," Richard said. "But it's better than biting my fingernails in the cockpit."

He waited for Andy to tell him—again—that he shouldn't go himself, expecting to reply—again—that the decision had been made, but Andy surprised him. "I hope the mission goes well," he said. "Good luck, Captain."

Richard blinked. "Thank you, Andy." He turned back to the straps and gave one last unnecessary tug. "I think we're set."

"Launch in fifteen minutes, then?"

Richard nodded. "Launch in fifteen, as planned."

"Very good. I'll return to the bridge." Andy held out his hand. "Good luck, Richard."

Richard shook Andy's hand firmly. "Thank you, Andy. Take good care of the *Victor Hansen*. She's the only starship we've got, unless we manage to drag that missing shuttle off the bottom of the sea."

"Makes me acting admiral as well as acting captain, doesn't it?" Andy said with a grin. He turned and pulled himself out along the ratlines still joining the shuttle, now floating free in the central tunnel of the *Victor Hansen*, to the curving walls of the tunnel's interior.

Richard pulled himself up out of the cargo hold into the passenger compartment. The shuttle could easily have carried a dozen or more, but for this trip the crew, all volunteers, consisted of just six, counting himself, evenly divided between nonmods and Selkies. Looking through the open hatch forward, he could see a young Selkie woman with black-and-pink hair: Melody Ashman, his pilot. Next to her sat her copilot, Pierre Normand, a slender Selkie with a fuzz of electric-blue hair covering his pate and lightning-bolt tattoos on each cheek, both contrasting sharply with his unadorned matte-black landsuit.

Strapped into passenger seats were Jerry Krall, another Selkie, bigger than Pierre but with more sedate taste in hair and tattoos—the former plain brown, the latter lacking—and Ann Nolan, a nonmod woman, older than Melody, so petite she looked childlike next to Jerry. They were the technicians who would explain the mak-

ing of the vaccine and program the first microfactories
to produce it, assuming all went well.

Finally, all by himself at the back, Richard saw the
remaining nonmod, Derryl Godard, tall, thin, wraith-
like, dressed all in black, hair and eyes just as dark. He
held a long black case across his knees, which Richard
knew contained a Holy Warrior sniper rifle. His job:
keep watch over Richard's first meeting with the supposed survivors and kill without mercy at the first sign
of treachery—or the first sign of Holy Warriors. He also
carried the control that would order the security chest
to destroy its contents.

Hope for the best, plan for the worst, Richard thought.
"Everyone set?" he said.

A chorus of "Yes, sirs," and "Aye, ayes," came back.
Only Godard remained silent, though he gave a slight
nod when Richard glanced back at him.

Richard strapped himself into the seat behind Melody, frowning. He only knew a little of Godard's story.
Like everyone else, he had lost people he cared about
in the Body's attack on Marseguro. Like many others,
he had responded by training hard with the Holy Warrior weapons that had become available in the after-
math of the plague, and had been one of those who had
helped ambush the follow-up landing by Holy Warriors
from *BPS Retribution,* sent from Earth to discover
what had gone wrong with the initial assault. But unlike most, he had continued to train, day after day, hour
after hour, becoming without a doubt the best shot on
Marseguro.

And then he'd volunteered for the *Victor Hansen.*

Yet Andy had assured Richard that although Godard
would shoot without hesitation, he was not on some private mission of revenge.

Richard hoped Andy knew what he was talking
about.

Jerry went back into the hold to sit across from Derryl,

while Ann took the other cockpit seat. Richard leaned forward. "We're in your hands, Melody."

She nodded and said briskly, "Computer, establish link to bridge; keep open until otherwise ordered."

"Link established," said the computer's uninflected male voice.

"Bridge, this is shuttle *Sawyer's Point*. We are secured and ready for launch." They'd named the shuttle in honor of the volcanic spire that Emily Wood had brought crashing down on the killerbot that had been tracking her . . . and Richard. It had been his first inkling that he wasn't who he thought he was, that he was literally a blood relation of the Selkies he had brought the Holy Warriors to destroy.

"Roger, *Sawyer's Point*. Reeling in ratlines." Through the cockpit window, Richard watched two of the lines retracting into the walls of the hold.

"Isolating launch bay."

Massive bulkheads irised shut in front of the shuttle, blocking off the bulk of the central tunnel of the ship. They would exit through the stern.

"Evacuating launch bay."

A gale sprang into existence outside, and for a moment the bay filled with fog as the air pressure dropped precipitously. Just as quickly the fog vanished, the roar of the pumps attenuating with it into silence.

"Opening rear hatch."

Richard couldn't see that, but flashing yellow light reflecting off the bulkhead separating them from the rest of the ship told him it was happening.

"Launch."

The bulkhead receded, faster and faster; then they were out in space, the sun glaring from behind them, lighting up the long cylinder of the *Victor Hansen*, sleek and silver, thicker at the stern where the drives and shuttle docking bays were located, and banded at the front by the fatter cylinder of the habitat ring. It fell away above them, and then slid out of sight behind them as Melody took control and began their descent.

"Here we go," Richard said to no one in particular.

The first thin screams of tortured atmosphere rose from outside the shuttle ten minutes later, and for the first time they touched the plague-infected atmosphere of Earth.

"They've entered the atmosphere," Grand Deacon von Eschen told Karl Rasmusson quietly.

"Good," the Avatar said. "Send the signal."

Chapter 6

ANDY KING SAT IN the captain's chair on the bridge of the *Victor Hansen* and watched the tactical display. The blip representing the shuttle entered Earth's atmosphere and began the descent to the resort island.

The display didn't show much else: just satellites and a few space stations. The satellites continued their automated functions, whatever they might be; the space stations were silent, floating tombs. The other ships orbiting Earth, the freighter, the two shuttles, the hotel ship, and most importantly, the Holy Warrior vessel *BPS Vision of Truth*, remained dead. They were alone in orbit.

About forty minutes after *Sawyer's Point* exited the ship, Pierre Normand's voice crackled onto the bridge. "*Victor Hansen? Sawyer's Point.* We're down in one piece. We'll update you shortly."

Andy touched the manual control that activated his end of the always-open communications link they'd established with the shuttle. "*Sawyer's Point, Victor Hansen.* Acknowledged."

Even as he spoke, a new blip appeared on the tactical display. It disappeared almost instantly: if he hadn't happened to have been looking at exactly the right part of the display, he never would have seen it.

He opened his mouth to say something, but his acting first officer, Cordelia Raum, beat him to it.

"Unknown vessel, bearing ..." She stopped. "Um ... it's gone, sir."

"I saw something, too, Cordie," Andy said. "Check it out."

Raum bent over her board. After a moment's silence, she looked up. "It read as a shuttle, but just for an instant," she said. "Then it disappeared. Some sort of atmospheric echo, maybe? If it were real, the computer would have said something."

Andy's eyes narrowed. "Maybe," he said. "But let's play it safe. Sound General Quarters." As klaxons sounded, he activated the comm link again. "*Sawyer's Point, Victor Hansen*. Captain, we may have a situation up here. Please respond."

Nothing. Andy frowned at Raum, who frowned at her board, fingers flying over the controls. "The comm link to the shuttle is down, sir!"

"Computer," Andy said. "Reestablish comm link to shuttle *Sawyer's Point*."

"Unable to comply," the computer said.

"Computer, why are you unable to comply?" Andy snapped.

"We are currently experiencing severe electromagnetic interference on all communications wavelengths," the computer replied.

We're being jammed, Andy realized. *And that blip was no atmospheric echo.*

He'd already sounded General Quarters. There was nothing else he could do but wait for the other shoe to drop.

Sawyer's Point burst out of low-hanging clouds and swept down the length of a broad valley, dark evergreen forest disappearing into the fog on either side. A few seconds later the forest ended in a cluster of buildings and four large piers, then they were roaring over gray-green tossing ocean. The island appeared out of the fog ahead of them, and the shuttle's braking rockets roared. Moments later, they settled onto a broad pad at one end of the landing strip, its concrete burned black by countless takeoffs and landings.

The shuttle creaked as it settled onto its landing struts. The engine noise died away, leaving only the faint hum of the ventilation fans and the ticking of cooling metal.

"We're down," Melody said unnecessarily.

"Let the *Victor Hansen* know," Richard said.

"Already done, sir," Pierre Normand said. Then he cocked his head, listening to his earbud. "Ground Control has contacted us. It's Jacob. He welcomes us to Earth and wonders if they can approach the shuttle now."

"Any visual?"

"No, just voice, like before," Pierre said.

"Let me talk to him." Pierre touched a control, then nodded.

"Hello, Jacob," Richard said.

"Captain Hansen! I can't tell you how wonderful it is to see you. Can we come out or do you need to secure things first?"

"Let's not rush anything," Richard said. "You'll forgive me for being cautious, and nothing personal, but this could still be a Body trap. I'll tell you what: I'll meet you on the landing strip, alone. Then we'll talk about what to do next."

Jacob chuckled. "I don't blame you at all, Captain. Okay. You're about a hundred meters from the control tower where I am. Do you see it? You're pointing right at it."

Richard leaned out of his seat and looked out through the cockpit window. Directly ahead, dim in the fog, a tower loomed at the edge of the concrete pad. "I see it."

"I'll meet you halfway."

"I'm on my way." Richard unbuckled. *You don't have to do this yourself,* he could almost hear Andy say. Those on board the shuttle expressed *their* disapproval with silent frowns. He ignored them, just like he would have ignored Andy.

He did, however, turn to Godard. "Get your weapon," he said. "I want you outside the shuttle . . . just in case."

Godard nodded, and unbuckled.

Andy King watched the tactical display. It didn't change.

But he felt something odd, a faint . . . bump. Barely perceptible. "Computer," he said. "Status."

"All systems nominal," the computer said.

"Computer," Andy began again, but got no further.

"Bridge, we're being boarded!" a voice yelled over internal communications. "Holy Warriors! They're coming through the . . ."

The voice cut off.

"Computer, secure all access routes against boarders!" Andy snapped.

"Unable to comply," the computer said.

What? Andy felt a chill. "Computer, why are you unable to comply with last order?"

"Order has been countermanded by higher authority," the computer said.

"Damn!" Andy slapped the internal communications controls. "Crew, report!"

"They're in the main access tunnel," an unidentified voice came back. "We can't even get there. All of the hatches are locked."

"Casualties?"

"One. Teddy Simons," came another voice, ragged, breathing hard. "He was right there when they came in through Hatch 12. The bastards killed him on sight. But they haven't fired another shot. They haven't had to. We can't get at them!"

"Computer," Andy said. "Location of party that has just boarded the ship."

"Command party has just entered the habitat ring," the computer said.

Command party!

"Weapons?" Raum asked.

"No," Andy said. "Stand down." He stood up, looked around at the four men and two women currently on the bridge. "All of you," he said.

They knew what he intended. They'd drilled it often enough. As one, the bridge crew shut down their stations, stood up and moved away from them.

"This is First Officer Andy King," Andy said to the ship at large. "Submerge. Repeat, submerge."

He looked around at the bridge crew. "Let's go."

The statue of Victor Hansen outside the bridge doors watched impassively as they filed out.

Richard stood outside the shuttle, breathing the air of Earth for the first time since he had boarded the *Sanctification* for the attack on Marseguro, more than half a year ago. The fog had lifted a little, just enough that he could see the base of the control tower clearly, though mist still wreathed the top. And there, right on schedule, came Jacob . . . or someone he presumed was Jacob. Not surprisingly, the man walking toward him was wearing a pressure suit . . . civilian, though, not Holy Warrior issue. A good sign.

"No one else visible," Melody's voice said in his ear.

"I'm going to meet him," Richard said, and he did.

Jacob appeared to be a bit shorter and slimmer than Richard. The half-silvered bubble of his pressure suit made it impossible for Richard to see his face. He raised a hand as Richard approached, then touched a control on the suit's neck. "Welcome to Earth!" he said, his voice tinny over an external speaker.

"You're Jacob?" Richard said.

"In a manner of speaking," the man said cheerfully. "Though you might know me by another name." And he touched another control that turned his suit helmet completely transparent.

Richard blinked. He knew that face, but he couldn't . . .

And then it hit him, with the force of a fist to the stomach. "You're . . . Karl Rasmusson. You're the Right Hand of the Avatar!"

"Ready," said Godard in Richard's ear. Richard's jaw clenched. All he had to say was the code word "Firstdip" and Rasmusson would die . . .

Along with himself and everyone on the shuttle. There could be no doubt now that Holy Warriors were nearby. He held his tongue.

"Well, not anymore. Now, I am the Avatar: Karl the First, at your service. Not through any choice of my own," Rasmusson added with a bit of a smile. "I much preferred being Right Hand. But thanks to you, I have Ascended, and taken the oath before God Itself to serve It and keep the Body Purified."

"You are also in the sights of a sniper," Richard said softly. "At my signal—"

"Look down, Mr. Hansen," the Avatar said.

Richard's eyes narrowed, but he glanced down. There were three small red dots in the middle of his chest.

Sniper laser guides didn't have to be in visible wavelengths. These were a message.

Richard looked up again. "Killing me won't do you any good. The vaccine is in a secure chest. Only I can open it. If anyone else tries, or if I give a signal . . . the vaccine will be destroyed."

"All of it?" Rasmusson said. "Surely some of it is aboard *BPS Sanctification*."

"*MSS Victor Hansen*," Richard corrected sharply. "Flagship of the Marseguroite navy. And any vaccine there is out of your reach."

Rasmusson smiled. "Is it?"

Richard felt a chill that had nothing to do with the fog. "Pierre," he said.

"Monitoring," Pierre said tensely.

Richard kept eyes on the Avatar. "Any communication from *Victor Hansen*?"

"Negative."

"Call them," Richard said.

A moment's silence. When Pierre's voice came back, it sounded strained. "No response, sir. But, sir . . . we just received a message from the ship."

"Replay it."

A crackle, then a voice Richard had never heard before: "This is *BPS Sanctification*. Bridge secured."

Karl Rasmusson cocked his head. "Trouble?" he said.

Richard's fist clenched. He wanted to smash it through Rasmusson's faceplate, but that would accomplish nothing except getting himself killed.

"We have your ship, and your crew," the Avatar went on conversationally. "Aboard that ship we will no doubt find a great deal more vaccine, and the data which will allow us to mass produce it. You have one unarmed shuttle, five crewmembers, a secure chest filled with entirely *redundant* vaccine, and three bright red dots over your heart." The Avatar smiled. "I suggest you surrender."

"I can still kill *you*," Richard said.

"I'm sure that's true," the Avatar said. "But if we both die within the next few seconds, it changes nothing. The Body will still control *Sanctification* . . . as it always has, of course; your so-called captaincy was essentially a work of fiction. Your crew will still be captive. Your shuttle and your crew here will be destroyed. All of you will die, and to no purpose."

"You'll be dead, too. Right now that seems a fair exchange."

The Avatar sighed. "Mr. Hansen, you know as well as I that upon Ascension to this position my own personal safety became secondary to the needs of the Body. If I die, God Itself will welcome me into the afterlife as a martyr and a hero."

Richard stared at him. Ice-blue eyes stared back. Richard's heart sank. "You really believe that, don't you?"

"I do."

"I didn't expect . . ."

"True belief in someone who has spent his life pulling strings in the shadow of Avatar Harold the Second?" Rasmusson shook his head. "Then you didn't think things through. I preferred to be Right Hand, never sought to be considered for Ascension, because I thought that being Right Hand allowed me to better serve and protect the Body. I am not interested in power for its own sake. I serve the Body; the Body serves God. It is the only way to ensure that It does not destroy Earth once and for all."

Richard stood stock-still for a long moment. He could bring this conversation to a bloody end with a word, but he had no doubt the Avatar was telling the truth. Karl Rasmusson was as much a fanatic as the First Avatar had been. His orders would already be in place: if he were struck down, not only would Richard die, so would his entire crew.

If the Body truly held them captive. Because therein lay his only hope: that Andy King had ordered the crew to Submerge. If he had, then the crew might be trapped in orbit, but they weren't imprisoned. They were in hiding in the rooms and access routes that they had systematically blinded the computer to during the months of retrofitting.

Simon Goodfellow, his pet computer genius, had assured Richard they'd left no traces of that tampering: that to the Holy Warriors, it would seem that the crew had fled aboard the (in-reality empty) escape pods launched automatically as part of the plan.

Goodfellow had promised Richard something else, too, offering him an option so drastic that Richard had hoped it would never be necessary. But now it sounded like it might be.

It wouldn't be his decision to attempt it, though. It would be Andy King's. Because for the moment, and quite possibly permanently, he was out of the fight.

He couldn't—wouldn't—sacrifice the shuttle and its crew. And at least one good thing could still come out of all this: the vaccine would be distributed. Lives would be saved. Even if ultimately that led to a resurgent Body, it was better than allowing the plague to continue killing innocent people indiscriminately. He'd said as much to Andy, when he'd raised the possibility he might eventually have to negotiate with the Body.

His own life might not be among those saved, of course, but in the grand balance, perhaps that wasn't all that important to anyone except himself . . .

. . . and, he dared hope still, Emily.

Glad yet again she had remained safe, at least for the time being, on Marseguro, he took a deep breath, then said, "Very well, Avatar. We surrender."

"Captain . . . ?" Melody said tensely in his ear. "Are you sure about this? Derryl's got a clean shot. Give the word, and—"

"You heard me, Melody," Richard said. "Godard, stand down. Everyone, stand down. Open the hatch. Let the Holy Warriors aboard." He kept his eyes on the Avatar, who never looked away. "They won't hurt you."

"Your crew won't be harmed, provided they cooperate," the Avatar said. "I promise." He turned away and spoke in a low voice into his helmet microphone, then turned back to Richard. "Now, if you'll perform the introductions . . ." He indicated the shuttle.

With the sense of failure settling on him like a heavy black cloak, Richard led the Avatar of the Body Purified to *Sawyer's Point*, already swarming with pressure-suited Holy Warriors.

Aboard the erstwhile *Victor Hansen*, Andy King held on to the zero-G webbing lining the walls of the giant cylindrical chamber that had once been a fuel tank but now no longer even existed as far as the ship's computer was concerned, and surveyed his crew. They were all there, every nonmod and Selkie ... all except for Able Crewman Teddy Simons, age twenty-four, promising splashball player and talented singer/songwriter, shot down by the Holy Warriors as they first entered the ship.

The Holy Warriors' method of precluding counter-attacks—ordering the computer to seal off all access to the route they took the bridge—had worked against them. It had given the crew time not only to respond to Andy's "Submerge" command and vanish into the hidden areas, but to take the entire existing stock of vaccine and the microfactory programming modules for creating more into hiding with them.

They had food and water enough for weeks stored in these secret spaces. But eventually they would run out. Before that happened, they had to retake the ship. And before they could retake the ship, they had to deal with the computer.

The nonmod hanging next to Andy in the webbing was thin and gray-skinned, with a sunken chest and sunken cheeks. Pale blond hair, almost white, stuck in wispy, sweaty strands to his mostly bald head. *He wouldn't last two minutes in a physical fight*, Andy thought. But right now Simon Goodfellow held the key to all their hopes.

"Can you do it?" Andy had asked the question a moment before, and it seemed to hang in the air between them. The rest of the crew, ostensibly out of earshot, somehow seemed to be holding its collective breath.

"It will take time," Simon responded at last. "I'll need uninterrupted access to a main data conduit for at least two hours. And a programming/diagnostic workstation, of course."

Andy frowned. "I thought you planted the databomb back on Marseguro. Why can't you just trigger it?"

"I did plant it," Simon said. "But these ship AIs are

extremely—insanely—well-protected. Not trusting types, Body engineers. Getting the activation command to the databomb through all the defenses designed to prevent tampering with the ship's brain ... we had weeks to get the thing in there. But if we'd made it too easy to access, it wouldn't have remained hidden. The AI itself would probably have found it and rooted it out before now. Two hours, minimum." He smiled a slightly superior smile. "I can explain in more detail ... if you have a year or two to study AI mechanics."

Andy took a deep breath, held it for a moment with his eyes closed, then let it out explosively. He didn't have to like Simon Goodfellow, but he sure as hell needed him. "Fine," he growled. "So where can we find a main data conduit, and where can we find a programming/ diagnostic workstation?"

"There's a PDW tucked away in here," Goodfellow said.

"That's a relief," Andy muttered.

"The best place to get at the main data conduit would be the corridor outside the bridge. There's an access panel there."

Andy stared at him. "Um, no," he said. "How about the second or third best? Preferably some place we can actually defend while you go about it."

Goodfellow grimaced. "Well ... I suppose I could do it from the VR training room. But there's no access panel. We'll have to cut through the wall. It'll add more time."

"Beats standing around outside the bridge waiting to be shot," Andy said dryly.

Simon turned a shade paler. "Um. Yes, I see your point."

Andy thought hard. "I might have an idea," he said at last. "It'll take some planning. And we'll have to be patient. If everything worked the way we planned, they'll believe we all fled to the surface. But we've got to give them time to search the ship, wait until they're off their guard." Andy wanted nothing more than to act *now*, this minute, to take the *Victor Hansen* back and turn the tables on the Holy Warriors . . . but he couldn't.

For the moment, the only wise action was inaction.

He sighed and looked around at the assembled crew. "So," he said. "Anybody got a deck of cards?"

Karl Rasmusson glared at the pressure-suited Holy Warrior in the vidscreen. Slightly out of focus behind him, the Avatar could see the bridge of the *Sanctification*. "Are you certain, Grand Deacon Byrne?"

"Yes, Avatar." Karl couldn't tell for sure through a faceplate but he suspected Michael Byrne—who, after all, had only been a Grand Deacon for about a day, since the Avatar had contacted the erstwhile captain aboard his orbiting troop ship, *BPS Vision of Truth*—was sweating. As he should be. "No crew left aboard. The computer confirms it. Ten escape pods launched as we approached the bridge. If they only had a skeleton crew, that would be enough to ferry them all down to the surface."

"We saw them launch," Karl said. He leaned forward. "But something else launched, too, Grand Deacon. Besides escape pods. Something larger."

Byrne paled even further. "The assault craft," he said. "All three of them. Unmanned, as far as we can tell. They seem to have laid in an emergency program to deny their use to anyone else should the ship be taken."

"Not surprising, considering the history of this particular ship," Karl said. "Do you have other bad news for me, Grand Deacon?"

"Yes, sir." Byrne swallowed. "The Orbital Bombardment System has been scrapped, ripped right out. Even the alloy rods are gone."

"Foolish of them, when they were sailing into Earth orbit. I'm surprised they didn't try to use it to threaten us into submission. But never mind that." Karl leaned forward. "What about the vaccine?"

Byrne shook his head. "Your Holiness, I'm sorry, but . . . nothing. There's none here. And the computer says it knows nothing about it. As a result . . ." Byrne spread his hands. "We don't dare remove our pressure suits while we're on board, and we're keeping vacuum between *Sanctification* and our shuttle. We return to it in shifts to sleep and eat."

Karl drummed his fingers on his desk and stared at the wall for a few moments. Finally he looked back at Byrne, who didn't particularly seem to welcome the attention. He gave the man a small smile: completely terrified underlings were of little use, after all. "Very well, Grand Deacon. You've done well. A shame about the vaccine, though. Keep your eyes open . . . for it, and for a possible counterattack. There are plenty of flight-ready spacecraft scattered around the planet that they could conceivably get their hands on. If you see a ship you don't recognize it, warn it, then destroy it if it doesn't identify itself. No second warning."

"Yes, Avatar."

"Avatar out."

Karl killed the circuit. He sat back in his chair, and looked around his office. Half the size of his old one, maybe a quarter the size of the Avatar's office in the Holy City, it had a determinedly faux-rustic appearance to match the fake-log-cabin exterior. Undressed "logs" of bioformed plastic formed the walls. The carpet, artfully worn, featured dogs hunting stags and foxes. The fireplace snapped and crackled just as if it contained real wood instead of a hologram, and the antlers above the hearth looked as though they might once have really belonged to a deer, possibly the victim of the equally authentic-looking muzzle-loading musket hung on hooks just beneath them.

His desk, though of polished wood, was crammed with electronics, of course. And although normally he could look across it through a huge plate-glass window over a descending slope of fog-wreathed trees to the Pacific Ocean, right now a half-dozen large vidscreens hung in that space.

The one he'd just been using blanked and withdrew into the ceiling. He turned his attention to the next one over, which showed Richard Hansen sitting on a bed in a room that contained nothing else except the security chest containing the vaccine—assuming Hansen hadn't been lying to him all along, of course.

Two pressure-suited Holy Warriors, only visible to the camera as disembodied legs, stood behind Hansen to ensure he didn't attempt to destroy the vaccine.

I've been a little too clever, or else not clever enough, Karl thought. *I thought they'd fight for the ship. I didn't expect them to just abandon it and take the vaccine with them. I didn't think they'd have time.*

Now that chest contains all the vaccine in my control. And I need it.

So . . . how best to convince Richard Hansen to give it to him?

Karl Rasmusson had been playing power games for a very long time. He specialized in using his opponents' weaknesses against them. And he had Richard Hansen's weakness pegged:

Richard Hansen cared about people.

Karl did, too, in his own way, but he cared about them as a mass far more than as individuals. He needed people to carry out the work of the Body, to bring God's will to fruition. When, someday, humanity had been completely Purified, when all the far-flung colonies had been brought under the Body and the last abominations rooted out, then God would open the universe to humans and death and pain would become a thing of the past. Those far-future people would thank the Avatars who had worked tirelessly to achieve their utopia. But unfortunately, he couldn't allow concern for here-and-now people to block the path to that future paradise.

Nor truth, for that matter.

He would talk to Richard Hansen in a few minutes. Let him contemplate the vaccine chest for a few minutes longer.

He glanced at a third screen, where the other five members of Hansen's crew were crowded together in the compound's only other quarantine room, but then turned to the fourth screen, where a Lesser Deacon stood at attention, awaiting his attention. "Report," he said.

"We lost tracking on the escape pods and the assault shuttles when they hit atmosphere, Your Holiness," the Lesser Deacon said. "We think the crew disabled the tracking signals before launch, and without them . . ." his voice trailed off.

Karl said nothing. Once not a sparrow could have fallen on the planet without it being observed by one of the Body's surveillance systems, but without people riding herd on them, those systems degraded quickly. Now the surveillance net had so many gaping holes in it that an entire invasion fleet could have already landed in, say, Afghanistan, and they'd be none the wiser. They were barely able to keep an eye on *BPS Sanctification*. "Best guess?"

"The escape pods all landed in remote regions that are sparsely inhabited or completely uninhabited, Your Holiness."

The whole planet is sparsely inhabited now, Karl thought, but didn't say.

"The escape pods aren't big enough to carry vehicles," the Lesser Deacon continued. "They're stuck, or at best weeks from walking out. I suspect they'll be entirely focused on staying alive."

"What about the assault craft?"

The Lesser Deacon shook his head. "The same situation, I'm afraid."

Then I hope Byrne was right about them being un-

manned, Karl thought. "Thank you, Lesser Deacon." Karl glanced at one of the smaller screens beneath the desk's polished surface. "Another matter, then. You've investigated these reports of aircraft being spotted near various Body compounds . . . ?"

"Yes, Your Holiness," the Lesser Deacon said. "And we have visual sightings that confirm your suspicion. The aircraft are manned . . . if that's the word . . . by Kemonomimi." And now the Lesser Deacon smiled for the first time. "And those we *have* been able to track: they're flying from the airport of a town called Newshore."

"I've never heard of it."

"It was built during the Third Wave of reconstruction following the Day of Salvation, Your Holiness." The Lesser Deacon's smile broadened, revealing teeth. "It's located on the coast of British Columbia. Less than three hundred kilometers north of Paradise island."

"Ah!" Karl returned the man's smile. "Thank you, Deacon."

"Lesser Deacon, Your Holiness," the man corrected.

"Not anymore."

The man grinned so broadly it looked like his face would split. "Thank you, Your Holiness!"

"Dismissed."

Karl flicked off the channel. That screen, too, rose into the ceiling. Now he could once again see down to the endlessly rolling waves splashing against the rocky shore. God Itself lived in that ocean, and in the air, and in the trees, and in space, and in the past few days, Karl had begun to feel Its presence more and more strongly.

First Richard Hansen had been delivered into his hand. And now . . . the Kemonomimi. The catlike moddies that had first come to his attention as First Hand.

The Holy Warriors had never been able to find a community of them, if such a thing existed, but sightings, though sometimes years apart, were consistent. Harold the Second had personally called off the expensive, fruitless searches that Karl kept mounting, reasoning (inasmuch as Harold the Second reasoned anything) that they weren't causing any trouble, so why not let them be?

God had answered that argument with the plague.

"We accept your chastisement, O God," Karl said out loud, still watching the ocean. "We understand why you have visited this disaster upon us. We failed to Purify the Selkies of Marseguro, and here on Earth the Kemonomimi abominations have also been left Unpurified. But we will not fail again. We will purge the Earth of the Kemonomimi. We will purge Marseguro of the Selkies. And then we will offer ourselves unblemished before you that you may extend your protection once more. As Your Avatar, I swear it!"

The waves rolled on unchanged, but Karl Rasmusson, Third Avatar of the Body Purified, knew in his heart that God had heard . . . and approved.

He turned his attention back to the screen displaying Richard Hansen's cell, and activated the communications circuit.

Richard sat in the isolation chamber and wondered when he would hear from the Avatar . . . and what the Avatar would have to say.

If Andy had successfully carried out Submerge, the Holy Warriors would have found no trace of the vaccine on board the *Victor Hansen*. Which would suddenly make the vaccine—and microfactory programming—inside the locked security chest far more valuable to the Avatar than before: and Richard's cooperation far more necessary.

If the Submerge had failed, then Richard had lost all bargaining power . . . and the Avatar would be able to do whatever he wanted with him.

It didn't surprise him at all that when the blank vidscreen in the isolation chamber came to life, his heart skipped a beat, then kicked into a much higher rate.

The Avatar's face appeared. He smiled pleasantly. "I'd like you to open the security chest now, Mr. Hansen," he said. "I will begin vaccine distribution the moment you do so."

That did nothing to slow Richard's heart. *Did Andy pull it off . . . ?* "Have you harmed my crew?" he asked.

"No," the Avatar said.

"Will you?"

"I will not," the Avatar said. "*If* you open the chest. If you do not . . . well, in the absence of a vaccine, you are a threat to everyone on this island. You are all carriers. I will have no choice but to treat you as hazardous material."

"You've got the vaccine from the ship," Richard said, but he was almost certain, now, that the Avatar did not.

"Of course," the Avatar said. *Of course, nothing!* "But delivering it here where we already have a supply is a waste of time. From orbit, we can quickly distribute it to our other enclaves around the world."

He doesn't have it! Richard thought.

But then, unbidden, came another thought:

So what?

So what if Andy had successfully Submerged the crew and hidden the vaccine? It could be days, if ever, before they regained control of the ship. In the meantime, people all over Earth continued to die, or fought an almost hopeless battle to keep the plague at bay.

It was just as he'd told Andy on the ship. The Avatar had access to everything needed to distribute the vaccine as quickly and efficiently as possible. The Marseguroites had . . . nothing. It was his fault, of course; he'd thought he was being overly cautious and in fact he hadn't been cautious enough. He shouldn't have come down himself, shouldn't have brought vaccine. He should have sent a scouting party first to find out if "Jacob" was on the level. But he'd been so anxious to start helping people. . . .

The road to hell is paved with good intentions. Clichés

became clichés because they contained truth, and he'd just proved the truth of that one in ... to use another cliché ... spades.

Mission of mercy. Not revenge. He'd made that point to Andy. Now he had to live up to his own high-minded rhetoric.

However good it would feel to destroy the vaccine in the chest ... it would benefit no one. Not the dying people of Earth, not his crew, on Earth or aboard *Victor Hansen*, not even the people of Marseguro. It would be a stupid, futile gesture. It would simply get him and the shuttle crew killed ... and ensure that unknown numbers of survivors died, even though help was at their planetary doorstep.

"All right," he said abruptly. "If you promise not to harm my crew."

"I promise," the Avatar said. "Before God Itself."

Richard took a deep breath. "Very well." He glanced at his pressure-suited guards. "May I ... ?"

"Let him go to the chest," the Avatar commanded.

Richard stood and crossed to the chest, a gleaming silver crate of roughly the same proportions as a coffin. He knelt and put his hands on the palm readers, bent and let the light beam scan his retinas, felt the nip of the DNA sampler against his index finger.

Without fanfare, the chest opened.

Inside were five thousand prepared doses of the hypervaccine and two microfactory programming modules for making more. The doses, each in a cylinder of gleaming black metal, shone in their padded racks. The silvery hyposprays for administering them lay in rows like weapons, but weapons designed to save lives instead of take them. The programming modules, each the size of a deck of cards, gleamed gold. It looked like, and in many ways was, a chest of treasure.

"Thank you, Richard," said the Avatar, using Richard's first name for the first time. Richard wished he wouldn't.

"Hildebrand, take Mr. Hansen to join his crew. Pufahl, stay put until the medical team gets there. They're suiting up now and should be along in a few minutes."

Richard followed Hildebrand out of the isolation cell and down a short corridor to the larger ward, where his crew waited. Hildebrand ushered him in, then closed and sealed the door. Richard looked around at them. "I gave them the vaccine," he said without preamble.

"What?" Pierre Normand's face darkened. "You gave the vaccine to the Body?"

"Otherwise they would have killed all of us," Richard said.

"They've already killed enough of us," Pierre snarled. "If a few more of us had to die in order to ensure the plague took every last Holy Warrior, it would have been a fair trade."

"They've already got the *Victor Hansen*," Richard said.

"But if Andy King—"

"I suggest you *submerge* your feelings," Richard snapped. "That's an order."

He saw the sudden recognition of the code word take hold in each of their faces . . . and with it, he hoped, the realization that everything they were saying must be being monitored. Pierre subsided, but he didn't look any happier.

"If the plague were only taking Holy Warriors, that would be one thing," Richard said. He didn't mind the Avatar overhearing *that*. "But it's also taking— has already taken—countless innocent lives. Vaccine distribution *must* begin as soon as possible. And . . . circumstances being what they are . . . only the Body can make that happen."

Silence. "What do we do, sir?" Melody Ashman finally asked.

Richard sat down on the floor and leaned his back against the wall.

"We wait." *And pray,* he added to himself but didn't say out loud.

The only God he'd ever worshiped didn't seem likely to be on his side.

Karl rubbed his arm where the vaccine had been administered, and stepped aside to watch as the long line of Holy Warriors and Body functionaries who had made it to Paradise Island stepped up one by one for their own shots. "Can we manufacture it?" he asked the tall, gaunt-faced woman who stood watching over the proceedings, her silver-gray hair drawn back in a tight bun.

Dr. Allison McNally looked around, then motioned the Avatar a few paces away, out of earshot of the assembled men and women. "There are difficulties," she said in a low voice. "The programming modules are for a very old kind of microfactory . . . and they're not even remotely compatible with any of the three on this island. We've tried to simply read the contents to burn new modules, but . . . there are also aspects of the programming we don't understand. The Marseguroites . . ."

"Are decades behind technologically," Karl said. "Are they not?" He kept his voice mild, but he could feel anger, like a corrosive acid, eating up at his control from below.

Dr. McNally must have detected something of his incipient rage, she paled. "In some ways," she said. "But not in others. Their technology has advanced over the past seven decades just as ours has, but in different directions. Their knowledge of genetic manipulation is superior to ours, as you'd expect, since research into such matters has been essentially stalled for—"

"—for very good reasons," Karl said. "To preserve us from the wrath of God."

Dr. McNally paled further. "I am not questioning the will of God," she said, very carefully. "I am merely explaining why the programming modules are not usable at this point in time. It will take work and study and experimentation to re-create this vaccine with our equipment, unless we can find a microfactory of the correct vintage, and frankly, I wouldn't even know where to begin looking for one."

"How long?"

Dr. McNally took a deep breath. "Days. Weeks. Months. I can't say with certainty. Perhaps if the Marseguroites helped . . . ?" Her voice trailed away.

Karl looked at the lines of personnel getting their vaccines, the stock diminishing with each hiss of a hypospray. "I'll think about it," he said. "In the meantime, there will be no vaccine distribution beyond this island. How many personnel do we have to vaccinate?"

"Three thousand, one hundred and sixty-four," Dr. McNally said instantly.

"Leaving us with one thousand, eight hundred and thirty-six doses."

"Yes, sir."

"Carry on."

Karl walked away, seething. The solution seemed obvious: ask the imprisoned shuttle crew for help. But theologically . . .

Theologically, Karl thought, *I can't.*

To go to subhuman monstrosities like the Selkies, cap in hand, begging for help, would be blasphemous. It would imply that Selkies were, in some measurable fashion, superior to normal humans. And clearly they were not: one only had to look at them to see that.

No. If God Itself had so arranged things that they could not manufacture the vaccine, and had not been able to retrieve any more from *BPS Sanctification*, then God wanted them to complete the Purification of Earth with the resources It had made available to them: five thousand doses of vaccine, no more. Destroy the Kemonomimi, and *then* God would provide the means to save all the people of Earth . . . and Purify Marseguro as it should have been Purified to begin with.

So, then. Time to be about it.

He quickened his pace. "Computer," he said to the air, knowing the microphone in his collar would transmit his command, "please ask Grand Deacon von Eschen to meet me in my quarters as soon as possible."

"Confirmed," the computer said in his ear.

The one thing they lacked, the Avatar thought, was detailed information about the Kemonomimi physical capabilities. They looked catlike, they were strong and fast, but how strong? How fast? How smart?

Well, he thought, *we have the clone of their creator imprisoned.* He altered his direction of travel to take him to the quarters where Richard and the others were being held.

Purification had been delayed, but not derailed. Karl Rasmusson, Third Avatar of the Body, would complete it . . . and save the Earth once and for all from the ever-looming wrath of God.

Chapter 7

HALFWAY BETWEEN MARSEGURO and Earth, the *Divine Will*'s computer cut the water rations. The first Emily knew of it was when she tried to soak herself in the zero-G bath, as she had been doing for hours every day ... only to discover she could no longer get water.

Floating naked in the empty bathtube, she stared through its transparent wall at the speaker in the ceiling. "Computer, repeat?"

"Water for baths is now restricted to every third day," the computer said. "This restriction will continue indefinitely."

Every third day? Starting from when?

"Computer, when will I next be able to take a bath?"

"In two days."

Emily felt a chill. She'd already delayed this soaking longer than she should have. Her gill slits already tingled, and her skin itched. Was this some nasty trick of Stone's?

"Computer, explain!"

"Recent prolonged submersion in salt water has damaged several systems," the computer said. "Corrosion has resulted in unintended venting of approximately one half of our water supply. Survival protocols dictate that water rations be cut to all crew."

Emily closed her eyes. She wanted to argue with the computer, but she knew that was futile. It could only follow its programming.

She'd have to talk to Stone.

Dry, she pulled herself out of the bathtube, tugged on a jumpsuit, and floated into the bedroom.

They'd been in space for a week now, and the drugs that had kept her mother calm had long since worn off. But to Emily's surprise, there had been no rages, no hysterics. Dr. Christianson-Wood remained calm, if confused. Half the time she asked after her husband, Emily's father, killed in the Holy Warriors' attack on Hansen's Harbor. Sometimes she seemed to think she was still a child, and Emily was *her* mother. And sometimes she simply sat staring into the distance.

At the moment she slept, snug in her landsuit, tucked into her sleeping bag. That suited Emily. She went to the vidscreen in the living area. "Computer, contact Commander Stone."

After a moment, the screen lit with Stone's face. "What is it?"

"The computer has cut the water rations," Emily said. "I can't fill the tube. I need—"

"We're short of water," Stone said. "We all have to put up with it."

"I don't need it to drink," Emily said. "I need— "

"You need to remember that you are a prisoner, not a guest," Stone snapped.

"Leaving me to dry is torture," Emily said quietly.

Stone laughed. "You can only torture a human being," he said. "You aren't one." And the screen blanked.

Emily's gills burned.

Two days, she thought.

God help me.

Shortly after Richard had handed over the vaccine, the crew of *Sawyer's Point* were shepherded from their isolation wards to what looked like a guest cottage, with four bedrooms, a large living area, and even a well-stocked kitchen. With nothing much else to do, they'd started a never-ending card game. Richard was up six hundred points over Melody Ashman and dealing the sixty-seventh hand of Blind Man's Hearts when the front door of the cottage opened and a Holy Warrior—Hildebrand, if Richard remembered right—stuck his head in.

He wasn't wearing a pressure suit.

They've been vaccinated, Richard thought. *It's begun.*

"Hansen," Hildebrand said. "Out here."

"Play this hand without me," Richard told the others. "I'll be right back."

He followed Hildebrand out of the cottage and across a gravel path to an artificially rustic lodge that had once served as the central meeting place for this neighborhood of the island resort. Its main room was a thicket of upended chairs on round wooden tables, and it took a minute for Richard to spot the Avatar. Karl Rasmusson sat in a big deerhide-covered chair by the enormous fireplace, in which what looked like real logs (though Richard suspected they were holographic) blazed away.

"Join me," the Avatar said, indicating the matching chair on the other side of the hearth.

Richard sat. Hildebrand stood behind him.

"Everyone on the island has now been vaccinated," the Avatar advised. "It's a great relief, as I'm sure you appreciate." He smiled. "The local wildlife appreciate it, too, since we're no longer blasting everything living out of the sky and sea. We even let a couple of sea otters ashore this morning, and the gulls are all over the docks again."

Richard said nothing.

"No doubt you are concerned about your crew," the Avatar went on. "I assure you no one was injured in the retaking of *BPS Sanctification.*"

"I'd like to talk to them," Richard said.

"That won't be possible," the Avatar replied smoothly.

"Just my first officer," Richard said. "Priscilla Wylie?" I'm sure she identified herself when you—"

"Yes, I know the woman," the Avatar said. "But I'm afraid I can't allow you to talk to her, or anyone else."

That clinched it. Priscilla Wylie had been Richard's kindergarten teacher. Andy had slipped the Body's clutches: the Submerge had worked. Richard allowed himself a touch of elation.

"Although . . ." the Avatar looked thoughtful. "Perhaps something could be arranged. If you can help me with something in return."

I know something you think I don't know, Richard thought. "I've already given you the vaccine," he said out loud. "I have nothing else of any use."

"You have information," the Avatar said. "Or at least you may." He leaned forward. "You're Victor Hansen's clone. He planted a gene-bomb in you to implant you with elements of his memories and his personality. So tell me . . . what do you know about the Kemonomimi?"

Richard blinked. *The what?* "Nothing," he said honestly. "I've never heard the name before."

"Are you sure?" The Avatar leaned back in his chair again, and gestured. From somewhere in the thicket of upended chairs appeared a woman in a black dress, wearing a white apron: she placed a tray containing a steaming pot and two cups on the low table between the two chairs. "Coffee?"

Richard shrugged. "Sure."

The Avatar poured. "Cream and sugar?"

"Both, please."

The Avatar put in a generous amount of sugar and cream, stirred the coffee, then handed him the cup. "The Kemonomimi," he said as he did so, "were your . . . original's . . . first creation."

Richard stopped with his coffee cup halfway to his mouth. "What?"

"A decade before he created the first generation of Selkies, Victor Hansen created the Kemonomimi. We don't know much about them. They're feline in appearance, and in ferocity. As with the Selkies, he brought several dozen modified embryos to term, then raised the children in secret. But something went wrong. He designed them to reach physical maturity very rapidly, in just nine years. In their tenth year, as they entered puberty, they became rebellious. They escaped the compound in the Canadian Rockies where he was raising them, and killed several normal humans in the process. They fled into the wilderness.

"That was long before the Day of Salvation, of course. They were forgotten in the ensuing chaos. But within the past fifteen years or so, we've begun to sight them occasionally. We've even captured one or two. But we've never been able to find where they're hiding.

"I was the one who discovered they were yet another monstrous creation of Victor Hansen's." He sipped his coffee.

Richard remembered the strange moddie he'd seen in the House of the Body on the Salvation Day, the one that had attacked the Voice and been shot down by Holy Warriors. Had that been a Kemonomimi? "I know nothing about them."

The Avatar sighed. "Well, it was worth asking."

"The gene-bomb didn't really work, you know," Richard said, perversely feeling he needed to explain.

The Avatar smiled. "Of course, I know," he said. "I approved the gene therapy that partially defused it . . . and quite possibly kept you from going mad, like your father."

"He wasn't my father," Richard said. *Though I thought he was.* "He was my elder twin brother."

"Touché." The Avatar sipped more coffee. "In any

event, if we hadn't modified the gene-bomb, you might have offed yourself even more messily than he did."

Richard remembered that time; he'd felt Victor Hansen inside his head like a second personality, trying to overwhelm him, blot him out, and he shuddered. "I can't believe I'm saying this," he said, "but thank you."

"You're welcome." The Avatar put down his cup. "Unfortunately, it appears that in the process we destroyed some of your memories. Or else Victor Hansen didn't include the memories of the Kemonomimi in your gene-bomb; that's quite possible. He was not a man to admit that he had made a mistake."

Then I'm definitely not like him in every way, Richard thought. *I know all too well how many mistakes I've made.*

"Well." The Avatar stood. "It was worth asking. Take your time with your coffee." He turned to Hildebrand. "When he's done, escort him back to his quarters."

Richard watched the Avatar pick his way out through the tables. Were the Kemonomimi, too, based on Hansen's DNA? Were they also Richard's cousins . . . brothers . . . sisters . . . children, even . . . like the Selkies?

Whether they are or not, they're in the Body's sights, Richard thought. *Marked for Purification. Another race of humans threatened with extinction at the Body's hands . . . and I've helped make it possible, by handing the vaccine over to the Avatar.*

Grandfather Hansen created races. I seem to be destined to help destroy them.

He put down his coffee cup and climbed to his feet. "Take me back to my prison," he told Hildebrand.

He didn't say it out loud, but inside he thought, *It's where I belong.*

Emily drifted in a sea of pain. She knew she was floating, naked, in a fetal position in the middle of her bedroom aboard *Divine Will,* but the knowledge was distant and unimportant. She couldn't focus her mind on anything except the agony in her gills, the fire consuming her skin. The tingling had progressed to burning, burning that intensified until it became an agony she had never imagined. At first she had attempted to wet her gills and skin with a washcloth, soaked in the little water the computer would allow, but it hadn't been enough, and as the pain had progressed, she had lost the ability to even do that much. Now she floated, and hurt, and hurt some more, and she doubted she could survive until the next allotted bath time . . . or even manage to get herself into the bathtube when that time came.

Except . . .

Someone was helping her. Someone was bathing her gills with water: not enough water, but enough to lessen the pain. Someone was sponging her drying skin. Someone . . .

She forced her swollen eyes open enough to see what was going on.

"There, there," her mother murmured, gently running the soaked washcloth over her parched gill slits. "I know it hurts, honey, but it will be better soon."

"Mom?" Emily croaked.

Dr. Christianson-Wood smiled at Emily, the first genuine smile Emily had seen from her mother in a very long time. "Take the cloth," she said, pushing it into Emily's hand. Emily gripped it and began sponging her own gill slits again. With both hands free, her mother began slipping out of the landsuit that, with its own constantly recycled, purified and oxygenated water supply, had kept her from suffering the same agony as Emily.

"Mom . . . no," Emily said.

"Nonsense," her mother said firmly. "I'll be fine for a few hours while you recover. Then we'll trade off again. Between that and the baths we're allowed, we'll manage the rest of the journey."

Her mother sounded so normal that Emily couldn't help it. She began to cry.

"Stop that," her mom said. "You can't spare the water."

That made Emily laugh, then cry even harder. She hadn't realized until that moment just how much she'd missed her mother.

But now, it seemed, at least for the time being, she had her back.

And, she thought as she wrapped herself in the blessed wet embrace of the landsuit, not a moment too soon.

Chris Keating had no way of knowing how many hours he had lain in the aircraft, dozing, awake, or somewhere in between, when suddenly the sound of the engines altered pitch. A few minutes later a solid bump banged his head painfully against the deck, then the engines roared so loud he feared for a moment that they would explode. Instead, they fell to silence, and he realized that his journey had ended.

Minutes passed and nothing happened; then he heard voices. A clunking sound, and fresh air swept across his face, damp and cool. He wriggled, so the owners of the voices would know he was awake, but they didn't seem to care: he was picked up unceremoniously, tossed carelessly and painfully over a bony, fur-covered shoulder, then carried down half a dozen steps into the open.

"Bring him over here," said a strangely familiar male voice. Chris was carried a few more steps. "He probably won't be able to stand after being tied up that long," the voice said. "Put him on that crate."

Chris was lowered off of the bony shoulder and manhandled into a sitting position on something hard, square . . . and wet. Cold water promptly soaked through his pants and chilled his buttocks.

"Untie him," the voice said.

The ropes binding his legs and hands were swiftly undone, and as blood rushed back into his extremities,

Chris gasped and tears sprang to his still-blindfolded eyes. If he'd been standing, he would have fallen, and probably screamed on the way down.

"Now take off the gag," the voice said.

The cloth binding his mouth went the way of the ropes, and Chris gulped a deep, damp, cool, and pine-scented breath. "Who are you?" he demanded, or tried to, but his voice came out in a barely audible croak.

The owner of the voice seemed to have understood him, though. "You'll see in a moment," he said. "Literally. Take off the blindfold."

Someone yanked away the blindfold, and Chris squeezed his eyes shut against the sudden, painful flood of daylight. Then he blinked away tears, looked up . . . and gasped.

He sat on a plastic crate in the middle of a long concrete runway. Beyond a stretch of open green ground rose a collection of modest one- and two-story buildings, interspersed with tall pines. And beyond those . . . unbroken forest, climbing up steep slopes until it disappeared into the fog.

At least a dozen of the catlike moddies . . . Kemono-mimi . . . surrounded him. And directly in front of him stood the last person he had expected . . . or wanted . . . to see.

"Richard Hansen!" he blurted out.

But the eyes in that hated face narrowed. "No."

"But you look—"

"I," said the man coldly, "am Dr. Victor Hansen."

The *Divine Will* took ten more days to reach Earth. They weren't comfortable days for Emily or her mother, but it appeared they would be survivable—thanks to the recovery, or at least partial recovery, of Dr. Christianson-Wood, and also thanks to help from an unexpected source.

Emily was so glad to have her mother back to something approaching normal that she didn't mind the constant switching back and forth of the landsuit or the hours spent in the bathtube until she couldn't stand the filthy, deoxygenated water any more.

She tried tentatively a time or two to talk to her mother about the nature of their trip, and their captors. But her mother brushed aside the efforts. "I don't want to think about that right now," she said. "I'm just . . . staying focused. On making sure we both make it okay."

Emily worried what would happen the first time a Holy Warrior made an appearance in their quarters. Four days after the computer announced water rationing, two days after Emily's last chance to use the bathtube and one day before she could use it again, she found out.

They had just exchanged the landsuit, so that Emily's mother was wearing it again and Emily momentarily wore nothing at all. The door swung open without warning. Emily looked up to see Biccum looking in. He took one look at her, turned bright red, and slammed the door shut again.

Emily couldn't help it; she laughed.

"Um, sorry, Miss Wood," came Biccum's voice through the annunciator panel. "I'm sorry. I should have knocked . . ."

"Don't worry about it," Emily said, pulling on her skinsuit with practiced ease. She glanced at her mother, but Dr. Christianson-Wood didn't seem perturbed by the fact a Holy Warrior had just walked in; she just looked amused. "I'm dressed now. You can come in."
We're your prisoners; you can do whatever you want, she thought, but didn't say.

The door opened. Biccum peered cautiously in. He still looked flushed and he didn't meet her eyes. "I really am sorry. I—"

"It's all right," Emily said. "What is it?"

"Um . . ." Biccum finally got up the courage to look her in the face. "I heard . . . you need water. I've brought you this." He held out something oblong and shiny.

Emily took it. "It looks like a datachip," she said.

"It is. It's my water. Uh, some of it. I mean, let the computer scan it and it will route some of my water ration to your quarters. So you can get wet . . ." He paused, blushed again, and mumbled, ". . . I mean, take a bath. A little more often."

Emily stared at him, bemused. "Um . . . thank you," she said.

"Yes, thank you," said Dr. Christianson-Wood firmly. "That's very decent of you."

Biccum gave her a startled look. "You're welcome?" He made it sound like a question. Then he backed out through the door. "I should . . . um, I hope it helps. 'Bye."

The door closed.

"You've made a friend," Dr. Christianson-Wood said. "Even if you embarrassed him horribly."

"It's not my fault he didn't knock," Emily said. She looked at her mother. "Are you . . . all right?"

Emily's mother looked away. "I . . . I think I will be," she said softly. "I'm . . . reintegrating, I think I'd call it. I've been focused inward, drowning in my own depths. You . . . when you were in so much pain . . . it pulled me out. Pulled me to the surface." She looked up. "I know we're prisoners of the Holy Warriors," she said. "I know we're going to Earth. I know that they want to punish me for . . . for what I did. I know all of that. And I'm terrified, Emily. But . . . but I'm not lost anymore. I've found my way out. I've found myself."

Emily felt a huge rush of relief, a tsunami of relief that washed her own fear away, at least for the moment. "Thank God," she said. "I've been so worried about you, Mama." She hadn't called her mother that in ten years.

Dr. Christianson-Wood smiled, wide green eyes bright with unshed tears. "I know, Emmy," she said. "I'm so sorry to have put you through all that worry . . . so sorry that you're suffering now because of what I did. I can't even claim not to deserve it. But you—"

"You *don't* deserve it," Emily said. "Don't start talking like that. You did what you had to to save us all. If not for you—"

Her mother made a brushing-off gesture. "My reasons don't matter, Emily. I made the best decisions I could at the time. But whatever my motivation . . . the results have been horrible. I'll have to live with the consequences when we get to Earth. Whatever they may be." She held up a hand, forestalling Emily's next protest. "Let's not talk about it now. Your boyfriend just gave you a present. Wouldn't you like to make use of it?"

Emily looked at the datachip, and laughed. "It was rather sweet of him," she said. "Which is not something I ever thought I'd say about a Holy Warrior."

"They're just people, Emily," her mother said. "People like us. Even the worst of them." Her face closed down again. "Even the ones who attacked Marseguro. Even the ones I . . ." Her voice trailed off.

Emily held her breath, afraid her mother would . . . go away . . . again, but Dr. Christianson-Wood shook her head and carried on. "Go on," she said. "Get in the bath. You know you want to."

She did. Silently thanking Biccum, she went into the bathtube, smiling to herself as she slipped out of her skinsuit again and remembered how red he'd turned when he'd walked in on her. "Just people," she told herself. "Just people."

She climbed into the tube, sealed it, and let it fill with clean water. As it closed over her cramped gills, and she opened them wide, wider than the landsuit allowed, she remembered how, for a time, she had relished watching Holy Warriors die, had even relished killing them.

Somewhere along the way she had lost that bloodthirstiness. She wondered if she could get it back if she needed it.

She wondered if she wanted to.

Sharing the landsuit and making use of the extra

water ration provided by Biccum, they passed the final few days of the journey to Earth comfortably enough. When they talked, they talked of shared memories, family stories, vids they'd watched and books they'd read.

The one thing they didn't talk about was the future.

The first they knew of their arrival at Earth was Stone's voice over the intercom. Emily was wearing the landsuit and Dr. Christianson-Wood the sedate navy-blue skinsuit she'd been wearing aboard the sub when they were taken. They were floating in the living room, playing a word game they'd found programmed in the entertainment unit. When the intercom came to life, Dr. Christianson-Wood's hand twitched, erasing her last move. Then she looked up, listening. So did Emily.

"All hands," he said. "We're entering Earth orbit. Our sensors and communications are barely functioning, so we're not sure what the situation is down below, though from what we can tell, things are . . . quiet. Too quiet." He paused, and Emily knew everyone in the crew must be thinking the same thing: the plague had hit Earth hard. "We're going to land and reconnoiter," Stone concluded abruptly. "All hands prepare for reentry."

Without a word, Emily shut down the entertainment unit. A moment later, someone knocked.

"Come in," Emily said.

The door opened, revealing Biccum. "I've come to make sure you're ready for reentry," he said. "You need to strap in to the acceleration couches. We've only got a few minutes."

"What was that about communications?" Emily said.

Biccum glanced over his shoulder, then lowered his voice as he started strapping her in. "We can receive, but we can't transmit," he said in a low voice. "*BPS Sanctification* is in orbit—"

Emily's heart skipped. *Sanctification*? Not *Victor Hansen*?

"—and it challenged us. Since we couldn't respond,

it warned us off, said it would destroy us if we tried to come closer. We've been challenged from the ground, too, but only by an automated system. If we try to land anywhere there's a Holy Warrior base . . . we may get shot down."

"So where—"

"We've picked up . . . another signal. A commercial homing beacon of some kind. No threats of being shot down. We're going to ride it down." He shook his head. "Aside from that, everything is just . . . empty. Like the whole planet is deserted."

Emily glanced at her mother. Dr. Christianson-Wood closed her eyes as though in pain, but then opened them again and focused on Biccum.

"So we're going to land away from any major population centers, and see what we can see," he went on. "If it's the plague . . ." He looked grim for a moment. "If it's the plague, we'll set up one of the microfactories we brought from Marseguro and start manufacturing vaccine. If there's some other reason, well, we'll sort that out when we get there." He finished tightening their straps, and gave them both a determined, if slightly forced, grin. "See you on Earth!" He went out, and the door closed behind him.

"Mom . . . ?" Emily said.

"I'm all right," Dr. Christianson-Wood replied. "I'm ready to . . . find out what happened. What I did."

Emily opened her mouth to reply, but a sudden jolt snapped her teeth shut so hard she was lucky not to bite her tongue. A high-pitched whine began, deepening to a steady roar. *Atmosphere*, Emily thought. The buffeting grew worse, and worse, and worse still, until it was as bad as it had been when she'd ridden *Sanctification* down during its automatic deorbiting procedure. *Something's wrong*, she thought, her fingers gripping the arms of the chair so tight they hurt. *This can't be right.*

Then Stone confirmed it. ". . . don't have . . . plete control," he shouted over an intercom now so full of static only portions of his words could be understood. ". . . slow our desce . . . can't control where . . . come down . . . ooks like . . . shit!"

That last word came through loud and clear.

Ten seconds later an enormous impact flung Emily hard against the straps of her acceleration couch. She heard a shriek of tearing metal, distant thumps and what sounded like an explosion, all mixed together. The lights went out, but were almost immediately replaced by the cold blue glow of the chemical emergency lights, strips embedded in the ceiling that turned everything a color Emily associated with sunshine filtered through four or five meters of seawater. And then . . .

It felt like utter silence in comparison to what had come before, though in fact she could still hear distant thumps and hissing noises and shouting voices. "Are you all right, Mom?" Emily called.

"I'm fine . . . oh!" The floor of the shuttle, once more emphatically the floor now they were back in gravity, had suddenly tilted. More shouting from panicked voices. The shuttle began to sway, a motion Emily recognized instinctively.

"We're in the water," she said. "We're sinking."

The floor tilted further, until they were hanging in their acceleration straps. More crashes and thumps came from somewhere inside the shuttle: it sounded like equipment breaking free and falling against bulkheads. The shuttle continued to sway for a minute or two, and then suddenly, with a final, solid thump, the motion stopped. The floor tilted back toward the horizontal, and finally, all was still.

"I'm going to get out," Emily said. "Stay put."

"Be careful," her mother said.

Emily unstrapped herself and picked her way across the slanted floor to the door. She put her ear against it, but could hear nothing on the other side but a distant roaring sound ...

... rushing water.

Then the door suddenly swung open, and water surged around her feet. Biccum stood ankle-deep in the corridor outside, blood streaming down his face from a gash on his forehead. His eyes were wide and panicked. "We're underwater!" he cried. "On the bottom! There's water coming in everywhere!"

"Pressure suits?" Emily said.

"We can't get to them. They're already underwater. We need—" He gave her a pleading look. "We need your help. If you can get to them, bring them back, please, there are only three of us in this section, we haven't heard anything from the rest of the shuttle, if you can just get us three pressure suits."

They're Holy Warriors, Emily thought, but then, *no. They're people.*

"I'll try," she said. She looked over her shoulder at her mother, who was also unstrapping. "Mom, you stay—"

"Not likely," her mother snapped. "I'm coming with you."

"But ..."

"Quit treating me like I'm made of glass, Emily," her mother said. "It's about time I started saving lives again."

Emily couldn't very well argue with that. "All right," she said. "Show us, Biccum."

"Dave," he said. "Call me Dave. This way."

The water in the corridor behind was already visibly higher than it had been when Biccum had opened the door. As he led them down the slight slope, it grew deeper still, until finally Biccum had to stop and grab hold of one of the curving metal handles of an equipment rack set in the wall.

"At the end of the corridor," he said. "There's a hatch. It's open. The pressure suits are inside. There's an air lock beyond that that leads out of the ship." He looked like he would say something else, but he didn't.

He's just told us how we can escape and leave them to drown, Emily thought. *But he's not going to beg us not to do it.* She looked at her mother, and saw that she had realized the same thing. But all she said was, "Let's go. This tub is filling up fast."

Emily nodded. "I don't need this," she said, reaching up to unzip the landsuit. She glanced at Biccum. "Maybe you should close your eyes."

He blinked, then blushed, said, "Oh," and squeezed them firmly closed.

Emily slipped out of the landsuit, its weight oppressive now they were back in gravity. Salt water swirled around her thighs. It felt good. "Go back up the corridor as far as you can," she told Biccum, putting the landsuit into his hand. "You might want to open your eyes once you've turned around. It'll probably help." Biccum nodded, turned and began climbing back up the corridor, the heavy landsuit held under one arm. He didn't look back. Emily smiled a little, then went the other way with her mother.

When the water was chest-deep, they plunged beneath it and opened their gills. The momentary shock of transition gave way to the pure pleasure of once again breathing seawater, albeit seawater with an odd tang to it. "It tastes funny," Emily chirp-clicked to her mother, and using the Selkie underwater language again after so long was a joy in itself.

"Different ocean," her mother said. "And possibly pollutants from the crash."

Emily chirped disgust, then looked around. The shuttle's emergency lights were more than bright enough for Selkie eyes, and she spotted the hatch at once. Together she and her mother swam down into the room below the corridor. As promised, three suits hung there. They freed them, then paused for a moment.

Just beyond the racks of suits was a closed air lock door.

"We could leave now," Emily said. "Escape. We don't owe the Holy Warriors any favors."

"No," her mother said. "We've had our revenge for the attack on Marseguro. That slate is clean. Maybe we do owe them: maybe we owe them ... some of them, anyway, the ones like Biccum ... the chance to live and grow into better human beings."

Emily couldn't decide whether her mother was being profound or hopelessly naïve. But she did know she didn't want to swim off and let Biccum or anyone else drown. She turned and swam back into the main corridor.

As she passed through the door, the shuttle shuddered, jerked—and suddenly tilted. In an instant the corridor's relatively mild inclination switched to vertical. The water around them boiled and foamed. For a moment Emily floundered, disoriented, then her Selkie senses reasserted themselves and told her emphatically that *that* way was up: and an instant later, as if to prove the point, something big plunged into the water from above.

A man. One of the Holy Warriors. He flailed helplessly, striking out in all directions. His left foot caught Emily in the ribs, and she dropped the two pressure suits she was carrying and grabbed it. "Hold still!" she clicked, but of course the Holy Warrior couldn't understand, or even hear her clearly. Her mother grabbed one of the man's arms. Together they drove toward the surface, and a moment later the man's head burst into the air. He gulped a huge breath, coughed, and choked out, "I can't ... can't ..."

"Swim?" Emily said. "Somehow I guessed."

She looked around. The water continued to rise, taking them up the corridor, now a near-vertical shaft with water cascading down its sides over the blue emergency lights. Far up, still ten or fifteen meters above them, a door stood open. Two pale faces peered down. "Is he all right?" one shouted. It was Biccum.

"Yes," Emily called back. "But I've dropped the suits I was carrying."

"I've still got mine," her mother said.

"Stay still and you'll be all right," Emily said to the man. "Mom will keep you on the surface. I've got to go back down." She flipped and drove downward with her broad, webbed feet.

The suits had settled at the far end of the corridor, past the hatch they had brought them out of. Emily grabbed them and started back up the corridor. The water's surface was now just three or four meters below the room where Biccum and the other Holy Warrior waited. She emerged into air, closed her gill slits, took a lung-breath and said, "Got them."

She looked at the man who had fallen on top of them. His eyes, so wide with fright they were almost as large as her own, looked back at her. She thought she remembered his name from Marseguro.

"You're Koop, aren't you?" she said.

He nodded. "Evan," he said. "Evan Koop."

"Well, Evan, let's try to get you into this one down here, before the water lifts us to the others," she said. "Then we'll have one less to deal with. Hold still." She passed one of the pressure suits to her mother, then plunged under the water. She unsealed the suit. It would have water in it, but as long as the helmet remained clear of it, that wouldn't matter.

The suit was bulky, designed to go over clothes in an emergency, and she had no trouble slipping the man's legs into it and pulling it up. She guided his arms into it. The life-support pack was only a pad a few centimeters thick built into the back of the suit, and the "helmet" was a transparent inflatable hood. She pulled it over his head, sealed it, and touched the suit's activation button.

The helmet expanded into a clear plastic globe, and the man grinned with relief. "It works!"

"Good."

They were within a meter of the room containing Biccum and the other Holy Warrior, whom Emily hadn't gotten a good look at yet; she was keeping her transparent nictitating eyelids over her eyes both to protect them and so she could see clearly underwater, but they tended to throw everything above water into soft focus. She tossed up the second suit she'd rescued; her mother tossed up the one she carried. "You two can dress yourselves," she said to Biccum and the other man. They grabbed the suits and disappeared.

Emily glanced at Koop. He wasn't looking up at all: his focus was entirely down into the water, and Emily suddenly realized that with his helmet in place he had a clear view of her nude body. She sighed. *Men,* she thought. *Nonmods or Selkies, they're all the same.*

The water reached the open doorway and suddenly poured into the room beyond. Emily stayed in the corridor, although any pretense at modesty seemed kind of silly at this point. "Are you two—" she began, then stopped. As he finished sealing his pressure suit, the man who had been with Biccum turned around, and at the same instant Emily finally recognized him as Abban—and realized he had a standard-issue Holy Warrior slug-thrower in his hand, small, but more than powerful enough to blow her head off.

"You two climb in here," Abban said. "I figure we've got just enough time to tie you up before the water fills the room." It was already approaching his knees.

"We just saved your lives," Emily snarled, fury almost choking her.

"Thank you. Now get in here."

Naked and dripping, Emily complied. Biccum looked away. Abban didn't. His eyes, clearly visible through the transparent helmet, ran over her body from head to foot, then back again.

Emily's mother climbed out beside her daughter.

"Biccum, tie them up," Abban ordered.

"I don't—"

"Do it!" Abban ordered. "We've got to secure them before the water rises. Then we can get them to shore, turn them in to the Body—"

"The Body doesn't exist anymore," Emily said. "The plague reached Earth. Haven't you been paying attention?"

"God wouldn't let the Body be destroyed," Abban snarled. The water was up to his thighs. "Do it!" he snapped at Biccum.

Behind Emily, Koop said "Abban, don't you—"

"Shut up, Koop. I outrank you and Biccum both. Follow orders or I'll see you up on charges of insubordination."

"All right, all right," Biccum said. He looked Emily full in the face. "I'm sorry, miss," he said. He stepped forward, past Abban—then half-turned and slammed his arm down onto Abban's forearm. The gun splashed into the water and Emily pounced on it.

She raised it to see Abban and Biccum struggling in waist-deep water. She couldn't shoot without hitting Biccum. She didn't want to shoot at all. But if she had to—

She didn't. As the two men struggled, they fell with an enormous splash. There was a strange popping sound, and when the men rose to face each other again, Emily saw that Abban's inflatable helmet had been punctured by something. It hung loosely on his face. "Abban—" Biccum said, reaching for him.

"Get away!" Abban snarled. "I swear, Biccum, I'll see you shot for—" His eyes suddenly widened. He looked down at the water, rising faster than ever; it was up to his belly. "Oh, God," he said. He looked wildly at the others. "I need—you've got to find another pressure suit!"

"There were only three," Emily said. "Biccum— Dave—are there any others in this section?"

Biccum shook his head. "No," he said hoarsely. "The others are up there—" he pointed toward what should have been the bow but was now straight up. "We can't get though the bulkhead without computer access. And the computer is dead."

"You've got to cut through—" Abban said.

"With what?" Biccum said. "God, Abban, I'll do whatever I can—but we have nothing."

"But . . ." Abban looked down at the water. It had risen to his chest. "But . . ."

Emily thought furiously. Maybe they could rig a diving bell, something that would hold enough oxygen to get Abban out of . . .

Or maybe . . .

But her thoughts went nowhere. The water was up to Abban's neck now. He began screaming, praying, begging. They lifted him up, kept him above the water as long as they could, hoping an air bubble would form and stabilize, but the air seemed to have some unseen escape path, and the rising water never faltered.

In the end, they all floated in the flooded compartment and watched Abban drown. He flailed for a few minutes, eyes wide and bulging, then suddenly opened his mouth and sucked water into his lungs. He spasmed, jackknifed, mouth opening and closing, and then abruptly fell limp.

Emily turned away. "Let's get out of here," she chirp-clicked to her mother.

They motioned to Biccum and Koop and started down the corridor toward the air lock. As they approached it, Emily heard a noise . . . a mingling of tapping and scraping sounds.

"What's that?" her mother asked. "Rescuers?"

"I don't see how it could be."

They swam into the pressure-suit locker and over to the air lock. Biccum moved up beside Emily. "Let me," he said, his voice sounding odd but perfectly audible to her Selkie ears even through the filters of helmet and water. "There are manual controls in case of emergencies . . ." He opened a panel next to the air lock door, revealing what looked like a hexagonal bolt head and a hand crank clamped to the wall. He pulled the crank free, attached it to the bolt head, and started cranking.

The door began to open. No air bubbled out of the crack that appeared. "The outer door must be open," Biccum panted. He cranked more, then stopped. "What the . . ."

Light streamed through the centimeter-wide opening, white light, not the blue-green light of the emergency strips, light that dimmed and faded as though its source were moving around on the other side. "There's somebody out there," Emily chirp-clicked to her mother.

"Looks like we haven't escaped the Body after all," her mother replied.

"There's somebody out there," Biccum said, echoing Emily though he had no way of knowing it. He gave her a questioning look; she wondered when exactly she had taken command. *Me, commanding Holy Warriors,* she thought. *That's a switch.*

She mimed continuing cranking, and Biccum nodded and kept turning the handle.

The door opened further. The light dimmed, as though its source had moved away. Emily looked through the opening, but all she could see was that light, surrounded by indistinct shapes, beyond the outer door of the air lock, which indeed stood wide open.

Finally the door was open wide enough for her to slip through. Emily motioned Biccum to move back. She looked down at her naked body. Well, at least they won't see me as a threat, she thought wryly, and slipped into the outer air lock.

The light steadied on her form. She floated, keeping stationary with gentle motions of her arms and legs, gills rippling. The water still tasted odd, but fresher than that filling the wreck of the *Divine Will*.

One of the shapes behind the light moved forward, came in front of the light, and swam toward her, a silhouette. She squinted, trying to see. Her heart suddenly pounded. The shape didn't have a pressure suit on, or scuba gear; it looked . . .

The swimmer entered the air lock, illuminated by the blue-green emergency lights, and Emily gasped.

A Selkie woman in a plain white swimsuit looked back at her with eyes as wide and green as her own.

Chapter 8

KARL RASMUSSON LOOKED at the projection on the largest screen in his office and let Grand Deacon von Eschen tell him what he was seeing. "This satellite image is a few months old, of course—we don't currently have control of any of our reconnaissance satellites—but obviously the topography won't have changed. The Kemonomimi haven't been entirely careless: Newshore is barely accessible by land. When normal humans still lived there, they flew in or came in by boat. Not a single road leads to it."

"Could this have always been their hiding place?" the Avatar asked.

Von Eschen shook his head. "No, this was definitely a Body town. There's a small meeting house, a school, a geothermal power plant, all the usual accoutrements for one of these reconstruction villages. A lot of them were built in remote places. The Avatar felt that seeding people around the planet could help preserve the race in the event of . . ."

His voice trailed off.

"Another catastrophe," Karl finished for him. "Like the plague. And he was right. Most of the survivors who aren't in Body enclaves are probably in towns like that one." He looked at von Eschen. "Are there any normal humans there now?"

"We don't know," von Eschen said.

Karl turned back to the image. "Why did the Kemono-mimi pick Newshore?" he said. "Why leave their hide-out in the mountains, wherever it was? It's kept them safe for seventy years."

"We *assume*," von Eschen said with careful empha-sis, "that wherever they were they didn't have access to aircraft. We also assume that their hideaway was some-where very close to this town, probably somewhere in this range of mountains that cuts Newshore off from the interior." A laser pointer highlighted jagged peaks just to the east of the small collection of buildings and the unmistakable lines of two intersecting runways that marked the town on the image.

"No roads," Karl said. "How do you propose to at-tack, then, Grand Deacon? By boat?"

Von Eschen shook his head. "We don't have enough boats. And they'd see us coming and melt away into the interior before we got there."

Karl frowned. "But you said—"

"Your Holiness," the Grand Deacon said quickly, as if suddenly realizing that making the Avatar feel foolish might not be a good career move, "*almost* inaccessible is not the same as *completely* inaccessible." The laser pointer moved again, and a winding path lit up, leading from a broad inland valley through the mountains down to the town. "There is a pass, along the river that eventu-ally flows into the sea at Newshore. It's narrow, but no trouble for men on foot."

"What about an air assault?"

"We have no air weapons systems," von Eschen said. "And our transport aircraft wouldn't stand a chance from any concentrated weapons fire on approach to the Newshore airport. If we had recovered the assault craft from *Sanctification* . . ."

"Yes, well, and if the Selkies hadn't ripped out *Sanc-tification*'s Orbital Bombardment System this whole discussion would be moot, wouldn't it?" Karl shook his head. "God is testing us, Grand Deacon. It has given us just enough vaccine for everyone on this island. It has stripped our forces down to men on foot, lightly armed. It has denied us air power and sea power, blinded our technology, thrown us back on our own resources. God, Grand Deacon, wants us to prove our commitment to Its command. And when we win the victory, God will know that we are once more worthy of Its continuing aid and protection, and a new Body will arise from the grave of the old: a better, stronger, more perfect Body to do the will of God Itself!"

"Yes, Avatar," the Grand Deacon breathed. His eyes shone in the light from the screen.

Karl found that he was standing, though he didn't remember getting up. His heart pounded and his head felt light. This *is what it means to be Avatar!* he realized exultantly. *God Itself is with me. I can feel Its touch. I can feel Its presence. It speaks to me . . .*

God speaks to me.

And I speak for God.

Avatar!

"Arm everyone, Grand Deacon," Karl said. "Everyone who can walk, everyone who can fire a gun. Gather supplies. Do whatever you must to enable us to cross to the mainland and march on the Kemonomimi. The sooner, the better."

"Forty-eight hours, Your Holiness," the Grand Deacon said. "Forty-eight hours."

"Good. Dismissed."

The Grand Deacon left. The giant screen drew back into the ceiling beam from which it had descended. Karl looked down the slope to the ocean. For once the sky was clear, and the setting sun drew a line of fire across the glassy water, a path of light that led to the horizon, and beyond.

A path to God, Karl thought. *A blood-red path.*

Red with the blood of the Kemonomimi. Red with the blood of the abominations of Victor Hansen.

The ancient religions were heresy, of course, but those high in the hierarchy of the Body studied them to recognize them when they saw them. Karl Rasmusson knew that in many of the old, false religions, blood sacrifices served to purify worshipers and turn away the vengeance of God.

A hint of truth in the superstitions of the past, he thought. *God trying to speak, but humanity unwilling to listen—until the First Avatar was born.*

We're listening now, God, he said in silent prayer. *I'm listening now.*

You will have the blood you demand. I swear it.

The sun sank into the sea, and the path of light vanished as though it had never been . . . but the sky still glowed red, the red of blood and fire.

"All set?" Andy King whispered into his mike. Pressure-suited, he hung in one of the shafts the computer no longer remembered existed, one that emptied up through a floor plate into the virtual-reality training room where Goodfellow's precious data conduit lurked behind the wall.

Below Andy, the shaft led down to one of their secret access routes, right up against the hull. Fifteen meters sternward from the bottom of the shaft, a shaped charge had been placed that, when detonated, would blow a hole in the hull. As the air rushed out, the computer would seal the two hatches into the VR room, isolating it from the rest of the ship.

Andy just hoped the makeshift air seals they had rigged in their own crawlspaces held, or everyone in his crew who wasn't pressure-suited—which was most of them; they only had access to a half-dozen suits—would be forced to flee into the areas of the ship the computer could still see, where they would be instantly detected.

Simon Goodfellow hung below him, his face pale and sweating through the transparent bubble of his helmet. He didn't speak, but nodded.

"Set," Cordelia Raum said in Andy's ear.

"Do it," Andy said.

Not all of the charge's force went out through the hull: he felt the explosion as a pressure wave that slammed past him, shoving him hard against the rungs of the ladder to which he clung. An instant later, air rushed the other way, howling out through the hole in the hull. A thick fog enveloped him momentarily, then was sucked away.

A few final phantom tugs of fleeing atmosphere, then the utter stillness and silence of vacuum. Andy looked down at Goodfellow. "All right, Simon?" he said.

"Yes," Goodfellow squeaked.

"Seals held," Raum reported.

"We're going in," Andy said.

He climbed up the last few rungs of the ladder and pushed aside the already loosened deck plate.

The VR training room contained the multipurpose simulators the Body used to train Holy Warriors in the operation of the ship's auxiliary vehicles. Everyone in the *Victor Hansen* crew had spent time in one of its four boxy simulators, learning to operate the shuttles, assault craft, boats, and submarines that filled the ship's equipment holds. The simulators, each about three meters tall, four meters wide and maybe five meters long, crouched down in tangled nests of hydraulics. Four curved white control desks for managing the simulations stood along the two longer walls of the room, two on each wall. The room was big enough that the curvature of the habitat ring's hull could be clearly seen, making it look as if the doors in the shorter walls were located slightly uphill from where Andy had made his unorthodox entrance.

Those doors, each about twice as wide as a normal door and taller, too, so that equipment could be easily moved in and out, were both closed: and above them, bright red lights flashed a steady warning rhythm. *Vacuum sealed for your protection,* Andy thought.

The rest of the room looked perfectly normal, except for frost glinting here and there on walls and floor.

Andy pulled himself up, then drew his laser pistol. "Get to work," he told Goodfellow. The tech climbed out clumsily, weighed down by a huge black backpack, and would have overbalanced backward and fallen back into the shaft if Andy hadn't grabbed his arm. He gave Andy a wan grin, looked around, then made a beeline for the wall between the two simulator control desks to his right. He set down his backpack, pulled out something that looked like an oversized handgun with a strange black shield surrounding the barrel, and pressed it to the wall. As he slowly moved it horizontally across the metal, a thin black line, edges glowing red, appeared behind it.

Andy turned his attention to the doors. The computer knew they were in there. The computer also couldn't do anything about it: the AI might be the ship's conscious brain, but the pressure seals were under the control of the ship's autonomic nervous system. The computer could no more open those doors than a man could command his heart to stop beating: not until the hull breach was sealed and the room repressurized. And since the hull breach had occurred in an area they had blinded the computer to back on Marseguro, it should be having fits trying to figure out exactly what had happened—and giving the Holy Warriors on the bridge fits in the process.

They'd figure it out eventually, of course. But with the computer out of the loop, the bots that would normally be sent out to fix a hull breach would be useless: they were all under central control. The Holy Warriors would have to go outside themselves, locate the breach visually, and then attempt to seal it. All that would take time.

Enough time?

Andy didn't know. But they'd thrown their dice. They'd either retake the ship, or die trying.

He sat down where he had a good view of both doors, and settled in to wait.

"Who are you?" Emily chirp-clicked. The woman cocked her head, obviously able to hear but not understand. She made noises in return, similar to the Marseguroite click-speech but unintelligible to Emily.

A second Selkie pushed into the air lock, a teenaged male, maybe sixteen, standard, wearing white trunks. He looked at Emily and his mouth fell open. The older woman elbowed him in the ribs, and he closed his mouth and dropped his eyes, but he didn't stop stealing looks.

Then Biccum stuck his helmeted head into the air lock and both Selkies backed up fast. The boy pulled a wicked-looking knife from the belt of his trunks.

Emily turned and shoved at Biccum. "Get him back inside!" she chirp-clicked to her mother. "And get me something to write on. I think the pressure suits have whiteslates."

Biccum's head jerked out of sight: Dr. Christianson-Wood had apparently pulled him back into the shuttle by his ankles. A moment later her hand extended a white rectangle with a silver stylus floating from it on a string.

Hoping the strange Selkies could read English, Emily grabbed the whiteslate and wrote, "Please help us."

She passed the slate to the woman, who took it cautiously. The boy's eyes were now locked on Emily's face—which showed great concentration on his part, she figured—and his knife remained ready.

"We don't help Holy Warriors," the woman wrote, the motion of her hand sharp and angry. Emily felt a surge of relief: they would be able to communicate.

She scribbled furiously. "Only two Holy Warriors alive," she wrote. "We were prisoners. These two saved us."

She passed the slate. The woman's eyes flicked over it.

He nodded, turned and swam back out into the open water, where the dark shapes of—presumably—other Selkies clustered, trying to see what was going on.

"Come with us," the woman wrote.

"The Holy Warriors?" Emily responded. She couldn't leave them to drown . . .

"Prisoners," the woman wrote. "Blindfolds."

Emily nodded, took the slate, and wrote on it for the benefit of Biccum and Koop, "They'll help us. But you have to go as prisoners. Blindfolds."

She passed the slate inside. Biccum looked at it, then looked at her. His mouth quirked. "Tables turned?" he said, his voice thin but loud enough for her Selkie ears to pick it up. "I can live with that. Since the other option would appear to be dying with it. But how do you blindfold a pressure suit?"

"I'm not . . ." Emily began, but then felt a touch on her foot. She turned back. The woman was holding out two opaque bags, probably used for gathering shellfish, easily large enough to go over the pressure suits' helmets. Emily smiled at her and passed them through.

Something else came out the other way: her mother must have swum back up to their quarters, and now held out Emily's zebra-striped yellow skinsuit.

With great relief, Emily pulled it on. Selkies weren't as body-shy as nonmods, as a rule, but she still felt she'd put on enough of a show for one day. *I'm not cut out to be an exhibitionist,* she thought.

She suspected the teenage boy with the knife would be disappointed.

With Biccum and Koop blinded by the bags, all four of them finally emerged from the *Divine Will.* The water outside was a deep blue-green: it had to be daylight up above. A dozen Selkies of both sexes, ranging from the teenage boy to middle-aged, floated outside, along with the same number of small transportation devices similar to the Marseguroite *sputa*: handheld, steerable torpedoes, essentially. Their headlights were the source of the illumination Emily had seen through the air lock door.

She felt the strange Selkies' eyes on her as she emerged, and was doubly glad to have her skinsuit.

Her mother swam up beside her. "I don't believe it," Dr. Christianson-Wood chirp-clicked. "Selkies? On Earth? How have they survived? Why hasn't the Body hunted them down? And why are they here in the first place? I've read Victor Hansen's diaries. He didn't say anything about leaving any Selkies behind on Earth."

"Maybe they'll tell us, once we're in air." Emily turned to look at the shuttle. Its hull was crumpled and torn in a dozen places, and its bow was a tangled mass of metal and glass: it must have taken the brunt of the crash, and it looked like something up there had exploded, too. She'd wondered if other Holy Warriors might still be clinging to life in the shuttle. Now she wondered how any of them had survived.

The woman in white held out her hand for the whiteslate. Emily passed it to her, and she wrote, "Follow us."

Emily nodded, and the whole strange party of Selkies towing Holy Warriors swam away from the wreck of the *Divine Will*.

Chris Keating looked around at the assembled Kemonomimi and debated the wisdom of telling "Victor Hansen" that he was full of crap. Assuming these catpeople were the original Hansen's creations, and in light of the fact that even those of them not armed *to* the teeth were armed *with* teeth—and claws—denying the identity of the person they apparently accepted as their creator didn't seem wise.

He opted for a cautious, "Really? I, uh, thought he was—uh, you were dead."

"As I wanted the world to think," Hansen said. His eyes raked Keating like lasers. "But as you can see, I'm very much alive. As, unaccountably, are you."

"Is that why you brought me here?"

"Why else?" Hansen gestured at the assembled cat-people. "My Kemonomimi were on an important ... errand ... for me in the Holy City when they spotted you: the only living human, so far as they could tell, in that entire metropolis. They radioed me for instructions and I ordered them to bring you back with them." He stepped closer. "Why haven't you succumbed to my clever little virus?"

"Your virus?" Chris blinked. "I thought ... uh, heard ... that it came from outer space. Marseguro."

Hansen's face darkened. "What you heard was a lie," he snarled. "A lie created by those hideous freaks, those ... fish-people."

"Selkies?" Chris said, and wished he hadn't.

"That's what they call themselves," Hansen said. "But to think such inferior creatures could have created anything as perfect as my virus ... it's laughable." He didn't look like he was about to laugh. He looked like he wanted to kill someone. But he took a long, deep breath and some of the color faded from his face, that face that was so much like Richard Hansen's.

It's true, then, Chris thought. He'd been told, while still imprisoned, that Richard Hansen was not Victor Hansen's grandson at all, but a clone. Which meant *this* "Victor Hansen" must also be a clone.

How many copies of himself did Hansen make? Chris wondered. *The man was a raging egomaniac.*

Which meant, he suspected, that so was the man in front of him, who seemed convinced he was the original.

Hansen was still staring at Chris. The anger had faded from his face. "How ... interesting ... that you heard this virus came from Marseguro," he said. "Considering only those at the highest levels of the Body Purified were told that particular lie." He abruptly turned on his heel, snapped, "Alexander. Napoleon. Bring him," and strode off.

Two towering Kemonomimi males, one glossy black, the other tiger-striped, stepped out from the encircling pack. Strong furred hands, retractable claws just showing from the tips of the fingers, gripped Chris' arms. He didn't resist; either one of them could have broken him in two, and both looked like they'd as soon eat him as escort him.

They propelled him in Hansen's wake across the runway to a broad sidewalk, and along it to the low building, punctuated by a control tower barely three stories tall, that had obviously been what passed for an airport terminal in the tiny town. A blue patch of sky had been showing when they'd removed his blindfold, but gray fluffy clouds swallowed it as they walked, and heavy drops of cold rain began to fall just as they reached the glass doors at the back of the building, clearly marked EXIT ONLY. They went through them anyway, into a large room decorated in earth tones, with comfortable-looking dark-brown chairs lining olive-green walls. Large windows gave a view of the runway. The crowd of Kemonomimi had dispersed: Chris could see them walking in twos or threes away from the field toward ground vehicles and other buildings. Just before Hansen led him through a door marked AUTHORIZED PERSONNEL ONLY, Chris thought he glimpsed much smaller Kemonomimi—children?—running through the rain to greet one of the couples.

Hansen, Chris, and his guards continued down a gray-carpeted corridor, punctuated at regular intervals by doors of dark, reddish wood, to an open door at the far end. Chris' guards pushed him into the room beyond in Hansen's wake.

"Wait outside," Hansen told them. They exchanged silent looks, but stepped back into the corridor. Hansen closed the door firmly behind them.

The room had obviously been the office of whomever had overseen operation of the airport. Two chairs upholstered in charcoal-gray leather faced a curving desk of the same dark-red wood as the door. Vidscreens covered one wall; a few personal knickknacks decorated a shelf nestled among the blank, glassy surfaces. Chris' gaze wandered to a photograph: a smiling woman, sun shining on her blonde hair, a small girl, her smile and hair matching the woman's, held protectively in the woman's arms.

Chris felt an unaccustomed pang. *All dead,* he thought. *All dead because I came to Earth . . .*

No. He pushed the thought away. *Not because I came to Earth. Because Richard Hansen betrayed real humans and helped the Selkies. Because Victor Hansen created those monstrosities in the first place. Because the Body failed to carry out God's wishes.*

Proof: Seventy years after the Day of Salvation and the supposed Purification, two cat-people stood outside this room, and a clone of Victor Hansen stood within it.

Chris tore his eyes away from the photograph, and bit down hard, clenching his jaw against the rage he felt. He had to play it cool, or he'd join that smiling family in death.

Hansen indicated one of the chairs that faced the desk. Chris sat. Hansen rounded the desk to the larger chair behind it. "Now," he said, sitting down, "I want answers. But . . ." He leaned back. "I'm generous. I know you must be curious about me, so I'll tell you about myself first.

"Yes, I'm Victor Hansen. The *original* Victor Hansen. I faked my death all those years ago and put out the ridiculous story that I fled Earth in the company of the worst mistakes of my career, the Selkies, to cover my true plan."

He spread his hands. "How old do I look to you?"

A trick question? "Um ... mid-thirties?" Chris said. "Maybe younger?"

Hansen laughed. Apparently he'd said the right thing. "Exactly," he said. "*Exactly*. And yet, seventy years ago when I supposedly hijacked a spaceship and fled Earth forever, I was already in my fifties." He leaned forward. "I have made many great discoveries in my life," he said, "and one terrible, terrible mistake.

"Of all my discoveries, three stand out." He held up one finger. "First, I discovered how to mold the human genome at will. And then, late in life, I made two more great discoveries." A second finger went up. "I discovered how to reverse aging." A third finger extended. "And finally, I discovered the secret of suspended animation."

Chris nodded. It seemed safe.

Hansen wasn't really looking at him, anyway. His eyes stared past him, off into the distance. He spoke as if he were talking to a large crowd, giving a long-prepared speech. In fact, the cadence of his voice as he told his story reminded Chris of the recordings of *The Wisdom of the Avatar* he had discovered among his parents' things, the recordings that had led him to activate the interstellar distress beacon that had brought the Body to Marseguro for its long-delayed Purification.

Not that that had exactly worked out the way he'd planned, but God Itself had a plan, of that he was certain. Just as he was certain that the plan involved him. Because why else would God have ensured he be brought to this strange place at this strange time?

Why else was he still alive?

To stay that way, though, he kept his mouth shut and listened to Victor Hansen's sermon.

"... and thus I reversed the aging process in myself, made myself decades younger," he was saying. "Then I entered a state of suspended animation. And when the time was right, I emerged from the darkness." A shadow crossed his face. "And a terrible darkness it was," he said softly. "There were ... unanticipated side effects. I dreamed terrible dreams in which I wasn't myself, dreams in which I wandered the world in the company of Holy Warriors and other functionaries of the cursed Body. But finally, one morning, I woke and found everything had become clear. I remembered who I was, and although I didn't remember what I had done to advance myself so far into the future, so young and strong, I soon reasoned it out." His voice softened. "A terrible loss, that particular memory. To know you have cheated death, and not to be able to remember exactly how you did it ... well. At least I remembered the most important things: my greatest triumph, and my greatest mistake.

"I remember creating the Kemonomimi." Hansen's eyes were bright, but he was still looking off into the distance, though his actual line of sight only encompassed an open door at the side of the room that appeared to lead to a toilet. Chris glanced at it longingly. He could *really* use a toilet.

"The Kemonomimi are what humans should always have been," Hansen said. "Stronger, faster, tougher. Their senses are superior. They need no clothes because they're almost impervious to cold. They're ... perfect. The perfection of humanity.

"I remember how proud I felt when the first youngsters, already sexually, physically, and mentally mature at age ten, escaped into the wild ... though I regretted the deaths of some of my employees during the escape, of course." He blinked, then carried on. "My beautiful Kemonomimi fled into the mountains, built a society, and successfully hid from every attempt, first by the government of the day, and later, after the Day of Salvation, by the Body Purified, to hunt them down."

He smiled proudly, but the smile soured into a scowl. "But then . . . I also remember creating the fish-people. The Selkies. And they were my greatest mistake.

"Humans' distant ancestors crawled out of the sea. We were never meant to crawl back into it. Water creatures are inferior. The fish-people can barely function on land. Keep them out of the water too long and they die a horrible death. They were *wrong*. I should have destroyed the embryos long before I implanted them in the artificial wombs. But . . . I didn't." He shook his head. "Why, I have no idea. My memories from that time are lost, wiped out by age reversal and suspended animation. I remember nothing after creating the Selkies.

"But no matter. The Selkies escaped to this other planet, this . . . Marseguro. A great pity, and someday I will rectify that, but for now the important thing is that there are no fish-people on Earth. Earth belongs to the Kemonomimi, *my* Kemonomimi. My virus made sure of that."

Chris had considerable personal experience with theories extrapolated from too little evidence. Right up until everyone on Earth started dying, he'd been convinced the deaths of the Holy Warriors on Marseguro, *Sanctification*, and *Retribution* had been due to some kind of diabolical poison cooked up by Richard Hansen. Now, of course, he realized that his judgment had been clouded by his own hatred of Richard Hansen and his belief—one he apparently shared with this clone of their creator, oddly enough—that the Selkies were too inferior to have created something as clever as the plague.

He didn't think his judgment was being clouded now, though, as he concluded that this Victor Hansen clone was one seriously deluded individual.

"You . . . remember creating the virus?" Chris said cautiously.

"No," Hansen said instantly. He rubbed his temple with one hand. "No," he said again. "I've tried and tried, but . . . it's not there.

"But I *know* I did it, just as I know I extended my life and slept through decades unchanged. I must have created the virus, for it is cleverly designed to kill almost everyone except those carrying a specific genetic sequence—a sequence from my genome, a sequence I put into my created races as a kind of artist's signature. In other words, this plague was clearly designed to free the Earth of inferior 'normal' humanity, in order to make room for my perfected version: the Kemonomimi."

Okay, then, Chris thought. *I think I know where we stand. You're crazy, and I'm entirely at your mercy.*

I hope this is all part of Your plan, God, because it's just a little nerve-racking from where I sit.

"Now it's your turn," Hansen said. He sat behind the desk and turned those intense blue eyes that Chris remembered so well from Richard Hansen's hated face toward him. "Why are you alive? And who told you that lie about the virus coming from Marseguro?"

Chris thought furiously. Hansen obviously would never accept the truth: that he had come from Marseguro himself and been vaccinated against the virus by its true creators, the Selkies.

"I was . . . a prisoner of the Body," Chris said after a moment. "For political reasons. I . . . um, did some work as a medtech and made the mistake of wondering why we weren't allowed to use gene therapy on humans. When they confronted me, I . . . said some other things. They locked me up."

"That would not stop my virus from finding you," Hansen said.

"No," Chris said, really wishing Hansen would quit using a possessive pronoun when referring to the plague. "But it kept me alive long enough for the Body doctors to experiment on me. They . . . developed a vaccine.

They gave it to me to see if it had any adverse effects. That's when I heard the story about the plague coming from Marseguro—the doctors talked about it. But then someone brought the plague into the prison, and within a day . . ." Chris let his voice trail off.

"A vaccine?" Hansen frowned, then said, reluctantly, "Possible, I suppose. But if what you say is true, how did you escape the prison?"

"A guard took pity on me, let me out," Chris said. It was always nice to be able to sprinkle a little truth in among your lies. "If he hadn't, I would have starved in that cell."

"Did anyone else receive this vaccine?" Hansen said.

"I have no idea," Chris said. "All I know is I didn't see anyone else alive in the City of God until the Kemonomimi showed up."

"What about the Avatar?" Hansen said. "Did you hear how *he* fared?"

"No," Chris said. "But I saw aircraft fleeing the Holy Compound after I'd been on the streets for a few days. They'd managed to keep the plague out that long, at least."

Hansen studied him. "Indeed they did," he said.

"What?" Chris blinked at him. "How did you—"

"The Avatar and as many surviving Holy Warriors and Body functionaries as he could muster have established themselves at Paradise Island, about three hundred kilometers south of here along the coast," Hansen said. "That's why we have decided to make this town our new home."

Chris waited for more explanation. Instead Hansen abruptly stood. "You must be tired and hungry," he said. "The Kemonomimi will look after you. I'll talk to you again before long."

Chris got hastily to his feet. "Thanks," he said. He squeezed his legs together. "Um . . . before I do anything else . . . may I use your toilet?"

Hansen blinked, then laughed. "Of course."

"Thanks." Chris dashed for the door.

Inside, he took care of business, then took a good look at himself in the mirror. He looked older than he expected, with chin stubble the same uninspired sandy brown as his ragged, shoulder-length hair, and dark circles under his eyes. His fine red shirt was torn and his tight-fitting black pants spotted with mud and covered in dust. "What have you gotten yourself into, Chris Keating?" he said out loud.

His reflection had no answer.

Chris sighed, washed his hands—*wouldn't want to spread disease*, he thought, wishing he could share the joke with someone—and stepped back into the office. "I'm all yours," he said: but though he spoke the words to Hansen, in his heart he directed them to God Itself.

Then Alexander and Napoleon came in and took him away.

Chapter 9

FORTY-FIVE MINUTES PASSED in the evacuated simulator room aboard the once—and future, Andy King hoped—*MSS Victor Hansen* with nothing much happening. Simon Goodfellow had cut a jaggedly rectangular section out of the wall, revealing neatly bundled cables of various colors. He'd hooked one of those cables to a strange black keyboard that he had unfolded like a fan and set up on its own thin-legged tripod of black metal, then donned a set of VR goggles. Mostly now he just sat, moving his head from time to time, and very occasionally dancing his fingers across the keyboard.

While he'd been setting up his equipment, Andy and the remaining four crewmembers who had volunteered to wear the pressure suits had been setting up a rough barricade of deck plates around him to shield him from any weapons fire that might make it through the doors if—more likely *when*—they opened.

That done, Andy placed two crewmembers at each end of the room, facing the doors. Two Selkies, Brenda Slade and Sam Hallett, crouched behind the control desks at one end and two nonmods, Arthur Schmidt and Hala Khoury, at the other. That some sort of counterattack would come, Andy was certain. How soon, and what form it would take, he had no idea.

And then he found out. His earphones crackled.

"There's a repair team on the outer hull," Cordelia Raum reported. "They're probing the hole."

Andy nodded to himself. "All right," he said. "You know what to do. Execute when you think the moment is right."

"Roger that."

A repair team on the outer hull was the best they could have hoped for. It meant the Holy Warriors wanted to seal the hole and then repressurize the room so they could open the doors and attack.

It also meant several Holy Warriors were even now gathered on the hull in the vicinity of the hole. Which meant . . .

"Executing," Raum said.

With no air to carry the blast, Andy felt nothing but a slight jolt as the two additional shaped charges they'd installed blew out sections of hull adjacent to the initial damage.

A moment's silence; then, "Repair efforts have ceased," Raum said. "I think they lost at least three men. The rest are retreating."

"Good work. They won't try to pressurize again. Which means they'll try something else. Stay alert, everyone." He glanced at Goodfellow. "Status, Simon."

"Getting there," Simon said. "Not there yet. Leave me alone."

"I was hoping," Andy said mildly, "for some indication of how *much* longer you need."

"At least an hour," Simon said. "Longer if you keep bothering me."

Andy started to reply, then thought better of it. He looked away just in time to catch an amused glance from Hala Khoury, ensconced behind one of the two nearest control desks, and shrugged.

"You think they'll try Plan B?" Raum said in his ear.

"What else can they do?" Andy said. "I just wish I knew how many men they can muster."

Plan B would be tougher for the Holy Warriors to arrange, but certainly not impossible. The computer wouldn't open the sealed doors as long as the corridors outside them were still pressurized. The only way into a depressurized area was to treat the next pressurized area as a giant air lock: put people into it in pressure suits, then lock down the next available pressure seal and depressurize the area with the people in it. Once that was done, the computer could be instructed to open the doors into this room, and the Holy Warriors could mount an attack.

Which was why Andy had his meager forces arrayed the way they were, watching for the flashing red lights above those doors to go out.

"First Officer Andrew King?" a voice said in Andy's ear. He jerked and looked around, then remembered the vacuum and felt like an idiot. He checked his data panel: the voice was coming over an overriding emergency frequency built into the Body-designed suit. With a tap on his wrist controls, he switched to that frequency.

"King here," he said.

"We can end this without bloodshed," the voice said. "Surrender your crew and you won't be harmed."

Andy laughed. "You expect me to believe that?" he said. "The Body has already killed my friends and family on Marseguro. The Body will always kill my kind. I'm a Selkie, you know. A moddie. A . . . whaddyoucallit? . . . oh, yeah. 'Abomination.' "

"I know what you are," the voice said. "And I'm Grand Deacon Byrne, acting commander of *BPS Sanctification*. You killed everyone I ever knew with your filthy plague. You've killed millions. I'd love to see you dead, and I'm sure the feeling is mutual. But I still say we can end this without bloodshed. Enough have died on both sides. Why add to the number?"

Andy looked at Simon. As long as Byrne was talking, he wasn't attacking.

"Why should I surrender?" he said. "Looks to me like I'm in pretty good shape right here."

"You're fooling yourself," Byrne said. "We know what you're trying to do, and it won't work."

"It won't?" Andy felt a chill, but he kept his voice light, aiming for a tone of polite interest. "Really? Why not?"

"You can't regain command of the AI," the Grand Deacon said. "The security protocols are unbreakable. It will only recognize the ranking Body officer as its captain, and even though you've convinced it that you're a Body officer, your fictitious persona doesn't outrank me, or any of my men. You can't change that with a data terminal, no matter how clever your programmer thinks he is."

Inwardly, Andy smiled. *He doesn't know what we're trying to do at all,* he thought. Out loud, though, he allowed a small hint of concern to creep into his voice. "I don't know anything about AIs," he said truthfully. "But why should I believe you instead of my own expert?"

"Your 'expert' comes from a planet that's been out of the mainstream for seventy years," Byrne said. "He's deluded. And he's deluding you."

Andy pretended to think. "Suppose I don't surrender," he said at last. "What then?"

"I think you know," Byrne said.

"You've already tried to repressurize this section. How'd that go for you?"

"There are other ways," Byrne said. "I'm not going to discuss it further. Surrender, or we'll kill you all."

"Suppose I make you the same offer?" Andy said softly.

"Fine," the Grand Deacon snarled. "Have it your way, moddie. Truth be told, I prefer it."

With no air to carry the sound as it contacted the deck, Andy might have missed the roof panel falling altogether if he hadn't happened to glance that way at just the right moment. But the instant he saw it dropping, he realized what must be happening, and flung himself to his feet and dashed forward.

He reached the fallen ceiling plate just as something small, round and black dropped from the newly opened shaft.

Acting on instinct, he grabbed the object and threw it back up the shaft as hard as he could, then dove to one side.

Just in time. The laser grenade went off somewhere inside the shaft, pumping out high-energy beams in all directions. Half a dozen came down the shaft, scoring the floor with white-hot gashes that slowly faded, a cloud of vaporized metal settling around them like mist.

A moment later a body dropped out of the shaft, its pressure suit holed in a number of places. It lay still, smoking. Blood began to pool on the deck plate.

After a moment, more blood began to drip from the hole in the ceiling.

Andy switched back to the frequency the Marseguroites were using amongst themselves. "Close one," he said. "Stay ready—"

Even as he spoke, he saw the light go out on the door he was facing.

"Here they come!"

He ran back to his place behind the corner of one of the simulators.

The door rose slowly. The instant it cleared the floor, the blank white backsides of the control panels Arthur Schmidt and Hala Khoury crouched behind smoked and sparked as lasers swept the room at floor level. A black line scored the barricade protecting Simon, and hydraulic lines at the base of the simulators ruptured, spraying fluid that exploded into a fine brown mist in the vacuum.

Then the door's ascent suddenly went from slow to fast, and two Holy Warriors rolled into the room and came up firing. Hala Khoury's laser burned one down instantly; the other vanished out of Andy's sight. He would have run around the simulator to go after him, but just outside the door another Holy Warrior crouched behind a long black tube on a black metal tripod.

Andy shouted a warning, but the heavy beamer had already fired. The control desk Hala crouched behind flared like a torch and fell apart. Hala jerked up, then fell over sideways and lay still.

Most of her head was missing.

An instant later Andy's laser found the helmet of the heavy gunner's pressure suit and sliced off its top, taking a chunk of the gunner's skull with it.

Andy looked around. The control desk Brenda Slade had been hiding behind had suffered the same fate as Hala's, but she wasn't lying there. He could see a body down by the door, and another slumped over a beam weapon like the one at his end in the corridor, but nobody alive.

He pulled back and ran to the other side of the room.

Brenda and Sam Hallett were struggling hand-to-hand with a Holy Warrior behind Sam's control desk. Andy looked the other way, and saw that another Holy Warrior, having somehow lost his weapon, was sitting on Arthur Schmidt's back, trying to undo his helmet. Andy fired, and the Holy Warrior's suit split across the back. The Holy Warrior stiffened, tried to reach behind him, then fell sideways.

Breathing hard, Andy looked around. Brenda and Sam had dispatched the Holy Warrior they'd been struggling with. That made five Holy Warriors dead, maybe six if there were another one up the shaft, and he'd only lost . . .

One, he'd started to say, but then he realized Schmidt wasn't moving. He ran to him and rolled him over, only to find dead, bloodshot eyes staring up at him: the Holy

Warrior had managed to rip out the suit's air hoses before Andy's laser had found him.

"Shit!" Andy gave the Holy Warrior a savage kick, then strode over to Simon. "Simon, status!" he snapped.

"I told you . . ."

"Damn it, you bloodless little robot, look around you!"

Simon sighed. "This isn't—" he flipped up the lenses on the VR goggles, and for the first time saw the bodies all around him. His face paled. "I didn't—what happened?"

"Arthur Schmidt and Hala Khoury just died so you can do your job, that's what happened," Andy snarled. "Now tell me: what is your status?"

Simon swallowed. "Five minutes," he said. "I swear. Five minutes . . ."

The doors suddenly slid shut again. "I hope you have them," Andy said. He looked around. Brenda and Sam were staring at Hala's body. Tom had his arm around Brenda, whose suited shoulders heaved. Andy went over to them. "They'll try again," he said. "If they get a chance."

"They can't have many more men," Sam said. "Can they?"

"They don't need many more," Andy said.

They waited. Andy could imagine all too well what was happening on the other side of those closed bulkheads. They'd be repressurizing. They'd be manning the heavy guns again. They knew there were only three of them, they knew they only had light weapons. They'd probably just stand back and sweep the room with the heavy beamers. If the *Victor Hansen* crewmembers were lucky, they might pick off one of the gunners, but . . . Andy looked at Simon. The deck plates protecting him wouldn't last ten seconds with a heavy beamer on them.

Simon's promised five minutes crawled into ten, then fifteen. Andy didn't say anything. He flicked his eyes from the shaft in the ceiling to the still-closed bulkheads, over and over.

"Last chance, Mr. King," Byrnes' voice said, so suddenly Andy jumped.

He keyed the Holy Warrior frequency. "You had our answer last time," he replied grimly.

"We both lost people," Byrne said. "But there are more of us than you. You'll be dead two minutes after those doors go up."

"So will some more of your precious Holy Warriors," Andy snarled. "And you all arrived on one shuttle. There can't be very many of you left either."

"Enough to do the job. Do you surrender, Mr. King?"

Andy looked at Simon, who had to be hearing the same broadcast over the same overriding emergency frequency ... and just at that moment, Simon straightened, took a deep breath, turned around, and gave Andy a thumbs-up. Andy grinned, pointed at Simon, made his thumb and finger into a gun, and "fired" it at the tech.

Simon nodded, turned around, and touched a single key on his keyboard.

"I believe the better question, Grand Deacon Byrne, is ... do *you* surrender?

"What the ..." Andy could hear confused, shouting voices in the background. "*What have you done?*"

"I just killed this ship's AI," Andy said. "Dead as a doornail. You have no command over anything."

"Neither do you!" snarled Byrne.

"Maybe," Andy said. "But I don't really need it, do I? Not like you do, Grand Deacon. Because you're trapped. Without the AI, you can't leave the bridge: security protocols have sealed it tight. You're stuck in there until your suits run out of air. Then you'll have to open your faceplates. And then ... well, you know what happens then. A tickle in the throat, a bit of a cough, a little nosebleed, and within a day you're puking your lungs out and dying in your own bloody vomit.

"So here's my ultimatum to you, Grand Deacon Byrne. We've routed manual control of the ship's systems to here. We can let you have safe passage to your shuttle ... so you can fly back to your ship and tell your precious Avatar that *BPS Sanctification* is once more *MSS Victor Hansen*."

"You're still dead," Captain Byrne snarled. "The ship's air won't last forever. Without the AI, systems will start to crash. You can't run something the size of this ship manually with practically no crew. And you've launched all your shuttles and escape pods. You've accomplished *nothing.*"

"My accomplishments," Andy said, "are none of your concern. All you have to do is," and he savored the next four words like bites of the most delectable dessert he'd ever eaten, "get ... off ... my ... ship." He waited one long moment. "Well?"

Silence for five seconds. Ten. Then: "All right."

Andy nodded to Simon. "Let them out."

Simon's fingers tapdanced across the keyboard. "They've got a clear passage to their shuttle ... they're leaving the bridge."

"Keep watching them until we know they've launched," Andy said. He clapped Simon on the shoulder. "Good work. You've saved us all."

Simon grinned awkwardly. "It was nothing."

"Glad to hear it," Andy said. "Because now comes the hard part. Once they're gone, you've got to get this ship's AI up and running again."

Simon's smile faded, and he gave his console a speculative look.

Andy's own smile disappeared as though it had never been as he looked back at Hala and Arthur, still lying where they'd fallen. *I'm tired of losing people to the Holy Warriors*, he thought. *It's got to stop.*

It's got *to.*

*   *   *

"We're ready," Grand Deacon von Eschen said quietly.

The Avatar stood in his office with his hands behind his back, looking through the window and down the once-again fog-shrouded slope to the Pacific Ocean, which today belied its name, smashing against the rocks of the island's west coast as though trying to tear it apart.

"What's the weather forecast?" the Avatar asked.

"Not good," the Grand Deacon admitted. "Of course, we don't have full meteorological capability, but what we've been able to piece together from the sensors scattered out west of the island and a handful of satellite photos ... it looks like we're in for a couple of days of this." He gestured out the window. Rain splattered against it, and the trees bent and swayed as violently as the ocean waves.

"Could we cross in this?" the Avatar asked, but he already knew the answer.

"Yes," the Grand Deacon said. "But not safely. Our boats are small and our crews inexperienced. There are rocks along the coast and the wind would be blowing us right at them. If something went wrong ..."

"God wants us to wait," the Avatar said. He looked up at the sky: though Body doctrine made it clear God imbued every part of the universe with Its life force, something in humans persisted in seeing the sky as more Godly than the Earth.

Well, he thought, *if God's everywhere, then there's more of It out there than there is down here on this puny speck of dust, isn't there?*

"Yes, Your Holiness," the Grand Deacon said.

The Avatar turned away from the stormy view. "Bring Richard Hansen to me," he said. "I want to talk to him."

"Yes, Your Holiness."

The Grand Deacon saluted and left. Karl wondered idly if he would bring Hansen back himself, or order someone else to do it. He'd noticed that people responded to the Avatar's wishes in unpredictable ways, and ways very different from how they had responded to the wishes of the Right Hand.

There's power, then there's absolute power, Karl thought. *And with absolute power comes absolute responsibility.*

Which was one reason he wanted to talk to Hansen.

He'd once suggested to Cheveldeoff that they sacrifice Hansen to the people, use him to cement Cheveldeoff's position as the next Avatar. But instead Hansen had led the Body to Marseguro ... and now he had returned, hard on the heels of Marseguro's killing plague.

He's been at the center of all that has happened, Karl thought. *And that means he's an agent of God, whether he realizes it or not.*

Karl believed he knew exactly what God wanted him to do. But that didn't mean he shouldn't try to discern God's wishes as clearly as possible.

A discreet knock sounded at his door. "Enter," he said, and turned to face the clone of Victor Hansen, ushered in by ... Karl smiled ... the Grand Deacon himself.

"You can leave," he told the Grand Deacon. "But post a guard."

The Grand Deacon gave Hansen a suspicious look, but withdrew.

"Sit," Karl said.

Hansen looked around at the office. "Kind of small for the Avatar, isn't it?" he said.

"Circumstances being what they are," Karl said, "it suffices." He indicated one of the seats across the desk from him. "Please."

Hansen sat. He looked ... tired, Karl thought. Defeated. He smiled. "I'd like to talk to you, Richard," he said. He sat behind the desk. "There's something I've been wondering about." He folded his arms on the desk and leaned forward. "Why?"

Richard didn't know what to expect when the Grand Deacon came to fetch him from the Marseguroites' prison cottage. As far as he knew, he had nothing else to tell the Avatar, nothing to offer him of any value. They'd established he knew nothing about the Kemonomimi. He'd already turned over their supply of vaccine. The Avatar was hardly in a position to threaten Marseguro— *Not yet*, Richard thought bitterly—so whatever knowledge he had of the Selkie planet was of no use.

He felt of little use to anyone. Bringing the vaccine to the island in person had been one more disastrous decision in a string of them that had begun with his determination to blot out his father's shame by helping to find the Selkies.

But the Grand Deacon took him to the Avatar's office, and the Avatar had him sit down, and then the Avatar asked him the one question he didn't expect: "Why?"

He understood the question instantly. But he pretended not to. "Why what?"

The Avatar leaned back in his chair and steepled his fingers. "You were raised in the Body. You were *loyal* to the Body. The gene-bomb Victor Hansen built into you was at least partially defused. You have been steeped since childhood in the teachings of *Wisdom of the Avatar of God*. You know that what the Body teaches is true: God Itself saved Earth from seemingly certain destruction. It was an obvious and unmistakable miracle. After it, no reasonable man could doubt that God exists, and has a plan for Earth that we thwart at our peril.

"Yet that is exactly what you did. You tossed aside God's plan. You tossed aside everything you had been taught, everything you believed. You threw in your lot with the kind of abominations that brought God's wrath down on Earth to begin with. You helped these abominations fight off the Body's Holy Warriors. And when they created a monstrously evil plague that only kills normal humans, not moddies . . . you still aided them.

"That plague has killed millions on Earth. Friends, en-

emies, everyone you ever met on this planet has most
likely fallen to it. And yet you continue to be loyal to the
monsters of Marseguro?"

The Avatar slammed his hands down on his desk so
suddenly that Richard flinched. "Why?" he thundered.
"How could you betray humanity?"

Richard could feel, deep in his heart, the pull of the
belief in which he had been so thoroughly indoctrinated.
Repent, it urged him. *Repent. This is the Avatar, God's
chosen vessel on Earth. Confess to him that you have
made a terrible mistake, that you will return to the fold,
that you will serve God again . . .*

. . . but another part of him pushed back, hard. He'd
made deeper and more lasting friends among the "monsters" and apostates of Marseguro than he had ever
found on Earth, and it was on Marseguro, for the first
time in his life, that he had learned to love.

He refused to see that love as monstrous or unnatural,
or the object of that love as an abomination.

He looked straight into the Avatar's ice-blue eyes. "I
do not deny that what happened on the Day of Salvation *seems* miraculous," he said. "But I deny your interpretation of it. I deny the Body's interpretation of it. I
deny the existence of a God that commands us to kill
in Its name. I deny the truth of a faith that labels fellow
humans monsters or abominations simply because they
look different or live differently. I deny a Creator of life
that would restrict Its creations from creating new life
in their turn. And as for the plague—" Richard's face
twisted. "No one on Marseguro wanted the plague to
reach Earth. We just wanted to be left alone. Chris Keating brought the plague here. Ask your God about *that.*
If It's so happy with your precious Body Purified, why
did It allow Chris Keating to bring back a virus that destroyed it?"

He sat back, but he didn't look away. The Avatar studied him for a long moment. "Fascinating," he said at last.

"How fascinating to catch a glimpse of the machinations of God. That It can use even an apostate like yourself to Its ends . . . astonishing."

Richard couldn't help it. He laughed. "God has been using me?" he said. "Then God has a weird sense of humor."

"Of course God has been using you," the Avatar said. "As it has used Chris Keating: to send us a message."

"A *message?*" Richard felt a hot stab of anger in his heart. "Millions died so you could receive a *message?* God couldn't just slip a note under your door?"

"Not for this." The Avatar leaned forward again. "The message from God is: the Body has been lax. The Body has grown soft. It has come to rely on its own strength, instead of on God's. It has mistaken its purpose on Earth. It is not here to govern, it is here to Purify. It is not here to make sure the crops get harvested and iron gets mined and people have pleasant little lives in clean, safe cities. God is not interested in individuals. God is interested in the survival of Its chosen race, Its ultimate creation: humanity.

"Now God has pared humanity down to a remnant. God will use that remnant to complete the Purification of Earth. And then God will have at last a *pure* human race, a *warrior* race, to spread out among the stars, as God has always intended.

"That Purification starts with the Kemonomimi. God used you to provide us with the vaccine for the plague. Now that we can leave this island, we will destroy those abominations once and for all. And once they are destroyed, God will bless the Earth again. The Body will rebuild: stronger, harder, sharper, a razor-edged blade to slash away the evil branches that have sprung from the pure stock of humanity.

"Marseguro will fall. Then the other colonies. Humanity, true humanity, pure humanity, will spread among the stars: planet by planet, until God's chosen race is so widespread nothing can threaten its existence again . . . except God Itself."

The Avatar sat back and smiled a satisfied, mocking smile. "And you . . . with Chris Keating's help . . . made it all possible. I was once the Right Hand of the Avatar, but you, Richard Hansen, clone of the foulest violator of God's law the world has ever known—*you* have been made the Right Hand of God Itself."

Once more Richard felt the pull of his old life, the majesty and terror of God Itself, all around him, pushing, guiding, forcing, threatening . . . and, if you did Its will, protecting.

But whether because of the gene-bomb Victor Hansen had implanted in his clones or his own experience, Richard Hansen no longer believed in a God like that.

And he was no longer afraid of that God's Avatar.

"Your reasoning is circular," he said. "Everything that happens is God's will, you claim: therefore everything I do, or you do, or anyone else does, is God's will. Nothing can happen that is not God's will.

"Which means, Your Holiness, that Victor Hansen's creation of the Kemonomimi and the Selkies was God's will, and this God you claim to worship is ordering you to destroy something, to kill hundreds more on top of the millions who have already died, that It caused to be created in the first place.

"I reject that kind of God, a God that is nothing more than a bored child pushing toys around in a sandbox. My decisions are my own. As are yours. To a greater or lesser degree, depending on our circumstances, we all have free will. We choose to do good, or we choose to do evil.

"I've made evil choices. But recently I've been trying to make good ones. And that's the only reason I'm here. I came—we all came, nonmods and Selkies alike—to offer help to the survivors of the plague that Marseguro unwillingly and unwittingly unleashed on Earth.

"We chose to do good. And now you, Your Holiness, rebuilding your army, withholding vaccine from other survivors, focusing instead on your determination to kill the Kemonomimi and the Selkies and anyone else who does not believe as you do—you are choosing to do evil."

He stopped. The Avatar looked at him. Richard didn't know what he'd expected—anger, perhaps, an order that he be removed, even executed, but the Avatar only looked faintly amused.

"And what," asked the Avatar, "are good and evil if God Itself is but a myth?" He shook his head. "You tell me these things as if they have never been considered before in the history of the world, instead of hashed and rehashed for millennia. But those arguments were settled, once and for all, when the First Avatar heard God's voice, and acted on it.

"Here's what it comes down to, Richard." Karl Rasmusson leaned forward. "I am the Avatar. I have been chosen by God to be the Avatar. And unlike the Avatar before me, I have listened to what God told the First Avatar: a man we know heard God clearly, since the miracle of Salvation Day attests to his connection to the Creator and Destroyer of All Things.

"What is good and what is evil are determined by God. Human opinions mean nothing. Human choice means nothing, if it is not informed by God. Your 'choices' are made without reference to the will of God, and therefore are not choices at all. Only those who believe and have submitted themselves to God Itself in the Body Purified have true freedom of will."

"But if that is so," Richard asked softly, "why hasn't God simply caused all of us 'unbelievers' and 'apostates' to believe and repent?"

"The decision to serve God is always made freely," the Avatar responded. "Once it is made, you have the choice every day of continuing to serve God, or to return to your old ways. But once you step outside the Body, your free choices are forfeit. Until you return to the Body, you serve as God's pawn, as a cog in Its great plan for the universe."

"Then the only 'choice' God allows is to serve It," Richard said. "You're saying I can choose to return to the Body and do God's will every day . . . or I can choose to remain outside the Body, in which case God will use me to do Its will anyway."

"Exactly," said the Avatar.

"Then freedom is a myth."

The Avatar's blue eyes bore into Richard's. "Exactly," he said again. "Richard Hansen, you could serve the Body again. Even though you claim to have none of Victor Hansen's memories of the Kemonomimi, you are still his clone—Victor Hansen himself, in very many ways. You could help us when we reach the Kemonomimi, help talk them into surrendering rather than fighting. If they surrender, we need not kill them."

"Just sterilize and enslave them," Richard said. "Like you planned to do with the Selkies."

"They cannot be permitted to continue to breed and pollute God's Holy Human Genome," the Avatar admitted. "But it is better to be alive and unable to reproduce than to be dead."

"And then I suppose you'll want me to help you retake Marseguro?" Richard said.

"It would be helpful," the Avatar said, "but not necessary. I understand you may have emotional entanglements with the Selkies. I would not force you to return to that planet. You could serve here on Earth, helping to distribute the vaccine, helping to rebuild the planet.

"It is the only free choice left to you," the Avatar said, and his voice hardened. "You have served God unwillingly and unknowingly. Continue to serve It like a puppet, or choose to serve it as a free man. But you *will* serve God."

Richard felt anger rising in him then, welling out of the same deep source from which he had earlier felt the tug of loyalty to the Body. *I gave myself to God freely once before,* he thought. *And the result was death and destruction, death and destruction that continue. Marseguro would remain undetected and hundreds there would still be alive, Earth would be uninfected and millions still alive here, if I hadn't made that choice.*

I sure as hell *won't make it again.*

"God," Richard growled, looking down, hands clenched, "can try to make me Its puppet. But I'm going to be pulling on those strings for all I'm worth. I'd rather be an unwilling puppet than a willing slave. In other words," he lifted his head and looked the Avatar straight in the eyes, "God Itself can kiss my ass."

Was that a flicker of anger at last in the Avatar's face? If so, it didn't carry over into his voice. "Very well," he said mildly. He looked out the window at the waves exploding in spray on the island's shore. "I believe God wanted me to offer you this last chance to serve It freely. I believe that's why we have been delayed by weather." He turned back to Richard. "And now that I have made that offer—and you have made your answer—I believe the weather will clear. We will sail to the mainland tomorrow, and from there march on the Kemonomimi."

He walked past Richard and opened the door. "Return him to his quarters," he said to the guards. As they entered and none-too-gently hauled Richard to his feet, the Avatar added, "You and your crew will remain here under guard. When we have completed our mission, we will return, and then I will deal with you as God instructs." He stared hard into Richard's eyes one last time. "I am being merciful," he said softly. "All of you will have one last chance to submit freely to the Body, and live. If you do not, then I am quite confident it will be God's will to see you shot." He stepped out of the way, and the guards pushed Richard out.

Richard didn't look back. *If there is a God,* he thought, *It may well have other plans for* you, *Avatar.*

He looked up at the sodden gray sky. Somewhere beyond those clouds, Andy would be trying to retake *Victor Hansen.* If he succeeded, all of the Avatar's plans could yet be seriously upset.

Not that he should mind, Richard thought savagely. *After all, it's all God's will.*

One of the guards gave him a shove that almost tripped him up, and he concentrated on the gravel path.

When the door closed behind Hansen, Karl Rasmusson allowed himself the luxury of slamming his hands down on his desk. The effrontery of the man! Raised in the Body, steeped in the truth of the First Avatar's words, witness to the recordings of the undeniable miracles of God on the Day of Salvation, and he *still* dared to deny God's will?

"Why did you want me to talk to him?" he asked God out loud. He looked out at the storm. As he had expected, it seemed to be easing. "You must have known what he would say."

And even as he asked the question, he knew the answer: God had wanted him to talk to Richard Hansen not for Hansen's sake, but for his own. God needed him to face head-on the doubts that might otherwise eat away at his faith. God needed him to see how powerless and hopeless were those who turned their backs on It.

His spirits suddenly lifted. Richard Hansen had served his purpose. He lived only at God's—and the Avatar's— pleasure. Karl no longer needed to think about him.

When the weather lifted, he would sail with his vaccinated army to the mainland. They would march on the Kemonomimi, whose polluting presence on the Earth had brought the plague down upon them all. He would Purify the Earth and, like the First Avatar, turn away God's wrath. And, unlike the second Avatar, he would not falter afterward. He would follow God's will wherever it might lead, whatever it might require: across the Earth, across the solar system, across the galaxy.

The clouds broke apart. Shafts of sunlight stabbed down on the restless ocean, striking diamond-bright sparks of light from the tossing waves, and Karl Rasmusson, Third Avatar of the Body Purified, knew without a shadow of doubt that it was a sign of favor from God.

Chapter 10

THE STRANGE SELKIES DROVE Emily, her mother, and the two pressure-suited Holy Warriors through the funny-tasting blue-green water, doubled up on the transportation devices Emily decided to call sputa, since they were close enough to Marseguro's Self-Propelled Underwater Towing Apparatus. The Holy Warriors were kept in the center, each riding with one of the largest men in the group, the rest of the Selkies surrounding them. Emily and her mother were shown a little more trust: Emily was put with the woman she had seen first, holding on tightly to her waist. Her mother was put with the teenage boy. From the looks the teenager shot in her direction, she suspected he would have preferred that the arrangement be reversed.

After an hour her arms were aching, and she began to wonder just how far they had to go. Then, suddenly, she saw something in the turquoise distance. As they approached and she got her first good look at it, Emily would have gasped if she had been in air.

An enormous artificial island rode the waves above them, tethered to the ocean floor by cables twice as thick as Emily's body. She couldn't begin to guess at it size—the metal underbelly disappeared into darkness in all directions.

And in the deep shadow of that steel ceiling: a sphere, attached to the island's underside.

At first she thought the sphere must be about the same size as a large Marseguroite habitat, but her sense of scale, already thrown out of whack by the enormous mass of metal floating overhead, kept adjusting itself as they approached it until at last she realized it was far larger than anything on Marseguro, at least a hundred meters in diameter. Tubes a good three meters in diameter led off from it in three directions to smaller spheres, just visible in the murk, and shadows hinted at further spheres beyond that.

It's not just a habitat, it's a whole underwater city, Emily thought. And it's completely hidden from above by . . . that.

Whatever *that* was.

A Marseguroite habitat would have blazed with light and been surrounded by traffic, from skinsuited Selkies to sputa and subs, but this one was absolutely dark. If she hadn't known better, she would have thought it dead and deserted.

She glanced at her mother. She, too, was staring upward at the metal ceiling looming above them.

When they were within five meters of the habitat's massive curved wall a section of it split open, spilling light into the water. They drove in, then up. Seeing a surface above her, Emily let go of the strange Selkie's waist with relief and kicked up on her own. A moment later they all broke into the air in a large pool surrounded by four men and two women, all armed, all aiming their weapons—odd, streamlined things that looked as if they were made out of obsidian instead of metal, but definitely weapons—at the center of the pool.

Emily found herself looking down a shiny black barrel. "Is that really necessary?" she exclaimed in English.

The man with the gun started so violently she was probably lucky he didn't shoot her by accident. "You speak English?" he said, then clamped his mouth shut even before the woman in the white bathing suit, who had surfaced just beside Emily, said, "Shut up, Herb."

Then she looked at Emily. "I think we have a lot to talk about," she said. "But before we get out of this pool you're going to have to explain *them*." She gestured at Biccum and his companion, both floating in the pool, still blindfolded. "Why are you protecting Holy Warriors?"

"They . . . well, one of them, anyway . . . was kind to me," Emily said. "He may have saved my life. He certainly saved me a lot of agony. I owe him." She paused. "And . . . I've seen enough dead Holy Warriors in my life."

"I haven't," the woman said shortly. "Very well. We'll let them into the Republic. But they're going to be prisoners."

The Republic? Emily thought, but, "Of course," she said.

"And they'll have to stay in their suits," the woman went on, looking at Biccum and Koop. "The station is infected with the plague. We made sure of it."

"No, they won't," Emily said. "They've been vaccinated."

The woman's head snapped around as though she'd been slapped. "What?"

Emily sighed. "You said we had a lot to talk about. That's part of it. Wouldn't it be better to do so somewhere more comfortable . . . and more private?"

Emily's mother swam up beside them. "I agree," she said. "And I can't speak for my daughter, but I'm starving."

Emily smiled at her. "In this case, you *can* speak for your daughter."

The woman looked from Emily to her mother, and her expression softened slightly. "Agreed," she said. "Take the Holy Warriors to the brig," she said to the man she'd called Herb. "Kujawa, you go with him." Another man nodded. "I'm assured they can safely remove their pressure suits, so get them out of those down here. They won't be trying to escape with no way to breathe.

"I'll take these other two to my quarters for questioning. The rest of you . . . get back to work."

Emily swam to the nearest ladder and climbed up onto the edge of the pool. Someone handed her a towel, and as she wiped off the excess water, she glanced around. Gray steel walls, gray steel ceiling, harsh lighting: utterly utilitarian. Whatever the place had been, it certainly hadn't been a luxury hotel.

She sniffed the air: humid, saturated, warm, just the way Selkies liked it. She glanced at Biccum, struggling out of his pressure suit under the watchful eyes and ready guns of Kujawa and Herb. Sweat poured down his face and he looked miserable—but at least he was alive. She caught his eye and gave him a smile; he gave her back a wan one of his own, then was abruptly taken by the arm by Herb and hurried away, Koop in the grip of Kujawa behind him.

"This way," their hostess said. She led them out a different hatch than the one the Holy Warriors had been taken through, and along a corridor every bit as gray and utilitarian as the pool room had been, lined with submarine-style doors. They hadn't gone far, however, before the woman stopped, looked behind them, and said sharply, "Where do you think you're going, Shelby?"

Emily looked back. She hadn't noticed the teenage boy was following them. He'd pulled on a plain white T-shirt over his trunks. She'd thought his short-cropped hair was black when she'd seen it underwater, but now she saw it was actually died a deep cobalt blue. He looked down at the metal floor and pushed at it with one bare toe. "I thought . . . I'd come along. Mom."

Mom? Emily glanced back at the woman. The same sharp chin and prominent cheekbones . . . she could see the resemblance, now that she looked.

"This is Presidential business," the woman said. "I don't need you spreading rumors and exaggerations all over the Republic."

"I won't say a word unless you tell me I can," the boy—Shelby—said. Like every other Selkie, he had big green eyes, and as he raised his head shyly and looked up at his mother through his long eyelashes, he looked so puppylike that Emily laughed. Her mother chuckled, too.

The woman's face softened some more. "All right," she said. "But if you breathe one word to anyone before I've made an official announcement . . ."

"I won't," Shelby said, and he hurried forward to join the group. He looked sideways at Emily but didn't say anything.

Several intersections and three flights of narrow metal stairs later, they reached another submarine door that looked exactly like all the others they had passed. The woman placed her hand over a panel to one side, and with a clank the door unsealed and swung inward.

They stepped through into the first room Emily had seen that wasn't gray. Instead, the walls were a warm, sunny yellow. The furniture looked handmade, from some kind of driftwood stained a deep chocolate brown. Throw rugs softened the black vinyl floor, and pillows were everywhere, most embroidered with sea motifs: fish, whales, coral, and seabirds. Through another door, Emily glimpsed a short hall with more rooms leading off of it.

One corner of the main room was filled by what, despite differences in design from any Emily had ever seen, was recognizably a cookbot. Emily's mouth watered at the sight of it, and she looked at their hostess hopefully, but the woman simply gestured to the couch and chairs. "Have a seat," she said. She looked at Shelby. "You can sit in the corner."

Shelby promptly threw a pillow into the corner by

the door, plopped down on it cross-legged, and watched with wide eyes as Emily and her mother seated themselves more sedately on the couch. The woman took one of the chairs.

"First, names," the woman said. "I'm Sarah McLean, and that, as you'll have gathered, is my son Shelby, age sixteen. I won't tell you my age." She smiled briefly, the first smile Emily had seen from her. "I'm the current president of the Free Selkie Republic, which is our rather grandiose name for this large habitat and ..." She hesitated. "Um, a number of smaller ones." She paused expectantly.

"My name is Emily Wood," Emily said. "And this—"

"I can talk for myself," her mother said. "I'm Dr. Carla Christianson-Wood."

"Emily. Carla," President McLean said. "Then here's the big question." She leaned forward. "Where are you from, and how the hell did you end up in that Holy Warrior shuttle?"

Emily looked at her mother, who looked back silently. Emily sighed. "That," she said, "is a very long story."

President McLean leaned back. "Then I suggest you get started," she said. "Because until I'm convinced you're not a threat to the Free Republic, you're prisoners. And if you are a threat ..." She left the sentence unfinished.

Emily cleared her throat. "Very well," she said. "First, where we're from." She looked into McLean's eyes, eyes identical to her own, eyes designed by Victor Hansen. "We're from Marseguro."

Shelby gasped. The president's eyes widened. "That's impossible!"

"Then you have heard of it."

"Of course I've heard of it. We were horrified when we heard that the Body had discovered it and sent an expedition to Purify it." She studied Emily and her mother. "I think some history is in order," she said. She looked at her son. "And since you're here, why don't you tell it? Assuming you've been paying attention in history class . . . ?"

Shelby straightened, bright-eyed. "Of course I have!" He cleared his throat. "When Victor Hansen fled the anticipated assault by the Body Purified against Luna aboard his stolen starship *Rivers of Babylon*, not all the Selkies he had created went with him. The initial Selkies gestated in artificial wombs, not in women's bodies, and were born within a few weeks of each other, and thus were all of the same age. But Hansen was only able to get one generation to Luna. The first generation—the original Selkies—were forced to fend for themselves on Earth. In the chaos of Purification, many were killed . . . but not all. Some fled into the oceans, and over time, they came together to form the Free Selkie Republic, which has now remained hidden from the Body Purified for seventy years." He stopped his recitation. "How's that?" he asked his mother.

"Succinct," she said. "Thank you."

Emily blinked. "I've never heard any of this!"

"That's because Victor Hansen didn't intend for the Selkies on Marseguro to ever find out about it," her mother said unexpectedly. Emily gave her a startled look, then suddenly realized . . .

"You had access to his secret diaries," she said. "You knew about the Earth Selkies!"

Her mother shook her head. "Not exactly. Hansen was convinced they had all been killed even before he left Luna. But he didn't want the Selkies of Marseguro to know they'd ever existed, because he was afraid it would drive the Marseguroites to attempt some sort of rescue, thus exposing themselves to the Body." She nodded at Shelby. "But everything he says . . . is true."

"Of course it is!" Shelby said. "I always tell the truth."

His mother cocked an eyebrow at him.

"Well, almost always," he said, and settled back on his cushion.

"The Body never talked about Marseguro again after announcing it would be Purified," the President went on. "I had begun to think it had just been a ploy, part of somebody's political maneuvering in the run-up to the selection of the new Avatar."

"It's very real," Emily said. "It's our home. And, yes, the Body attempted to Purify it. But we defeated them."

"How?" the President said harshly. "I know what Holy Warriors can do—*have* done, to crush dissent all over this planet. How did *you* defeat them?"

Emily looked at her mother, who nodded. Emily turned back to the President. "The plague," she said simply.

"What?" McLean sat up straighter. "The Body said it was a virus that escaped from some old gene engineering lab. When it started, the Body kept talking—well, until there was nobody left to talk—about how it proved once again the dangers of modifying God's Holy Human Genome and how the Holy Warriors would redouble their efforts to bring all rogue genetic engineers and moddies to 'God's implacable attention.' "

"The plague did not originate on Earth," Dr. Christianson-Wood said. Emily looked at her with concern, but her voice, though it wavered a bit, remained strong. "It originated on Marseguro. And it is in no way natural. We created it." She closed her eyes, opened them again; gave Emily a long look, then turned to President McLean. "*I* created it."

"No way," Shelby breathed. His mother shot him a look that made his shoulders hunch, then turned her laserlike gaze back to Dr. Christianson-Wood.

"A rather grandiose claim," she said. "You're saying you, personally, designed a virus that is almost one hundred percent fatal in unmodified humans?"

"Yes," Emily's mother said.

"And then you unleashed it on Earth?" McLean's voice gave no indication of how she felt about that, but Dr. Christianson-Wood reacted violently.

"No," she snapped, slamming her hand down on the low table in front of the couch. "I created it as a last-ditch *defense* of *Marseguro*. I created it because I knew—*all* of us knew—that if the Body Purified found us, they would sterilize us, enslave us, slaughter us. It was *only* intended to drive off nonmod invaders and ensure they could never invade again."

"You appear to have overachieved," McLean said levelly.

"But I never wanted this!" Emily's mother's voice broke for the first time. "When I heard . . . it almost drove me mad. I've barely started to climb out of the depression it plunged me into. I never wanted all these deaths on my conscience. All the millions—every one of them—dead because of something I cooked up in my lab, something I nurtured, something I tucked away at night in liquid nitrogen. That virus might as well be my own child."

Emily winced, but said nothing. McLean still sat straight and still, watching Dr. Christianson-Wood. "If you didn't send it deliberately," she said, "then how did it get here?"

"A traitor," Emily said. "A traitor to Marseguro. The same traitor who triggered the interstellar beacon that allowed the Body to find us in the first place. Chris Keating. He managed to get aboard a Body ship and rode it back to Earth. He'd been exposed. He carried it here."

"Why didn't he die?" Shelby asked, his eyes wide. His mother shot him a look, but didn't tell him to be quiet.

"Because he was vaccinated," Emily said.

"Like the Holy Warriors from the shuttle?"

Emily nodded.

"But why vaccinate him?" McLean demanded. "Why vaccinate *them,* if you created this virus to destroy them?"

Emily's temper snapped. "He got vaccinated because the person vaccinating him didn't know what he'd done. The Holy Warriors stole vaccine and vaccinated themselves. And I'm getting sick of this. We're Selkie. You're Selkie. Do you really think we're all part of some elaborate scheme to betray you to the Body?"

"Emily," her mother said, but Emily ignored her.

"The Holy Warriors on that shuttle kidnapped us. They dragged us into space against our will and flew us here with only one landsuit between us. They threatened to gang-rape us, for crying out loud. And they planned to put my mother on trial for genocide.

"Now it sounds like you're planning to do the same. Damn it, we're on your side!"

"How do you know what side that is?" McLean said, and now Emily could hear anger rising through the infuriating icy calm the President had maintained until then. "You—and you—*all of you*—you haven't been here. You've been enjoying your freedom on Marseguro all the years we've been struggling to avoid being found and slaughtered. Every year I've lost people, people who were glimpsed by fishermen or Holy Warriors on patrol, people who killed themselves rather than face interrogation that might have revealed the Free Republic. Two years ago, I had to order the scuttling of an entire outpost. We evacuated a hundred Selkies, but their homes, their belongings, everything they'd worked for their whole lives—gone.

"Every year, we grow fewer. There aren't enough young people, and there aren't enough women." She gestured at the walls around her. "There used to be more than two thousand of us living in this complex. Now most of the smaller habitats are deserted: we only visit them to tend the hydroponics and the vortex power generators and the microfactories. We're down to fewer than a thousand Selkies here, maybe half that many again in all the smaller outposts combined. We're aging and dying out. We've only survived this long because we've been smarter than the Body."

"We've been hiding from the Body, too," Emily pointed out. "We just had a larger hiding place. And when we were found, we fought back . . . just like you would. And we lost hundreds. Maybe thousands." She leaned forward. "We're not your enemies. The Body is."

McLean blinked and looked down. "Old habits of paranoia die hard," she said. She looked up again. "And to answer your question—no. We're not interested in putting you on trial for genocide, Dr. Christianson-Wood. Quite the contrary. If what you've said is the truth, we'd rather honor you as a hero. Because as far as we can tell . . . you've almost killed the Body Purified."

"I'm not a hero," Emily's mother said savagely. "Don't you *dare* call me that. I did what I had to do, but I never intended . . ." Her voice shook. "All those deaths—"

"Landlings," McLean said.

"People," Dr. Christianson-Wood snapped.

"People who would cheerfully kill you on sight."

"Not all of them."

"Enough of them."

"Women. Children."

"Breeders of Holy Warriors. Future Holy Warriors." The two women glared at each other, and Emily, her own anger fading somewhat . . . but only somewhat . . . stepped into the momentary silence.

"I have a question." She thought. "Two, actually."

McLean looked at her, face still tight with anger. "Go ahead."

"First. Earth isn't as much a water planet as Marseguro, but if I remember right, it's three-quarters of the way there. How did our shuttle happen to land almost on top of your 'Free Selkie Republic'?"

"If your shuttle hadn't fallen apart during descent, it *would* have landed on top of us," McLean said. She pointed up. "That artificial island up there is an old commercial spaceport. It's been abandoned since the Day of Salvation; just a dead hunk of metal tethered to the top of a sea mount in the middle of the Pacific Ocean. This," she gestured at the walls around her, "was where the workers lived, safe from typhoons and launch disasters. The first-generation Selkies found and moved into it.

"Because it was a spaceport, we've been able to use its old equipment to hack into System Control. There hasn't been much to see for the past few weeks . . . until just recently. A Holy Warrior starship showed up a few days ago . . . and then, your shuttle.

"When your shuttle got warned away by the starship and automated systems at the various Body outposts, we decided maybe we could use a shuttle . . . and so we activated an old landing beacon to bring you here. But you crashed instead, and . . ." she shrugged. "Here you are."

Emily nodded slowly. "I see," she said. "All right, I buy that."

"Good," said the President. She glanced at her son. "Because I always tell the truth." She looked back at Emily. "Your second question?"

"You said the plague had 'almost' killed the Body. What did you mean by that?"

McLean stood up abruptly. "That, I'll have to show you," she said. "Shelby, stay here."

"Aw . . ." the boy had stood up, but now he sat down again.

"You have homework to do," McLean said. As she led Emily and Dr. Christianson-Wood out, Emily glanced back to see the boy, crestfallen, dragging himself toward the bedrooms.

The President led them down this time, eventually swimming them through water-filled tubes lit by yellow glowstrips, then up into a wet porch. "Main control for the whole complex," she said as they climbed out into the air and toweled off. "We've made it as hard as possible for landlings to get to . . . just in case we're ever boarded."

Emily looked around. The room reminded her of the bridge of the *Victor Hansen*, but on a larger scale. Several Selkies sat at consoles, monitoring . . . what?

"Heating and cooling, fresh water extraction, protein synthesis, swimway oxygenation, the usual things," McLean said when Emily asked. "That's not what I brought you here to see." She paused in front of a particularly large console built into the curving wall. "This is central communications. Hello, Patrick."

The tech at the controls, a skinny young Selkie in a bright-orange landsuit, waved a hand. He had headphones clamped to his ears and was watching a screen that seemed to be displaying fuzzy surveillance video from . . . where? Emily could see pine trees, but it was either foggy where the camera was or it had serious technical difficulties.

"Any change?" the President asked.

Patrick pulled off the headphones. "No," he said, rubbing his nub of an ear. "They seem to have finished loading their boats hours ago. My guess now," he nodded at the screen, "is that they're waiting for the weather to improve."

"Who's they?" Emily asked.

"The Avatar," President McLean said. "And his army."

Emily jerked.

Dr. Christianson-Wood turned pale. "But you said—"

"I said 'almost killed,' " McLean said. "Almost isn't entirely. The Avatar—whoever he is; he could have been a janitor before the plague hit for all I know—has been holed up on an island with several hundred Holy Warriors and other Body survivors.

"We've known about Paradise Island for years. It's a luxury resort for the most important members of the Body hierarchy. We've got an outpost just fifty kilometers south of it, and we do our best to keep a watch on it, without getting close enough to get detected. That's how we knew the Avatar had fled there. But the only reason we've got that—" she pointed at the fuzzy vidscreen, "—is because Patrick here is a genius who managed to hack into a supposedly unhackable undersea data line. This video comes from a hidden camera that used to send video directly to Body Security in the City of God."

"I doubt even the Avatar knows it exists," Patrick said. "We think Cheveldeoff installed it as a way to gather material to blackmail Body officials with. This island saw some wild parties under the old Avatar."

"In any event," McLean said, "a few days ago, something happened. A shuttle came down from the Holy Warrior starship that had just arrived in orbit. It wasn't long before we saw *this*."

Another vidscreen flicked to life above the first. Emily looked up and gasped. Holy Warriors in long lines were moving past men in white coats, who methodically dosed each with a hypospray. "They're being vaccinated!"

"So it appears," McLean said. "Which is one reason I still have one or two doubts about your story." She looked at Emily, her face hard once more. "If they're being vaccinated . . . where did the vaccine come from?"

On the lower of the two vidscreens, Emily suddenly saw movement: a man being half-dragged by two Holy Warriors. Something about the man seemed familiar . . .

Ignoring McLean's question for a moment, Emily said to Patrick, "Can you zoom in on that prisoner?"

"Eh?" Patrick looked at the screen, then glanced at McLean. She frowned, but nodded. Patrick turned back to his controls. "Sure, just hold on a second . . ."

He pushed at a slider. The prisoner seemed to leap toward them, and Emily thought her heart would stop as an enormous surge of both fear and joy swept over her. "We didn't bring the vaccine," she said, her voice sounding distant, barely audible above the sudden roaring in her ears. "He did." She pointed.

"My God," her mother breathed beside her.

McLean looked at the man on the screen. "Who is he?"

"Richard Hansen."

Patrick spun in his chair to look at her; McLean froze for an instant, then turned more slowly. "Hansen? As in . . . ?"

Careful, Emily thought. *We don't want to . . .*

"As in Victor Hansen," her mother said. "Richard Hansen is a clone of our creator. And he brought the vaccine here to try to save as many people as possible."

"A clone of—?" Patrick said, but McLean had already jumped onto the latter half of Dr. Christianson-Wood's statement.

"As many Holy Warriors as possible, you mean."

"People," Dr. Christianson-Wood said sharply. "Just . . . people."

So much for not telling them everything we know, Emily thought. She watched Richard hungrily until he was pulled out of the frame by the guards.

Richard a prisoner. Vaccine going to the Body instead of the general population.

How did everything go so wrong?

"We've got to rescue him," she said.

"We?" President McLean gave her a cool look. "You mean *us.*"

"Yes," Emily said.

"But you just said *he* brought the vaccine," McLean said. "He gave it to the Body. Now the Avatar and his Holy Warriors will be able to leave that island.

"We know there are other enclaves of survivors around the world. We've heard some of them talking to each other. They're free of the Body right now—that's the one good thing the plague has accomplished. But now that it has the vaccine, the Body will regain power. Survivors will have to submit to it again, or die. And we Selkies . . ." She stepped close to Emily, until their faces were just centimeters apart. "We could have inherited the Earth. Now we'll be forced to stay in hiding. Or else the Body will find us, and kill us." She thrust out one finger at the screen. "Why the hell should I rescue *him*?"

"Because," Emily said, but her throat closed down on whatever she had been about to say.

And what had that been exactly? *Because I love him?* She didn't think that would sway Sarah McLean.

"Because he's *not* one of the Body," Emily's mother said sharply. "He's their enemy. He fought them on Marseguro. He seized control of an entire Body starship, for God's sake. That starship? That's ours now. And he's its captain. He's on our side."

"He's got a funny way of showing it," McLean said. She started to say something; stopped, then finally shrugged.

"However. As it happens, a rescue mission is already underway."

Emily gaped at her. "But you said—"

"Not for him," Sarah said. "He didn't figure in our plans. But he's not alone there. Patrick, show them."

Patrick's fingers flicked across the controls. The top screen's image changed. Now it showed prisoners being hustled across the compound by Holy Warriors. Some were nonmods.

Some were Selkies.

"That's Melody Ashman," Emily said. "And Pierre Normand . . . Jerry Krall . . . they're all from Marseguro. They must have been aboard the shuttle with Richard."

"We couldn't figure out how there could be Selkie prisoners we didn't recognize," McLean said. "But we knew we had to find out. And we knew we couldn't leave Selkies in the hands of Holy Warriors.

"So we sent a sub from our outpost near the island. At around two AM—" she glanced at a time display on Patrick's console, "—that's about six hours from now—a rescue party will put ashore."

"But they're going after the Selkies," Emily said. "You're not planning to rescue any of the nonmods, are you?"

McLean said nothing.

"You have to—"

"I don't have to do anything," McLean snapped. Then her voice softened. "In any event, I can't. I have no way of communicating with them. They'll report back when they're well clear of the island. If all goes well, that will be early tomorrow morning our time."

She turned. "I'll show you to quarters."

The Marseguroites followed her silently, each lost in her own thoughts.

Chapter 11

IN THE MIDDLE OF the night, Richard woke to gunfire.

He had no idea how long he'd been asleep, but it didn't feel like very long: he'd tossed and turned for hours after he'd lain down, unable to brake the endlessly turning wheel of self-recrimination and worry in his brain.

All of that had been ramped up by what they'd witnessed out the windows of their cabin/prison at dusk: lines of Holy Warriors marching down to the quay and boarding the ships that waited there, leaving behind only a skeleton staff to look after the buildings, and an unknown number of guards to keep watch on them.

As the ships had sailed away in the gathering night, Richard had glanced at the others. "They're going to attack the Kemonomimi," he said.

"Poor bastards," Melody said. "I wish we could warn them."

Richard said nothing and turned in early.

Now, head still fuzzy from too little sleep, interrupted too soon, he sat up in bed and listened, wondering if he'd dreamed—

No, there it was again. The unmistakable crack of Body-issued firearms. He'd heard the sound too often on Marseguro—sometimes with his own finger on the trigger—to mistake it for anything else.

But who—?

He got up and pulled on his green Marseguroite navy uniform, then emerged into the hallway beyond to see the rest of his crew already gathered there, in various states of undress. The cabin had four rooms; he had one to himself, as did Ann Nolan. Melody and Pierre, to his surprise, though apparently no one else's, were sharing another one. *The captain is always the last to know,* he thought. By necessity, Jerry Krall and Derryl Godard were sharing the remaining room, though Richard didn't get the feeling either one of them much cared for the arrangement.

Melody, a sheet wrapped around her, said, "What's going on?"

"I wish I knew," Richard said. "Everyone get dressed, then come to the common room. Be quick."

They disappeared back into their rooms. He went down the dark hall, not daring to turn on a light, and knelt on the sofa to look out the window.

The hall across the road from the cottage, where he had had coffee with the Avatar, was ablaze, flames leaping high into black billowing smoke. He glimpsed dark figures in front of the fire. Two grappled; one fell, joining at least two other motionless forms he could see on the ground.

Abruptly, the door rattled. Richard leaped off the couch and turned to face it. A pause, then suddenly, with no warning at all, the lock exploded. Something stung Richard's cheek; he touched the spot, and his finger came away red.

The door smashed inward. A black figure stood silhouetted against the flame, a bright white light shining from the side of its head. Richard could see no details, but he could tell the figure held a handgun in one hand and a knife in the other. He held himself still as the light found his face.

The figure gasped, and lowered its weapons. "Creator?"

A woman's voice. "I . . . doubt it," Richard said. "Who are you?"

Her hand went out, fumbled on the wall—and as the lights switched on, it was Richard's turn to gasp.

A Selkie woman stood in the door. The light came from a headset that looked similar, though not identical, to the standard comm headsets of the Holy Warriors. She wore a black skinsuit not that different from those worn on Marseguro. But the thing that astonished him was that he'd never seen her before.

She wasn't from the *Victor Hansen*, and that meant she wasn't from Marseguro.

"Richard, what . . . ?" Melody Ashman led the rest of the group into the room. They were all fully dressed now, the Selkies in the black landsuits they wore during the day, the nonmods in pale-green Marseguroite uniforms like Richard's own. Melody froze so suddenly when she saw the strange Selkie that the others barreled into her from behind with classic slapstick timing. "Who—?"

The strange Selkie tore her eyes off Richard and looked at Melody. "I don't know who you are either," she said cheerfully, "and I sure as hell don't know how that's possible, but some of you are Selkies, and that's good enough for me." She holstered her gun and sheathed her knife with practiced ease, and grinned. "Hi. I'm Lia Wu, and I'll be your rescuer this evening."

"Rescue?" Richard said. "How—?"

"Well, we were planning to swim everyone down to our submarine just offshore, but I see that won't work for all of you. Fortunately, the Holy Warriors made things easy for us by leaving *en masse* earlier this evening, so I think we can safely use boats."

"The guards . . . ?"

"Are no longer a problem," Wu said. She turned her light back on Richard. "Does that concern you?" she said softly.

"No," Richard said. *Just a few more deaths to add to my account.*

"Good. As for the ordinary staff—they're not going to cause us any trouble either. They're all locked up. By the time they break out, we'll be long gone." She touched something on the belt of her landsuit, and spoke to, apparently, thin air. "Are you copying all this?"

She listened, then laughed. "Roger that." She jerked her head toward the door. "Grab anything else you have to take, and let's go."

Richard looked at the others. No one moved. "We're wearing everything that belongs to us," he said.

"Except for the deck of cards in the kitchen," Jerry said.

Richard groaned. "Leave it. I never want to play cards again."

Wu nodded. "Then follow me." She led the way into the smoke-filled air, past two Holy Warrior corpses on the gravel path, and then into the woods, down toward the rocky beach where the Pacific rolled in, the surf still heavier than usual after the recent storm. A nearly full moon gleamed through wisps of ragged, fast-moving clouds, alternately illuminating and casting into shadow the white-capped breakers. As they drew nearer, Richard saw a dark shape on the water: an inflatable boat, one man sitting in its stern, another waiting on shore. They had to get closer still before he could hear the soft thrum of its propulsion unit above the noise of the waves.

"All aboard," said Wu. "I hope none of you are subject to seasickness."

"Can Selkies get seasick?" Richard murmured to Melody, the closest Marseguroite to him.

"Oh, yes," she said. "Yes, they can."

He glanced at her. She gave him a wan smile, teeth and huge Selkie eyes gleaming in a momentary ray of moonlight, then vanishing into darkness again. "You?" he said in surprise. —

"Selkies were designed to live underwater, not float around on top of it," she said defensively. "It's not natural!"

Then they were climbing aboard the boat, its rubber bottom heaving in time with the surf. Richard sat down much harder than he intended on one of the semirigid benches that spanned the boat's width.

With everyone aboard, the boat pulled away from the shore, and Richard held on for dear life. He'd mostly gotten over his tendency toward spacesickness, but he hadn't been on a surface boat since that day months ago when he'd joined the Holy Warriors tracking the hunterbot as it chased John Duval—that day that had ended with him floating in a survival suit and being chased by the hunterbot himself.

Of course, in hindsight it had been quite a special day, because it was the day he'd met Emily Wood.

Even if, later, she'd wished she'd let the hunterbot blow him apart.

Memories of Emily, wonderful as they were . . . well, memories from the later, less potentially lethal, part of their relationship, anyway . . . were apparently not an effective prophylactic against seasickness. Abruptly, he had to scramble for the starboard side of the boat, and threw up into the heaving water.

He heard Melody retching off the port side.

Nobody else seemed to be having any problem with the motion, and they studiously ignored him as he sat up and wiped his mouth and wished he had clean water to rinse it with. He looked back at the island. The flames from the burning hall flickered above the trees, and he wondered if the Avatar were still close enough to see it. If he did, would he bring the Holy Warriors back?

Probably not, Richard thought. *The Avatar would*

note that everything and everyone he'd left behind had just been burned to a cinder, and praise God for telling him so clearly that he is doing the right thing and mustn't turn back.

His stomach, to his annoyance, heaved again. He didn't think he had anything left in it.

A moment later he was sure.

At last he spotted a low, dark shape in the water. A few minutes later they were clambering aboard a sub larger than anything on Marseguro. With the others, guided by Lia Wu, he descended a ladder through an open hatch near what he guessed was the bow, though he couldn't see enough detail to be sure, and a moment later stood shivering in the compartment at its base, surrounded by landsuits plugged into recharging hoses. The Marseguroites stood shoulder to shoulder in the cramped space.

"Next stop, the Free Selkie Republic . . . or rather, its nearest outpost," Wu said. "We'll be there in a couple of hours. I'd tell you to make yourselves comfortable, but this isn't a particularly comfortable conveyance. However, we've cleared out the forward cabin—" she indicated one of the two doors, currently dogged shut, that led out of the room, "—and put in two extra cots. As long as you don't mind close quarters . . ."

"As long as it's warm," Richard said. His teeth were chattering; he glanced at Ann, who looked just as miserable, and Derryl, who looked . . . exactly the same as always, stone-faced, unmoved. The Selkies, with their extra layer of subdermal fat, all looked comfortable enough—except Melody, whose pale skin had an unmistakable tinge of green about it.

"It's warm," Wu said. "Steve?"

"Follow me," said one of the men who had crewed the rubber boat. He led them through the forward hatch down a typical submarine corridor, narrow, with storage lockers of some kind on either side, then finally into a chamber that spanned the width of the sub—maybe four meters—

crammed tight with six narrow cots, three abreast, two deep, with barely enough room to squeeze among them. No hatches exited the room forward, and the curve of that wall told Richard they were right in the bow.

He picked a bed and flopped down on it. The others quickly sorted themselves into the other bunks. The Selkies left their landsuits on.

Nobody spoke until Steve had left the room. Then they all started at once.

"Can you believe it?"

"More Selkies?"

"Here on Earth?"

"But I thought the Body killed them all."

"Obviously not. They must have been in hiding."

"For seventy years?"

"Just like us."

"Yeah, but we had a whole solar system . . ."

Richard let the conversation and speculation roll over him, but kept his eyes closed, one arm thrown over them. His stomach felt more settled. His brain did not. He had all the same questions as his crew, and no answers.

Wu had said she was taking them to an outpost of the "Free Selkie Republic," whatever that was. Presumably they'd get some answers when they got there.

At least they were out of the Avatar's hands.

But what was happening on board the *Victor Hansen*?

With us free, and the ship back in our hands . . . we might be able to do something to save the Kemonomimi.

Assuming that the Free Selkie Republic has any interest in doing anything of the sort.

What would they think when they found out the Marseguroites had come to Earth to offer a vaccine to the nonmods?

What would they think when they found out that he had handed that vaccine over to the Avatar—and that that decision had led to a plague-proof army of Holy Warriors?

What would they think when they found out that that army was on the march against another race of Victor Hansen-created moddies?

He didn't have any answers to any of those questions. He suspected he might not like them when he did.

"Damn it!" Andy King glared at Simon Goodfellow. "You *promised* me you could do this."

"I said I *thought* I could." Goodfellow looked even paler than usual, and his hair hung across his balding head in greasy strings. He'd hardly left his console in the simulator room for days. *He certainly hasn't showered*, Andy thought, wrinkling his nose.

"You said," Andy said, "that you had successfully made a copy of the AI's kernel. You said, once you wiped the AI, you could reboot it, and then enter our names as the properly assigned crew. That's what you said."

"I said I *thought* I had successfully copied the AI's kernel. I said I *thought* I could reboot it. I never promised." Goodfellow blinked at Andy. "If I'd been *certain* I could do it, we would have done it on Marseguro and made sure the Body could never take control of the ship. But we didn't do it, because the risk was too great."

Andy clamped down on his temper. "So now you're saying you *can't* do it?"

"No," Goodfellow said. "I still think I can do it. But it may take longer than I'd thought. It's not just a matter of plugging in the datasphere and dumping its contents into the kernel. There are physical defenses that have to be dismantled, shunts to be installed, careful testing to be done before we even make the attempt."

"In case you haven't figured it out," Andy said, "we're in a hurry. We don't know what the Body will do next. If they can get control of another ship, or a ground-based space defense system . . ."

"And if I make the attempt and it fails," Goodfellow said, "we won't get another one. The computer will be permanently dead, incapable of being revived. The ship will need a whole new AI. And I don't happen to have one in my pocket. Do you?"

Andy took a deep breath and looked away. They were in the simulator room where they had fought off the Holy Warriors, but Goodfellow had a lot more equipment spread around the data conduit than he had before. "If I ever design a spaceship," Andy growled, "I'm going to make damn sure you can control everything on it manually if you need to."

"Fine," Goodfellow said. "But in the meantime, we're stuck with *this* one. And the longer you harass me, the longer it will take me to get everything lined up for our one and only chance to take control of it again."

Andy closed his eyes. "Fine," he said in resignation. "Keep me posted."

"Of course," said Goodfellow, and turned back to his terminal, effectively dismissing the First Officer.

I thought I *was in command here?* Andy thought as he walked back to the shaft leading down into the now resealed and repressurized spaces where they had hidden during the Holy Warrior occupation.

He snorted. *Yeah, right.*

The motley fleet of vessels carrying the Avatar's remnant of Holy Warriors reached the mainland at first light. Karl Rasmusson stood on the bridge of what had once been the cruise ship *Ocean Breeze* and was now redesignated *Fist of God*, watching through binoculars as the first Holy Warriors began unloading materiel onto the pier of Blackstone, the deserted town that had once served primarily as the embarkation point for ferries to Paradise Island. The ships would have to take turns unloading, the pier wasn't big enough for more than two or three to dock at a time.

"Your Holiness," said a voice from close beside his elbow. He lowered the binoculars and turned to his

Right Hand, Ilias Atnikov. "If you could come to the bridge . . . there's a message from the island."

"Not good news, I suspect from your tone of voice," the Avatar said. "Lead the way."

He refused to speculate on the message's content. Instead, as he climbed the narrow metal stairs to the bridge, he took a moment to appreciate the irony of a ship like the *Ocean Breeze*, intended only to transport Body functionaries and their families on pleasant sight-seeing cruises along rocky, forested shores to see calving glaciers, suddenly transformed into *Fist of God*, the flagship of the Body navy, a task it was monumentally unqualified for.

He suspected more than a few of the surviving Body members saw him in similar terms. As Right Hand, he'd been almost invisible, apparently little more than a glorified secretary. The higher-placed members of the Body hierarchy, like the late Samuel Cheveldeoff, knew who *really* controlled things as Harold the Second sank further and further into hedonistic somnolence, but the rank and file did not. For Karl Rasmusson, of all people, to emerge as the Avatar after the catastrophe of the plague must have shocked them—and brought home just how great the disaster that had befallen the world was.

Karl's own moments of doubt were now past. God Itself had proved to his satisfaction that It had complete confidence in him, and that gave him complete confidence in himself. He could only hope that his actions would assuage the doubters. Failing that, he could only hope that their own faith would see them clear to giving him unqualified support.

Because failing *that,* he would have no choice but to follow the Purification of the Kemonomimi with a cleansing of his own ranks, and they were thin enough he would prefer not to have to thin them further.

It's a test of faith for all of us, the Avatar thought. *God rewards those who pass Its tests . . . and terribly punishes those who fail.*

"Here you are, Your Holiness," Atnikov said.

The Avatar looked at the only lit screen on the board, and recognized the face of John Duncan, chief administrator of the former resort. "Your Holiness!" he blurted the moment he saw the Avatar. "We've been attacked. All the Holy Warriors are dead, and two of my staff. They burned the mess hall. We were locked up, we just escaped—"

"Slow down," the Avatar said sharply. "When did this happen?"

"This morning, early, maybe two AM," Duncan said. "We were asleep, then we heard shots, and the next thing we knew they were hauling us—"

"And who are *they*?" the Avatar said. There were plenty of "revolutionary" groups that had promised over the years to bring the Body to its knees, but any such group must have suffered from the plague as much as the Body had. That left—

Duncan confirmed his suspicion. "Selkies, Your Holiness."

Selkies! Crew from *MSS Victor Hansen.* They'd fled the takeover of their ship . . . at least some of them must have managed to guide their escape pods somewhere close to Paradise Island, so they could try to rescue Richard Hansen. "The prisoners?"

"All freed," Duncan said. He pressed his lips together nervously, then blurted, "Will you be returning, Your Holiness? We're defenseless now. We need—"

"They got what they wanted," the Avatar said. "They won't attack again. No, I won't be returning. Bury the dead and repair the damage. Report in if anything else happens . . . but I don't think it will." He paused, remembering something Duncan had said. "My condolences on the loss of your staff members. Did they have family?"

"Not since the plague," Duncan said. He blinked hard a couple of times. "None of us have family anymore."

"Things will get better," the Avatar said. "Tell your staff that. When we have finally finished the Purification of Earth, under God's renewed protection, things *will* get better."

"Yes, Your Holiness," John Duncan said, but he didn't meet the Avatar's eyes.

Don't you believe me? Karl wanted to snarl at him. *Don't you believe* God?

But it would have accomplished nothing. "Avatar out," he said instead, and touched the control to manually end the transmission.

He looked out the big glass windshield at the handful of buildings that made up Blackstone, only slightly dimmed by mist this morning. "Ready a boat for me," he told Atnikov.

"Yes, Your Holiness." Atnikov crossed the bridge to confer with the captain. Karl kept his gaze on the shore.

No looking back, he thought. *If Hansen is free, it's because God wanted it that way. Maybe he still has some part to play in God's plan that I can't see yet. All I can do is carry out* my *part.*

The Kemonomimi were ten days away on foot. In ten days, the Earth would at last be free of Victor Hansen's foul legacy, truly Purified at last, ready to receive God's blessing.

Ten days.

Karl Rasmusson smiled. *No time at all, really.*

Chapter 12

THE KEMONOMIMI treated Chris well enough, except perhaps for the tiny Kemonomimi woman who came in twice a day with a syringe and took a sample of his blood. She wouldn't tell him why.

In fact, nobody would tell him anything.

For days they held him in a small suite in what had been a small hotel. Meals appeared at regular intervals in the discreet room-service dumbwaiter, hidden behind a rather ugly red-and-brown abstract painting; the first time the elevator beeped to announce there was a tray inside it, it took him fifteen minutes to figure out where the noise—and the maddeningly delicious smells—came from.

The suite boasted an entertainment unit well-stocked with vids and feelies and games and texts, and Chris made good use of it, but after the first couple of days, he began to feel pangs of stir-craziness. After a week, he dreaded waking up to face another day in his comfortable prison . . . and found himself looking forward to the visits by the taciturn blood drawer.

At least the windows gave him a clear view of the airstrip. Aircraft continued to come and go. Kemonomimi moved hither and yon, often unloading bundles from aircraft and hustling them into one of the storage buildings alongside the runway.

And then, without any warning at all, Victor Hansen summoned him again.

The sun was actually shining that day, and Chris blinked in its bright light as Napoleon and Alexander, his guards from a few days before, led him along the sidewalk between landscaped flower beds, now gone to seed, to Hansen's appropriated office.

The first thing Chris noticed, after Napoleon and Alexander ushered him in and closed the door on him, was that the photograph of the previous owner's family had vanished. So had every other personal knickknack. Now the office was as impersonal as Chris' hotel room, although with better art.

The second thing he noticed was that Hansen wasn't alone. One of the chairs had been pulled into the corner, and sitting cross-legged on it was a Kemonomimi woman with fur as white as fresh-fallen snow over all of her body except her hands and feet, which were pitch-black. She looked like she was wearing gloves and boots, when in fact she wasn't wearing anything at all—and the fur didn't entirely cover what clothes would have. Chris tried not to stare at her. She had no such compunction about staring at him. Her eyes, amber yellow, narrowed as she looked at him.

Hansen stood with his back to Chris, hands folded behind him, looking out the window at the sunlit runway. An aircraft taxied along it, the sun glinting off its clean white flanks.

"Keating," Hansen said without preamble. "I have a question for you."

Chris looked at the clone's back warily, then glanced at the woman. Her eyes narrowed further, and he quickly looked away again. "I'll . . . answer it if I can," he said.

"Yes," Hansen said. "You will." He turned. "Do you serve God?"

Chris blinked, sensing a minefield. "I . . . guess," he said. "I've never thought about it very much."

Hansen snorted. "A prudent answer. A politician's answer. You're afraid if you say yes, I'll have you killed as someone too loyal to the Body to keep around.

"But you're wrong." Hansen spread his hands. "I, too, serve God. I always have. Though perhaps not the God you know.

"The Body Purified has done its best to stamp out not only all genetically modified life, but much of humanity's religious heritage. What do you know about Christianity, boy? Or Islam? Judaism? Buddhism?"

"Nothing," Chris said, which was almost true. There were Christians on Marseguro, a few Buddhists, a vanishingly small number of Jews, no Muslims that he was aware of, a smattering of other religions. Chris had never paid much attention to any of them. Having grown up in a family that secretly adhered to the Body, he knew that all other religions were both false and abhorrent, targets for God's wrath. The fact they existed among the nonmods who had accompanied the original Victor Hansen—unwillingly, in his parents' case—to Marseguro was only one more sign that the planet needed Purifying.

A few Selkies had taken up some of the nonmods' religions—Buddhism was particularly popular—but the closest most Selkies came to religion was venerating Victor Hansen. He very carefully didn't look at the woman. He suspected the Kemonomimi were the same, only their "god" still lived among them.

The real Victor Hansen, according to the history books, had tried very hard to stop his Selkies from treating him like a god. This Victor Hansen, Chris suspected, had no problem with it at all.

"I don't follow any religion," Hansen said abruptly. "Yet I serve God—at least, God as I conceive It—in my own way.

"Christianity and Judaism have in their holy book a mythological account of the creation of the world.

In it, God creates various aspects of the world—day and night, sea and dry land, sun, moon and stars, green plants, etc.—over seven days. On the penultimate day, He—they saw God as a male—created the first man. On the seventh day, He rested. The book notes that God created man in 'His' image.

"To the ancients, that may have meant that God looked like a man. But I see it differently. As I see it, God created us in Its *spiritual* image, not its physical one, for, of course, It *has* no physical image. And at the core of God's spiritual nature is Its creativity. Why did it create the universe? Because It could. Because creating things gives It joy.

"If we are indeed created in God's image, than creativity must also be at the heart of our spiritual nature." Hansen walked over to the woman and sat on the arm of her chair, putting his arm around her shoulder. She bumped her head against his side and spread her lips in an alarmingly sharp-toothed grin. "And so, in obedience to God's will, I, too, create. And of all the humans that have lived on this Earth, I have come closer to God than any other, because I have created a new race of humans. This, by the way, is Cleopatra." He caressed the woman's furred cheek, and she took his hand and kissed it.

The sight sickened Chris. Maybe that was why he said, "*Two* races," then instantly wished he hadn't.

Hansen gave him a hard look. "Two races," he said. "But then, since I am *not* God, I sometimes make mistakes." He kissed Cleopatra on the forehead, then stood and came over to the desk to face Chris once more. "So," he said. "I serve God. Do you?"

"That's what I've tried to do," Chris said, still hedging.

"But you say you were imprisoned by the Body for daring to suggest that life, God-created life, could be improved upon."

Chris tried to remember the cover story he'd made

up on the spur of the moment days earlier. "Um, yeah, that's right."

"Were you imprisoned justly?"

Think fast. "No. I don't think so. It's ... well, I've never thought of it quite the way you've put it, but I guess that's the way I feel. God made us creative and gave us the tools to modify life. Why shouldn't we use them?"

Because using them brought God's wrath down on us! he thought, but didn't say. God frowned on dishonesty, but It didn't actually forbid it—not in a good cause. Which keeping Chris Keating alive certainly was, at least as far as Chris was concerned. And since he was the only properly God-fearing loyal member of the Body Purified within the Kemonomimi camp, staying alive *had* to be a service to God.

"Good." Hansen sat down behind the desk. "The Avatar plans to attack us."

Chris' heart jumped. "How do you know?"

"Reconnaissance drones. The Avatar left Paradise Island with most of his remaining Holy Warriors last night. Today they are landing at Blackrock—"

"Stone," said Cleopatra. She had the same lisping accent as the other Kemonomimi he had heard speak.

Hansen looked at her, obviously irritated. "What?"

"Blackstone, not Blackrock." She smiled. "You made a mistake."

"I ..." Hansen pressed his lips together. "Oh. Very funny." He turned briskly back to Chris. "They are landing, as I said, at Black*stone*, the nearest town on the coast."

"But ... the plague ..."

"Either they've decided it's burned itself out or they've been able to produce enough of the experimental vaccine that saved your life to inoculate their troops," Hansen said.

Which would have made perfect sense, except, of course, Chris had entirely fabricated said vaccine. "Where are they headed?"

"Here, of course," Hansen said. "To Purify us. You grew up in the Body. You know how the Avatar thinks. He sees the plague as a punishment from God for allowing moddies like the Kemonomimi to survive." He smiled. "It's funny, really. It has been my plan for a very long time to eventually mount an attack on Paradise Island. The old Avatar visited it regularly—so regularly that we could have been assured of killing him and most of the highest members of the hierarchy. When my plague hit, and I realized the Body still clung to Paradise Island like barnacles on a rotting boat, the attack made even more sense. And rather than hide out like pirates in a cold, wet camp somewhere along the shore, we were able to make use of this no-longer-occupied town . . . and its idle aircraft. With the ability to move freely at last, with no fear of Body detection, I sent a team to the Holy City to pick up a . . . vital component which I had arranged for but had not yet been able to smuggle out. They brought it back—and you along with it.

"But now we don't have to attack Paradise Island. The Avatar has left it and is coming straight to us."

"So . . . where will you run to?" Chris said.

Cleopatra laughed. It didn't sound entirely human to Chris; there was a hint of a feline yowl to it that made the hair stand up on the back of his neck.

Hansen chuckled, too. "Run? We're not running anywhere." He leaned back in his chair. "We're going to sit right here. And when the Avatar gets a bit closer, we're going to kill him and all the Holy Warriors with him . . . just like we planned from the beginning."

He pointed at Chris. "And you're going to help us."

The quarters President McLean showed Emily and her mother to were pleasant enough, though depressingly military in appearance: gray walls, gray floor. "Most of the Selkie quarters have their own air locks for slipping outside," McLean said. "I'm afraid these quarters do not. If you would like to swim, the deck below is flooded."

"Still don't trust us?" Emily said.

"I don't trust anyone." McLean left, closing the door behind her. It sealed with a hiss.

"Nice," Emily muttered.

"Don't be too hard on her." Emily's mother dropped onto the dark-blue couch. The rest of the furniture consisted of a small round table and two chairs in the corner, by a door Emily presumed led to the bedrooms . . . and, she hoped, a bathroom. "She's responsible for keeping her people safe. She does what she has to."

Emily sat beside her. "You sound tired."

Dr. Christianson-Wood laughed. "Really? I can't imagine why." She leaned her head back and closed her eyes.

"How are you . . . feeling . . . otherwise?" Emily said cautiously.

"You mean am I going to go catatonic on you again?" Dr. Christianson-Wood asked without opening her eyes.

"Well, um . . . yeah."

Now Emily's mother did open her eyes. "No," she said quietly. "I don't think so. Whatever that was, it's past. Though, in some ways, I wish I could go back there."

"Mom!"

"I didn't have to think," her mother said. "No thoughts, or very few. Just a blank grayness. I didn't have to . . . deal. With the consequences of my actions." She closed her eyes again—squeezed them tightly. "God, Emily. All the people who died here . . ."

"Not your fault. We've been through this."

"Intellectually, I know that's right," her mother said. "And someday that knowledge may help me feel better. But right now . . ." She shook her head. "What I think and what I feel are two different things."

"Richard's here," Emily said. "That means the vaccine is here, too. There'll be survivors. *Many* survivors. Without the amplifying effect of Marseguroite life-forms, they can ward it off with strict quarantine. Right? Just like any other infectious disease."

"But for how long?" Emily's mother said. "And if the Body has Richard, *they* must have the vaccine. They'll give it to Holy Warriors first. They'll use it to reestablish the Body's control. Marseguro may be safe for a generation, but eventually the Holy Warriors will come again." Her voice fell to a whisper. "I haven't even saved Marseguro. I've just delayed the inevitable."

"A generation is a long time," Emily said. "Things can change. Here, and on Marseguro. A new war isn't inevitable."

"I'm beginning to think war is always inevitable."

Emily took that disquieting thought to bed with her— the hallway did indeed lead to bedrooms, two of them, and a small but functional bathroom.

She lay in the darkness of the tiny bedroom, alleviated only by the glow of a clock on a table by the bed, and stared up at the ceiling.

Was her mother right? Was war inevitable? Was violence built into the human genome? *The "Holy Human Genome,"* she thought bitterly.

Once she wouldn't have thought so. She'd thought Marseguro was as close to utopia as humans had ever come. Nonmods, Selkies, different people, different opinions, different religions, even, all living together, arguing sometimes, sure, but never resorting to violence.

But then . . . Chris Keating had shattered it all and brought violence down upon them. And once Marseguro had been attacked, Emily and her mother had both discovered that they, too, could use violence in the service of a cause: self-defense, perhaps, but the people they killed were dead just the same.

Why didn't Victor Hansen remove our capacity for violence, while he was at it? she thought.

But she answered her own question. *If he had, we'd*

all be dead or imprisoned now. The Body would have seized Marseguro and slaughtered, enslaved, and sterilized the Selkies without resistance.

Humans, she thought bitterly. *We're just a thin layer of civilization painted onto the grinning skull of millions of years of bloody battles.*

She wasn't sure how the religionists explained it. If God had created everything, why did murder lurk in every human heart?

She supposed they'd blame sin, tell her that humans had once been perfect and peaceful, but had chosen to follow the path of death and violence.

And yet, they could not have followed that path if the capacity for it didn't lurk within them from the beginning; hadn't been placed there, in fact, by God.

If humans really were created in God's image, as she'd heard the Christians say, then maybe the God of the Body Purified *was* the true one: a God whose own capacity for capricious violence when disappointed by Its creations was perfectly mirrored in those creations' own ability to hurt and kill.

When she finally did drift off to sleep, Emily's dreams were full of blood.

She woke to knocking. It took her a few minutes to figure out where she was, and then she stumbled to her feet and pulled on the robe she had found in the closet of her room. She half-staggered through the darkened apartment, banging her shin painfully on the coffee table, and opened the door.

Shelby stood there, wearing only skimpy blue trunks. His skin glistened with water; he'd obviously made his way to them through one of the flooded decks. "We've heard from the sub," he said. "They rescued *all* of the prisoners—Selkies and nonmods alike."

Emily's heart skipped a beat.

"They'll be at the outpost near Paradise Island in a couple of hours," Shelby went on. "And Mom . . . um,

President McLean ... wants me to take you to main control as soon as you can get ready."

"What's going on?" her mother said from behind her. Emily turned and gave her a huge hug.

"They got them all," she said in a choked voice. "*All* of them. They're safe."

"Thank God," her mother said, hugging her back.

Emily said nothing, but her dark thoughts of the middle of the night came back to her.

God, she thought sourly, *had nothing to do with it.*

As far as she could tell, It didn't really believe in happy endings.

Lia Wu woke the *Sawyer's Point* crew with a cheery, "Good morning!"

Richard opened his eyes. *Where? ... Oh!* Remembering, he sat up and turned to look at Wu, standing in the aft door. "Um, good morning."

"I hope you're all well-rested after your ... oh, about two-hour ... night," Wu said. "We're almost to the outpost. I'm afraid I can't offer you breakfast, but you'll be able to eat once we've disembarked. Which we need to prepare for. The Selkies can swim, but the rest of you will need waterbreather gear, unless you can hold your breath for, say, fifteen minutes?" She looked at him expectantly.

"Um ... no," Richard said. "I might manage three or four."

"Is that all?" Wu looked intrigued. "Interesting."

These Selkies don't interact with nonmods, Richard thought. *We're as exotic to them as ... well, as Selkies were to me.*

"Well, the Free Republic has some old suits: original equipment, I think. We'll have them swum across. As far as we know, they still work."

As far as we know ... ?

Wu crouched beside his bunk as the others begin to

stir and stretch. "There's something else," she said in a low voice. "Apparently there are a couple of friends of yours at the main complex."

"Friends?" Richard blinked. "You mean others from the *Victor Hansen*?"

"I don't know," Wu said. "They just said to tell you that Emily and her mother are waiting to talk to you."

Richard felt like he'd been punched in the gut. He stared at Wu, stunned.

"I take it you're surprised," Wu said wryly.

Richard found his voice. "That's . . . impossible. Utterly impossible. We left them on Marseguro!"

Wu shrugged. "I'm just telling you what I was told." She stood up. "We'll be tethering in about half an hour. I'll see if I can round up some swimwear." She went out.

"I can't tell you how glad I'll be to get out of this land-suit and go for a proper swim," Melody said. She sat on the bunk across from Richard, looking at him. "Did she just say what I thought she said?"

Richard spread his hands helplessly. "I don't see how it's possible, but it must be true. How else would they know Emily's name?"

"But we have . . . had . . . Marseguro's only starship. They *can't* be here."

"I know."

No one could offer even a far-fetched explanation. If the Body had returned to Marseguro and somehow captured Emily, she certainly wouldn't now be in the company of the Earth Selkies the Body didn't even know existed. But the Earth Selkies couldn't possibly have gone and fetched her: they had no access to space-craft and couldn't possibly know Marseguro's location anyway.

I guess I'll have to ask Emily in person, Richard thought, and felt almost giddy at the thought.

Wu returned with swimwear for everyone, and the

sexes demurely turned their backs to each other while they stripped and put on the simple white suits. After a few minutes Wu came back and took away the nonmods' uniforms and the Selkies' landsuits. She held one up and looked at it closely. "Interesting design," she said. "Better than what we've come up with. It's hard to cobble together new technology when you're having to obtain all your supplies surreptitiously. We do have a couple of microfactories, but the feed stocks . . ."

Richard stiffened. "You have microfactories?"

"Yes," Wu said. "Three at the main complex, one in each outpost. Older models—pre-Day of Salvation, in fact—but the nanofabricator juice is still viable and of course they're self-repairing—"

Richard looked at Ann Nolan. "Older models," he said. "Like ours."

She grinned. "I'm way ahead of you. We'll have to download the software from *Victor Hansen*, but if we can program new modules . . ."

"What?" Wu said, looking from one to the other.

"Not now," Richard said. "But I think we may be able to make good use of those microfactories, if you'll let us."

"That'll be for the President and Council to decide," Wu said. "Way above *my* level of responsibility."

A bell clanged twice, then twice again. The vibration of the engines changed pitch, then died away altogether.

"We've stopped," Wu said unnecessarily. "Time to go."

She led them back to the landsuit-packed room through which they had first entered the sub, but carried on past it and down a flight of spiral stairs to a lower deck. From there they went aft, into a room where water lapped at the sides of an open floor hatch about a meter and a half in diameter. A couple of large Selkie men stood beside it, both with strangely rounded, shiny black riflelike weapons slung over their backs: something that could be used underwater, Richard guessed from the look of them. A third Selkie, likewise armed, stood back a little way. The Free Selkie Republic obviously wasn't taking any chances. "They'll escort the Selkies over first," Wu said. "Then they'll bring back the waterbreathers for you landlings." She nodded to the Earth Selkies. "Whenever you're ready."

"Aye, aye, ma'am," said one, and jumped into the pool. The other guided in the Selkies from Richard's crew: Jerry Krall, Pierre Normand, and finally Melody Ashman. Once they'd all entered the water, the second Earth Selkie jumped in, too.

Richard, Ann, and Derryl sat and waited in silence, while Wu spoke in a voice too low for them to hear with the remaining armed guard.

Maybe twenty minutes after they'd disappeared, the two Selkie men returned. They climbed out, then hauled up a huge mesh bag that they dumped on the deck at their feet.

Wu came over. "Let's see . . . anybody know how these things work?"

"Let me," said Ann. "They look a lot like what we used to use on Marseguro years ago." She started pulling things out of the bag. "Here we go. Slip into this backpack. Pull this hood up over your head . . ." She demonstrated as she talked. "Pull down the goggles, bite down on the mouthpiece . . . mmph mere moo mo!" She spat out the mouthpiece. "I mean, and there you go!" She looked at Wu. "What depth are we at?"

"Ten meters."

"Shouldn't have to worry about decompression, then," Ann said. She began handing out the waterbreathers.

The backpack had two straps that went across chest and stomach; the top strap had a small glowing readout on it. Ann twisted it up and took a look. "Not fully charged, but good for half an hour. We won't need it that long. The pack will expel or suck in water as necessary to ensure you keep neutral buoyancy."

"Great," Richard said. He pulled on his own rig, with a little help from Ann (Derryl, not surprisingly, needed no help), stuck in the mouthpiece, and took an experimental breath. The air tasted like sweaty socks, but it was breathable. He pulled on the goggles and gave Wu a thumbs-up.

"Off you go, then," she said.

As before, one Selkie jumped in ahead of them, the other guided them through the hatch. Richard jumped and sank through a welter of bubbles. For a moment he thought he would keep on sinking, but as promised, the backpack vibrated, jetting out ballast, and in a moment he stabilized.

He looked around. It had to be daylight up above, because a deep green light suffused everything, fading to blue in the distance. The sub was a long black cigar shape looming overhead. And the outpost of the Free Selkie Republic . . .

A cylindrical habitat, maybe fifty meters in length and half that in diameter. He couldn't see much detail, but as he followed the "come-along" gesture of their Selkie leader and swam toward the structure, writing on its side came into focus. "Commonwealth of American States Pacific Ocean Administration," it said.

The words gave him a shiver. The Commonwealth of American States had been the last secular government for this part of the world before the Day of Salvation and the rise of the Body. This thing must be almost a century old.

A time before the Body, he thought. *When will we see a time* after *the Body?*

They entered through a water lock, swimming up into a water porch. Richard climbed onto the deck, unbuckled the backpack, and pulled off the goggles. Within a few minutes Derryl, Ann and Wu joined him. Their Selkie guard took their waterbreathers, then Wu led them down the habitat's long central corridor to a control room at its centre and up a spiral stair. Vidscreens and blinking lights lined the walls of the circular room, the only other light coming through the clear dome overhead. Four Selkies were stationed around the room, watching consoles or listening on headphones.

But Richard hardly saw any of that. The moment his head rose above the surface of the control room floor, his eyes were drawn like magnets to the largest of the vidscreens, and the face of the young Selkie female who filled it. That face split into a delighted grin as he came within range of the video pickup, and Richard felt something hard and frozen deep inside him dissolve into warmth as he saw it.

"Emily!"

Chapter 13

IT TOOK THE HOLY WARRIORS most of the day to unload and divvy up equipment. They had six all-terrain cargobots, twenty-seven packhorses (part of the recreational complement of Paradise Island)—and lots of strong backs.

"We can't surprise them," Grand Deacon von Eschen had told him back on the island. "They have aircraft. Possibly reconnaissance drones. They'll almost certainly see us coming."

"Let them," the Avatar said.

"What if they flee inland?"

"Let them," the Avatar said again. "We'll track them down. They've come out into the open. They can't disappear again. And I don't think they'll even try."

The Grand Deacon frowned. "I don't follow."

"They believe the Body is finished," the Avatar explained. "Why else show themselves? And when they look at our forces, they won't see what *I* see—a dagger, small but deadly, hand-forged and honed by God Itself to Purify the Earth. They will see only a tiny, lightly-armed, ragtag army. They will believe they can defeat it."

"But they're outnumbered, even so. You can't be sure—"

"I'm sure," the Avatar had said. "God has made me sure."

The Grand Deacon, of course, had no answer to that.

And sure enough, as the day waned and the Holy Warriors made camp, preparatory to starting the march on the Kemonomimi the following day, Karl, standing outside his tent, heard, faintly but unmistakably, the droning buzz of an aircraft engine. He looked up and saw it, a tiny silver speck, still catching the rays of the sun that had just slipped behind the ocean horizon.

Grand Deacon von Eschen came to stand beside him. "The Kemonomimi know we've left the island," he said softly.

"And so God's plan continues to unfold," the Avatar responded. Von Eschen said nothing, but after staring up at the aircraft another long moment, he went back to his own tent.

Karl watched the aircraft until it was out of sight. He knew the Grand Deacon had his doubts that the Kemonomimi would do what the Avatar predicted, but Karl felt only calm certainty.

Once I had doubts, he thought. He could remember those days, those dark days when the Avatar had been a shambling, drunken, drugged-out wreck, concerned only with the next dissolute party, the next night's bed partners. Karl Rasmusson had kept the Body going, making decisions for the Avatar and in the Avatar's name, but as he'd watched the Avatar destroy himself, he'd begun to doubt God.

How could such an animal be the Avatar of God? How could he believe in a God that would set such a thing up as Its representative on Earth? How could God Itself actually *live* inside that . . . thing?

But now Karl understood. The previous Avatar had been part of God's plan to humble the Body, to humble Earth, to remind them both God was in charge.

More: the travesty that had been Harold the Second had helped to shape Karl Rasmusson into the perfect tool for God to seize when he needed a new Avatar, a

strong Avatar, one who would understand what needed
to be done . . . and be willing to do it.

And so he watched, with perfect equanimity, the Kemonomimi aircraft disappear into the gathering dusk.
Whatever the Kemonomimi did or did not do, God
would deliver them into Karl Rasmusson's hands.

He knew it, as surely as he had ever known anything.

Chris Keating sat very still after Victor Hansen's extraordinary announcement. *He's bought it*, he thought.
*He thinks I'm on his side. This could be my chance . . .
my chance to finally, finally prove to the Avatar himself
that I am loyal to God and to the Body, to finally earn the
rewards I've worked so hard for since I first activated the
distress beacon on Marseguro.*

My big chance. As long as I don't blow it.

"I'll do whatever I can," he said carefully. "But I don't
see what use I can be to you."

"Really? Take a good look at yourself."

Chris looked down. They'd found some clothes his
size somewhere in the town, so he wore new black pants
and a soft plaid shirt. Brown hiking boots. Otherwise,
he was as thin as always, no taller than ever, completely
unimpressive—and he knew it.

He looked up. "I don't get it."

Victor Hansen laughed. So did Cleopatra. "You're
alive," she said. "You're immune to the plague. That
makes you, if not unique, extremely rare."

Hansen glanced at her, and Chris thought he saw annoyance on his face. But his expression smoothed as he
turned back to Chris. "Cleo is exactly right. Your obvious immunity will make you of great interest to the Avatar. If you approach his forces, he'll certainly have you
brought to him for questioning."

"And what do I tell him?" Chris said.

"The truth. Well . . . up to a point. That you received
the experimental vaccine, that a guard released you. But

then you have to convince him that you saw the error of your ways and want to return to the fold, that once you were captured by those hideous abominations, the Kemonomimi—"

Chris glanced up at Cleo. She raised her eyebrows and he looked away again.

"—you realized the wisdom of the Body's prohibition against genetic modification. Tell him you escaped and came to warn him.

"And then you tell him that you know our plans: that we are going to flee inland before he reaches the town, and that you know a place where he can take us by surprise." Hansen reached down and opened the middle drawer of the desk; he took out a map and slid it across the desk to Chris. "Here."

Chris looked at it. He wasn't very good at reading maps: there'd been little need of them on Marseguro, where a plain blue sheet of paper would have been a perfectly accurate map of most of the planet's surface. "What's special about it?"

"It's a narrow valley, a pass through the coastal range from the inland valley they'll have to follow to get here. And it's where we'll have a surprise waiting for the Avatar."

"An ambush?"

"Not exactly," Hansen said. "A bomb. A very special bomb. A bomb that will destroy the Avatar and all his forces."

"Nuclear?"

"Close enough," Hansen said. "Matter-antimatter, actually."

Chris blinked. "Where did you get *that?*"

"The Holy City, of course," Hansen said. "It was supposed to be smuggled to us by a . . . friend. I'm afraid he fell to the plague before arrangements could be made. Fortunately, with the Body essentially out of the way, the team that also discovered you was able to retrieve it from its hiding place."

"A friend?"

Hansen sighed. "Mr. Keating, the Body has many enemies. The Body has also had firm control of all channels
of communication, however, so the actions those enemies have taken have been little known among the general population . . . except locally, among those members
of the general population injured or killed when bombs
go off or water supplies are poisoned."

Chris had never dreamed . . . "Terrorists have attacked
the Body?"

"Repeatedly, if not very effectively," Hansen said.

"The Kemonomimi?"

"No. The trouble with . . . I prefer the term 'direct action' to 'terrorism,' by the way . . . is that the Body is very
good at rooting out and destroying groups that take that
route. This has limited the number of attacks over the
years, but certainly hasn't stopped them entirely. And it
has made it clear to me that if one is going to strike, one
must make that strike decisive. Hence our original plan:
to decapitate the Body by destroying Paradise Island
while the Avatar and many of his top officials were va-
cationing on it. To do that, we needed a special weapon.
Which the Holy Warriors themselves were kind enough
to invent for us."

"But how did this . . . friend . . . of yours get his hands
on it?"

"He was one of the scientists who invented it," Hansen said. "He was also, fortunately, highly susceptible to
bribery and blackmail." He shrugged. "And now he's
dead. But we have the weapon . . . and the codes needed
to arm and detonate it remotely."

"What if the Avatar takes me with him to this valley
where you intend to blow him up? You're asking me to
commit suicide!"

"Offer to fight," Hansen said. "Enlist in the Holy Warriors. You should be able to find an opportunity to slip
away before the force enters the valley. Put a mountain

between it and yourself, and you'll be fine. Don't worry. We'll be shadowing the force and will make sure you're clear before we do anything . . . irrevocable."

Chris wanted to laugh out loud. *He's handing me everything I wanted on a platter,* he thought. *I'll talk to the Avatar, all right. I'll tell him exactly what's going on. He'll never go near that valley. And I'll not only enlist in the Holy Warriors, I may damn well be in charge of them by the time this is all over!*

But he kept his expression troubled and modest. "If you really think I can pull it off," he said, "I'll do it. I want the Body ended as much as you do."

"I doubt it," said Hansen. He nodded to Cleo, who got up and gave Chris an exciting, if morally troubling, look at her long-tailed backside as she bent over and opened a cabinet door. From a hidden refrigerator, she pulled three bottles of beer. She put two on the desk, then took the third herself and returned to the corner chair. Hansen picked up the two on the desk, flicked them open with his thumbs, and handed one to Chris. "There's a huge stock of this stuff in the basement under the airport restaurant," he said. "Good thing, because I'm pretty sure the brewery's out of business." He raised his bottle. "To the end of the Body," he said.

Chris clinked bottles with him. *To the end of you and all your kind,* Chris thought, and took a swig of the bittersweet brew.

"Now let's talk about Marseguro," Hansen said. "Because once the Body is out of the way and the Kemonomimi are finally free to follow their destiny, it will be time for me to set about rectifying my most serious mistake and ridding the universe of those water-breathing freaks." He took another swig of beer. "The Body made a tactical error. They tried to capture the planet, instead of simply killing everyone on it. I'll know better." He held the beer bottle up to the light, examining the play of light on its dewed surface. "Nor will I need an army ... well, not an army of Kemono-mimi, anyway. Not with the special weapon I've already prepared for the task." He smiled, as if to himself, then suddenly lowered his gaze back to Chris.

"But I need more information about my target," he said. "So ... tell me about Marseguro."

He wants me to tell him about Marseguro so he can destroy it? Chris thought. *Now that's a conversation I can enter into without any reservations at all.* He settled back. "What would you like to know?" he said, and took another long pull on his beer.

Richard couldn't believe it. He drank in Emily's image on the vidscreen and could feel a grin as big as hers splitting his face. He couldn't have suppressed it if he'd wanted to.

Emily stepped back from the vid pickup and, for the first time, he saw who was standing beside her. He blinked. "Dr. Christianson-Wood?"

Emily's mother smiled. "Yes, I'm really here," she said. "All of me."

On the other side of Emily stood a Selkie woman he didn't know, in a white swimsuit that made a stark contrast to Emily's bright-yellow zebra-striped skinsuit. Emily indicated her. "Richard, this is Sarah McLean, President of the Free Selkie Republic."

"Pleased to meet you ... Madame President." Richard said.

McLean seemed immune to all the smiling going on around her. "I'm not sure I can say the same about you," she said. She stepped forward, until she filled the screen, her image blocking out his view of Emily and her mother. "We need to talk. And not over this vidlink. In person."

"Of course," Richard said. "Um ... where are you?"

"You don't need to know." The President glanced at something out of frame. "I'll come to you." She looked back at him again. "You and your crew make yourselves comfortable. I'll arrive within . . ." she glanced off screen again . . . "eight hours."

"Emily—"

"President McLean out."

The screen went blank.

Wu had come up the ladder behind Richard. He looked at her, and she shrugged. "I'll show you to your quarters."

The next few hours would have passed with agonizing slowness if Richard hadn't been so tired. Wu showed him to a tiny cabin with a cot and not much else in it except for a bubblelike porthole. Once he'd taken a good look at the view it offered of blue water and drifting plankton, there was nothing to do—and, for that matter, nothing he wanted to do—but sleep.

Which he did, waking to a knock on the cabin door. "The President will be boarding the habitat in five minutes," Wu said when he opened it.

Richard nodded. He found the head, two doors down, and looked at his unshaven face, framed by mussed, tangled hair, in the round, steel-rimmed mirror. He stuck out his tongue at his reflection, then headed toward the wet porch.

The President was climbing out onto the edge of the pool as he entered. Her gaze slid right over him, though, because she was too busy turning to glare at the teenaged Selkie boy climbing out of the water after her. "Shelby Alister McLean, I've a good mind to lock you in your room until you're eighteen. What the hell did you think you were doing, stowing away? You know weight tolerances are tight on the sub-planes. What if you'd overloaded it? You could have killed us all!"

The boy looked down at the deck plates, one bare foot sliding back and forth in a puddle. "I didn't . . ."

"You didn't think at all, did you?"

"I don't . . ."

"Oh, never mind. We'll settle this later. Now get out of the way."

The boy shuffled off to one side as another Selkie swam up to the air. Violet hair broke the surface, and Richard's heart skipped a beat. "Emily!"

She erupted out of the water almost like a dolphin, hit the deck with both feet, and an instant later barreled into him like a Richard-seeking missile, a large, muscular missile that wrapped its arms around him so tightly he could hardly breathe.

After what seemed both an eternity and all-too-brief an instant, Emily disentangled herself from Richard and stood back, grinning at him.

Over her shoulder he saw that the boy had raised his head and was looking straight at them. He looked . . . well, Richard still couldn't read Selkie faces as well as he could nonmods', but he could have sworn the boy looked . . . jealous.

Dr. Christianson-Wood was now hauling herself out of the water much more sedately than Emily had. Richard went to her and shook her hand. "Dr. Christianson-Wood," he said. "I can't tell you how happy I am to see you looking so . . . well."

"Thank you, Richard," Dr. Christianson-Wood said.

He turned to the President. "Madame President?" He held out his hand.

McLean didn't take it. Instead, she looked past his shoulder at Wu. "Where can we talk?"

"I've cleared the forward wardroom," Wu said.

"Take us there." McLean walked past Richard, who raised an eyebrow at Dr. Christianson-Wood. Emily's mother's mouth quirked in a half-smile, then he turned to follow the president. Emily fell in beside him, and the teenager brought up the rear. But not for long. "Shelby, get lost," McLean said without looking around as they reached a hatch at the end of the main corridor.

"But—"

"Go!"

The boy gave the President a dark look, gave Richard an even darker one ... and then gave Emily a completely different sort of look, one Richard, who had once been a teenager himself, immediately recognized. As the boy walked back down the corridor, his bare back somehow radiating sulkiness, Richard whispered to Emily, "You've got an admirer."

Emily's mouth quirked. "Tell you why later," she whispered back.

The wardroom was probably the largest room in the habitat, since it spanned the full width of the cigar-shaped hull. Big curving overhead windows provided a view of the underside of the waves ten meters above. There were four rectangular tables and, in one corner, a miniature galley: microwave, sink, refrigerator, counter space.

President McLean planted herself at the head of one of the tables and gestured for the others to sit down. Richard sat to McLean's right, Emily at his side, while Dr. Christianson-Wood sat across from them.

"I've heard part of the story of how and why you came to Earth, Richard Hansen," McLean said without preamble. "But now I, as President of the Free Selkie Republic and representing the full Council, want to hear it all ... and whatever reasons you can offer why we should not consider you a sworn enemy of our state for the aid you have provided the remnant of the Body Purified."

Richard looked up at the green light filtering down into the room. "Ah," he said. "It's a long story—"

"You've got nowhere to go," said President McLean. "And neither do I."

Emily's hand found Richard's under the table and squeezed it reassuringly. He squeezed back.

"For me," he said, "it all began when the man I thought was my father committed suicide ..."

It took him well over an hour to relate all the events that had led him to Marseguro and everything that had transpired there and since. McLean frowned through much of his tale, and the frown deepened when he explained how he had been tricked into delivering the vaccine to the Avatar on Paradise Island.

But the biggest reaction came when he mentioned the Kemonomimi.

McLean had been looking down, hands folded quietly in front of her; suddenly, her head snapped up. "The Avatar asked you about the Kemonomimi?"

"Another race of moddies? Created by Victor Hansen? Here on Earth?" said Dr. Christianson-Wood.

Richard nodded. "So the Avatar said. I haven't seen them, but he was convinced enough that they existed that he left the island with all his forces to destroy them." He frowned. "Or maybe I *have* seen them," he said. "One of them, anyway. The Salvation Day service, just at the time I began to figure out where Marseguro must be ... during the Penitents' Parade, a moddie jumped the Lesser Deacon. She looked ... feline. The Holy Warriors shot her."

"Fascinating," Emily's mother said. "Victor Hansen's diaries ... there were strange references that hinted at some previous genetic experiment that had gone wrong. But he was never specific. And there were gaps ... huge gaps in his diaries, years' worth where he'd either recorded nothing or destroyed what he'd written." She nodded at the President. "He never mentioned Selkies left behind on Earth, for instance. And in his scientific papers he sometimes cross-referenced work we have no record of elsewhere."

"And I had no inkling of their existence from the shadows of memories that his gene-bomb imprinted on me," Richard said. "He obviously excised them from that, as well."

"He didn't want us know about them," Emily said. "But . . . why?"

"Because they're savages," President McLean said.

The three Marseguroites looked at her. "You've heard of them?"

"Yes," she said. "About five years ago, we managed to steal some pretty sophisticated AIs, one of which we set up to monitor Body communications for mention of moddies, thinking it might give us warning if the Body discovered our existence. We got more than we bargained for. Within a week, the AI just about scared us to death when it overheard numerous mentions of expeditions trying to find some mysterious moddie camp.

"But they weren't searching for us. They were in the mountains. People had been slaughtered in their homes in remote areas of the Canadian Rockies. Transports had been ambushed, aircraft shot down. All by these other moddies.

"I've got no love for the Body or most nonmods," she looked straight at Richard, "but I don't condone murdering civilians."

"Nor do I," Dr. Christianson-Wood said sharply. "But I did. On my world, and on yours. Millions have died horribly simply because I did what I thought needed to be done to protect my kind. Your Kemonomimi may no more be savages than we are. They're simply trying to survive. Those 'murders' may have been necessary to prevent their eradication."

"Well, they won't be able to prevent it much longer," Richard said. "Not if the Avatar reaches them." He looked at President McLean. "You may not approve of what you've heard of their actions," he said. "But they're not your enemy. The Avatar is. You openly attacked Paradise Island. Unlike the Kemonomimi, you left people alive. He knows there are Selkies out here, now, or he soon will. And the plague is no longer a deterrent. Once he's dealt with the Kemonomimi, he'll come looking for you—and sooner or later, he'll find you."

"Which brings us back to your choice to give him the vaccine," President McLean said. "By your own account, you had the chance to destroy it, once you found out you'd been tricked . . . but you didn't. If the Body attacks, it will be because you enabled it to." Her eyes narrowed. "Just like you enabled it to attack Marseguro."

Emily squeezed his hand again, but Richard pulled it free almost angrily. "You aren't telling me anything I haven't already told myself. I did what I thought was best at the time. I didn't know about the Free Selkie Republic. I didn't know Emily was here. I didn't know about the Kemonomimi. All I knew was that people were—*are*—dying all over the planet, and it looked like the only hope to get the vaccine to them was to put it in the hands of the Avatar.

"None of us can change our past actions. All we can do is choose what we do next." He locked gazes with the President. "Warn the Kemonomimi. Join forces with them. Together, you can overcome the Avatar."

"Fight him?" President McLean laughed. "We can't take on an army of Holy Warriors—on land!"

"But I can," Richard said. "A small, lightly armed one, anyway, which is all the Avatar has left to him." He looked up through the blue-green water. "Up there, in orbit, I have a starship. And that starship has assault craft and holds full of weapons and ammunition."

"Your starship has been taken."

"I have every reason to believe she has been, or soon will be, taken back. Even if she hasn't, there's only a skeleton crew of Holy Warriors aboard, and my crew is in hiding, ready to strike back.

"Give me a shuttle, and I'll give you my ship." *I hope.* "And then *we'll* have the upper hand, and the Avatar will have no choice but to give up his dreams of Purifying Earth of all of us . . . abominations."

"What do you mean, 'us?' " McLean said. "You're not a moddie."

"No," Richard said quietly. "I'm a clone."

McLean sat very still for a long moment. Then, "I'll have to talk to the Council," she said abruptly. "I'll let you know what we decide."

She got up without another word and stalked out of the wardroom.

Dr. Christianson-Wood looked at Richard and Emily. "I'm going to ... explore," she said, and followed the President.

"Why—" Richard began, but didn't get any further, because Emily was kissing him, almost devouring him, as though he were drink and she were dying of thirst.

An indeterminate time later they both surfaced for air. "I have a cabin," Richard said.

"I was hoping you might," Emily said.

Thinking about it afterward, it seemed to Richard they somehow teleported down the corridor to the tiny room he'd been given. And some time after that, as he spooned with her in the tiny bed, both of them naked, sweaty, and very, very happy, he said into her ear, "I take it you're ready for this, now."

She laughed. "I think so," she said. "But I may have to try it a few more times to be sure."

He tugged at her earlobe with his teeth, then murmured, "I'm not going anywhere."

For now, a voice whispered.

He ignored it.

Emily woke to the brightening that signaled morning, and for a moment wondered where she was; then she remembered, and smiled. She turned her head to look at Richard asleep beside her. For a while last night she'd thought they'd never sleep, and hadn't minded in the slightest. She knew they'd missed a meal, but somehow, no one had come knocking on their door, though it must have been obvious, in such a small habitat, where they'd disappeared to.

So much for being discreet, she thought.

Richard lay on his side facing her, and she studied his face, so much like the photographs of a young Victor Hansen in the museum back in Hansen's Harbor. She knew he was a clone of the creator of her race, and that they shared a not insignificant amount of DNA; but then, so did all the Selkies on Marseguro. That hadn't stopped them marrying and having children, and the tweaking Victor Hansen had done to the first generation of Selkies had ensured that the sometimes dire consequences of inbreeding hadn't befallen the population, though Emily couldn't remember exactly how he'd achieved that.

Her smile faded a little. She and Richard could never have children. Victor Hansen had seen to that, too. And yet, Victor Hansen had also given the Selkies a strong sex drive, to ensure they reproduced. Her attraction to Richard was part of that drive, but no matter how long they drove, or how hard and fast—and they'd driven long, hard and fast indeed last night—they could never reach that particular destination.

I don't care, she thought. *So we can't have children. We'll have each other.*

If we both survive the next few days, a part of her warned. She tried to ignore it.

The knock on the door that hadn't come the night before came now. "The President wants to see you both," said a voice Emily recognized as Wu's. "Half an hour."

"We'll be there," Emily called.

Richard stirred and opened his eyes. "What . . . ?"

"The President," she said. "Half an hour. She and the Council must have made a decision."

"I hope it doesn't involve shoving me out an air lock without a waterbreather," Richard said. He stretched and yawned.

Emily tried to speak, but her throat closed on her words. "I won't let that happen," she finally managed.

Richard blinked at her. "It was a joke."

"It wasn't funny."

"Um. No. Perhaps not." He grinned at her. "Breakfast?"

They found the rest of the crew of *Sawyer's Point* in the wardroom, along with a couple of Selkies Emily didn't know—and who kept to themselves—and, inevitably, Shelby. The teenager had only half-finished his breakfast—a bowl of some unidentifiable glop that looked inedible to Emily—but when he saw the two of them come in together, he shoved away from the table in a hurry and strode out without looking back.

"Um," Richard said. "Well, can't say I blame him." Emily had told him the story of how she'd first met the Selkies of the Free Republic.

"I hope that's not going to cause any problems down the road," Emily said.

"It's not your fault he's a teenage boy," Richard said. "He'll grow out of it."

They spent a few minutes catching up with the others from *Sawyer's Point*, who kept exchanging grins when they didn't think Richard was watching. Everyone had had a long, long sleep and expressed their readiness for anything . . . everyone but Derryl who, as usual, said next to nothing beyond, "Captain Hansen. Emily."

Dr. Christianson-Wood was not in the wardroom, but she met them at the ladder leading up to the control room. She raised a hand in greeting as they approached. "You two look . . . relaxed," she said.

"Mom!" Emily said.

Her mother laughed.

"You can come up, now," said Wu. The three of them climbed into the rather cramped control room. President McLean turned to face them. On the screen behind her, Richard saw an indistinct image of half a dozen other Selkies gathered around a table.

"I and the Council of the Free Selkie Republic have discussed matters," she said. "We agree that we must stop the Avatar now, while he is weak.

"Richard Hansen," she went on, looking at him directly. "Although the decision was not unanimous, we have decided to trust you.

"We'll get you a shuttle. You get your ship."

Chapter 14

ANDY KING SPRAWLED in his landsuit in the captain's chair on the still essentially useless bridge, legs hung over the armrest, watching the Earth spin in the tactical display, still showing the last view the Holy Warriors had chosen. Footsteps sounded behind him, and he turned around to see Simon Goodfellow.

"The reboot sequence is underway," Goodfellow said without preamble.

Andy's feet slammed to the deck plates. "You started it *without informing me?*"

Goodfellow blinked. "You've been going on and on about how important it is to get the computer working. I didn't think I needed to tell you I was about to do what you've been telling me to do."

Andy closed his eyes, took a deep breath, then opened his eyes again and let the matter drop. Simon seemed congenitally incapable of grasping the finer points of shipboard protocol—like the need to always check with one's commanding officer before beginning a technical procedure that could turn the ship into a useless lump of orbiting junk. "How long?"

"Two hours, twenty-nine minutes from start," Simon said. "Or . . ." He glanced at his watch. "Two hours, thirteen minutes from now."

"When will we know if it's working?"

"When it works," Simon said. "In two hours and thirteen ... twelve ... minutes from now, the computer will either wake up and ask for instructions, or it will remain silent forever."

"And the ship will shut down."

"And the ship will shut down," Simon said. "It's all or nothing. Either the reboot works, or else it wipes out everything. You might say that right now the AI is in a coma, but its brain stem is functioning. If the reboot fails, the brain stem dies, too."

"Life support, power, everything gone."

"Right," Simon said.

Andy nodded. "Very well," he said. He got to his feet. "I'll get down to the crew quarters and make sure everyone is ready for—" He stopped. Something had just happened: a sound, or maybe a vibration. Distant, but distinct, and definitely not part of the ship's normal, if currently rather subdued, function. "Did you feel that?"

"Feel what?"

Andy looked at the tactical display. Earth continued to swing below; they were just crossing the terminator, currently somewhere over North America. Nothing unusual there. He began moving from station to station, checking each in turn. All were frozen in whatever state they had been in when Simon had pulled the AI's plug, but some of their vidscreens showed exterior views.

There. Andy stared hard to be sure. The vidscreen was small and the lighting uncertain, but that bump on the hull ... that shouldn't have been there. *A shuttle,* he thought. *The Holy Warriors. They didn't return to Earth. They just put themselves into a slightly different orbit. They knew we wouldn't be able to track them with the computer down, and now they've come back.*

We're being boarded!

"Simon," Andy said. "Go back to your data terminal. Stay there. Do whatever you can to make sure this reboot succeeds."

"There's nothing I can—"

"Then do nothing, but stay there!" Andy roared. "That's an order, damn it."

Simon blinked. "Um, okay. Uh, sir." He went out.

Andy pulled on one of the microcomm headsets they'd been using since they'd cut themselves off from ship systems. "Cordelia," he said.

"What is it, Andy?" Cordelia Raum's voice came back.

"The Holy Warriors are back," Andy said. "And we're in the middle of the reboot. The computer can't tell us where they are, but I'd say it's a safe bet they're heading to the bridge. We have to cut them off."

"I'll gather some people."

"Not some," Andy said. "All. Everyone who can hold a gun." He looked at the image of the shuttle. "They've come in through one of the external work air locks about three-quarters of the way to the stern. There's no way into the habitat ring from there. They'll have to come up the central shaft."

"Zero-G fighting," Raum said. "They're probably trained for it. We're not."

"We're Selkies," Andy said. "Well, some of us, anyway. We live in zero-G, remember?"

Raum laughed. "Affirmative," she said.

"Delegate four crew to guard the bridge," Andy said.

"Where will you be?"

"I've got a laser rifle. I'll be heading up to the shaft. See you there." He cut the connection before Cordelia could protest that the commanding officer shouldn't put himself in danger, that he should wait at the bridge in case the computer came back up . . .

Screw that, Andy thought. More than two hours? By then the Holy Warriors would either have the ship, be running away again . . . or be dead.

Andy preferred the latter option, and why should he let everyone else have all the fun of making it happen?

He found the nearest Jefferies tube and climbed up

it toward the central shaft, weight dropping away as he progressed. As he neared the top, he slowed. The Holy Warriors had only just docked. They'd still be getting organized, slipping through the corridors toward the central shaft. Probably none of them had entered it yet.

Still, getting his head sliced off because he'd been too eager would be an embarrassing way to end his brief stint as acting commander of Marseguro's only starship.

He looked out carefully. The central shaft was pitch-black; its lights had gone out with the computer crash. A faint light shone up the Jefferies tube, though, and realizing it could silhouette him to anyone down the shaft, he cautiously pulled himself up and out. The spin here imparted just enough weight to keep him bobbing against the wall of the shaft like a balloon, but he could easily leap too high and be stranded in midair.

He closed the hatch, then pulled himself along webbing he couldn't see toward the elevator hut he knew was there somewhere.

He found it by the simple if somewhat painful expedient of bashing his head against it, and stood slowly upright, hooking his feet in the webbing, keeping his back to the elevator hut and the elevator hut between himself and the shaft. Then he unshipped the laser rifle and held it out at arm's length.

The rifle had an aiming vidscreen at the top that could be turned at right angles to the weapon, allowing him to shoot around corners.

It also let him see in the dark.

In the screen, the shaft glowed dimly green. Areas heated by machinery or with warm spaces beneath them glowed brighter than others.

And far down the shaft, one by one, small, bright dots were emerging into the shaft.

The Holy Warriors.

The shaft's atmosphere was too dense for him to make any effective shots at this distance, but he lined up one of the dots and activated the automatic tracking system. When the rifle's computer decided the range had lessened enough, it would automatically fire at that dot ... and then the next ... and then the next ...

Which sounded like a surefire way to take out the whole troop, except, of course, the Holy Warriors had built the weapon ... and had their own versions of it, and their own defenses against it.

He thought he might get one, if he were lucky. He doubted he would get two.

But one would be something.

He stood where he was, watching the screen and the approaching dots, wondering idly which man he had selected to die.

The screen flashed green. The laser fired. And then ...

Holy shit!

The shaft exploded with light as the Holy Warriors opened up, not with lasers, but with automatic rifles. Tracers left blue-and-green streaks in the atmosphere.

Something smashed Andy's laser rifle from his hands, dislocating a finger in the process. He yelped in pain and pulled his hands in, then pressed his back against the elevator hut.

Suddenly, coming up here by himself seemed like a monumentally bad idea.

The gunfire ceased, leaving him in the dark, half-deafened, hand hurting. He debated crawling back to the Jefferies tube, but they were surely alert now and they'd have their own night-vision apparatus. If he showed even a sliver of warm body, they'd blow it off.

Which meant he'd just set up his own crew for ambush.

"Shit." He activated the microcomm headset. "Cordelia, come in. Come in!"

"We're almost there," Raum said. "We'll be popping up in—"

"No!" Andy said. "Don't. I did something stupid. I took a shot. It alerted them. They're bound to be using night vision. And they're using projectile weapons. Explosive bullets, I think. They don't have to nail you to nail you."

"Projectiles? In a spaceship?" Raum sounded shocked.

"Guess they figure they're unlikely to punch a hole in the hull from here," Andy said.

"But . . . that means you're stuck. Wherever you are."

"Yeah, well. As long as I keep my head down, no reason they should spot me."

Raum didn't say anything, but Andy could feel her disbelief and disapproval even over the comm link. "What do you want us to do?"

"With the elevators out, they'll have to come down a Jefferies tube themselves," Andy said. "I'll try to tell you which one they pick. You need to be waiting for them at the bottom."

"What if . . . you can't?"

"Then you'll just have to do the best you can," Andy said.

Silence for a moment. "Roger that," Raum said. "Good luck."

"You, too, Cordelia." Andy cut off the comm link.

We're all going to need it, he thought.

Once the President and Council of the Free Selkie Republic decided to trust Richard, things moved quickly. Now, just one day later, he and the crew of *Sawyer's Point* were once more aboard Lia Wu's sub, heading in the opposite direction from Paradise Island: south toward the Cape Scott spaceport at the northwestern tip of Vancouver Island, just a few hours' journey from the Republic's hidden habitat.

One difference: this time Emily was with them.

He'd urged her to stay behind. She'd refused. "You and I took *Sanctification* all by ourselves last time," she'd reminded him as they lay entwined in bed after another lengthy demonstration of moddie/nonmod unity.

"I don't want anything to happen to you," Richard said. His finger traced the lower curve of her left breast. "Not now."

"And what makes you think anything is more likely to happen to me than to you?" Emily said.

Richard sighed. "Can't I be chivalrous if I want to?"

"No." Emily had kissed the tip of his nose. "Chivalry is dead. I read that somewhere."

Richard looked at her now, standing at his left in the sub's control room, watching the crew at work, and hoped that no one would join chivalry in death once they got to the *Victor Hansen*.

If they did. They were betting on the spaceport having a ready-to-fly shuttle that could be piloted manually, and that sufficient information continued to flow through the orbital tracking systems of the Body that the shuttle's computer would be able to locate and rendezvous with the *Victor Hansen*.

Not impossibly large odds, at a spaceport the size of the Cape Scott one . . . especially since, Richard knew from his days at Body Security, Cape Scott had been developed in this remote location by the secretive Cheveldeoff as Body Security's private facility for launching missions into space. That implied to Richard that there would be a wide variety of spacecraft available. Still, it was hardly a sure thing. And they didn't know if Holy Warrior survivors still stood guard there or not.

The Earth Selkies understood they needed the *Victor Hansen*'s resources if they were going to have any hope of halting the Avatar's advance. But they didn't trust the Kemonomimi; as far as Richard could tell, the Council's view was that the Kemonomimi were a failed experiment, whereas the Selkies were a successful one.

Richard wondered what the Kemonomimi's view of the Selkies was . . . if they even knew they existed.

The Selkies were willing to attempt to stop the Avatar, with the *Victor Hansen*'s resources. But they refused to warn the Kemonomimi first. If they stopped the Avatar, they'd consider talking to the other moddies. If they failed to stop the Avatar, then the Kemonomimi could face him alone. The Selkies would not expose themselves further to the possibly resurgent Body.

Richard thought they were wrong, but he had no way to persuade them, being essentially a beggar with his hand out.

"ARV launched," a crewwoman announced behind Richard.

"Let's see," Wu said. She went to look over the crewwoman's shoulder at a curving triptych of vidscreens. The images relayed from the dragonfly-sized aerial reconnaissance vehicle hovering just above the waves all showed variations of the same thing: gray water splashing on gray rocks and gray sky above. Only a few gray roofs showed inland. "Not very informative," Richard said.

"Or aesthetically pleasing," Emily put in.

"Another reason to hate the Body," said Wu. "Bad architecture. But the important thing is, nothing's moving. Radar and sonar are both clear, as well. And there's no radio chatter of any kind, open or encrypted."

"Because *everyone* there has been encrypted," Melody said.

Every turned to look at her.

She blushed. "Because . . . they're dead? In crypts? Encrypted? Get it?"

"I won't even dignify that with a groan," Richard said, but he smiled as he said it.

"Push the ARV up to a hundred meters," Wu said. "Let's get a better look."

The images shifted, the water falling away and the view inland opening out. Dark-forested hills surrounded the spaceport, and waves splashed against rocky headlands in the distance. And in the spaceport itself . . .

"Yikes," Melody said softly.

"My sentiment exactly," Richard said. It looked like something large had crashed on landing and skidded across the spaceport at a forty-five-degree angle to everything else, smashing trees into kindling, other ships into flinders, and finally buildings into rubble. The control tower, its windows blown out, stood at an angle more appropriate to an Italian postcard. The crashed vehicle itself, a battered and blackened cigar-shaped hulk, had fetched up just twenty or thirty meters from the sea. "A spaceship?"

"Orbital cargo vessel," Wu said. "Either the pilot or the ground controller probably had the plague and made a wrong decision—or dropped dead—at just the wrong moment." She pointed at something on the screen. "Zoom in." The shoreline seemed to leap toward them. "Made things easier for us, though. The fence is down." She tapped the screen.

It wasn't just down, it had been rolled up like baling wire and wrapped around a denuded tree.

"Let's surface," Wu told her crew. "Launch a boat."

Twenty minutes later the Marseguroites, accompanied by Wu and two of the sub's larger crew members, splashed ashore. One other sub crewman remained with the boat.

No one challenged them except for a crow that rose cawing from a dead, white-streaked tree jammed between two black rocks. They entered the spaceport through the hole in the fencing without difficulty, and headed to the flight line.

Richard saw a couple of bodies at a distance, but didn't suggest they investigate. He'd seen the bloody and bloated remains of plague victims often enough on Marseguro. He didn't need to see them on Earth . . . or any more evidence of the horror Chris Keating had unleashed.

Though there were surely many more bodies tucked away around the huge port, most people had probably died in their quarters, too sick to get out of bed. *A blessing, maybe . . .*

He snorted. A blessing? "With blessings like this, who needs curses?" He muttered the old Body saying under his breath, but Emily heard him, of course. Probably half the party did, with their damnable Selkie hearing.

"Are you all right?" she said, coming closer and taking his hand.

"Yeah," he said. "Just thinking." He gestured with his free hand. "All this destruction. All the deaths. I hope Chris Keating is proud of himself."

"I hope Chris Keating is dead and rotting," Emily snarled. "Or better yet, still locked away in solitary confinement somewhere wondering why nobody brings him food and water anymore."

"Maybe we should be grateful to him," Richard said. He squeezed her hand. "After all, he brought us together."

Emily didn't let go, but she turned to look at him. "I love you, Richard, but I would give you up in an instant if it meant I could roll things back to the way they were before Keating did what he did. If I could bring back my father . . . my friends . . ." Her voice choked off, and she looked away.

Richard didn't know what to say, because he couldn't tell her the truth: that he very well might make the opposite choice.

Of course, that attitude was incredibly selfish, and he felt bad about it, but ultimately the brain and body were primarily concerned with themselves. Altruism required work.

And, yes, of course those thoughts were incredibly egotistical, as well, but then, he came by that part honestly: as he sometimes forgot but his genome never could, he was the clone of Victor Hansen, the man who had created not just one, but two races of modified humans out of his own DNA.

Talk about thinking the world revolves around you . . .

Wu stopped suddenly. "There," she said, pointing off to the right. "I think we may have lucked out."

Richard looked. Tucked in between a couple of helicopters was a delta-winged craft that looked a bit like a miniature version of the assault craft carried by the *Victor Hansen*. "It's the right style to be set up for manual flight," she said. "And the fact it's on the flight line means it could be juiced up."

"Let's find out," Richard said.

Of course, it was really Melody Ashman and Pierre Normand, who'd be required to fly the thing, who gave the craft the once-over—and proclaimed it ready to go.

"What about navigation?" Richard said. He stood between and behind Ashman and Normand, who were tucked into the pilot and copilot seats. "No point going up there if we can't find the ship."

Melody tapped a screen. "It looks like we're getting automated tracking information from somewhere; probably an AI under the tower that's still doing the best it can." She pulled out a keyboard and typed on it for a few seconds. "Good old manual controls," she said. "Gotta love 'em." More typing. "There." She banged a final key emphatically and let the keyboard retract. "Course laid in. Unfortunately, with where they are now, we're in for a bit of a chase to rendezvous. I'll know more once we're in orbit, but we're probably . . . six hours away from docking."

"Assuming they don't shoot us out of the sky."

"There is that," Melody admitted.

Richard turned and looked back into the tiny cabin. Pilot and copilot in the front, room for two passengers behind them. The reality hit him like a blow to the stomach. He turned to Emily, who stood close behind him. "Emily . . ." he said. He swallowed. "It's too small."

"What?"

"It's too small." He gestured. "We can't take . . . everyone."

Her face froze. "Richard—"

He shrugged helplessly and repeated, like a robot, "It's too small."

Emily looked down for a long moment. When she raised her head again, her eyes glistened. "Then I'll stay behind."

"Emily, I can't—"

"You can't do anything about it. I know." She put her hand on his chest. "But you *will* come back to me. Or else—"

"Or else?"

"Or else I'll kill you." She looked him in the eyes a long moment, then took a deep breath, turned, and went out.

Richard followed her. No one argued about who should go and who should stay: the choices were obvious. Richard had to go. Melody and Pierre, as pilot and copilot. And since they might have to fight when they got to the *Victor Hansen*, the logical fourth choice was Derryl, their silent warrior.

Jerry Krall and Ann Nolan would stay behind, because they would be needed if and when *Victor Hansen* was firmly in Marseguroite control once more, to download information from it that could be used to create vaccine-creation modules for the Earth Selkies' microfactories.

And Emily . . . Richard took her aside. "Keep working on McLean and her Council," he said in a low voice. "Convince them to warn the Kemonomimi."

Emily's face suddenly lit up. "I'll volunteer to go myself," she said. "That way she's not putting any of her people at—"

"No!" The word exploded out of him. "You heard what she said. The Kemonomimi are dangerous. Let her—"

"—send someone else?" Emily snapped. "Possibly sacrifice a friend?"

Richard shook his head stubbornly. "It doesn't make

sense for you to go. You don't know anything about Earth, or the Kemonomimi. You—"

"It sounds like nobody knows much about them," Emily said. She gathered his hands in hers. "Richard, I won't take foolish chances. I'll volunteer to go, but I'm not going to run up to the first Kemonomimi I see and yell ... what's that old expression? 'Take me to your leader!' But if I show how important we think it is by being willing to put myself in danger ... then maybe McLean will change her mind. And even if she doesn't ... well, the Kemonomimi still have to be warned." She squeezed his hands. "It's as simple as that."

"Damn it." Richard pulled her close and hugged her tight. "I hate it when you're right," he whispered into her ear. Then he pulled back a little ways and kissed her, long and lingeringly. Reluctantly, he stepped away at last and stared deep into her iridescent green eyes, the ocean-colored eyes he longed to drown in. "Be careful."

"Look who's talking," she said, her voice breaking a little. Another quick hug, then he forced himself to turn and walk toward the shuttle. Derryl Godard was the only one of the crew still waiting outside. He gave Richard an unreadable look, moved aside to let him enter, then followed him in through the tiny air lock, turning to close the double doors behind them.

Richard sat down in one of the blue-upholstered acceleration chairs and buckled up the five-point harness. Derryl sat beside him and did the same. Melody and Pierre were already in place.

"Let's go," Richard said.

"Aye, aye, sir," said Melody.

The ascent was only a little rough, and smoothed out as they pierced the upper atmosphere and powered into orbit. Melody studied her controls as their acceleration ceased and Richard felt himself lift slightly from the chair, kept in place only by the harness. "Okay," she said. "I've got a better ETA." She leaned forward and peered at one of her screens. "Five hours, forty-nine minutes from . . . now."

The passenger section of the shuttle didn't even have any windows. Richard sighed and closed his eyes. Well, a nice long nap sounded like a good idea anyway.

Thanks to Emily, he hadn't been getting much sleep the last couple of nights.

He dozed off at once. He woke to a sound like someone striking a small silver gong in the distance. "What—?" It took him a moment to remember where he was. "What's going on?"

"I'm not sure," Melody said. "I don't know the system's audio cues." Her eyes flicked from screen to screen. "I'm trying to spot—Pierre, do you see—?"

"There," he said. He pointed at something. She peered at it.

"Ah," she said. The pilot's chair swiveled: she turned to look at Richard. "There's another Body shuttle already docked with the *Victor Hansen*. It's using the exterior lock I had programmed us to mate with."

Richard frowned. "It must be the shuttle the Holy Warriors used to board her. But . . . why wouldn't they have gone into the main boat bay? If they had computer control—"

"I don't think anybody has control of the ship right now," Pierre said. "*Sanctification—Victor Hansen* to us, but not to this shuttle's computer—is not responding to attempts to communicate." He tapped the console. "Our computer's getting frustrated. It keeps cycling through its communication options, faster and faster. But nothing. Can't even raise a proper identification code."

"Simon Goodfellow's databomb," Richard said. "Andy must have managed to activate it. They flatlined the AI."

"But that doesn't explain why that shuttle is where it is," Melody said.

"I can think of a good reason," Derryl said, startling

Richard. They all turned to look at him; his dark eyes looked back from a face like stone. "The crew drove the Holy Warriors off the ship, but only temporarily . . . and with the AI out of commission, they had no way of knowing when the Warriors came back."

Richard blinked at him, astonished. He'd never heard Derryl say that many words in sequence before. Derryl frowned. "What? Why are you all looking at me like that?"

I guess he just hasn't had anything to say until now, Richard thought. "I think you're right," he said out loud. He turned to Melody. "Any way to tell how long that shuttle has been there?"

"It couldn't have been there when we made the boost to higher orbit," Melody said. "*Its* ID beacon is working just fine. If it had already been docked where it is now when I programmed in our course, our computer would have warned us sooner. I doubt it's been there more than an hour. Maybe less."

"Then they've just boarded," Richard said. "And we've got a chance to surprise them from the rear." He tried to lean forward, but of course his harness stopped him: weightless, he'd forgotten it was fastened. "Where else can you dock?"

"There's an emergency access hatch directly opposite," Melody said. "But we can't mate with it."

"Can we even open it?"

Melody nodded. "It's got manual controls."

"Get us as close as you can," Richard said. "We'll jump the rest of the way." He glanced at the sniper. "Derryl, get out the weapons."

"With pleasure," Derryl said. He unbuckled and floated to the back of the cabin. Richard followed.

They'd loaded the locker at the back before they'd left with standard-issue Body automatic rifles, "liberated" from some depot or other, laser pistols, Holy Warrior body armor, and visored helmets with built-in night vision and magnification capabilities. Those would have to wait until they were in the ship, though; they'd have to don pressure suits first to make the transition.

Neither the pressure suits nor the body armor appealed to Richard. "We're going to look just like Holy Warriors," he said to Derryl. "Any of our guys see us, they're liable to shoot us on sight. I'm sure they'd be really sorry about it afterward, but . . ."

"Nothing to be done," Derryl said.

He was right, of course. Richard put that worry aside and focused on a different one. "I'm also not wild about the prospect of using projectile weapons inside a spaceship."

"Nothing here that could hole the hull from the central shaft," Derryl said. "The main reason lasers are commonly used shipboard is that a nonrecoiling weapon has some obvious advantages in a zero-G environment. But as long as you remember Newton's Third Law and brace yourself accordingly . . ."

"Mmmm," Richard said. No need to mention that he was about as clumsy in zero-G as . . . well, as a nonmod trying to swim stroke-for-stroke with a Selkie.

"Ready," Melody said. "Holding station."

"Then let's get suited up." Richard shoved his feet into the legs of a pressure suit. "I want our ship back."

"Aye, aye!" said Melody, and "Copy that," Pierre said. Derryl said nothing, but he picked up a rifle and sighted along it with practiced ease, then put it down again with a grim half-smile and started climbing into a suit.

They didn't bother with the air lock. Once they were all suited up and had secured their weapons and body armor in carry bags, they opened both doors at once and blew the shuttle's air out into space in one brief, violent hurricane of wind and fog.

They followed more sedately, gently launching themselves the three meters from shuttle to ship, grabbing the stanchions surrounding the emergency hatch as they hit. Richard went first, and as the others followed, tried his luck at opening the hatch using the external controls. Final proof that the computer was offline, if any was needed, came when he simply touched "Enter" on the keypad without entering his security code, and the hatch slid silently open.

The air lock was big enough for all of them, though barely. They crowded into it. Richard closed the outside door, cycled the lock, pulled a laser pistol from the bag of weapons, and opened the inside door.

There was nothing beyond but an empty spherical room, lit by the eerie blue-green of emergency lights. Webbing covered the walls, and ratlines crisscrossed the middle. There were openings above, to both sides, and directly ahead. Richard skinned out of the pressure suit, the others copying him, then strapped himself into body armor and grabbed a rifle. He jammed a helmet down over his ears. "Don't talk over the helmet radios," he said. "We just might be on the same frequency as the Holy Warriors.

"If we are," Derryl said dryly, "shouldn't we be listening to them?"

Richard blinked, then laughed. "Yes," he said. "And I'm an idiot." He flicked down his visor and the heads-up display kicked in immediately. "How did this thing work again?" he muttered to himself, trying to remember long-ago and cursory instruction in the helmets' use. "Look and blink . . . look at the menu you want, blink two times fast . . . aha." It worked: he found the communications menu, made sure his own microphone was muted, and then activated the helmet radio.

Nothing but static, but with maybe, just maybe, the tiniest *soupcon* of voices mixed in: unintelligible, but there.

Quickly he explained to the others how to work the helmet controls. "Experiment as we move," he said. "I don't know what's going on out there."

"Where do we go?" Pierre asked.

"Central shaft," Derryl replied, before Richard could. "Only way to the bridge."

The others looked at Richard. He nodded. "You heard him. Central shaft."

The corridors at least had some light, even if its green tinge made them all look like they'd been dead for a week (to Richard; he suspected to the Selkies it suggested sunlight through shallow water, or something else appropriately soggy). But the shaft . . .

The shaft was pitch-black. "Night vision," Richard whispered to the others. "Third menu from the left, fourth . . . no, fifth item." He double-blinked at the words apparently floating in space in front of him, and his vision shifted as the goggles began registering infrared and displaying it as visible light.

Now the shaft was a huge tube, mostly colored a very dark blue, although faint greenish and yellowish patches along its walls indicated warmer spots, probably where bits of the ship's power distribution network or hot pipes were close to the surface. At the far end, where the habitat ring rotated, the blue shaded to a deep emerald green: there was a lot more life support at work down there, warming up the multiple decks between the shaft and the hull.

And just approaching that habitat ring were half a dozen bright yellow dots, crawling along the side of the tube like some strange kind of glowing beetle: and now that they were in the shaft, Richard could hear over his helmet earphones what those distant Holy Warriors were saying.

". . . got the bastard?"

"Doubt it. Ducked behind the elevator head. But we'll get him soon enough. Nowhere to hide."

"The rest of them'll be on their way," the first man said.

"Then you'll just have to SHUT UP AND MOVE

FASTER!" a new voice roared, obviously the commanding officer; after that, there was no more chatter.

"Derryl?" Richard whispered to the sniper.

He shook his head. "Not in this light, not at this distance, not with this weapon. If I still had my sniper rifle . . ."

"We'll have to get closer, then," Richard said. "Quietly. They've got no reason to look behind them. Let's keep it that way."

The quartet moved off, hauling themselves along the webbing that lined the shaft. Richard remembered the last time he'd made this journey, with a broken arm, Emily tugging him along like a balloon on a string.

"Transitioning," a low voice said in his ears, and it took him a second to realize it must be one of the Holy Warriors. Ahead, the Holy Warriors' glowing shapes suddenly swept up and around the curve of the shaft. They'd crossed into the rotating habitat ring, which here moved at about the speed a man could walk, though at the hull it whirled around at something close to 100 kilometers an hour. Which, of course, was why there was no way to dock directly with it.

"Nothing yet," the same voice whispered. "Todd, Barker, left side of that elevator head. Hough, you're with me. You others spread out. If anything moves, shoot it."

As far as Richard could tell, his group still hadn't been seen.

And then, with absolutely no warning, the lights came on.

Four glowstrips spaced equidistantly around the circumference of the shaft belied their name: they didn't glow, they blazed. His earphones erupted with startled shouts and Richard himself let out a shocked yelp. He couldn't possibly have reacted fast enough to save his eyes, but he didn't have to: his helmet visor instantly cut off the night vision and darkened, so swiftly he only felt a quick stab of pain. All the same, for a moment he was even more blind than he had been in the dark: the visor seemed to have gone completely opaque. *Designed to react to an explosives flash,* he thought. *It will come back in a—*

Ahead of him, weapons spoke. "Lie flat!" Richard shouted, hurling himself to the webbing. He looked at the heads-up display, calling up menus, trying to find the one that would adjust the visor's tint to let him see, and then suddenly he realized he *was* seeing. The visor had adjusted itself.

A firefight had broken out in the habitat ring. The only weapons he could hear were the rifles of the Holy Warriors: the defenders had to be armed with lasers. At least two bodies already floated in the middle of the shaft, tumbling over each other in a broken ballet, trailing blood, one in a Holy Warrior pressure suit, the other in a pale-green Marseguroite uniform. Richard felt sick, and wondered who it was.

Richard looked at Derryl. He nodded. "The spin won't make it easy, but I can do it."

"You split off, then. Pierre, Melody, follow me. We'll get as close as we can and jump 'em from the rear. Derryl, wait until we're . . ." Richard judged the distance. "Past the third segmentation ring. See it?"

"Aye, aye," said Derryl. He stuck his feet into the webbing and unslung his rifle.

"Let's move." Richard led the way, his heart pounding as he watched the battle ahead. The Holy Warriors seemed to have the defenders pinned down, and were slowly, bit of cover by bit of cover, moving closer. Richard guessed the defenders were using the Jefferies tubes as foxholes, but there were only four of those, and that meant only four people could be firing at any one time. There were a dozen of the Holy Warriors—*well, one less now,* he thought, as the bodies that had been in the habitat ring drifted by overhead.

The Marseguroite, a nonmod, didn't have a recognizable face anymore, or much of a head. Richard still didn't know who he was.

He ground his teeth. The third segmentation ring, a broad band of shining metal, lay just ahead. He gripped his rifle tighter with one hand and pulled ahead. Once they opened fire, they'd have the Holy Warriors in a crossfire with the defenders—but they'd also be firing from a completely exposed position. The constant spinning of the habitat ring should make it difficult for the Holy Warriors to shoot back at them with any accuracy, but it made it just as hard for them to shoot at the Warriors.

Derryl said he could compensate. Richard hoped he was right.

They crossed the ring. "Fire at will," Richard said. He dug his feet and one arm into the webbing to hold himself in place, raised his rifle—

And heard the flat cracking sound of Derryl's.

The Holy Warrior just easing past the elevator head jerked and quit moving, falling in slow motion to the webbing. And with astonishing speed, the other Holy Warriors turned and discovered Richard and his crew behind them.

Richard pulled the trigger. The shots went wild, missing the Holy Warriors completely, ripping out chunks of the insulating padding that lined the ring like a giant quilt, as the Holy Warriors rotated over their heads. The Holy Warriors fired back, but nothing found its mark.

But Derryl's rifle spoke again, and the helmet of another Holy Warrior suddenly burst apart in a cloud of red and gray.

The ring kept coming. The Holy Warriors were getting closer. And Richard suddenly realized that staying put would get them killed. "Move!" he yelled.

He lurched upward as he said it and jumped, soaring across the shaft as the Holy Warriors opened fire again.

Halfway across, something slammed into his chest so hard it knocked the breath out of him and he tumbled out of control, but the body armor saved him, and another Warrior died as Derryl fired again.

Spinning so fast he could hardly see, Richard slammed into the far side of the shaft, barely holding on to his rifle. Nauseated, he clung for a moment. Bullets tore into the padding just two meters from his legs, and almost without thinking he grabbed his rifle and fired back.

By pure luck, the Holy Warriors were at the closest point. His burst of automatic fire stitched a bloody line across the chest of one Warrior's pressure suit.

Behind that Warrior was another, though, and Richard saw the rifle swinging toward him that would surely finish him off—except the Warrior didn't fire. A puff of gray smoke erupted from his chest, and he stiffened, then just stopped moving, feet caught in the webbing, gun falling in slow motion.

The defenders had emerged from their foxholes.

Four Holy Warriors still lived. They threw down their weapons and held up their hands.

A moment later only three of them were alive as a final laser found its mark, but then the fighting stopped.

Richard tried to catch his breath. His chest hurt. Bodies floated in the shaft or bumped bonelessly against the habitat ring's inner padding, and a haze of blood and smoke swirled through the air.

Richard looked back at Derryl and gave him a wave. Then he looked around for Pierre and Melody . . .

. . . and saw them where he had left them, still tangled in the webbing, now soaked with blood, more blood floating in glistening scarlet globules all around them.

"God, no," Richard whispered. He jumped across the shaft, almost losing his breath again when he slammed into the far side, tossed his rifle and helmet away and pulled himself hand over hand to where his two crewmembers lay motionless.

They were dead, gaping holes torn in their bodies. From their postures, it looked like Melody had been tangled in the webbing and Pierre had tried to help free her . . . and then the Holy Warrior's bullets had found them.

My fault, Richard thought, a black roaring in his head, not wanting to look at their mangled bodies, but unable not to. *My fault. Pride. Hansen pride. I thought I knew what was best, just like Victor. I thought I could do whatever I want. I thought I could save the* Victor Hansen. *I thought I could save Earth. I thought . . .*

I thought wrong.

He was still sitting there, staring at their bodies, when Andy King found him.

Andy enjoyed adventure vids as much as the next person, but he usually only watched the latest Marseguroite efforts. Nevertheless, he'd once had occasion to visit the home of a friend whose hobby was ancient Earth "movies," and had been subjected to several risible and largely incomprehensible entertainment programs from the early twentieth century. When he'd expressed skepticism at the fortuitous timing of the arrival of military aid in one particular "western," his friend had laughed. "It's one of the clichés of the period," he said. "The cavalry always shows up in the nick of time."

Andy felt a new empathy for the rescued heroine of the western when, just as the Holy Warriors were threatening to overrun the *Victor Hansen* defenders, someone started shooting them from behind.

Not that he assumed they'd won yet, at that point: he'd already been disappointed that the sudden illumination of the central shaft (and God bless Simon Goodfellow for getting enough computer control back to make that happen, and his crew for rushing up the Jeffering tubes when it did.) hadn't blinded the Holy Warriors completely. His men had known it was coming and simply closed their eyes. The Holy Warriors must have been using night vision and hadn't had any warning, but their pressure suits seemed to have some sort of automatic mechanism for dimming the faceplate, because they'd resumed their attack faster than he'd thought possible.

It soon became apparent that there weren't enough Holy Warriors to fight a two-front battle, however, and within minutes the last of them surrendered, and if Andy was just a bit slow about realizing they had surrendered and shot one more of them anyway, who would ever blame him?

Only then did he see who their rescuers were.

Only then did he see Richard Hansen clutching the webbing, staring at two blood-spattered bodies, and realize that the cost of keeping *Victor Hansen* for Marseguro had been higher than he'd realized.

They gathered the dead, took them by elevator down to the full gravity of the outermost deck, and laid them out in two rooms, the crew of *Victor Hansen* in one, the dead Holy Warriors in the other. Byrne, the commander, was among the dead; none of the remaining three outranked the others. Andy left them, under guard, to perform whatever rites they considered appropriate before the bodies were recycled, and went in search of Simon Goodfellow.

Of course, now that Richard was back on board, Andy was no longer the commanding officer of the *Victor Hansen*, but Richard seemed to be in no condition to take over. He'd barely spoken. Andy had last seen him sitting in the room with the bodies of Melody, Pierre, and Munish, the other Marseguroite casualty, head bowed, hands clenched in front of him.

Andy found Goodfellow in the simulator room. "Good work with the lights," he said. "I take it you've successfully rebooted the computer?"

"Sort of," Simon said. He sat at his data terminal, watching monitors and chewing on his lower lip. "There's . . . resistance."

"Resistance? To what?"

Simon pointed at a display on the screen that looked to Andy like a tangle of multicolored noodles. "The AI is . . . confused."

"Confused? It's a machine!"

"It's a very smart machine. Artificial 'intelligence,' remember?"

Andy sighed. "*Why* is it confused?"

"I couldn't wipe its memory completely and still have it be any use to us," Simon said. "It's finding gaps in its data. It knows something has happened to it and it's wasting processing cycles trying to reason it out. In human terms, it's suffered a massive concussion and partial amnesia."

"Uh-huh," Andy said. "So what are you doing to . . . de-confuse it?"

"Holding its hand," Simon said. He held up his own. "Figuratively. I'm watching it work its way through its memories. When it runs into a hole, I plug it with a reassuring subroutine that essentially tells it to move along, there's nothing to worry about there. It's worked to a certain extent. The lights came on when I asked for them, and I seem to have control of various other systems throughout the ship, but everything is still . . . uncertain. Not every command is obeyed, or even acknowledged."

"So we still don't have complete control."

"No," Simon said. He frowned at Andy as if seeing him for the first time. "Didn't you go to see if the Holy Warriors were sneaking aboard again?"

"Yes," Andy said neutrally. "Some time ago."

"And . . . ?"

"They were. We fought them off. They're mostly dead."

"Ah, good." Simon turned back to his console.

"Captain Hansen is back aboard," Andy said, mainly

just to see if he could puncture Simon's geekish focus on the computer. To his surprise, Simon swung around at once, a huge grin on his face.

"Excellent! Just what we need!" He jerked a thumb at the console. "One reason the AI is struggling is that it is missing its captain. I've completely wiped any memory of the Holy Warriors taking command, so as far as it's concerned, Richard Hansen should be issuing its orders . . . although it's confused enough that it's been letting me issue a few. When it shuts me out, though, it seems to be because it has suddenly realized I'm not the real captain. If Captain Hansen can come down here, we might be able to shock the system into some sort of stability."

Andy thought of Richard, sitting numbly in the makeshift morgue, and his jaw clenched. "The AI isn't the only system that needs to be shocked into stability," he growled. He'd been crouched down on his heels while he talked to Simon; now he snapped to his feet. "Captain Hansen will be down in a few minutes," he said, turned, and went to fetch him.

When Andy King returned, Richard tried to ignore him as he had before: but Andy wouldn't let him.

"Why the hell," Andy snarled, "are you still sitting there?" He grabbed Richard's arm and hauled him to his feet. "Captain. Sir. Technician Goodfellow requests that you assist him in the rebooting of the ship's AI."

"You go," Richard said. He tried to pull free. Andy didn't let go. In fact, he pulled Richard's arm behind his back and shoved his face up against the cold metal wall.

"I am not the captain," Andy said into his ear, his voice a burning whisper. "You are."

"You can't—" Richard tried to struggle, but Andy was a Selkie. He pushed Richard hard to the wall again.

"I can't make you act like a captain? No, I can't. But if you aren't the captain anymore, Richard, then I can damn well try to knock some sense back into you. You didn't answer my question. Why the hell are sitting in here with three dead bodies when you've got a ship to get back up and running?"

Cheek stinging, Richard felt a flicker of anger. "You don't understand, damn you," he grated, his words slightly distorted. "I got them killed. All three of them. If I'd made better decisions when we reached orbit . . . if I'd never gone down to meet 'Jacob' . . . hell, if I'd never insisted we come back to Earth in the first place . . ."

"Don't be so full of yourself! Everyone on the *Victor Hansen* is a volunteer. Everyone knew the risks. Some of us even knew the risks of having an inexperienced captain at the helm—lots of sailors on this ship, 'sir'—and yet we still decided to come. And as for you 'insisting' this ship come back to Earth with the vaccine, I seem to remember a certain Council of duly elected representatives having a little something to do with that decision. Or did you get yourself crowned king sometime while I wasn't paying attention?"

The flicker of anger fanned to a flame. "I'm still responsible," Richard snarled. "The Council agreed, but I pushed for it. They felt they owed—"

"Owed you what? Gratitude for saving them from Cheveldeoff? Who wouldn't have shown up at all if you'd never found Marseguro in the first place?" Andy said. "Hell, Richard, I don't see why you should be so cut up over the deaths of three Marseguroites, considering how many thousands you helped kill."

The flame roared into a bonfire of fury. Richard shoved back hard, threw Andy off him, and spun to face his First Officer, fists clenched. "You know how much I hate what I was, what I did. How dare you—"

"How dare you risk all the rest of our lives letting yourself sink into self-pity?" Andy snarled. "The mistakes you made when we entered this system are *nothing* compared to what you did before. But you managed to move on. You redeemed yourself. So move on again.

Redeem yourself again. Snap out of this stupid funk and start acting like the captain again or, by God, maybe there'll be four corpses cooling in here."

"That's enough!" Richard roared. "You want a captain? Fine. I'm captain. And you're—"

Under arrest, he'd started to say, but he suddenly realized just how ridiculous that would sound. His anger evaporated like a puff of air in a vacuum.

"—absolutely right," he finished, almost under his breath.

"Sir?" said Andy. "I couldn't quite hear that last bit."

Richard snorted. "Yeah, right. Okay. You win. Take me to Simon. Let's get this ship up and running." He managed a wan smile. "And, uh... confine yourself to quarters for insubordination. Not now. When it's convenient."

"Aye, aye, sir!" Andy snapped off a salute. Then he grinned. "Welcome back, Richard."

"Thanks," Richard said. He took one long final look at the bodies, each tucked neatly beneath a blue Holy Warrior blanket. If he'd gotten them killed, the least he could do was make sure their deaths weren't wasted. Down below, the Avatar was on the march. Another race of moddies was threatened with extinction. Around the planet, unknown thousands of survivors squatted in hiding in deathly fear of the plague.

Their mission wasn't over: far from it.

He turned away from the corpses of his crew. "Lead on." Then he followed Andy back into the corridors of the *Victor Hansen*.

Chapter 15

BACK AT THE FREE Selkie Republic outpost, Emily found Sarah McLean in the wardroom, eating a nondescript slab of something that might have been animal, vegetable, or mineral—it was hard to tell. With Captain Wu standing a diplomatic distance behind her and Shelby watching from the corner, bare feet pulled up onto the bottom of his chair, arms around his knees, Emily made her plea. The President chewed and swallowed automatically while she listened, but as Emily wound down, she lowered her fork and pushed her plate aside. "The Council decided not to warn them," she said. She sounded tired.

"Because of the risk to your people," Emily said. "But you wouldn't be risking any of *your* people. Just me."

"My people would be at risk escorting you . . ."

"I'm not asking for that," Emily said. "Just get me close. I'll walk in."

Silence. Emily glanced at Shelby: his wide green eyes were locked on her.

"It sounds foolishly dangerous," McLean said finally.

"It's important to me," Emily said. "I know you have decided that you do not want to risk any of your people contacting the Kemonomimi until the Avatar has either been dealt with, or . . . not. That's your decision. But as a Marseguroite, with fresh memories of what the Holy

Warriors did to us, it's important to me to try to save the Kemonomimi from the same horror." *Seize the moral high ground!* she thought. "They're family, in a way: we all carry some of Victor Hansen's genes."

More silence. Emily hoped the President was feeling at least slightly ashamed. Maybe even enough to provide her with support after all. She didn't really relish the idea of walking into the Kemonomimi camp on her own.

But if she'd shamed the President at all, she hadn't shamed her that much.

"Very well," McLean's said suddenly. "Captain Wu."

"Yes, Madame President?" Wu said, coming up to stand beside Emily.

"Do not risk detection, but deliver Miss Wood as close to the Kemonomimi village as you safely can. Provide her with food and water and a landsuit. Give her a communicator. If you succeed, Miss Wood, or if the Kemonomimi allow you to leave, you may use the communicator to call the sub. You may also use it to call for assistance if you run into trouble *before* you reach the Kemonomimi. But if you call for assistance after you reach the Kemonomimi, you will not receive any. We will not attempt a rescue. Do you understand?"

"Yes," Emily said.

"Do you understand, Captain Wu? You are not to attempt to rescue Miss Wood, even if the Kemonomimi arrest her and threaten to kill her and you learn of it."

"I understand," Wu said.

"Miss Wood," McLean said. "We have no wish to see the Kemonomimi eradicated. But we do not trust them, and we will not expose ourselves to them. We have, however, chosen to trust you, and to trust that you will not do anything that would harm the Free Selkie Republic. Please do not betray that trust."

Of all the— "I won't," Emily grated.

"Then good luck." The President, stood, tossing the

napkin that had been spread on her lap onto the table as she did so. "If you'll excuse me . . ." She glanced into the corner. "Shelby?"

"But, Mom—"

"Now."

With an exaggerated sigh, Shelby plopped his feet onto the floor and followed his mother out of the wardroom.

As the door closed behind them, Wu looked at Emily. "I won't disobey her," she said quietly. "If you get into trouble, we won't be there to rescue you."

"I know."

Wu sighed. "All right. If we leave in a couple of hours, we can have you there by first light. It means traveling all night, but you can sleep on the sub, and we're divided into day and night watches here, anyway. The crew will be fresh. Will that suit you?"

Emily shrugged. "I don't suppose it matters."

"I'll go prepare the sub, then, and get your supplies loaded." Wu gave her a long, level look. "I hope you know what you're doing." She turned and went out.

"So do I," Emily muttered. "So do I!"

Two hours later she entered the sub through its wet porch, toweled herself off, and padded forward to the control room. Wu greeted her. "We mostly just have bunks in this sub," she said, "but you can have my cabin if you want. It's the first hatch on your left as you go forward."

"Thank you," Emily said. "What about you?"

Wu laughed. "Don't worry about me. I'm a night person."

"Wake me when we're close."

"I will." Wu made shooing motions. "Go on. Rest. You're going to need it."

Emily nodded and went through the forward hatch. She found Wu's tiny cabin at once, but then her stomach growled. She hadn't eaten anything since . . . well, she couldn't remember. *Better fuel up,* she thought. There was a tiny galley in the bow of the sub; she headed that way along the narrow corridor, feeling the throbbing of the engines under her feet.

They were underway.

Three days into the Holy Warriors' ten-day march to the Kemonomimi, the Avatar sat on one of the two camp stools at the mouth of his tent and looked out at falling rain. It had started around noon, and by midafternoon had been coming down so hard he'd been forced to call a halt. Their tents could keep them dry, and they had enhanced-vision equipment that ensured they could see despite the sheets of falling water, but nothing could keep them from getting bogged down in the mud and slipping on rain-slicked vegetation and lichen-covered stones. They'd have to wait it out.

Which he was doing, with ill humor, wondering why God Itself couldn't make things just a little easier for Its servants, when Grand Deacon von Eschen, hooded and cloaked in rain gear, splashed across the ankle-deep stream running down the middle of the camp and trudged up the slope to Karl Rasmusson.

The Avatar gestured for von Eschen to sit on the second camp stool. "I hope you're here to tell me the scouts have spotted blue sky headed our way," he said.

"I'm afraid not, Your Holiness." Von Eschen shook his head. "But we've just had a message from *Sanctification*."

"They've found more vaccine?" the Avatar exclaimed, his spirits lifting.

"No," the Grand Deacon said. "The message was not from Michael Byrne. The message was from Richard Hansen."

The Avatar froze. "Impossible."

"So I would have thought," von Eschen said. "But there is no doubt about it."

"How did he . . . ?"

Von Eschen said nothing.

Damn it, God, why are you testing me like this? Karl snarled silently. "And the message?"

"I brought it with me." From underneath his dripping navy-blue rain vestments, he pulled a datapad, and thumbed it to life.

Richard Hansen's face appeared on the tiny screen, and his voice, tinny but recognizable, rang out in the tent. "Your Holiness," he said. "It is my pleasure to inform you that *MSS Victor Hansen* is once again in the hands of her Marseguroite crew, though I must sadly say that this was not accomplished without considerable loss of life, primarily among the Holy Warriors you sent to board her.

"The three surviving Warriors have been vaccinated and imprisoned. Please don't concern yourself about their safety.

"I'm contacting you now to urge you to reconsider your attack on the Kemonomimi. By now they must know you are coming, and will either fade away into the mountains, or will stand and fight. In either case, you will not find their Purification an easy task. It will be made less easy now that we control this starship.

"I propose that you return to Paradise Island while I talk to the Kemonomimi. There is no need to start the reconstruction of Earth with a war. Peaceful coexistence and cooperation would—"

"Kill it," the Avatar snarled.

Von Eschen turned off the display. "The message ends with a request for a response," he said. "If you do not agree to his terms, Hansen says, he will use the resources of the starship to stop our advance."

The Avatar snorted. "What resources? His crew scattered *Sanctification*'s assault craft to the four corners of the world when we took the ship. They can't retrieve them quickly, if they can retrieve them at all. He only has a handful of Selkies and nonmods to begin with, hardly enough to turn the tide against our army. And

they themselves dismantled *Sanctification*'s Orbital
Bombardment System." He shook his head. "We do not
answer. We ignore his 'demands.' I don't know how he
managed to retake the ship, but it's of no concern. Our
concern is with the Kemonomimi. We must Purify them
to prove to God we are worthy of Its blessing and protection once more." He looked up; a patch of blue sky
had just drifted over the mountain peak to the west, and
the rain had definitely lessened. "Ah," he said. "Grand
Deacon, I believe we may have just passed a test." He
got to his feet. "We'll be able to continue our march in
the morning. Make sure everyone is ready."

"Yes, Your Holiness," the Grand Deacon said. He
stood, saluted, then splashed back across the camp.

The Avatar looked back up at the clearing sky. "Rot in
orbit, 'Captain' Hansen," he said. "You gave us the vaccine. Your role in the work of God is done." He looked
around the camp. "Mine remains unfinished."

Chris Keating stood with Victor Hansen and Cleopatra
inside the waiting area of the air terminal building Hansen had made his headquarters, watching the rain sluice
down the runway. "It won't last the day," Hansen said,
looking to the west, where the sky was already notice-
ably brighter, although to the east the mountains were
still completely lost in the clouds. The higher elevations
were, no doubt, receiving a prodigious dump of that
strange white stuff Chris had read about but had never
encountered in person: snow.

Only the highest of the inaccessible peaks along the
western shore of Marseguro's lone continent sported
a crown of snow, and Chris had never been up there.
No one on Marseguro had, as far as he knew. Certainly
no Selkie would dare attempt to climb a mountain in a
landsuit. They had enough trouble staying comfortable
in warm, moist air. The cold, dry air of a mountain peak
would be torture.

Wish I could haul Emily Wood up there, he thought.

"Tomorrow morning, then," Victor Hansen said. He put his arm around Cleopatra's waist and gave it a squeeze, then looked at Chris. "I'll have your pack prepared tonight. Warm coat, good boots, plenty of food and water. You'll have an escort, of course. They'll get you as close as is safe for them. You won't need to fear getting lost."

And you won't need to fear I'll simply take off, Chris thought. "I'm ready," he said out loud.

"Good." Victor returned his gaze to the rain-spattered windows. "We haven't been able to get a good read on the Avatar's position for a couple of days, but he can't be making good time in this weather. You should reach him in about four days. Five at the outside."

Chris nodded. "Does that give you enough time to get your bomb into position in the pass?"

Cleopatra nuzzled Hansen's neck. "The bomb will be where it needs to be," he said, rubbing his cheek against the top of her head. "I promise you that. You do your job, and we'll do ours. And then, once the Body Purified has been ... well, Purified, in their own twisted sense of that word ... then you and I can turn our attention to the Selkies of Marseguro."

"I wish you'd tell me more about this weapon of yours,' Chris said. "The one that will wipe out all the Selkies. I'm dying of curiosity."

"All in good time," Victor Hansen said. "All in good time."

A shaft of sunlight speared down on the runway.

Tap tap tap. Emily jerked awake in the pitch-darkness of her borrowed cabin. *What was ... ?*

Tap tap tap. "Miss Wood?" said a voice muffled by the steel door. "Miss Wood? Captain Wu sends her compliments and asks you to join her in the control room."

Emily sat up and flicked on the lights, winced, squinted, and called, "Thank you. I'll be along shortly."

She used the head, brushed her teeth, put on her skinsuit, and within half an hour joined the captain in the control room, still yawning. Wu held two steaming cups of something; without a word she handed one to Emily, who sipped it cautiously. It was hot and not *too* unpleasant, if you concentrated really hard on the short list of all the worst things you had tasted in your life. "I can't send an escort with you," Wu said, "but nobody told me I can't help you with a little offshore reconnaissance."

Emily blinked at her. "I don't understand."

"We're about two kilometers out from Newshore and we've just launched a micro-ARV," Wu said. "Thought you might at least want to have a look at where you're going before you head there."

"I appreciate that," Emily said. "I hope you won't get in trouble."

"No reason I should," Wu said cheerfully. She drained her mug. "Finished with that?"

Emily nodded and handed her her own mug, still half full. Despite the liquid's foul taste, she had to admit she somehow felt more awake than she had just moments before. Wu handed both mugs off to a crewman, then led Emily to one of the stations along the walls. Large vidscreens curved around the seat there, occupied by a young Selkie woman who gave Emily a quick smile before turning her attention back to her controls. "All right, Malia, let's see what we can see."

"Aye, aye, ma'am," the crewwoman said, and pushed a tiny joystick forward with her right thumb while her left hand played over a keyboard. The screens lit up.

The ARV was currently just a few centimeters above the almost perfectly flat water. Emily could see the coastline, rock-strewn and dotted with trees, a cluster of buildings, a pier. Forested hills rose all around the town, climbing up in the distance to jagged mountains, silhouetted against pink eastern sky. A good-sized river emptied into the sea through the town, a curved wooden bridge spanning it not far from its mouth.

"A little more elevation, if you please, Malia," said Captain Wu. "And then zoom in on the town."

Malia nodded and pushed the joystick further forward, tapping again with her left hand. The buildings seemed to rush toward them at the same time as they dropped away below them, and now Emily could make some kind of sense out of them. An aircraft sat motionless on a runway. That low building with the single tower with the glass-walled room atop it must be the terminal. Houses were scattered among the trees, and just visible further inland slightly taller buildings rose, the largest maybe four stories—presumably Newshore's commercial district, if it had such a thing.

But then Emily forgot all about Newshore's buildings as she caught her first glimpse of its people.

Two figures strolled around the aircraft, apparently inspecting it, and although they were quite small on the screen, she could see them well enough to realize they looked . . . odd.

"Can we zoom in even more?"

"Of course," Wu said. "Malia."

Again the scene rushed toward her. The image danced and flickered, but now she could see the people more clearly.

They were heavily furred over every inch of their naked bodies. One had fur of almost pure white, with black stripes circling his torso and legs and . . . was that a tail?

It lashed as he turned to say something to his companion. Yes, definitely a tail.

His ears were large and pointed and tufted with black, and though located on the side of his head, not the top, seemed capable of independent movement, like a cat's. His eyes, too, looked catlike, with slit pupils instead of a normal human's—

She caught herself, shocked at her own turn of thought. Since when did a Selkie think of a nonmod as a "normal human"?

Since she came face-to-face with a version of humanity as different from her as she is from a nonmod, she thought. She glanced at Wu, who was staring at the screen with fascination and a hint of disgust on her face. *No wonder the Free Selkie Republic doesn't want to have anything to do with the Kemonomimi,* she thought. *They're not just different, they're* too *different. Too animallike.*

And what will they think of us? she wondered.

Well, I guess I'll find that out soon enough.

The second Kemonomimi, a female—a *woman,* Emily consciously corrected herself—laughed at something the man had said. She was pitch-black from nose to tail, sleek and muscular and glistening and . . .

. . . beautiful, Emily thought. *She's beautiful.*

But oh, so strange.

"Pull out again," Wu said. "Let's see if we can find any more."

The image expanded. The two Kemonomimi disappeared around the back side of the aircraft. At the same time, though, a much larger group came out of the terminal building. "Zoom in on those," Wu said. Malia nodded and adjusted her controls. The image shifted, swelled—

—and Emily gasped out loud.

Wu turned on Emily, her face suddenly hard and unfriendly. "What is *he* doing there?" she snarled. "Have you been lying to us?"

Emily didn't answer. She couldn't.

On the screen, moving easily alongside half a dozen Kemonomimi wearing body armor and carrying rifles, she saw someone she'd never thought to see again: Chris Keating.

But even more impossibly, standing next to him was a man who looked exactly like Richard Hansen, holding hands with a sleek white Kemonomimi woman.

"Richard is in space," she said finally. "You saw . . . we all saw . . . him launch in the shuttle."

"We saw him launch. We don't know where he went after that," Wu said. "Maybe he flew here. And maybe your volunteering to warn the Kemonomimi was just your way of rejoining him. Maybe you're planning to betray us to the Kemonomimi."

"What?" Emily turned to stare at her, honestly bewildered. "To what possible end?"

"To . . ." Wu paused. "To . . ." She blinked, and then suddenly laughed. "I have no idea." Her laugh faded. "But whether it makes sense or not, that's what the President and Council would think if they were here."

"Good thing they're not, then," Emily said. She shook her head. "I don't know what's going on. That can't be Richard. But I do know who the other man is."

"Who?"

"Chris Keating." Emily said the name like it left a bad taste in her mouth, which wasn't too far from the truth.

"I take it you don't like him," Wu said dryly. She looked at the screen again. Keating and the man-who-looked-like-Richard were talking. One of the Kemonomimi handed Chris a large backpack and helped him struggle into it.

"I hate him," Emily spat. "He's from Marseguro. But he betrayed us. He activated the signal that brought the Holy Warriors down on our heads. And he's the one who brought the plague to Earth."

"Yeah?" Wu looked at Emily. "Maybe we should thank him."

Emily's mouth tightened, but she let that pass. "I don't know how he's survived. And I sure as hell don't know what he's doing with the Kemonomimi. He's a fanatic. He hates moddies, *all* moddies; lives and breathes the *Wisdom of The Avatar*. If he's helping them, or they're helping him, then either they're deluded or he is."

"Like your friend, there?"

"That's not Richard!"

Wu held up her hands. "Whatever you say. But you have to admit it looks—"

It suddenly sank in. "It's another clone," Emily said. "It must be."

Wu's eyes widened. "Another clone of Victor Hansen?" She stared at the man on the screen, who gave the Kemonomimi woman a lingering kiss on the lips, then took Keating by the arm and turned him inland, so their backs were to the sub. "But why is he here?"

"I don't know," Emily said. "But I think it's about time I went ashore and found out."

Wu stared at the screen for another long moment, then said. "I think you're right. Helm, take us south around the headland."

"Aye, aye, ma'am," said the Selkie at the sub's main controls.

Wu looked at Emily. "There's a good place to swim ashore there, and you'll be out of sight of Newshore. And if you change your mind, we can pick you up again there before you make contact."

Emily shook her head. "I won't change my mind." She pointed at the screen. "Especially not after seeing *him*."

Twenty minutes later they hovered in twenty-five meters of water at the mouth of the narrow cove just south of Newshore's wider bay. Emily, wearing her black land-suit, with her waterproof pack of supplies strapped to her back, sat on the edge of the wet porch with her webbed feet in the cold water. "Last chance to reconsider," said Wu, the only other Selkie in the compartment; this close to Kemonomimi territory, Wu had doubled up everyone at the duty stations on the bridge, so twice as many eyes were watching the sonar, radar, and visual displays.

"Thank you for your help," Emily said. "Tell President McLean I'll be in touch."

"I'll tell her," Wu said. "Don't make me into a liar."

"I'll do my best." Emily gave a final wave, then slipped into the water.

She swam ashore uneventfully, never looking back at the sub. She clambered out onto wet rocks, turned to take a last look out to where she had left the sub . . . and jumped back so suddenly she tripped and fell painfully onto her rear end as a head rose out of the water directly in front of her.

Then, as the rest of the Selkie's body appeared, surprise gave way to dismay. "Shelby?"

He stood in water waist-deep, four or five meters offshore, holding his own dripping waterproof pack in his right hand. "My mother's wrong," he said. "She should have sent help with you."

"So you decided to come yourself?" Emily climbed to her feet and winced as she rubbed her bruised bottom. "Shelby, this is nuts! I can't let you do this."

"You can't stop me," he said. "I'm volunteering, just like you. I've thought long and hard about this. We need to warn these people. They're moddies, just like us. I don't know why my mother won't—"

"She's President," Emily said. "Her responsibility is to her people. *Your* people. The Free Republic has stayed hidden for decades. Warning the Kemonomimi could expose the Republic to the Body, if the Body prevails. She doesn't want to risk that. And she certainly doesn't want to risk her son. Nor do I." She shook her head violently. "No, Shelby, you can't come. You don't even have a landsuit, for God's sake!"

He held up his pack. "Want to bet?"

Emily ground her teeth. "Nevertheless, you can't come."

"You can't stop me."

"Oh, yeah?" Emily said. "There's a communicator in the backpack. I'm going to call Captain Wu and—"

Something in Shelby's expression stopped her. He

wasn't even looking at her: he was looking beyond her, and his eyes had widened.

Already knowing what she would see, Emily turned around to face the armed Kemonomimi on the shore.

There were half a dozen of them, five men and one black-furred woman who held Emily's backpack in one hand and a pistol in the other. They wore helmets and body armor. Four of the men carried rifles, all of which were pointed in their general direction. The fifth man carried something else: a massive rocket launcher that Emily was sure a nonmod would have had to set up on a tripod. He had it aimed out to sea. It took her a moment to realize what that meant.

"No!" she yelled, but it was already too late: with an earsplitting shriek, a missile blasted from the launcher and lanced across the water of the cove. Emily whirled, Shelby following suit, just in time to see the missile plunge beneath the surface of the water. A moment later, with a dull whump!, a column of water and steam erupted into the still morning air.

Then furred arms seized Emily from behind and she was dragged across the beach. Another Kemonomimi grabbed Shelby and pulled him after her.

Behind them, the suddenly troubled water of the cove splashed erratically against the rocks.

Chapter 16

THE LOADED BACKPACK Victor Hansen gave Chris was heavy, but not much heavier than he'd often carried when he hiked on Marseguro. Inside Hansen's office, with Cleopatra sitting on the edge of the desk most distractingly, Hansen had gone over its contents: ultralight tent and sleeping bag, collapsible heater/stove, dried food, a water purifier bottle, flashlight, rope . . . the usual accoutrements of any hiking trip. The camouflage-patterned clothes he'd been given were warm, flexible, and tough. So were the boots. A self-adjusting warm/cool coat rounded out his equipment.

The one thing he *didn't* have was a weapon, unless you counted his belt knife. "They're more likely to shoot you on sight if you're armed," Hansen said. "And right up until you get there, you'll be escorted."

Chris didn't buy Hansen's excuse for a minute, but he was hardly in a position to argue.

"Any questions?" Hansen asked.

"No, I don't think so," Chris said. He adjusted the pack on his back. "I'm set."

"No more delay, then." Hansen held out his hand to Cleopatra; she took it, and they all went out onto the runway, where they were promptly joined by six waiting Kemonomimi, wearing helmets and body armor (but still no pants or boots), and carrying rifles, sidearms, sword-like blades and backpacks bigger than Chris'. Two more Kemonomimi, a man and a woman, were inspecting the aircraft Chris had arrived on. The sun hadn't cleared the mountains yet, but the cloudless sky was washed with pale pink, fading to deep blue out over the ocean.

Victor Hansen turned him away from the view and pointed inland. "You're heading toward that notch in the ridge where the river comes down. You should make it by nightfall. There's a good campsite near the top. We'll send up reconnaissance today to pin down the Avatar's location, but with any luck you'll get to him the day after tomorrow." He turned and kissed Cleo full on the lips, lingeringly; she rose on her toes and pushed her hips against him. Chris swallowed and looked away. A moment later Hansen took his arm and led him inland; Chris glanced back to see Cleo walking, hips and tail undulating in a most . . . interesting . . . fashion, back toward the terminal.

The six armed Kemonomimi fell in behind Hansen and Chris. Hansen led them to where the river ran along the airfield's border, stopping when the short-cropped bot-mowed airfield grass gave way to the longer, untidier flora of the wild. There Hansen held out his hand. Chris took it. "Good luck," Hansen said. "With your help, Earth will finally be free of the Body . . . and soon, Marseguro will be free of the Selkies." He released Chris' hand, then stepped back.

There didn't seem to be anything to say to that, so Chris took the hint and started up the trail that ran alongside the river, shadowed by his taciturn escort. Hansen hadn't introduced him to any of them—the *only* Kemonomimi Hansen had introduced him to so far had been Cleopatra—and looking at their grim, fur-covered faces, Chris guessed they weren't particularly interested in his introducing himself. *It's going to be a quiet trip,* he thought.

Well, that suited him. Making small talk with the

abominations that had caused God to turn Its hand against Earth didn't exactly appeal to him anyway.

He had work to do . . . if not *quite* the work Victor Hansen thought.

"No reply," Cordelia Raum told Richard.

It had been twenty-four hours since he'd issued his ultimatum to the Avatar. The Avatar, it appeared, had no intention of responding.

"Did you really expect one?" Andy said.

Richard shook his head. "Not really. But I didn't see the harm in offering him a way out."

Andy snorted. "A way out. As if his fate is sealed if he refuses to surrender to us. Do you know something you haven't told me?"

Richard rubbed his forehead. "I wish," he said. "But you know as well as I do what resources we have to draw on." He stared gloomily at the blue curve of the Earth on the main bridge display. "I think we were too smart when we set up the Submerge routine."

"If we'd left the assault craft on board, the Body would probably have them now," Andy pointed out. "And if they did, the Kemonomimi would already be dead."

Richard sighed. "I know, I know. So. What *have* we got that we can use against the Avatar?"

"Some pretty heavy weapons," Andy said. "Some ground vehicles, but I don't think they'll do us any good in that terrain. Light aircraft, unarmed. Cargo shuttles, too unmaneuverable to be of any use. And, currently, two personnel shuttles: the four-person flyer you came up in and the one the Holy Warriors . . . won't be needing anymore."

"Can we command that one?"

"Simon Goodfellow says yes," Andy said. "The reboot is proceeding smoothly, and that shuttle has been slaved to our AI. It will recognize the same chain of command."

"And it will hold . . . ?"

"Maybe twenty people at most, lightly armed," Andy said. "Fewer if they take some of the heavier equipment."

"Not enough, in other words."

"No."

"And no chance of getting one of the assault craft back."

Andy hesitated. "Define 'chance.' "

Richard straightened in the captain's chair. "You've pinpointed their locations?"

"Define 'pinpoint.' " Andy held up a hand. "I'm not being funny. We know within, say, a hundred kilometers, where each one went down. Presumably, if we took one of our surviving shuttles down, we could, eventually and with luck, locate them all."

Richard sighed. "I hear a 'but' coming."

"Good ears. Are you sure you're not Selkie?" Andy nodded. "But . . . although we know approximately where they are, we have no idea whether they're intact. They were never meant to fly themselves out of orbit. Simon programmed them as best he could, but he won't guarantee—"

"Simon won't guarantee that the sun will come up tomorrow," Richard said. "But it always has so far."

Andy made a noncommittal sound.

Richard rubbed his forehead again. "Let's start with the basics. Where are they?"

"One is somewhere in the Himalayas," Andy said. "Quite possibly in a crumpled heap in a glacial crevasse. One came down near the southern tip of Africa. Fairly flat there, it might be okay. And one is actually remarkably close to the Kemonomimi and the Free Selkie Republic . . . but since it's about two hundred kilometers offshore, I suspect it's too deep for any Selkie to reach."

"Even with a sub?"

Andy shrugged. "Unknown."

Richard nodded slowly. "All right. We have two shuttles. We send one to Africa with a recovery team. As for the other, perhaps if I ask nicely, President McLean will—"

"Transmission from the surface for Captain Hansen," the computer said suddenly.

"Computer, identify source," Richard said.

"Source self-identifies as President Sarah McLean of the Free Selkie Republic."

Richard shot a look at Andy. "Maybe Earth Selkies are telepathic." He raised his voice. "Computer, put it through."

The main display screen suddenly showed Sarah McLean, and Richard knew instantly something was wrong. For the first time since he'd met her, she looked flustered. Selkies' eyes always looked a bit watery to him, since they were so much larger, but hers looked so watery he could only think she'd been crying. And her gray-streaked black hair, longer than that of any Marseguroite Selkie he'd ever seen, but usually kept tightly under control in a bun or pony tail, hung loose around her face.

"President McLean?" Richard said. "What—"

"The Kemonomimi captured Emily as soon as she landed," the President said, her voice tight. "They must have spotted the sub. One of the Kemonomimi had a rocket launcher loaded with some kind of antisubmarine depth charge. Lia Wu's sub was severely damaged, but she managed to slip away before a ship rounded the headland from Newshore. She may still have to abandon ship before she gets back to this outpost."

Richard found he was gripping the arms of his chair so tightly his fingers hurt. He forced himself to relax them. "She's made contact, then," he said, keeping his voice steady. "That's what she wanted."

"She wasn't the only one the Kemonomimi took," McLean said. "They've got my . . ." A hard swallow.

"They've got Shelby. My son. He apparently stowed away on the sub. I thought he was just sulking in his room here on the habitat. I never thought . . ." She swallowed again. "He swam ashore behind Emily. The Kemonomimi have him, too."

"Emily will look after Shelby," Richard said. "She won't let them hurt him."

"How will she stop them?" The President's eyes suddenly blazed. "Two of Wu's crew were injured in that attack, Captain Hansen. One of them may not make it . . . absolutely won't, if the crew has to abandon ship. And now my son is being held by those . . . savages? I want him back, Captain Hansen." She leaned forward, so her face almost filled the screen. "I gave you your ship back. Now I want you to forget the Avatar for the time being. I want my son back!

"I can't attempt a rescue myself," she went on. "The whole Free Selkie Republic only has half a dozen subs, the nearest is three days away, and Wu's is the largest. But *you* can be down there within hours."

Richard sat silent for a long moment. "If we attempt a rescue, we may get them both killed," he said.

"If we don't, they may kill them anyway," the President said. Her face hardened. "This is not a negotiable request, Captain Hansen. If you want the cooperation of the Free Selkie Republic in distributing your vaccine— distributing it to nonmods who some of our people might well think we'd be better off leaving to die—you will attempt to rescue my son. Do I make myself clear?"

Richard felt his temper rising, but pushed it down. "Perfectly," he said in as even a tone as he could manage. "But I hope you know what you're doing." Richard glanced at Andy. "Change of plan. Forget the assault craft in Africa. We need to get whatever forces we can on the ground near Newshore as soon as possible."

"Aye, aye, sir," Andy said. He turned on his heel, went

to his station, pulled on a headset and began talking in a low voice.

Richard turned back to McLean. "I have very limited resources," he said. "Far fewer than I'd hoped. But we'll bring down as many people as we can. We should be able to land within a few hours' walk of Newshore without the Kemonomimi seeing us. We'll reconnoiter on foot and then decide on a course of action."

"The Free Selkie Republic thanks you," McLean said formally. Then her voice softened. "And I thank you. I won't forget this, Captain."

"I'll keep you posted," Richard said. "Captain Hansen out. Computer, discontinue link."

The screen blanked, and Richard, keeping a tight hold on his own emotions, went to talk to Andy.

The Kemonomimi tied Emily's and Shelby's hands behind their backs, gagged them, then propelled them up a muddy track to a badly deteriorated paved road that ran along the shore until it plunged through the woods above the headland. The black-furred female led the way, with Emily walking between two of the males right behind her and Shelby, accompanied by his own pair of guards, behind her. The big Kemonomimi with the rocket launcher brought up the rear.

She became aware that the Kemonomimi on her left was staring at her. She stared back just as boldly.

His red-furred face had a hint of a stripe pattern, darker fur forming a kind of W shape over his eyes radiating out from his mouth and nose. Unlike a true cat, he didn't have long vibrissae, and his mouth and nose were close to human: no harelip. Thicker, darker hair, rather like a mane, swelled out from under the back of his helmet and flowed partway down the back of his armored vest.

"Can you talk?" he said suddenly.

The words shocked Emily. She realized she'd been thinking of him as an animal, not a human. *Just as the Holy Warriors think of us,* she thought.

"Do you understand me?" he said.

In fact she had a little trouble in that regard. His canines were sharper and longer than a nonmod's and they gave him a kind of lisping accent, with barely-there plosives. He made up for it with harsh gutturals, though.

The gag kept her from speaking, of course, but she nodded at him. His eyes widened, she felt a moment's satisfaction to think he had probably been thinking of her as something as inhuman as she'd been thinking of him ... and then she felt shame. She'd claimed she wanted to talk to the Kemonomimi. It looked like she'd get her chance. And all she could think about was how weird they were.

I didn't want to talk to them this *way,* she thought. *Not trussed up like a feastfish on Landing Day. Not a prisoner taken by force.*

What had happened to the sub?

How could she offer hope for a peaceful alliance after that unprovoked attack?

"Quiet," snarled the black-furred female, turning her head so that Emily could see her gleaming teeth. "It is for the Creator to talk to these creatures, not you."

"I am sorry, Ubasti," said the male, and after that he kept his eyes resolutely forward.

So she's in command, Emily thought. *Interesting.* And then ...

They're taking me to meet their Creator?

A few minutes later they came out of the patch of pine trees and left the road, striding across close-cropped green grass toward the landing strip Emily had seen from the sub, and the cluster of buildings alongside it. Looking to her left, she saw the water of Newshore Bay, houses close to the shore, small boats tied up to little piers, and the arched bridge she knew took the road they had been on over the river that emptied into the bay.

The nonmod who looked like Richard Hansen stood waiting for them by the terminal building, his arm around the white-furred female Kemonomimi she had seen from the sub, his own all-black attire—black pants, black boots, a black T-shirt, a black leather jacket—making a striking contrast to her, which Emily was quite sure was intentional. The stranger had a pistol holstered on one hip and a long knife or short sword sheathed on the other.

"Good work, Ubasti," the man said as they approached.

"Thank you, Creator," Ubasti said. She walked up to Emily and pulled the gag off her face with sudden, brutal force. Emily jerked her head and glared at her, but the black-furred Kemonomimi had already stepped past her to do the same to Shelby.

"What's your name?" the man said, his voice very much like Richard's, but full of an arrogance she'd never heard from her lover.

"Emily Wood," she said. "What's yours?"

The man cocked his head to one side, a gesture so much like one she had seen Richard do a thousand times that it made her heart ache; but his next words shocked her. "I'm Victor Hansen," he said. "And I'm your creator."

"That's impossible," Shelby said in the kind of sneering, contemptuous voice that only a teenager could manage. "Victor Hansen left Earth seventy years ago. He never came back."

"A lie," said the man who called himself Victor Hansen. "A lie told by the Body . . . and apparently by the Selkies, too."

"Prove it," Shelby said. Emily wanted to tell him to be quiet, but "Victor Hansen" just laughed.

"My dear fishboy," he said, "I don't have to prove anything to you. Now be quiet."

Shelby drew in his breath as though about to speak, but Ubasti's hand, still holding the pistol, lashed out. The butt of the gun clubbed the boy behind the ear, and he cried out and dropped to his knees, gasping, blood dripping onto the concrete.

Emily jerked at her bonds, but Ubasti's flat eyes turned toward her and she subsided. "There was no need for that!" she cried. "You could have killed him!"

"He won't interrupt again," Ubasti said.

"Now, now, Ubasti," Victor Hansen said. "I appreciate your devotion, but that was perhaps a little extreme. Please don't damage either of them further unless I tell you to."

Ubasti inclined her head in his direction. "Of course, Creator." She stepped back, but she didn't holster her gun and she resumed her watch on Emily.

Victor . . . Emily didn't know what else to call him . . . came closer to her. "So," he said. "Emily Wood. From Marseguro."

She blinked. "How did you . . . ?"

Victor laughed. "Where else could Selkies have come from?"

A light went on in her head. *He doesn't know. He doesn't know about the Free Selkie Republic. He thinks all the Selkies he's seen came with us from Marseguro.*

She wished she could warn Shelby.

"Yes," she said. "From Marseguro . . . like Chris Keating," she added, watching to see if the name meant anything.

If it did, Victor didn't let on. Which was also very Richard-like: Richard had the best poker face Emily had ever seen, when he wanted to use it.

"Tell me, Miss Wood," Victor said, looking at her once more. "Life on Marseguro, before the Body so unfortunately managed to locate you . . . was it good?"

"Better than we knew," Emily said. Those days before

the Holy Warriors announced their presence with blood and thunder seemed like a golden age from ancient history.

"My Kemonomimi, too, are working toward a world without the Body," Victor said. "So that they can enjoy, here on Earth, what you Selkies had for so long on Marseguro."

Emily said nothing.

"But there is a problem," Victor admitted. He looked from her to Shelby, who still sat with his head down, his breathing ragged. "You Selkies."

"Why is that a problem?" Emily said. "We're happy in the water, you're happy on land. We'll take the oceans, you can have everything else."

Victor laughed. "Miss Wood, are you trying to bargain with me? To negotiate?"

"There's no reason Kemonomimi and Selkies should be enemies," Emily said. "We're all moddies. Victor Hansen . . ." She hesitated. *Humor the insane,* her father used to say. *Just don't vote for them.* "*You* made us both."

"True, Miss Wood." Victor came close to her, uncomfortably close, and looked her in the eyes. "But there is one great distinction between you."

"They've got fur, we've got gills?" Emily said. It might have made Richard laugh. Victor only smiled.

"Besides that." He reached up and touched the side of her neck, where the high collar of the landsuit hid her gills. She had to hold on to herself to keep from flinching, though when Richard had touched her naked gills just two nights before . . .

Another difference between them, she thought.

"You were my biggest mistake," he said softly. "I had already created the perfect race of moddies, and yet I created another. If I believed in sin, or believed in any god, I would say I suffered from hubris.

"But there is no sin, no God, and no such thing as hubris. There is only life, a brief stumble from nothing-

ness to nothingness. What I did was not sin, but it was . . .
unwise. I thought that since I had created one race, I
should create another. But I was wrong."

He stepped back and put his arm affectionately
around the white-furred Kemonomimi woman. Ubasti's
eyes flicked from Emily to Victor as he did so, and Emily
thought she didn't look pleased. "I had already created
perfection. I could not create it twice. The Selkies were
inferior in every way to the Kemonomimi. I kept thinking I could improve them, somehow raise them to the
level of my first creation . . . but no. It wasn't to be.

"And then I made my second mistake—or so I presume, for I no longer remember making it. Nevertheless, it appears, from the evidence, that I felt pity for
your kind, my flawed, water-breathing creation. And so
I arranged for you to flee to Marseguro and escape the
Body Purified. I even sent along an imposter who could
pretend to be me, so that you would not be deprived of
your Creator; then (so I surmise) used my new life ex-
tension techniques to make myself younger and put myself into suspended animation until the time was right
to emerge and lead my Kemonomimi to their rightful
place as rulers of this planet."

Emily's eyes widened. *Oh . . . kay*, she thought. *He's
even crazier than I imagined. Good to know . . . I think.*

"I never dreamed you would one day return to Earth.
But now that you have . . . well. There is no room on this
planet for both my Kemonomimi and you Marseguroites. You will leave voluntarily, or I will drive you from
this planet. And soon," he said in a perfectly matter-
of-fact voice, "I will eradicate you. I should never have
allowed you to live in the first place. Always clean up
your messes: that's one of the first things I learned in lab
classes in university."

Emily didn't know what to say, because how *do* you
respond to the clone of the scientist who created your

entire race when he expresses his determination to wipe
it out? She felt a bit like Noah, except she didn't think
her version of God was going to tell her she would be
spared if she only built an ark.

Shelby raised his head. Blood had run down the side
of his neck and across his chest and belly, but his voice
was clear. "The real Victor Hansen is dead," he snarled,
"You're just a crazy clone." Ubasti made a move toward
him and he flinched, but Victor raised his hand sharply
and she stepped back again.

"I'm surprised to find," Victor said, "that the Selkies
of Marseguro have so willingly accepted the Body's pro-
paganda. Well, no matter. I know the truth, and so do
the Kemonomimi." With the hand that wasn't wrapped
around the woman's waist, he made a grand gesture,
encompassing sea, sky, and mountains. "This world is
theirs," he said. "The plague I engineered to kill the nonmodded humans has given it to them."

That was too much. "*You* didn't create any plague,"
Emily snapped. "My mother created it to protect Marseguro from the Body. Chris Keating brought it here by
accident. We would have done anything to stop it reaching Earth, if we could have."

Victor shook his head. "You are deluded," he said. "The
Selkies are inferior. They could never have engineered
something like this perfect plague. I have examined the
plague organism in detail, since it appeared and it became apparent I and my Kemonomimi were immune. I
have taken it apart and put it back together again. It is
clearly the work of a genius: clearly, in other words, mine.
I don't know how you Selkies got your hands on it, I confess. Most likely I sent samples along with you and the
man you falsely believed was Victor Hansen, back when
you fled Earth seventy years ago, as insurance against the
Body eventually finding you."

Emily was beginning to realize that arguing with Victor was a waste of breath. *Nothing I say will make the slightest dent in the self-centered fantasy world he's constructed,* she thought.

It's the gene-bomb. Victor Hansen's damned gene-bomb. He thought he could live forever through his clones. Instead, he just screwed them all up.

All except Richard . . . and that had been close.

Richard had told her what it had been like when the gene-bomb, partially defused in his case by the efforts of Body Security scientists, had gone off. He'd felt as if he were splitting in two, as if he had a new and unwanted personality in his head: the ghost, almost literally, of Victor Hansen.

All her life Emily had revered Victor Hansen as the creator of their race, the man who had, against all odds, successfully stolen, outfitted, and launched a starship with the first generation of Selkies on board in the very teeth of a Body assault and founded a new world where moddies and nonmods could live in peace.

And there was no doubt it was an amazing accomplishment, and he deserved to be honored for it.

But the great hero, the great founder of their world, the man whose statue she'd seen almost every day of her life growing up, had had more than one skeleton in his closet and quite possibly a few bats in his belfry. At the very least, he had been, without question, the biggest egomaniac old Earth had ever produced.

Unlike Richard, the clone in front of her seemed to have all of the original Victor Hansen's faults and none of his redeeming qualities. He had obviously filled in the gaps in his Victor Hansen-installed memories with an elaborate fantasy of his own devising so solid that it could not be shaken by mere facts . . . even the fact he couldn't actually remember creating the plague he now claimed as his own.

He's got all of Victor Hansen's genetically determined characteristics, untempered by the experiences of his later life, she thought. *He's like a teenager, so full of himself and his wants, so convinced that he's unique—not just unique, but superior—that he sees everything in black and white . . . and for him, the Kemonomimi are the good guys, and we, clearly, are the bad ones.*

She looked at the white-furred woman. She met Emily's eyes, opened her mouth—revealing alarmingly sharp teeth—and licked her lips with a long pink tongue. "What are you staring at, fishface?" she said.

"Now, now," said Victor. "Be polite, Cleo."

Cleo turned her head. "Why?" she said. "She's a Selkie. Subhuman. Why should I be polite to a subhuman?" She nuzzled his neck. "Ubasti got to blood the young one," she said, her voice almost a purr. "Let me try my claws on the female."

Victor's face went cold and he released her waist with a jerk. "No, Cleopatra," he said, his voice like ice. "You will obey me."

Cleopatra's own eyes narrowed, and she showed her teeth again. For a bare instant, claws flicked from the ends of her fingers. Then, suddenly, the tension evaporated from her body, and she flowed up against Victor again. "Of course, Creator," she said, her voice purring even more than before. "I'm sorry."

Ubasti watched the interplay with eyes narrowed and ears ever-so-slightly laid back.

It's not all sweetness and light between the Kemonomimi and their "Creator," Emily thought. *Or among themselves.*

Not that that knowledge did her the slightest bit of good at the moment.

"There's no reason for Kemonomimi and Selkies to be enemies," Emily said again, though she suspected an appeal to reason would do her no good either. "And there was no need to attack the sub."

"You landed here to spy on us," Victor said. "An act of war."

"I landed to talk," Emily said. "I would have walked into your town on my own within an hour."

"Really," Victor said dryly. "Pray tell me why?"

"I came to warn you."

"Warn me?" Victor's fingers ran up and down through the fur on Cleo's belly. "How unexpectedly . . . kind. . . . of you. Warn me about what?"

Emily nodded at Shelby. "Let the boy go, and I'll tell you."

Shelby's eyes flashed. "Emily, I—"

"Be quiet, Shelby." The boy subsided, his blood-streaked face sullen.

Victor smiled. "Well, even though he's a Selkie, I'll grant you I've no interest in seeing him hurt at the moment. It would be like kicking a puppy." He paused. "I'll make a deal. Give me your warning. If it is of any value to me, I'll let him go."

Emily hesitated. She didn't trust Victor, but she had no way to drive a harder bargain. "Very well." She took a deep breath. "The Avatar is still alive. He and a sizable army of Holy Warriors are marching through the mountains right now. They're coming to destroy you."

Victor's smile grew wider, as if he were delighted. "Really?" He looked at Cleo. "Did you hear that? The Avatar himself, coming to destroy us."

"Oooh," said Cleo, sounding bored. "Eeek."

Emily had a sinking sensation. "You know."

"Of course we know," Victor said. "I've known for a long time about the Avatar's little hideaway on Paradise Island. That's why we came here: to kill the Avatar. We would have done it on the island, but then he chose to march toward us—which makes things even easier.

"When the time is right—very soon now—we will destroy him and all his forces . . . and that will be the end of the Body Purified, and the beginning of the reign of *Homo sapiens hanseni*: the Kemonomimi."

"And then you plan to launch a fleet and try to take

Marseguro, do you?" Emily said. "We fought off the Holy Warriors. We can damn well fight off you."

Victor laughed. "We will not be attacking Marseguro."

"You said you would eradicate us."

"Soon, yes. Very soon."

"But how—"

Victor laughed again. "Now, why on Earth would I tell you that?"

Shelby's head suddenly snapped up. "You're crazy!" he snarled. "A fucking lunatic! You can't—"

Victor nodded to the Ubasti. She took two steps forward and kicked Shelby hard in the stomach. The blow drove the breath from the boy's body and he doubled up and fell onto his side, mouth stretched wide, gasping for breath.

"You should have listened to Miss Wood," Victor said, "and shut up." He looked up at her. "Now," he said. "I require some information from *you*."

Emily felt rage rising inside her, a fury she recognized, first cousin to the burning hunger for revenge that had set her soul aflame on Marseguro. She'd killed without a qualm then, on the ground and on board *Sanctification*, and she hadn't lost a moment's sleep over the horrors her mother's plague had visited on the Holy Warriors who had died at their posts, vomiting blood.

She'd thought she'd put her own warrior side behind her. She'd come here hoping for peace, not war. But at that moment, if she could have reached him, she would have snapped the grinning clone's neck in an instant, no matter how much he looked like Richard.

"I have nothing to tell you," she snarled.

"But you do," Victor said. "I need to know how many Marseguroites are on Earth, and how many more in orbit. I need to know what kind of weapons they have, and if they are likely to use them. And I need to know everything there is to know about Marseguro itself, and exactly how my pet plague was used to destroy the Holy Warriors who attacked it.

"I need to know so many things, Miss Wood." He smiled and pulled Cleopatra close; she put her arm around his shoulders and her tail around his waist, leaned in close, and nuzzled her head against his neck. "And you're going to tell them to me." His smile faded slightly. "One way or another."

Emily clenched her jaw, and said nothing.

Victor sighed. "You're going to make this difficult, aren't you? Well, no matter. The end will be the same." He nodded to Ubasti, who still stood over Shelby. The boy had finally managed to start breathing again but showed no signs of getting up. "Lock them up where I told you. Provide the boy with whatever first aid is required. I'll be along shortly to question them." With Cleo still clinging to him, he turned and walked away.

Ubasti nodded to one of the male Kemonomimi, who picked Shelby up like a sack of grain and slung him over his shoulder. The boy groaned and promptly threw up all down the back of the man's armored vest. The Kemonomimi grimaced and his tail twitched like an angry cat's, but he set off in the direction of the taller buildings Emily had seen earlier, the ones she thought marked the miniscule town's downtown core, such as it was. Her own guards grabbed her arm and propelled her in the same direction. Ubasti moved forward to once more take the lead.

"Downtown" seemed a little grand to describe a single street with a dozen storefronts, a restaurant/pub ("The Tipsy Sasquatch"), a Body Sanctuary, a town hall—and, next door to it, Newshore School, a two-story building of red brick trimmed with white limestone, with what looked like two classroom wings and a larger central section. The Kemonomimi dragged them up the broad flight of stairs at the front of the school, through the glass doors into a dark, musty-smelling lobby, and down the hallway to the right.

Doors opened on either side of the corridor, lit only by the light that made it down its length from the fire doors at the far end and the lobby behind them. Three doors down, they stopped. Ubasti pulled a keycard from her belt and opened the door. The Kemonomimi carrying Shelby disappeared inside with him. "Patch up his head," Ubasti ordered through the open door, then led the way one door closer to the lobby on the opposite side of the hall. Ubasti opened it, Emily was propelled through it, and then it slammed behind her.

She looked around. "You've got to be kidding me!"

They'd locked her in the girls' toilet. The walls were bare and a most unappealing shade of pink. High windows, far too small to climb through, let in a modicum of the morning light, while a recessed light ring in the ceiling provided a modicum more. Someone had set up a cot along the wall under the window, where it blocked one of the six stalls. *Well, after all,* Emily thought sardonically, *how many stalls do I really need?*

And that was that. She couldn't talk to Shelby. She'd had her chance to talk to Victor Hansen, and he wasn't buying what she was selling. Instead, he wanted information that would help him . . . what? Eradicate all the Selkies? But how, since he denied any plans to actually attack Marseguro?

He's crazy. You can't expect him to make sense.

But crazy or not, it sounded very much as if he intended to torture her to get her to answer his questions.

Emily had never been tortured, but she already knew one thing she would not—could not—let slip, no matter what: the fact that Selkies already lived beneath Earth's oceans. She hoped Shelby would have the presence of mind to keep that monumental secret.

She hoped *she* would.

She lay down on the bunk with her arms under her head, stared up at the pink ceiling, and waited.

Half an hour later, the door suddenly opened. Victor Hansen stepped inside the washroom. The same two Kemonomimi who had guarded her since she'd been first seized followed him, though there was no sign of Ubasti. "So," Victor said. "Ready to answer questions?"

"I won't betray my people," Emily said.

"Really?" Victor grinned, as though delighted by her refusal. "Oh, good, because I've been dying to try something, and now I have the perfect excuse." He nodded to the Kemonomimi accompanying him, who stepped forward. Emily drew back against the cot, but she had nowhere else to run.

"They won't hurt you," Victor said. "They just want your landsuit."

"What?" Emily felt as if she had just stepped into thin air from a thousand-foot cliff. "But I—"

"You'll gradually dehydrate without it," Hansen said conversationally. "Yes, I know. What I don't know— probably because of my unfortunate memory loss—is *how* gradually. Or what your reaction to the process will be. So this is the perfect opportunity for me to gather some solid data on Selkie physiology, potentially valuable should I find the need to question more Selkies in the future."

Emily felt cold. She'd had a taste of dehydration aboard the *Divine Will*, but that had been mitigated by her mother's sharing of her landsuit and the access to the shower. Here . . . she looked around. No shower. And simply wetting her gills from the sinks . . . wouldn't be enough. Not nearly enough.

"So," Victor said. "Will you remove your landsuit, or shall they?"

Emily's rage threatened to choke her, but she pulled off the landsuit and let it fall, heavy with water, to the ground, and stood there in her striped skinsuit, glaring at Victor.

"Now," he said. "I think we'll have the skinsuit off, too."

What? Her hands clenched. "No," she growled.

He sighed. "I'll have *them* do it, if you prefer. I'm sure they'd enjoy that."

Emily ground her teeth, but there was nothing for it. Defiantly she slipped the skinsuit off of one shoulder, then the other, then shoved it to the floor and stepped out of it.

The Kemonomimi's lips parted in toothy grins. Victor stepped closer. "Interesting," he said, running his eyes over her form.

"Is that why none of your Kemonomimi wear clothes, Hansen?" she snarled. "So you can ogle naked women?"

"They're not naked," he said. "They've got fur. And as for ogling naked women, my interest in your body is purely scientific, I assure you. I haven't had the opportunity to examine my handiwork before. Perhaps it will bring back some of my lost memories. Now stand still."

Emily's instinct was to fold her arms over her breasts, but instead she forced herself to stand proudly, arms at her side, glaring at Victor Hansen, imagining how his throat would feel in her grip, how it would sound as he choked for breath . . .

"Ah," he said. He walked back and forth as if examining a sculpture. "An extra layer of fat, I see; makes sense for an aquatic creature. And completely hairless." He looked up. "I wonder why I didn't get the hair off your head while I was at it? Seems useless for a sea creature." He stepped back. "Well. Very interesting. Inferior to the Kemonomimi, of course, but still, quite an amazing accomplishment on my part."

"May I get dressed now?" Emily grated.

Victor sighed. "Oh, every well. But no landsuit." He went to the door, then glanced back as she bent down and pulled up the skinsuit. "In eight hours, I will ask you some questions, and you will answer them; or if you do not, I will wait another eight hours and then ask them again. And then another eight."

"You'll have a long wait."

Victor shook his head sorrowfully. "Please, Miss Wood, spare me the bravado. You've been living a lie, all those years on Marseguro, convinced you were free. You have never been free. I am your creator, and I own you, as I own the Kemonomimi. And like all the creators in all the myths that have come down to us from Earth's ancient history, I play favorites. The Kemonomimi are my Chosen People, and the Selkies . . . the Selkies, in the words of the Christian Bible, 'I will spew out of my mouth.' " With that, he exited. The Kemonomimi followed, one carrying the landsuit. The door slammed shut behind them, and locked.

I won't tell him anything, Emily thought fiercely. *I won't.*

But as she sat down on the bed and wrapped its navy-blue blanket around her shoulders, she couldn't help thinking about his threat. Eight hours without water would be no problem; Selkies slept dry, after all. But they also went for a swim first thing in the morning, typically even before breakfast.

Sixteen hours without water . . . or more . . .

She remembered what she had gone through on the *Divine Will,* and her stomach roiled like a witches' cauldron at full boil.

He can't mean it, she thought.

But the way he had looked at her . . . the Kemonomimi had looked at her and seen a naked woman, an object of lust. She didn't like it, but she much preferred it to the way Victor had examined her, utterly coldly, as if she were simply an interesting scientific specimen.

He saw her whole race that way. And he would throw out any specimen in an instant if it no longer suited his purposes.

He would let her die, and not lift a finger, if she didn't answer his questions.

She sat and stared at the pink concrete floor. *Eight hours*, she thought. *A lot can happen in eight hours. The Free Republic knows we're here.* She looked up at the blue door, wishing she could see across the corridor, see how Shelby was doing. *He could have a concussion . . . or cracked ribs . . . or both!*

I was a fool. I didn't believe . . . the Kemonomimi, the Selkies, we're all moddies. The Body Purified is our enemy. We should have been able to help each other.

But we—I—didn't count on an insane clone of Victor Hansen.

The Free Republic had made it clear that they wouldn't rescue her if she were imprisoned by the Kemonomimi. But Shelby . . . Shelby, the son of the President . . .

Shelby was a different matter.

They would rescue *him*. And in the process, perhaps they would rescue her, too.

All she had to do was hold on . . . eight hours at a time.

She lay on the bed with the blanket up to her chin, put her hands behind her head, stared up at the ceiling, and resumed her wait.

Chapter 17

ANDY KING HAD HEARD Richard's order to forget the assault craft in Africa. He'd immediately gone to his station and begun issuing directives that would provide Richard with the force he needed to take the ex-Holy Warriors' shuttle down to the coast of British Columbia to attempt to rescue Emily and Shelby.

But those weren't the only directives he'd issued.

Andy had had plenty of time to sound out the crew on the journey to Earth and in the days since. He knew exactly how each member of that crew felt about the mission, and how they were pursuing it.

He knew several crew members who, while willing enough to distribute vaccine to innocent nonmods, had had something on their minds more than just a mission of mercy when they had signed on, no matter what they'd paid lip service to when asked.

They wanted revenge. They wanted to make the Body pay for what it had done on Marseguro. They had come to Earth because Earth was the only place where they could still find Holy Warriors to kill, the plague having ensured they were fresh out on Marseguro.

The Avatar had proved that his only interest in the vaccine was to enable him to attempt genocide once more: he'd made no effort—none—to distribute the vaccine to civilians anywhere on the planet. He had ordered an attack on the *Victor Hansen* that had led to several Marseguroite deaths.

Now, though—now he had assembled his remaining Holy Warriors and marched them out into the open; and down in Africa one of the same assault craft used to attack Marseguro lay waiting.

Richard had promised to rescue the President's son and Emily, and Andy agreed wholehcartedly with that attempt; so he gave the orders that would enable Richard to do what he wanted to do: but at the same time, he gave a few additional orders.

He rode the shaft-transport with Richard and the fifteen crew members they'd manage to scrape together to accompany him down to the hatch that gave access to the air lock where the Holy Warriors' shuttle was still docked. As the transport slowed, Simon Goodfellow emerged into the shaft.

"Hello, Simon," Richard said, holding up while the rest of the crew launched themselves through the hatch with varying degrees of zero-G aplomb. "What's our status?"

"You're good to go, sir," Simon said. "The shuttle's AI is fully slaved to the ship AI. It'll help you fly the shuttle, no questions asked. And if anything does go wrong, you can disconnect the AI and fly manually."

"Well, *I* can't," Richard said. "But I hope Claude can."

"He can," Andy said. "Claude Maurois is the best pilot we've got, since . . ." he realized what he was about to say, and stopped.

"Since Melody and Pierre were killed," Richard said quietly. "I'm sure he'll do fine." He held out his hand. "Take good care of the ship, Andy," he said. "Not that I have any doubt you will, after what you managed last time."

"Good luck, Captain," Andy said. He shook Richard's hand, then did something he almost never did: he saluted. "I hope you get Emily back."

"I will." Richard said it with grim certainty. "Count on it." He returned the salute, then pushed himself off the transport and disappeared through the hatch.

Andy turned to Simon. "Take the transport back to the habitat ring," he said. "I need to check a couple of things while I'm down here."

"All right," Simon said. "Um, I mean, aye-aye." He pulled himself onto the transport; it slid away toward the bow.

Andy watched him go, then jumped across the central shaft and began pulling himself further aft using the webbing. Shortly he came to another hatch—the one Richard, Melody, Pierre, and Derryl Godard had come through when they'd ridden to the rescue.

The crew members he had contacted surreptitiously were waiting in the tiny shuttle. Derryl was one; he'd requested permission not to accompany Richard, and the captain, mindful of everything he'd been through, had agreed to let him stay behind. Sam Hallett, who had fought the Holy Warriors in the simulator room with Andy, was another. Annie Ash, a young Selkie, was the third. Andy made four.

"You don't have to do this," Andy told them. "Leave now, and no one will be the wiser. We're about to go against Captain Hansen's direct orders. That makes this the first mutiny in the history of the Marseguroite Space Navy."

"I volunteered my services to help get the *Victor Hansen* to Earth," Hallett said. "I never promised anything about what I'd do when I got here."

Annie looked nervous, but determined. "They killed my parents and my little brother," she said. "They'll kill the rest of us if they get the chance. We have to kill them first. I don't blame Captain Hansen for wanting to rescue Emily, but he's too softhearted to do what has to be done. He wants to save everyone. I don't think the Body Purified is worth saving. I'm with you."

Derryl just gave him a cold, flat look. "You're wasting time."

Andy nodded. "All right, then." He pulled himself into the cockpit and maneuvered himself into the pilot's seat. "I've given the shuttle computer the coordinates of the assault craft, as near as we can determine them, in Africa. Once we're almost down, I'll take over manual control and we'll see if we can spot it. There's no reason to think there'll be any humans around at all, due to the plague, but stay alert. We don't really know what we'll find."

He strapped himself in. Annie settled into the copilot's seat and pulled on her restraints, and behind him he heard the click of seat buckles as Sam and Derryl likewise secured themselves. "Computer," Andy said. "Execute program Andy 1."

"Executing," the shuttle's computer said. Andy had had Simon dumb it down so far it would answer anyone's commands, with no regard to their actual authority, if any. He looked out the cockpit windows at the vast silver bulk of the *Victor Hansen*, which his brain insisted was looming above them, threatening to fall.

The air lock door closed. There was a faint mechanical murmur, a bump, and then the *Victor Hansen*'s hull began to recede. The shuttle nose dipped, and the hull moved out of sight, replaced instead by the blue green curve of the Earth.

As Andy had expected, the communications link snapped to life. "Shuttle! Report! Who's on board? Who gave you permission to launch?"

Andy powered up his end of the link. "Relax, Cordelia," he said. "It's me, Andy. I'm on board. I've got Hallett, Ash, and Godard with me."

"Andy?" Raum sounded bewildered. "I didn't know anything about this . . . where are you going?"

"Bit of a secret," Andy said. "You'll see soon enough. In the meantime, you have the bridge. Take good care of the ship until we get back."

"But, sir, I—"

"King out." Andy killed the link.

The Earth now filled more than half his field of view out the cockpit windows. They had nosed down.

They were heading to Africa.

"Message from *MSS Victor Hansen*," said the computer in the erstwhile Holy Warrior shuttle *Creator's Glory*.

"Computer, accept link," Richard said.

The screen lit up with Cordelia Raum's worried visage. "Sir? Andy King has left the ship."

Richard sat up. "What?"

"With Sam Hallett, Derryl Godard, and Annie Ash. He wouldn't tell me why. Sir, I'm concerned that we won't be able to hold the ship if the Holy Warriors try to take her again. We're down to about fifty crew."

"I don't think the Holy Warriors will be back," Richard said absently. His mind raced. "Are you tracking Andy's shuttle?"

Raum nodded. "Yes sir. They appear to be heading for Africa."

The assault craft. Damn! I should have guessed.

But there was nothing he could do about it. "Keep me posted," he said. "Hansen out."

He glanced at Claude Maurois in the pilot's chair; the young nonmod kept his eyes on his readouts. They'd re-entered the atmosphere some time ago, and the ride was getting a little bumpy.

Then Richard looked back into the crew compartment. With the cockpit door open, everyone must have heard the message. How many secretly thought Andy was doing the right thing?

He looked back out the cockpit window as they plunged into thick clouds. He couldn't blame his crew for wanting revenge, after what the Body had done on Marseguro. But he didn't believe any of them would put that desire above the need to rescue Emily, hero of the resistance. She was the nearest thing to a princess Marseguro had, and they'd go through hell and . . . he smiled to himself . . . low water to free her.

The trick would be freeing her without turning the simmering conflict between Selkies and Kemonomimi into a full-scale war. And the first part of that trick involved being very careful to land where the Kemonomimi wouldn't see them. Richard and Andy had pored over satellite images and, with the computer's assistance, plotted an approach shielded by high mountain peaks, leading to a landing in a valley several hours' hike from Newshore.

At least the weather was cooperating: the whole valley was awash in clouds and rain. Richard looked at Claude's intent face and hoped he and Holy Warrior collision avoidance technology were up to the task.

They were. Half an hour after the message from the *Victor Hansen*, he and fourteen of his fifteen crewmembers (Claude would remain to guard the shuttle) stepped out of the shuttle's main hatch onto the lichen-stained rock of a very soggy alpine meadow.

"Everyone set?" Richard said, when the bustle of pulling equipment out of the shuttle and hoisting backpacks had subsided. There were ten Selkies—six men and four women—and five nonmods—three men and one woman, plus himself.

He hoped he could remember everyone's name, although just recognizing them might be the biggest challenge, since everyone looked the same in dappled green-and-gray Holy Warrior camouflage (though carefully stripped of its Holy Warrior insignia, of course). The Selkies wore it over their black landsuits.

"You know the plan," Richard said. "Stealthy approach, careful reconnaissance. When we've got a better idea of where Emily and Shelby are being held, then we can figure out how to get them out. But the important thing right now is not to be seen. If the Kemonomimi know we're out here, we don't know what they'll do to their hostages. Any questions?"

None. He didn't really expect any: they'd talked about this before they left the ship.

He glanced at the navcomp Simon Goodfellow had found, explained to him, and personally strapped to his wrist. It laid out his path for him in bright red, with simple written instructions. "Five kilometers due west to start," he said. "We'll be descending gradually, but the footing should be good and there's not much vegetation to slow us down." He readjusted his own pack. It hadn't felt that heavy when he'd first shouldered it, but it was already weighing him down. He'd never thought he'd miss zero gravity, occasional nausea and all.

"Let's go," he said, and the Marseguroites set off, single file, into the swirling mist.

Emily had had too little sleep for days. Prepared to wait, awake and alert, for eight hours, she instead woke with a start as the door to the washroom opened. She sat up. She could tell by the quality of light from the high windows that a great deal of time had passed. And since Ubasti was here ...

"Eight hours already?" she said.

"I said get up!" Ubasti moved with blurring speed, grabbing Emily's arms, pulling her wrists behind her, binding them with strips of plastic, then propelling her into the corridor, where one of the men who had entered earlier with Victor waited. The door to the room they'd locked Shelby in was still closed, and Ubasti pushed Emily past it and on down the hall to a door near the very end. The man unlocked it with a swipe of a keycard, and Ubasti pushed Emily in, followed her, and locked the door behind them, leaving the male guard in the hall.

Emily found herself in a small room set up as a theater, with maybe twenty seats in four rows facing a screen, the windows blocked by metal shutters. And on the screen . . .

Shelby, his image obviously captured by a camera in one corner of his room. It was no more a prison cell than her washroom: its walls were pink and blue and had pictures of teddy bears playing among oversized flowers. It looked like a child-care facility, but whatever furniture and toys had been there in preplague days had been removed, replaced with a cot like the one in the washroom.

Shelby, still in his bloodstained white trunks and nothing else, lay on that cot, one arm thrown over his face. At some point someone had dressed his head wound with a large white bandage and cleaned the blood from his face and hair. A big purple bruise marked his right side where Ubasti had kicked him. His gill slits showed pink along the sides of his neck, pulsing slightly.

Emily's, she'd gradually become aware since waking, were doing the same. It was the first sign of dehydration. The pulsing would continue. Over the next few hours, it would become a tickle; then a burning pain. Eventually, the slight pulsing would evolve into throbbing agony, like someone slamming a hammer again and again on an already crushed finger.

Emily had been far along that road aboard the *Divine Will*. She didn't look forward to beginning that journey again. And Shelby didn't deserve to make it at all.

"Miss Wood," said Victor Hansen's voice. Emily jumped and looked around her, but except for Ubasti, she was alone. "I promised I would wait eight hours before I asked you any questions, and so I have. But it occurred to me I may have left you with the wrong impression.

"It is not my intention to deprive *you* of water, in order to get you tell me what I want to know. The school you are in has a swimming pool, your escort will take you there. It's filled and kept warm by a natural hot spring, so I think you'll find the water to your liking."

"That sounds like a carrot," Emily said. "What's the stick?"

Victor Hansen laughed. "I'm surprised you know that metaphor."

"I read a lot."

"I see. Well, the 'stick' is that while you may have free access to the pool . . . your young friend there may not."

Emily froze. "You bastard," she breathed after a moment.

Ubasti growled deep in her throat.

"Ubasti doesn't like it when you call her Creator names," Victor said; he'd obviously heard her reaction. He might even be observing them as they observed Shelby, though Emily hadn't spotted a camera anywhere. "Although I suppose an argument could be made that a clone, being fatherless, is indeed a bastard. In any event, I gather you understand the situation."

"You're going to torture that poor boy until I tell you what you want to know," Emily snarled.

"I'm not going to torture him at all. He's in a comfortable room, and will be provided with ample food and water . . . but only for drinking, I'm afraid. That's not torture. At least, it wouldn't be for a normal human being, or my Kemonomimi."

Bastard, Emily thought again, but didn't say. "He's already hurting," she said. "In eight hours he'll be in agony. In twenty-four to thirty-six, he'll be dead. You'll be murdering him in cold blood!"

"Not I," Victor said. "You. His fate is entirely in your hands."

"And not in yours?"

"You should be thankful it is not," Victor said. "Since I consider you both mistakes that by all rights shouldn't even exist. Allowing you to live so I might learn from you is an honor you do not deserve. Placing your friend's fate in your hands is likewise." His voice hardened. "Eight more hours until I come to call in person, Miss Wood. You are welcome to use the pool for a period not to exceed twenty minutes, once every two hours. The rest of the time you will remain in that theater and observe what your stubbornness has wrought.

"Hansen out."

Emily spun to face Ubasti. "Take me to the pool," she snapped, wishing, as she followed the black-furred woman out, that she could drown Victor Hansen in it.

Decorated with white-and-blue tile, lit by fluorescent lights, the pool was purely utilitarian, but the water was as wonderful as Victor had indicated. She'd been worried the mineral content might irritate her gills, but in fact it seemed to soothe them.

But nothing could soothe her spirit. She swam in clean water; Shelby tossed and turned on dry bedding. She could come back here every two hours; he could only continue to suffer, and the suffering had barely begun.

Would it be so bad if she answered Victor's questions? What difference could it make if he knew how many Marseguroites were on Earth? As long as she didn't tell him about the Free Selkie Republic . . .

Besides, she could lie. He'd never know the difference. And the other stuff he'd asked about . . . why *not* tell him about Marseguro? What could he do? He couldn't very well steal a Body starship and launch an attack.

But it was the fact she didn't *know* what he could do that concerned her. They'd already underestimated the Kemonomimi once. And Victor Hansen, either the original or any of his clones—and how many of them had there *been*, anyway?—wasn't stupid. His claim he would destroy the Selkies without attacking Marseguro seemed crazy, but . . .

Richard. President McLean. Between them, a rescue *would* be coming. Shelby only had to hold on until then. It couldn't be long . . .

It could be days, she told herself as she flipped over and began her fourth lap of the pool. *Days. Shelby won't survive.*

She stopped in the middle of the pool, let herself sink to the blue-tiled bottom, gills working, and stared up at the distorted images of the fluorescent lights. If Victor had only tortured *her,* she would have resisted as long as possible. But with Shelby involved . . .

Like a lead weight settling in her stomach, she knew Victor had beaten her.

She had to answer his questions. She had to buy time for the rescuers to find them.

And if they don't find you?

Then I'll think of something else.

Won't I?

She rolled over, swam as fast as she could toward the edge of the pool, leaped out, and landed on her broad, webbed feet, drenching Ubasti, who snarled and drew her sidearm. One of the pool room's big double doors swung open with a crash and the red-furred man leaped in, weapon in hand. He skidded to a stop when he took in the scene, then burst out laughing.

"Stuff it," Ubasti said. "And you, fishhead—" she pointed at Emily, "—do that again and I'll slice you into sushi."

"Well, what do you know, you can speak whole sentences," Emily said. "I was beginning to think all you Kemonomimi were really Victor Hansen's puppets and he was the only one who could actually talk."

The man's laugher ended instantly. "We are the Kemonomimi," he growled. "We are a free people. We follow the Creator of our own free will."

"Right," Emily said. "Whatever. Well, tell your glorious leader I'm ready to talk to him."

The two cat-people smiled, and with those teeth, the smiles weren't pleasant. "The Creator told you when he will return to see you."

"But that's hours away. The boy will be in agony by then. There's no need for it!"

"If the Creator feels there is need, then there is need," said Ubasti.

Emily felt the old rage burning inside her again. "Free people, my ass," she snarled. "Slaves, to let a boy suffer just because some nonmod says so."

The man's eyes narrowed and he hissed just like an angry cat. "We are not slaves!"

"Prove it."

Ubasti looked from Emily to the man. "Augustus—" she began warningly.

"I will pass your message to the Creator," Augustus said. "But it will do you no good." He turned and banged out through the double doors, snatching his tail clear just before they closed on it.

"Back to the theater," Ubasti snapped at Emily. "You've swum enough."

Emily picked up a towel from a table near the door and began wiping herself dry. "Indeed I have," she said. "Hadn't you better get one of these yourself?"

Ubasti hissed . . . but she picked up a towel just the same, and rubbed down her fur, which stood up in spiked tufts which might have been humorous on anyone less murderous.

They returned to the minitheater, where Ubasti forced Emily to sit in one of the chairs in the front row. In the other room, Shelby no longer slept. Instead he prowled the room, pacing along each wall over and over like a caged animal. Occasionally, he reached up as if to touch his gills, but then he snatched his hand away. Emily knew his predicament. They itched, but they were becoming inflamed, so touching them hurt. His skin must be feeling dry, too: he kept scratching, wincing when his fingers found his bruised side.

Around and around the room he went. And the second eight hours had just begun.

Augustus returned from wherever he had gone to contact Victor Hansen. He looked . . . smaller. Emily and Ubasti turned toward him as he entered. "No," he said, looking at Emily. "The Creator will return when he has said he will return, and not a moment sooner."

Emily gripped the arms of her chair so hard her knuckles audibly cracked. She forced herself to look back into the room where Shelby paced.

"He's teaching you a lesson," Ubasti said. "Are you capable of learning it, I wonder?"

Emily didn't turn around. She kept watching the suffering Selkie boy.

She was learning a lesson, all right.

She was learning that she still knew how to hate.

Chapter 18

THE ASSAULT CRAFT GLEAMED in the South African sunlight two kilometers from where Andy and his crew lay on a tree-covered ridge. The shuttle had set itself down in a vineyard, tearing a huge gap through vines heavy with rotting grapes once intended to produce fine Pinotage for rich Body officials.

The winery and what had presumably been the owner's house and outbuildings lay about a hundred meters past the shuttle. Beyond that, a jagged mass of shining granite rose against the blue sky: Paarl Mountain, the computer had called it when Andy had asked on approach.

But Andy's attention now was entirely on the immediate vicinity of the shuttle. He was examining the scene with binoculars: Derryl, ever the pragmatist, was examining everything through the scope of the new sniper rifle he'd obtained from *Victor Hansen*'s armory. Sam and Annie had to make do with their own eyes.

"I don't see anyone," Andy said. "Derryl?"

Derryl lowered the rifle. "No," he said. "But that does not mean they are not there."

"Very Zen," Andy said. "But let's advance just the same." He got to his feet. "Single file. I'll go first. Tom, you follow me. Annie, you bring up the rear." He led the way down the slope and into the vineyard. The smell of rotting fruit was almost tangible.

They hadn't gone a dozen meters when Andy suddenly held up his hand and stopped. "Why aren't there any birds?" he said. "All this fruit, and no birds . . ."

"Birds carry the plague, don't they?" Annie said.

"Yes," Andy said. "But it doesn't kill them . . ."

He suddenly heard something moving nearby, something mechanical, turning toward them . . .

"Everyone down!" he yelled, flinging himself to the ground. Derryl acted instantly; Annie was close behind; Sam was a second slower . . .

. . . just enough slower that when the automated bird-killer fired, the load of birdshot slammed into his shoulder, twisting him around and throwing him against one of the wooden posts supporting the vines.

Sam screamed and writhed, trying to clamp his hand over every one of the dozens of tiny holes in his flesh as blood oozed out, soaking his shirt and the ground beneath him.

"Quiet," Andy snapped as he scrambled over to him, being careful to keep his head lower than the top of the grapevines, reasoning that the vineyard's defenses wouldn't be designed to unload buckshot directly into the vines. "At least you didn't get it in the face."

"It hurts," Sam moaned.

"I'm not surprised. Hold still." Andy unzipped Sam's shirt and eased it over the damaged shoulder. "They barely penetrated," he said. "You'll live. But getting all the shot out isn't going to be easy and we need to stop the bleeding." He looked toward the assault craft, out of sight now they were below the vines. "The assault craft has an autodoc. We need to get you there."

"But if we stand up, we'll get our heads blown off," Annie protested.

"So we crawl," Andy said.

Which they did, though it was a slow process, having to help Sam every inch of the way, one of them always supporting his good arm and thus taking most of his weight as well. The ground was sandy and stony and thoroughly unpleasant to crawl on, although the layer of water in their landsuits helped pad the Selkies' knees, at least.

They were only about halfway to the shuttle when they ran across the vineyard's ground-level defense. With a bloodcurdling chittering sound, something silvery bright rushed at them along the row, waving sharp-edged claws that glittered in the sun. Andy swore and tried to bring his laser pistol to bear. But the . . . thing . . . skittered almost comically to a halt a few meters away. Andy had the distinct feeling he was being stared at: then as suddenly as it had arrived, the bot spun around, raising a cloud of dust, and raced back toward the wincry.

Andy blew the air out of his lungs. "Too big for it, I guess," he said. "It's probably designed to attack rodents."

Annie looked after it thoughtfully. "You don't suppose it's smart enough to come back with a swarm?"

Andy blinked. He hadn't thought of that. "I hope not," he said. "But let's pick up the pace just the same, shall we?"

Easy to say, hard to do, but at least they kept moving. Then, just when Andy had begun to allow himself to think that they might reach the assault craft with no more trouble, the vineyard sprang its last surprise on them.

"You're in our sights," a voice boomed. "Stop moving, or we'll open fire."

"Damn," Andy breathed. "Hold up."

They stopped. The bottom hatch of the assault craft dropped open and a man jumped out of it. He wore a white surgical mask and rubber gloves, carried a massive shotgun, and had the darkest skin Andy had ever seen. Victor Hansen had designed Selkies to express a wide range of skin pigmentation, and Andy himself was chocolate-brown, but this man's skin was more like ebony.

"Who are you and what do you want?" the man demanded in a strongly accented voice. He looked closer. "Let me rephrase that. *What* are you? And why aren't you dead?"

"Why aren't *you?*" Andy said. He pointed at Sam, lying panting on the ground next to Derryl. "He's hurt. We want to put him in the autodoc. We know there's one on that spacecraft."

"Yes?" The shotgun never wavered. "And how would you know that?"

Andy sighed. "Look, we're not attacking you. In fact, we came to this planet to help you."

"You're . . . aliens?"

Andy blinked at him. "What?" And then he realized that the man had never seen a Selkie before. "No. There aren't any aliens. Well, none that anybody has found, anyway. No. We're . . ." He hesitated. If the man were of the Body, admitting he, Derryl, and Annie were moddies might convince him to do a little freelance Purifying. ". . . just different." The man would be seeing their overlarge eyes, their tiny noses and ears . . . but he couldn't see their gills, which were safely tucked away in the cool embraces of the landsuits. "It's a birth defect. Runs in our family." He pointed at Sam. "He's the lucky one. Missed out."

"You must live a long way from any Body outposts," the man said. "People that look like you get sterilized when they run afoul of the Body."

"We do," Andy said. "Very isolated, our home. The Body's not in charge there."

The shotgun still didn't move. "Assuming I believe you, why did you come here?"

"We . . . heard about the plague." He paused. "And we have a vaccine."

At that, the man jumped to his feet, banging his head on the hull. He crouched again, rubbing his skull with one hand, finally letting the shotgun droop toward the ground. "You have a vaccine?" he said, eyes locked on Andy with burning intensity. "You're telling the truth?"

"Yes," Andy said. He glanced at Sam. "Unfortunately, it doesn't protect against buckshot."

"What? Oh . . ." The man looked up into the assault craft; down at Andy again. He took a deep breath. "Very well. He can come in. You, too. You others . . . stay put for now. But don't think you can try anything. There's been more than just this shotgun aimed at you for the past few minutes."

"Do what he says," Andy said. He went to Sam's side. Sam's eyes fluttered open, but it took them several seconds to focus on Andy. "Come on," Andy said. "Let's get you into the autodoc."

Sam nodded, and, with a groan, climbed back to his knees. Andy supported him on the side of his good arm and helped him shuffle toward the access hatch where the man waited, his eyes flicking between them and the other two Marseguroites waiting in the background.

Sam managed to climb up the ladder more or less on his own, with Andy supporting him from behind. Together they emerged into the main crew compartment of the assault craft, designed to hold maybe twenty Holy Warriors and their equipment. Andy immediately turned toward the rear of the compartment, knowing that was where he would find the autodoc, only to pull up short at the sight of a young woman and two small girls, one maybe six, the other no more than three, sitting in a kind of nest of mattresses, pillows, and blankets that was blocking his way. The children stared at him with wide brown eyes and held on tight to their mother, whose arms held them protectively.

"I'm sorry, I didn't . . ."

"Tseliso said you have a vaccine," the woman said. "Is that true?"

Andy smiled at the children. "It's true."

The woman's eyes suddenly glistened with tears. "Will

you give it to us?" she said, voice choked with emotion. "Will you give it to my girls?"

Andy nodded, a lump suddenly forming in his own throat. "It's why we came. But . . . my friend . . . ?"

"Of course, of course," the woman said. She pulled the children aside. "Let the nice man through," she told them. The girls stared up at Andy as he picked his way through the family's belongings, Sam leaning heavily against him.

"That man's bleeding," said the older girl.

"Owie," the littler girl agreed.

"Yes, he has a bad owie," Andy said solemnly. "But he'll be all right." *And so will you,* he thought, and for the first time the importance of the *Victor Hansen*'s mission really struck home. All over the world survivors were living like rats, hiding, afraid that any gust of wind or passing bird or nighttime rodent might spell their death warrant.

The vaccine they had brought would end their fear, allow them to emerge into the light again, to rebuild their world.

Am I doing the right thing?

He settled Sam by the door to the autodoc. "Computer," he said. "Power up."

Like a beast awakening from sleep, the assault craft, long cut off from the AI on *Victor Hansen* and thus still recognizing Andy's authority without question, rumbled. Ventilation systems whispered, the interior lights flickered to life, controls lit in the cockpit. Andy heard the woman's gasp, but didn't turn around. "Computer," he said, "open autodoc."

The blank metal panel in front of him slid aside, revealing a chamber like a very small bedroom: so small it was all bed, no room. "In you go, Sam," Andy said, and helped his wounded crewman to his feet. "We'll need to get your shirt off."

"I was afraid of that," Sam said, but with Andy's help,

he managed it, though his already pale face turned almost pure white during the process and at one point he staggered as though he would fall. Andy caught him, and helped him crawl into the autodoc.

"Autodoc," Andy said. "Examine and treat."

The door slid shut, cutting Sam off from his sight.

Andy turned around to see that the big man had climbed up into the passenger compartment—and had his shotgun aimed squarely at Andy. "Explain to me how you have voice control over a Body assault craft," he growled. "Explain it to me very carefully. Because if you are a Holy Warrior, I will shoot you down where you stand, before my own children."

Andy stood very still. "I'm not a Holy Warrior," he said. "Far from it." He very slowly raised his hands. "I'll show you, if you'll let me."

"Slowly," the man said. "Carefully."

Andy nodded. He touched the controls on his landsuit, and felt it sucking the water away from his skin, storing it for later use. Then he reached up and squeezed the collar release. The landsuit came apart down the front, and Andy let it slip down off his shoulders, feeling his gills tingle as the dry air hit them. The woman gasped. The older girl said, "Mommy, what—" and was hushed. The little girl stared at the pink slits on his neck. "Owie," she said again. And the man . . .

. . . laughed.

It was a deep, booming laugh, a laugh full of such pure joy and relief that Andy couldn't help but smile himself, though admittedly the smile would have been broader if the shotgun hadn't still been aimed at his head.

But a moment later it wasn't. The man threw it aside. "You're a Selkie! The planet you came from is Marseguro!"

"You've . . . heard of it?"

"Of course, of course," the man said. "The Body told us all about Its great victory over 'Victor Hansen's abominations,' how God's blessed Holy Warriors had Purified the last stronghold of his evil Selkies. But then they stopped talking about it, and we knew something had gone wrong . . . and I was glad. A lot of us were glad. A lot of us around here are . . ." he lowered his voice, as though by force of habit so strong changing circumstances couldn't break it ". . . Christians. We pray nightly to our God, the God of love, not their demon of hate and destruction. We pray for deliverance. And shortly after the Body stopped talking about Marseguro . . . our prayers were answered.

"We heard reports of a strange disease cropping up all over the world. Then those reports stopped coming, and we knew the disease must be worse than the Body was admitting.

"Shortly after that, the Body was telling us that the strange new disease was nothing to worry about, and we knew it must be very bad indeed. Shortly after that, the Body, still insisting the disease was nothing to worry about, was telling us to avoid crowds and stay away from animals. And then, shortly after *that*, the Body stopped telling us anything because the people who told us things were mostly all dead, like everyone else."

"But not you," Andy said.

"Not us," the man said. "And there are many other survivors scattered through the countryside. The cities . . . very bad. The plague liked crowds. But even in the cities, there are survivors. A few people are immune. A few . . . a very lucky few . . . even recovered.

"We didn't wait to find out if we were either immune or lucky. When we heard how the plague was coming closer and closer, even after the Body banned all travel, we fled here. We were fortunate, we had this place." He looked around the inside of the assault craft. "Well, not *this* place. But the vineyard. The winery. In my family since before Salvation Day. At first we lived in the house, but it was too hard to keep the birds away. And then, in the middle of the night, this thing came roaring down, planted itself in the middle of my best vines, turned itself off, and opened itself up."

I should have a word with Simon about how he programmed these things, Andy thought.

"And that's when I realized we could live in here. I modified the bird-bangers to fire something more than compressed air, left the ratbots to chase down the rodents, and moved us in. I go up to the winery, get food from the pantry, bring it back. So far I haven't been infected. But . . . it's no life. Not for me and my wife. Not for our little girls. It's like . . . waiting to die." His smile faded. "You really have a vaccine?"

"Yes," Andy said.

"Praise God!"

Andy didn't know how to reply to that. He'd never bothered with religion, even though religion, in the form of the Body, had certainly bothered with him.

Instead of saying anything, he refastened the landsuit, and felt the water flow over his skin and gills again. Then picked up his pack, opened it, and took out a hypospray. "Who gets it first?" he said.

"The girls," the man said.

Andy nodded, adjusted the dosage for the girls' small bodies, and stepped over to them. Both girls shrank back and the older one started to cry. The mother shushed her. "Give it to me, first," she said. "See, Asha, Mommy will go first so you can see it doesn't hurt." She pulled down the neck of her dress to bare her shoulder. "Go ahead," she said.

Andy adjusted the dosage upward again, then leaned forward and pressed the trigger. The hypospray hissed, and that was that. "It didn't hurt at all," the woman said to the girls. "Just a little cold, like someone put a dollop of ice cream on my arm."

That made the girls smile. "Now you, Asha," the woman said. "Show Ani how brave you are."

The older girl held out her arm. Andy adjusted the dose, sprayed her. Her arm jerked a little as the spray entered her skin, but then she held still. "See, Ani," she said to her little sister. "It's okay. It doesn't hurt."

Ani cried after she received her dose, but only for a moment.

Andy vaccinated the father next. As the big man rubbed his shoulder, the autodoc door opened, and Andy turned to look at Sam, sitting up now, his arm in a sling, his shoulder bandaged. "Autodoc, report," Andy said.

"Patient suffered multiple puncture wounds to his left upper arm," the autodoc said. "Blood loss was substantial but not life-threatening. Removed foreign objects from wounds, cleaned and dressed the shoulder, administered anti-shock medication and analgesics. Patient should make a full recovery with no residual physical ill effects and only moderate scarring."

Andy looked back at the family. "You're safe from the plague now," he said. "You can go anywhere you like."

"Praise God," the man said again. "And praise you, too . . . Andy, is it?"

Andy nodded. "Andy King."

"Andy King. My name is Tseliso Mathibeli. My wife is Letlotlo. My girls are Asha and Ani." He held out his hand. "I haven't shaken hands with anyone in months. I would like you to be the first."

Andy took the proffered hand. The man squeezed hard once, then released his fingers. He looked around the passenger compartment. "You came for this craft, didn't you," he said.

"Yes," Andy said. "And you don't need it now. You can go back to the winery."

The man nodded slowly. "There are other survivors in the area," he said. "How much vaccine do you have?"

"We can't stay and vaccinate everyone," Andy said.

The man's brow furrowed. "I thought that was why you came."

"Why we came to Earth, yes. But not why we came to your vineyard." Andy studied him. A Christian, persecuted by the Body, unfazed by the fact his prayed-for salvation came in the form of a moddie . . .

The truth, Andy thought. *He deserves it.* "The Avatar is still alive," he said. "He has an army of Holy Warriors. They stole vaccine from us—" *well, not all of the truth: effectively, Richard handed it to them on a silver platter,* "—and are on the move. They're planning to attack a community of moddies. After that, they will send vaccine around the world, but they will start with the survivors in the Body enclaves. It will mean the Body once more taking control of Earth, even more firmly than before, because it will decide who does and does not receive the vaccine. It will be able to wipe out its remaining enemies just by withholding the one thing that can save them from the plague.

"But we have a chance, now, while the Avatar and his men are on the march, on foot, to stop them once and for all." He looked at the man. "That's why I need this assault craft."

Mathibeli nodded gravely. "Then you may have it."

"You'll turn off the weapons targeting my other two crewmembers?"

Mathibeli smiled a slow smile. "I would, of course . . . but they don't exist." He shrugged. "I was bluffing."

Andy blinked, then burst out laughing. "After the bird-blasters and the ratbots, it was a very good bluff."

"Thank you," Mathibeli said. His smile faded. "If you cannot stay to vaccinate the other survivors in this area," he said, "then please, I beg you, let me have the vaccine. Show me how to administer it."

"We don't have very many doses with us," Andy said. "We didn't really expect to find survivors."

"Then give me what you have, or at least what you can spare. Please." He looked at Letlotlo, already rolling up their bedding, and Asha and Ani, who sat quietly holding hands, watching the men. "There are other children. Have you seen a child die of this plague, Andy King?"

"No," Andy said quietly. "I have seen victims of it, but they were all Holy Warriors."

"I have seen friends, and family, and children die," Mathibeli said. "It is only by the Grace of God that we still live. If you can give me the means to save even a dozen people . . . a dozen children . . . please. You must."

"You'll put yourself in danger," Andy said. "If you have the vaccine, word will get out. Desperate people will come looking for you. They won't believe you when you say you have no more . . ."

"I have friends, neighbors, who still live. We will band together. We will protect ourselves, and our families. We can do that. But no one can protect themselves indefinitely from the plague. Only this vaccine of your, this miracle from heaven, can do that." Mathibeli suddenly dropped to his knees and held up his arms. "Mr. King," he said, "I am begging you."

"Don't!" Andy said. "Don't." He held out his hands, pulled Mathibeli to his feet. "I'll give you the vaccine I have. And I will do my best to get you more. Somehow."

"Thank you, Mr. King," Mathibeli said, shaking his hand again. "Thank you. But . . . if I may ask . . . if you came to Earth hoping to vaccinate the survivors, why is the supply so limited?"

"We intended to manufacture it here, using Earth's microfactories," Andy said. "But the Body controls those."

Mathibeli blinked. "But . . . I have a microfactory."

Andy stared at him. "What?"

"The winery. We make . . . made . . . our high-end wines using very traditional methods. But we also made lower-end wines—still high quality, I assure you, but far less expensive. And those are made by microfactory. It's an old model, one my grandparents installed when they bought the property more than seventy years ago . . ."

"It's a seventy-year-old microfactory?" Andy said.

"Yes . . ."

Andy laughed out loud. "Then, my friend, you're out of the wine business . . . and into the vaccine production business."

A vast smile split Mathibeli's face. "God has doubly blessed us this day!" he said. "Are you sure you aren't an angel?"

Andy's smile faded. "Oh, I'm sure, all right," he said. "Very, *very* sure." He turned to Sam, who had climbed out of the autodoc. "Get Annie and Derryl up here. And then . . ." he looked back at Mathibeli. "We'll get your microfactory set up and producing vaccine in no time." *Assuming Cordelia lets me download the programming,* Andy thought. "But before we head to the winery . . ."

"Yes?"

"Could you please turn those damn bird-blasters off?"

Mathibeli laughed. "With pleasure!"

Richard sat panting on a boulder beside the trail and looked at his navcomp again, hoping it would tell him something different. But its instructions remained stubbornly the same: leave the trail, a well-groomed hiking trail complete with occasional text panels highlighting geological or botanical points of interest, and climb the ridge to the south. Newshore lay on the far side of that ridge.

The problem was that the "ridge to the south" looked more like the "sheer cliff to the south."

A mess of boulders and dirt and tangled trees and a massive scar showed well enough what had happened: some seismic shrug had brought the path the navcomp was cheerily pointing them toward sliding down the mountainside sometime since the navcomp's database had last been updated.

Richard instructed the navcomp to provide him with

an alternative route. It took it a lot longer than he thought it should have, rather as if it were pouting, and while he waited, he looked around at the rest of the rescue party. None of them seemed to be breathing as hard as he was. The Selkies he could understand: even weighed down by their landsuits, they were stronger than he could ever hope to be. But he couldn't understand why the other nonmods weren't finding the going as tough as—

He sighed. Actually, he could understand it all too well: he just didn't want to admit it. He was in his mid-thirties, and despite the exertions of the last year, had led an essentially sedentary life: certainly sitting in front of computer screens in Body Security hadn't done much to buff him up. They were, in Earth years, barely past twenty. The youngest was probably more like eighteen.

I'm getting too old to save planets, Richard thought.

The navcomp buzzed to get his attention, and he looked down. A yellow route had appeared on the map, winding down to the ocean and along the shore. He frowned. It looked awfully exposed—

Richard's microcomm crackled. "Point One here," a voice whispered. "We've got company. Four Kemono-mimi just came out of the woods. They're heading your way."

Richard jumped up. "Everyone off the trail!" he ordered. "Company's coming."

Ten seconds later the trail looked as deserted as it had before they'd come along half an hour before.

"Point One," the voice said again. "They'll be at your location in thirty seconds."

Crouched in the woods with the others, Richard waited. Right on schedule, the Kemonomimi came into sight. It was Richard's first glimpse of them in the flesh, at least since he'd seen one shot down in the House of the Body last Salvation Day.

They're just modified humans, he told himself. *That's all. Certainly no stranger than the Selkies.*

But human beings had no built-in fear of gilled water-apes, whereas millennia of life on the African veldt had hard-wired a fear of big cats into them. Despite his best mental efforts, Richard felt the hair on the back of his neck rise as he watched the four males—*men,* he corrected himself firmly—come into view. One was glossy black; another had leopard spots; another was all white except for black points on his face, ears, tail, hands, feet and groin; one boasted tiger stripes that reminded Richard of Emily's favorite skinsuit. All were naked except for belts hung with sidearms, what looked like short swords, and other equipment he couldn't identify. All carried Holy Warrior rifles. They moved with uncanny grace, ears flicking, eyes bright as they glanced this way and that.

A hunting party, Richard thought. *That's all. Keep on going. Keep on going . . .*

But they didn't. They stopped, right at the boulder where Richard had been sitting moments before. As Richard watched, they sniffed, mouths opening as they did so, revealing alarmingly white and alarmingly pointed teeth. And then their heads came up in unison and—

—they looked straight at him.

Crap, Richard thought, and dove for cover.

Bullets ripped apart the trunk of the tree he'd been kneeling behind moments before and the fallen tree he cowered behind now. A splinter stung his cheek.

"Don't kill—" Richard started to shout, but it was far too late for that. The Marseguroites' weapons chattered. One of the Kemonomimi fell, chest shattered, but the others, lightning fast, vanished behind the rocks.

"Damn it!" Richard crawled on his belly over to the line of boulders where the others had taken cover. "We're not trying to start a war here!"

"They fired first," said one of the Selkie women—Angela, that was her name.

"Anybody hurt?" Richard said

Nobody had time to reply before the Kemonomimi's weapons opened up again. Richard hugged the nearest rock.

"Point One here," said a voice in Richard's ear. "Point Two is with me. We're flanking them. We should be able to take them out with—"

"Negative," Richard said. "*Don't kill them*. Just drive them into cover."

"I can do that," said a new voice—Point Two. A moment later the Kemonomimi's fire stopped as a new weapon spoke from the other side of the valley. A bullet ricocheted, whining off into the distance.

"Captain," said Point One, a Selkie named Chang, "they've got communications equipment on their belts. If they tell the town—"

"They already have, unless they're idiots," Richard said. "But they don't know why we're here. They haven't even seen us. They probably think we're Holy Warriors. We don't have to kill any more of them. We fade away, leave them chasing phantoms, slip on toward the town while they're searching the woods."

"They sniffed us out once," Chang said. "They can probably track us wherever we go."

Should have thought of that, Richard thought. "So we split up. A decoy party to lead them on a wild goose chase. Another party to conduct the rescue." And, damn it, he knew which one he was going to have to be in, though he wanted with every fiber of his being to be part of the team that would enter Newshore to bring out Emily. "They can't smell in the water. So here's the plan. We nonmods keep this bunch pinned down while you Selkies slip away on down the valley. Get down to the sea . . . then swim someplace where you can land unobserved. Watch the town until you locate Emily and Shelby. When you're ready, go in and get them. Don't kill anyone if you can help it. We'll lead as many as we can away from the town."

Angela gave him a long look. "The Kemonomimi have been evading Holy Warriors in these mountains for decades. You think you can keep ahead of them?"

"I'm going to try," Richard said grimly. "Point One, Point Two, do you copy?"

"Yes, sir," Chang replied.

"Yes, sir," said Point Two.

"Wait where you are. The other Selkies will join you. Nonmods, you're with me."

"Good luck," Chang said.

"You, too," said Richard. "Covering fire," he told the other four nonmods. "But try not to hit anything vital. On my mark . . . fire!"

As they raised up and sprayed the rocks below with bullets, the Selkies ran upslope, deeper into the woods.

When he was sure they were away, Richard looked at the other four nonmods, reinforcing their names in his mind. Eric. Tembe. Akim. Dominique. "Ready for a game of cat and mouse?" he said.

Dominique snorted. "I'd rather be the cat."

"Me, too," Richard said. "But I'm afraid that role is taken." He took a deep breath. "Okay. One more volley, and then we run . . . back up the valley, away from the town. On my mark . . . three, two, one . . . fire!"

They sprayed the rocks, then scrambled off into the woods in the opposite direction from that the Selkies had taken, every step taking them farther away from those they had come to rescue.

There goes my chance to play knight in shining armor, thought Richard; but then he heard a very cat-like yowl behind them, and put everything out of his mind except running.

Chapter 19

EMILY SAT IN VICTOR Hansen's office in the air terminal building. For once, Cleopatra wasn't with him, but Ubasti stood behind her, hardly blinking as she watched her, one hand always resting on the butt of her gun.

Victor poured himself a glass of ice water out of a metal pitcher beaded with sweat, then tapped the pitcher against a second glass. "Drink?"

Emily ignored him. "Let the boy go. I'll talk."

Victor sipped his water, then held it up so the light of the softly glowing floor lamp in the corner shone through it. Outside, it was pitch-black; past midnight. Shelby had been without water now since early that morning, more than eighteen hours in total. Victor had deliberately stayed away long past the time he had said he would return, leaving Emily to watch, hands gripping the arms of the observation room chair, as Shelby went from prowling the room to curled in a fetal position on the bed, arms locked around his knees, moaning. Twenty minutes before Victor finally showed up, the moaning had stopped and Shelby had fallen into a restless stupor.

It had taken all Emily's self-control to keep from leaping at Victor the moment he entered. She longed to feel his neck in her hands, fantasized about killing him with the wrist-mounted dart guns built into her landsuit on Marseguro. But attacking Hansen would only have gotten her shot by Ubasti, and would have accomplished nothing for Shelby. Instead, she had meekly accompanied Victor back to his office. Then Victor had left there for another hour, still guarded by the apparently tireless Ubasti. He'd only returned a few minutes ago. She watched as he considered her offer of cooperation.

"I think not," Victor said at last.

This time Emily did surge to her feet in fury—or tried to; clawed, furred hands gripped her shoulders and pushed her, hard, back down into the black leather chair. "Then kill him and be done with it," Emily snarled. "And me, too. Why put us through this?"

Victor contrived to look hurt. "I'm not a monster, Miss Wood," he said. "The boy has already been taken to the pool and is now resting comfortably."

Relief flooded Emily; relief, then confusion. "But you said—"

"You asked me to let the boy go. I can't do that," Victor said. "He's obviously the perfect lever and leash where you are concerned. To ensure your cooperation, he remains a prisoner, just as you do."

Emily closed her eyes. It enraged her to look at that face, almost identical to Richard's, attached to such a . . .

Well. Her rage vanished like air from a pricked balloon. Whatever she thought of him, he had her number, didn't he? He knew she wouldn't let Shelby suffer to placate her sense of honor, not when the information she could provide Hansen probably wouldn't do him any good anyway.

Probably.

Though if she could figure out exactly what he was up to, she'd feel more certain of that.

Praying to any God but the Body's that what she was about to do wouldn't hurt Richard or Marseguro, she said, "All right. Ask your questions." She took a deep breath. "And I'll have that drink now."

"Excellent." Victor poured her a glass and pushed it across the desktop. It left a shiny black comet's tail of moisture behind it that he swiped away with his sleeve. "Let's begin with the basics. Tell me how many are in the crew of the . . ." He grinned. "*MSS Victor Hansen*."

We're going to have to change the name after this, Emily thought, sipping her water. She put it down, cleared her throat. "I didn't arrive on the *Victor Hansen,* but if I remember right . . ."

Victor kept her talking for the next hour. What was the population? What weapons did they have? What ships? What were the principal towns? Describe the vegetation. The weather. The style of architecture. The level of medical knowledge. The . . .

On and on the interrogation continued, until suddenly Victor held up a hand to stop her in the middle of her description of the Marseguro Planetary Museum and its (in his view) "laughably fraudulent" displays. He yawned hugely. She remembered Richard yawning just like that the morning after they'd . . .

She clenched her teeth.

"I think that's enough for now," Victor said. "We'll carry on in the morning." He stood and held out his hand to Ubasti, "Let me have your handgun. I'll escort Miss Wood back to her quarters myself."

Ubasti hesitated. "Sir—"

"Do as you're told!" Victor snapped.

A soft hiss, but, "Yes, sir," Ubasti said, and handed the gun to him.

"Good." Victor waved a hand at her. "You're dismissed. Get some sleep."

"Yes, sir." Back ramrod straight, Ubasti turned and disappeared down the hall.

Victor turned, gun held loosely, not even pointed at Emily. "Let's go," he said.

Emily didn't move. "Are you sure you want to risk taking me back to the school all by yourself?" she said. "Aren't you afraid I might jump you? I'm faster and stronger than you are."

"And I'm holding Shelby," Hansen said. "If you kill me, the Kemonomimi will tear him apart. And they're faster and stronger than *you* are, Miss Wood. They'll hunt you down and tear *you* apart, too. You're not stupid enough to risk it."

"Then why do you need the gun?"

"Just in case you *are* that stupid. Now come on." He motioned with the gun.

Emily walked past him, down the hall, and out of the terminal building into the night. Lights, blurred by fog, glowed here and there among the trees. Two yellow pole lights at the end of the pier shone like cat's eyes, watching her. *How appropriate,* she thought.

They trudged toward the school. "I want to see Shelby," Emily said suddenly. "I don't trust you. Prove to me he's been allowed to rehydrate, or I won't tell you another thing." She stopped so abruptly Victor's pistol jabbed her in the back. "And if you have lied to me, Victor Hansen," she said without turning around, "then *I* will tear *you* apart, gun or no gun, no matter what happens to me afterward."

Victor sighed. "Oh, very well," he said. "We can look in on him before you're locked up again."

They passed through the empty downtown. The school loomed ahead of them, dark except for a single light in the entryway. Augustus lounged there, but he jumped to his feet as Victor and Emily climbed the steps. "Sir?" he said.

"I've brought her back to be locked up," Victor said. "But I promised her she could look in on the boy." He glanced at Emily. "You'd better come with us," he told Augustus.

Good, she thought. *I rattled him. Just a little.*

A miniscule victory, but she savored it.

They walked through the darkened hallway to Shelby's prison room. Augustus unlocked the door. Emily put her head in, intending only to take a quick look, but Shelby rolled over as she did so and sat up. Only a small amount of light made it through the room's high windows from a streetlamp somewhere outside, but she could see him clearly with her Selkie eyes, bare-chested, blanket covering his legs. He stared at her. "Emily?" he said. "What—?"

"Just checking to see that you're all right," she said. "Have they let you swim?"

"Yes, thank God," Shelby said. He pulled his knees up and wrapped his arms around them. "It was . . . awful." He sounded very young. "I've never hurt like that in my life."

"I know," Emily said, anger flaring inside her again. "I know."

"Are you finished?" Victor said. "Because I'd really like to—"

Gunfire interrupted him. Victor swore, gave Emily a sharp shove that drove her into Shelby's room, then slammed the door on both of them. Before she turned around, she heard Victor's and Augustus' footsteps pounding down the hallway.

She turned back to Shelby. He stared at her. "What's going on?"

"I don't know," she said. "Holy Warriors, probably." She prowled the room, but there was no way out: the door was locked, the windows too small to fit through. She sat down on the bed next to Shelby.

"Did they torture you, too?" he asked.

"Not . . . directly," she said. "They were torturing *you* to get *me* to tell them about Marseguro. Hansen has some scheme to destroy us once he's somehow wiped out the Avatar's forces . . . although he also says he has no intention of actually attacking Marseguro. I don't know what he's thinking." She suddenly thought of something and leaned in very close to his ear. He tensed. She whispered as softly as she could, "He doesn't know about the Free Selkie Republic. Whatever you do, don't mention that you're from Earth."

Shelby nodded. Emily leaned back, and he visibly relaxed.

What . . . ? she wondered, and then it hit her. Teenage boy, in bed, girl sits next to him, she leans in close . . .

Oh, good grief, she thought. *Boys! You'd think a little thing like gunfire in the streets outside the prison where you've been tortured by the clone of your creator would cool your libido.*

Apparently not.

So she casually got up and went to sit in the chair instead.

"But then . . . why did they *stop* torturing me?" he said.

Emily met his gaze. "Because I told him what he wanted to know. I don't see what use the information will be to him, and . . . I've been through dehydration. I didn't want you to suffer because of some stupid sense of heroism on my part."

Silence. Shelby looked away. *Have I managed to destroy his hero worship?* she wondered. *My feet are as clay as they get.*

But then his gaze returned . . . and he smiled, a little. "Thank you," he said.

She did her best to smile back. "You're welcome."

The gunfire had continued intermittently since she'd been shoved into the room, and once she'd thought she heard shouts. Now footsteps raced down the corridor toward them.

Emily jumped to her feet just as the door slammed open to reveal Victor Hansen and Augustus, large packs on their backs. Augustus leveled his rifle at the two Selkies, while Victor tossed something onto the floor with a grunt. Emily recognized the black bundle at once: their landsuits.

"Put those on," Victor said. "We're leaving."

Emily grabbed one, tossed the other to Shelby, and pulled hers on as quickly as she could. She checked the readouts on her wrist. The water supply was still good, the batteries strong. She glanced at Shelby; he had his on, too. She turned back to Victor, who now held a pistol. "What's going—" she began, but Augustus, who had slung his rifle on his back alongside his pack, rushed in, grabbed her arm, and practically threw her out into the hallway, so hard she banged against the far wall. When she spun, furious, she found Victor's gun leveled at her stomach.

"No talking," he growled. "Just do what I say."

Augustus reemerged, hand wrapped around Shelby's upper arm. "That way," Victor said, and gestured down the corridor, away from the main entrance. Augustus shoved Shelby in that direction, and Emily caught him before he could fall. She gave another furious glare over her shoulder, but Augustus had his own pistol out now, and with two guns pointed at their backs, she had no choice but to follow orders.

The door marked EXIT at the end of the corridor took them into a stairwell. There was a door leading outside at their level, but they didn't take it, instead descending into the basement where there were two more doors, one to their left that probably led to the janitor's workspace, and one to their right, painted bright red and padlocked. Augustus stepped forward and hammered the lock open with the butt of his rifle, then kicked the door in.

Beyond stretched a long, straight corridor, lit at irregular intervals by ancient fluorescent bulbs. Pipes, some copper, some insulated with white foam, some plain black plastic, ran along the walls and ceiling. "Go," Victor said. Once they were all through the door, he closed

it behind them. Then they hurried along the corridor for
what Emily judged to be at least two hundred meters,
maybe more; right under the soccer field, if she remembered the layout of the school grounds, and then well
beyond it.

At the far end, the corridor ended in another red
metal door, while the pipes turned and disappeared up
and out through the ceiling and walls. This door was already open a crack; the guard pushed it the rest of the
way, took a quick look inside, then led the way into what
appeared to be some kind of heating plant. Other doors
led off in other directions. *All the public buildings must
get their heat from this one plant,* Emily thought. She
didn't know enough about the technology to figure out
the heat source. Big metal tanks and boxes, a bewilder-
ing maze of pipes . . . geothermal, maybe?

"Up," Victor said. They climbed stairs made of metal
honeycomb and stepped off onto smooth concrete.
Some of the pipes and tanks from the lower level extended into this level, as well. A room off to one side,
enclosed in glass, glowed with vidscreens: presumably,
the control room.

Prodded by Victor and Augustus, Emily and Shelby
hurried past the control room to another door. This one
led into a carpeted corridor, dark except for pale blue
glowstrips in the ceiling every two meters or so. Doors
to either side opened into pitch-black rooms. At the far
end, glass double doors let them into a reception area.
Its lights were off, too, but two stories of glass wrapped
around it, and although it faced away from downtown,
distant streetlights bleeding through the fog made it
easy enough for Emily to see the furniture scattered
around the big room, and, above the massive wooden
slab of the reception desk, a sign: "Newshore Community Geothermal Plant." Beneath that, smaller letters
proclaimed, "God is the One True Power."

A not-so-distant explosion shook the building. "Keep

moving," Victor said. "If they're in the school, it won't take them long to find the door into the steam tunnel."

Augustus grunted and led the way to the main doors. They opened at his approach, and all four of them slipped into the fog.

Once outside, Emily could clearly hear shouts and shots. But she couldn't see anything of the town: on the other side of the driveway that curved around the front of the geothermal plant dark forest marched up a slope, fading away into the fog.

A moment later, they plunged in among the dripping trees.

Chris Keating was getting very tired of his Kemono-mimi escort.

At first he'd tried to talk to them, but they'd ignored his efforts. They didn't even talk to each other, at least not where he could hear them. Of course, he usually only had two of them in close proximity: the other four ranged through the woods ahead and behind and to either side, alert for Holy Warriors who might spoil the surprise they had planned for the Avatar before it could be delivered. For all he knew, they chatted up a storm out there in the trees, but whenever they were around him, grim silence prevailed.

The silence had finally been broken as they'd been setting up camp near the top of the ridge Victor Hansen had pointed him to, but none of the talk had been directed at him, and although he could hear low voices all around him as he lay alone in his tent that night, he couldn't understand a word. The Kemonomimi could murmur to each other at a far lower volume than a normal human would have found intelligible.

He wondered what they were saying, and how much of that low murmuring, just on the threshold of hearing, concerned him.

He sighed and looked up ahead along the steep, switch-

backing path they were following in what seemed like yet
another endless series of ridges between him and the pass
where he was to allow himself to be captured by the Avatar. Not that he could see very far. It vanished into the fog
that had descended with the night.

His back ached, his legs ached, and the warm/cold
coat's supposedly hypoallergenic lining made his skin
itch. He couldn't honestly say he'd never felt as miserable as he did right then—he'd lived through some pretty
miserable times recently—but *just give me a couple of
days*, he thought.

The path was too narrow for them to walk abreast,
so he and his two Kemonomimi companions moved in
single file. And then the one in front stopped, so suddenly Chris almost planted his nose in his body-armored
back.

"What are you—" he began in irritation, but the big
moddie whipped his head around and snarled at him,
excessively sharp teeth bared. Chris bit off the rest of
his question for fear of having it bitten off for him, along
with his head.

He glanced back. The trailing Kemonomimi had
stopped, too. Both of the moddies stood motionless,
heads raised, nostrils flaring and ears flicking as they
surveyed the surrounding trees.

And then two shots rang out almost simultaneously,
and both Kemonomimi fell, squalling, the one in front
clutching his arm, the one in back his leg. Chris felt
something warm on his face and when he touched it his
hand came away red: Kemonomimi blood. He stared at
the scarlet stain, too shocked to move.

An instant later four men and a woman in hooded,
camouflaged coats burst out of the trees and ran toward
the fallen moddies. The Kemonomimi who'd been shot in
the leg tried to bring his rifle around, but the lone woman
kicked it out of his hands and then banged him firmly and
expertly on the head. The Kemonomimi slumped.

The one at the front of the line had been similarly dealt with. But then, to Chris' bewilderment, one of the men knelt down and began treating the bullet wounds, flipping back the hood of his jacket as he did so. Chris stared. "I know you," he said. "You're . . . oh, God." He felt a cold chill that had nothing to do with the fog. "You're Eric Hingston. You're from Marseguro!"

"So are you," said a voice behind Chris, and he turned to see another man pushing back his hood, revealing the face of the man he hated more than any other.

Richard Hansen.

Chris couldn't speak. Richard Hansen had been his nemesis since the moment they'd met. Richard Hansen had derailed everything Chris had planned for himself, and for Marseguro. He'd fantasized about killing him so many times he'd almost convinced himself he must be dead. And yet . . .

Here he was.

How? *Why?*

To finish what he started, Chris thought. *He's here to kill the Avatar.*

He doesn't know he's on the same side as these Kemonomimi.

And Chris wasn't about to tell him.

"Richard Hansen!" he said. "Thank God."

Richard stood a mere two meters away from Chris Keating, and he still couldn't believe it.

So far, the day had been one of unpleasant weather and unpleasant news. They'd managed to stay ahead of, and eventually lose, the Kemonomimi patrol that had found them, without having to do any more fighting. Then, in the middle of the night, they'd heard from the Selkie party sent to rescue Emily and Shelby . . . the party that had failed.

They'd tried to sneak into town when they spotted Emily being escorted through the town by a single man.

But they'd been detected—they weren't sure how—and a firefight had broken out. No one killed on either side, as far as they knew, but there'd certainly been some injuries.

When they'd finally reached the school where Emily had been taken, she was gone. Apparently, she and Shelby had been taken out through maintenance tunnels that led to the community's geothermal generating plant. By the time the Marseguroites had figured that out, Emily and Shelby and an unknown number of Kemonomimi with them had vanished into the fog-shrouded forest—and the Kemonomimi in the town were beginning to regroup. The Selkies had gotten out while they still could, swimming down the river into the bay, then landing far up the coast. Now they were hiking back toward the shuttle, where the nonmods would rendezvous with them.

But then, this morning, Richard and his companions had seen, in the distance, another nonmod, not one of theirs, who was apparently a prisoner of the Kemonomimi, and had doubled back to "rescue" him. Only to discover . . .

Richard shook his head. That Keating still lived seemed a not-so-minor miracle. But that he not only lived but was here, being escorted by Kemonomimi . . . that was a miracle on the order of raising the dead.

Yet here he was.

And being escorted . . . where, exactly?

"Thank God?" he said in response to Chris' greeting. "I'd have thought you'd have given up on your God by now, Keating. *It* certainly seems to have given up on the Body Purified."

"Oh, I have," Keating said. "I . . . you have no idea, Richard, what I've been through. The plague . . . when I realized that I had brought it back, what it was doing . . ." He looked at the ground. "It was more than I could bear, almost. It almost destroyed me."

Richard looked at the young man. "Did it?" he said. "How lucky for you it didn't. It certainly destroyed pretty much everyone else."

"I'm sorry," Keating said. "That's all I can say. If I could change things, I would. But I can't."

Richard glanced at the fallen Kemonomimi. "You have strange friends for such a staunch Believer."

"They're not my friends," Chris said, with such vehemence that Richard fully believed him for the first time. "They're my guards. I don't know where they were taking me." He hesitated. "Do you know who their leader is?"

Richard shook his head.

Keating smiled an odd smile. "It's you."

"What?"

"Another of you. Another clone. Only this one actually thinks he's Victor Hansen—the original, not a copy. And the Kemonomimi think he is, too. They call him 'Creator.' "

Richard blinked. "Another clone . . . like me?"

"*Exactly* like you. Even the same age, or close to it."

Only in him the gene-bomb worked . . . more or less, Richard thought. *Victor Hansen, you son of a bitch.*

"One of his scavenging parties found me in the City of God. They wanted to know why I was immune. They brought me back here. I didn't tell him about Marseguro, or the vaccine . . . I didn't tell him anything. So he ordered these Kemonomimi to take me . . . somewhere. I don't know where. Maybe a laboratory. I think 'Victor Hansen' is planning to . . . experiment on me." Chris looked Richard in the eye. "I know we've had our differences—"

"That's one way to put it."

"But I swear to you, Richard Hansen, I'm glad to see you now. I'll take my chances with you over these abominations any day."

Abominations. That sounded more like the Chris Keating Richard knew and loathed.

His crew had finished treating and tying up the Kemonomimi. Now they stood looking at Chris. Richard saw the hatred on their faces, and suddenly realized how much danger Chris was in ... not from the Kemonomimi (if he were even telling the truth about that) but from the Marseguroites, all of whom had lost family and friends when the Body attacked.

Up until that moment Richard had been assuming he'd keep Chris with him as a prisoner. But now he realized that if he took Chris Keating prisoner, Chris Keating might very well be dead within hours—if not from a knife in the back or a stray bullet, then from falling off a cliff or being hit by a falling rock. And even if Richard kept him alive, he would be an unending source of tension and friction among Richard's already troubled crew.

"Keating," Richard said, "I don't believe a word you've told me. I don't know what you're really doing with the Kemonomimi, and I suspect I wouldn't like it if I did. But I've got other things to worry about. So here's my best offer: get lost."

Chris blinked at him. "What?"

"Get lost. Now." And looking at the scrawny, barely-bearded boy/man in front of him, Richard felt his own anger suddenly erupting to the surface. He barely stopped himself from raising his rifle: if he did, he suspected the others would shoot Chris in cold blood seconds later. But his fists clenched and he let the anger into his voice as he roared, "Now!"

Chris took one look at him, eyes wide, then turned and ran into the foggy woods. Dominique, standing next to Richard, made a move as if to follow him, but Richard put his arm out to stop her. "Let him go," he said.

"He's a bloody-handed traitor," the woman growled. "He should be executed."

"He should be tried and, if found guilty, punished according to the law," Richard said. "But we don't have time to try him, and we can't afford to lug him along with us back to the shuttle. And we've waited here long enough as it is. There are more Kemonomimi out here somewhere."

"We should have killed these two," Dominique said. "What's the point of winging them and knocking them out? If we end up in a fight with them—"

"We don't want to end up in a fight with them," Richard said. "We want to make friends with them." He looked down at the motionless Kemonomimi at his feet, arm wrapped in a blue field dressing whose nanobots were already hard at work repairing the damage. "Although I admit that's looking harder to achieve all the time."

Dominique looked after Chris again, still visible occasionally between tree trunks, toiling up the slope. "You're the captain," she said at last.

Richard let out a breath he hadn't realized he'd been holding. "Yes," he said firmly. "I am. Now let's get moving. We don't want to get to *Creator's Glory* only to find the Kemonomimi got there first. Besides, Claude must be lonely."

He looked up the slope one last time, but Keating had disappeared into the trees.

Richard hoped he hadn't just made a fatal mistake by letting him go.

Chapter 20

EMILY HAD BEEN EXHAUSTED even before Victor and Augustus forced her and Shelby into the woods. By the time the first gray light of morning began to seep through the unyielding fog, she could barely put one foot in front of the other. The landsuit she had welcomed when she'd first put it on now weighed her down like a suit of armor.

Shelby had at least had some sleep before being rousted out, but he'd also barely begun to recover from forced dehydration. He, too, began to stumble as the night wore on and still they didn't stop.

The Kemonomimi didn't seem fazed by their wearying midnight trek. Neither did Victor, which annoyed her. He was the only nonmod in the group; shouldn't he have been the first to flag?

When Shelby stumbled for the fifth time and dropped to his knees, she knelt down and helped him up, then glared at Victor, who had watched impassively. "Where are you taking us?" she demanded for the umpteenth time. Every other time her request had been met with a curt order to shut up, but this time, to her surprise, Hansen answered her. "There's an abandoned mine a few more kilometers up this ravine," he said. "It's where I set up my research lab. I had intended to bring you up here in a day or two, but last night's attack advanced my schedule."

"Who was attacking?" Emily demanded. If Victor were in a talkative mood, she wanted to get all the answers she could. "Holy Warriors?"

Victor laughed. "Not likely. They're still slogging through the forest toward their doom, although they don't know it yet. No. Your kind. Selkies."

Richard? Emily thought. "Funny how your 'superior' Kemonomimi couldn't fight them off."

"I'm sure they did, in the end," Victor said. "But they were obviously after the two of you, and in the confusion, there was always the possibility they might find you. And as long as I held you in the town, I would be inviting more attacks. So I removed the temptation." He shrugged. "It doesn't make any difference. I can continue your interrogation just as easily at my lab. I still have the necessary leverage." He looked at Shelby, leaning most of his weight on Emily and oblivious, it seemed, to everything being said. "And as I said, I intended to bring you up here anyway."

"Why?"

Victor's lips quirked in the smile she knew so well from Richard. "Enough talk. Get him moving."

Emily pressed her lips together, put her arm more firmly around Shelby's chest to support him better, and waited silently for Victor to move on.

Fifteen minutes later they reached the edge of the forest. The trees resumed another hundred meters up the defile, but in between was nothing but lichen-covered boulders, some the size of houses, and scruffy grass. Victor called a halt. "Augustus, go ahead and check it out."

The Kemonomimi nodded once and slipped ahead, padded feet silent on the needle-strewn path. He disappeared around a rock.

"Cleopatra. Augustus. What's with these names?" Emily said to Hansen.

"The Kemonomimi are mostly named after figures

from classical literature or ancient history, from a variety
of cultures," Hansen said. "As befits superior beings."

Emily started to make a retort as befitted a smart-
alecky Selkie, but it died on her lips as a single gunshot
rang out from up the path, echoing in the ravine like
thunder. Victor spun, lifting his own rifle. From around
the rock that had hidden Augustus a moment before
came half a dozen figures in blue uniforms.

Holy Warriors!

Victor turned and ran without a word, vanishing
among the trees. Emily stared after him, shocked by his
sudden disappearance, then spun back to see the Holy
Warriors moving down the slope toward her and Shelby,
rifles leveled.

She very carefully raised her free arm.

Shelby looked up, blinked, and did the same.

Karl Rasmusson had had just about enough of God's
tests.

Now it was fog. Rolling in two nights ago, it hadn't
lifted yet, and it made his army's progress painfully slow.
Slick rocks and slicker grass posed both a nuisance and
a hazard, and visibility was so poor they were in constant danger of the rear of the column losing contact
with the front.

All of which made it perfect weather for an ambush
by the Kemonomimi, who presumably knew these mountains like the backs of their ... paws ... and could un-
doubtedly hear better, if not see better, in the fog than
his men could. If he were in charge of the Kemonomimi
and planning to attack, he would do it now.

Against that chance, he had triple the usual number
of scouting parties ranging far and wide ahead, to either flank, and behind: and he had called a halt for the
day and made camp, though it was barely noon, to await
their reports.

The last thing he thought his scouts would bring him

was two Selkies in black landsuits, a young woman and an even younger boy.

The woman had short hair died a deep violet and, like all the Selkies, emerald-green, oversized eyes. She didn't look cowed as the Holy Warriors brought her to the door of his tent, where he sat on a camp stool, leafing through *The Wisdom of the Avatar of God*. In fact, she looked angry. The black-haired boy simply looked exhausted. Exhausted to the point of collapse, in fact, leaning heavily on the woman, and when the Holy Warriors tugged them to a stop, he sank to the ground and sat with his head on his knees, arms folded around them. One of the Holy Warriors put a hand on the boy's shoulder as though to force him to his feet, but the Avatar waved him off. "Leave him," he said. "He obviously needs the rest."

He got to his feet, putting aside the book reader. "I'm Karl Rasmusson, Avatar of the One Just God, By Its Grace the Head of the Body Purified." *Even if I still can't believe half the time I have the right to say that.* "Who are you?"

The woman drew herself up to her full, and not inconsequential, height. "I'm Emily Wood. I don't believe in your God, and I don't accept your authority. Let me go."

The Avatar almost laughed out loud at the sheer gall. He settled for a smile. "I'm afraid I can't do that, Miss Wood. You're a genetically modified human, which immediately makes you subject to arrest. Furthermore, you've wandered into the middle of a military operation. Operational security demands—"

"I didn't wander into anything," Emily snapped. "I was *dragged*—dragged *up* the mountain by one man, dragged *here* by others. And there is no security about your operation, Avatar. You're marching to destroy the Kemonomimi. The Kemonomimi know you're coming."

The Avatar let his smile widen. "Of course they do,"

he said. "But if they were going to flee, they would have done so already. Now they can't. We're too close, and my scouts are everywhere. They've missed their opportunity. They've trapped themselves.

"But never mind that. You're obviously from Marseguro. I know your kind freed Richard Hansen from Paradise Island. I want to know what Hansen is up to. Is he going to betray his own kind again? Is he planning to help the Kemonomimi the way he helped you Selkies? He won't find it as easy this time. No miracle plague can save *this* race of moddies. They *will* be Purified."

Emily Wood looked at him for a long moment, her eyes drilling into his. He found the directness of her gaze uncomfortable: none of the Holy Warriors ever looked at him that directly, that long—but he'd be damned if he'd look away first.

"I have nothing to tell you," she said at last, and looked down.

I win, he thought with satisfaction. "Perhaps not yet. But you will." He looked at the Holy Warriors. "Take their landsuits. Both of them. And ask Right Hand Atnikov and Grand Deacon von Eschen to attend me." He turned his gaze back on Emily Wood. "In a few hours," he said, "we'll talk again."

He sat back down on his camp stool and picked up the book reader, and, as the Holy Warriors seized the two Selkies and hauled them away toward the middle of the camp, said a silent apology to God Itself, which had obviously used the fog to deliver the moddies into his hands.

All things work to God's purpose, he read on the first page he looked at. He smiled.

With a familiar feeling of dread, Emily submitted to being stripped of her landsuit. A Holy Warrior gave them both standard-issue pale-blue jumpsuits to put on over her still-wet skinsuit and Shelby's wet trunks. She pulled hers on, then helped Shelby with his. "Emily . . ." he said as she zipped it up. "What's going to happen?"

She gave him a quick hug. "It will be all right," she said. "We have friends looking for us. It will be all right."

Shelby blinked around at the armed men moving among the camp's fog-shrouded tents. "How?" he said.

Emily didn't have an answer.

Having taken away the landsuits—and not incidentally left them barefoot—the Holy Warriors left the two of them alone. The tent they'd been ushered to was half the size of the Avatar's and contained two fold-up cots, a coldlight lantern, and nothing else.

It also came equipped with two armed guards outside the flap, as Emily discovered when she looked out. Two pairs of cold eyes turned to glare at her, and she pulled her head back inside.

Shelby lay on one of the cots, arm thrown over his eyes. They were both well-hydrated for the moment, at least: they had maybe eight hours before dehydration would begin to make itself felt.

But this time, Emily wouldn't—*couldn't*—answer her interrogator's questions. Not to save Shelby, and not to save herself. She could not betray Richard, her fellow Marseguroites, or the hidden Free Selkie Republic. Not to the Avatar.

There had been one piece of information she'd almost shared with the Avatar, though, one piece she still held tight in her mind, worrying it like a dog with a bone.

Victor Hansen had told her he expected to destroy the Avatar and his Holy Warriors when they reached the pass providing the only ready access to Newshore.

The pass they were in now.

He hadn't told her how.

If she warned the Avatar, she could save a lot of lives . . . but they'd be Holy Warriors, vaccinated Holy Warriors, Holy Warriors who would then be available to hunt down the Earth Selkies, her fellow Marseguroites, and the Kemonomimi.

But if she didn't warn the Avatar . . . and if Victor Hansen had been telling the truth . . . then soon, possibly at any moment, the Avatar and all his Holy Warriors would be killed.

And presumably, if they were still imprisoned, so would she and Shelby.

She remembered her mother, just before they unleashed the plague, explaining to her on Marseguro that those nonmods whom they could not vaccinate would die along with the Holy Warriors.

Until now, she hadn't fully comprehended how difficult it had been for her mother to decide to deploy the plague anyway. But she didn't doubt that her mother had made the right decision.

And now . . . so would she.

The Avatar would learn nothing about the Kemonomimi's plans from her. And as for dehydrating them . . . well, if they were going to die tomorrow anyway, how bad could it get?

If there were any comfort in that thought, it was extremely cold, and did nothing to help her to sleep when she lay down on the second cot and closed her eyes.

Richard sat in the copilot's chair of *Creator's Glory* and stared at the blank communications vidscreen. Beside him, Claude Maurois slumped in the pilot's chair, eyes closed.

Richard didn't want to make the call, but he had no choice.

He keyed in the frequency he'd been given. For several moments there was no response, and Richard sat in silence broken only by the heavy breathing of the members of his crew, who were mostly collapsed in various stages of exhaustion in the body of the shuttle. When the screen finally lit with the image of President McLean, her appearance shocked him: she seemed to have aged years in the past couple of days.

It reminded him uncomfortably of one truth he'd done his best to ignore: Selkies didn't live as long as nonmods.

Emily . . .

Well, Emily was several years younger than he was. Maybe their life spans would even out over the long term.

If he ever found Emily.

If her life hadn't already ended.

"You have them?" McLean said.

It tore a hole in Richard's heart, but he had to shake his head. "No," he said. "We don't. And we don't even know where they've gone."

McLean's face stiffened into a grim mask. "Explain!"

Richard related the events of the past two days as baldly as he could. When he had finished, McLean looked even grimmer. "Your crew screwed up," she said. "They moved too soon."

"They seized their best moment," Richard retorted sharply. "They saw Emily being escorted by a lone man through empty streets in the middle of the night. They saw where he took her. It was reasonable to assume Shelby was being held there, too. They successfully reached and entered the school. They can't be blamed for being unaware that a network of tunnels ran under the town."

"Really?" McLean snapped. "They never saw a central geothermal plant before?"

"No," Richard snapped back. "They're from Marseguro, remember? There are no geothermal plants on Marseguro."

"You're from Earth."

"I wasn't there."

They glared at each other for a long moment. Finally, Richard took a deep breath. "I know it's hard for you. Shelby is your son."

McLean pressed her lips together for a moment, then said softly, "And I know it's hard for you, too. Emily is your lover."

It took Richard a moment to answer. "Yes," he said slowly. "I guess she is."

"And they're both still missing," McLean said. "So what next?"

Richard rubbed his temples. "We'll take to the sky. See if we can spot them from the air. They couldn't have gone far after they left the power plant. They were on foot. We'll do a search, and—"

A strange sound filled the cabin, a buzzing alarm Richard had never heard before. Claude jerked upright, then ran his hands over the control board. "Assault craft," he said. "Heading this way."

"Holy Warriors?" Had the Avatar found them?

"Yes," Claude said, then, "no. No, wait, it's ..." He looked up from the controls. "It's one of ours," he said. "One of the assault craft jettisoned from *Victor Hansen*."

Richard sat up straight. "Andy!"

"What's happening?" Sarah McLean demanded.

"I don't know for sure," Richard said. "I'll get back to you." His hand reached out to disconnect, then he pulled it back. "Tell Emily's mother ... I'm doing my best," he said.

The President looked at him a long moment. "I will," she said at last.

"Richard Hansen out." He killed the connection, and turned to Claude. "It's heading *here?*"

"Currently on course to ... no, wait." Claude reached out, tapped controls. "Not quite here. Further inland." He looked up. "I think he's attacking the Avatar."

Richard looked out the cockpit window and into the fog, as though there were the slightest chance he could somehow peer through twenty or thirty kilometers of the stuff and a mountain range to boot. "Can you contact the assault craft?"

"If anyone's listening," Claude said, and tapped controls again. Then he nodded to Richard.

"Andy, can you hear me?" Richard said.

Silence.

"Andy, I know it's you in that assault craft. It must be."

A brief crackle of static.

"First Officer King, answer me!"

"Hello, Richard," came a reply at last. "No need to get testy. How's the rescue mission going?"

"Badly," Richard snapped. "Andy, what the hell do you think you're doing?"

"What we should have done the moment we knew where he was," Andy said. "Taking care of the Avatar."

"You've only got a single assault craft. You can't take out an entire army."

"I'm not so sure, Richard," Andy replied. "They're on foot. I think it will be like . . . mowing the grass."

"It's bloody murder, is what it is," Richard said. "Those aren't squigglefish you're clearing out of a habitat intake. They're men."

"Men who would cheerfully kill me," Andy said. "And you. And everyone on Marseguro. Men who are going to kill those other moddies, those Kemonomimi you're so anxious to protect. You're too soft, Richard. Too . . . squeamish. You don't want to kill anybody. But sometimes you have to."

"I've killed," Richard said. "When I had to. You know I have. But this—there's no need for it."

Andy laughed. "Yeah? Before you went on your rescue mission, you were planning to use this assault craft against the Avatar, too. Or did you have some other plan in mind?"

"I was going to use it stop their advance, force the Avatar to negotiate," Richard said. "And give the Kemonomimi time to escape."

"Even if it worked, and you saved the Kemonomimi,

it would only be a temporary reprieve," Andy said. His voice hardened. "You handed the Avatar the vaccine, Richard. Maybe you didn't mean to, to start with, but you did. The plague crippled the Body Purified—the monstrous religion that decimated our population, killed my wife, killed my friends, destroyed our cities—but you personally gave the Avatar what it needed to get back on its feet. You thought the Body would start helping the survivors scattered all over the planet. But you were wrong, Richard.

"I've met some of those survivors. They don't need the Body. They don't want the Body. Down in South Africa they've already started manufacturing the vaccine themselves. Cordelia Raum can give you the details; she allowed me to download the programming for their microfactory. There are other microfactories available besides those that belong to the Body, all over the world.

"So with all due respect, Richard, I've decided not to take orders from you anymore. I'm going to do what we should have planned to do from the beginning, if we found the Earth in this state: finish the job the plague began, and finish the Body Purified forever."

Richard felt cold, then hot . . . then cold again. Marseguro military culture was . . . nonexistent. He was captain and leader only because the *Victor Hansen* had obeyed him, and through whatever respect he had earned with his actions during the battle against the Body Purified.

Could he even call it mutiny? Because, God knew, Andy King was right. He *had* handed the Avatar what he needed to relaunch his campaign to Purify the Earth. He'd miscalculated every step of the way since they'd come to Earth. Andy had successfully driven the Body off of the *Victor Hansen*. Richard . . . Richard hadn't even managed to rescue his lover, or the son of the Earth Selkies' president.

"Andy," Richard said. "I'm asking you to reconsider.

I know I've made mistakes. But you promised, back on Marseguro. Everyone in the crew. You took an oath."

"An oath to protect Marseguro," Andy said. "An oath to serve our world. And that's what I'm doing."

"You promised to obey orders."

"Not blindly. Nor to follow a blind leader. And you've been leading blindly, Richard."

"Andy—"

"That's it," Andy said. "I've said what I have to say. Our attack run commences in thirty seconds. King out."

Another burst of static, and then silence.

Richard looked out into the fog again. Just tens of kilometers away, one of the very assault craft that had rained death and destruction on Marseguro was about to return the favor on the Body Purified.

And the truth was ... Richard didn't know whether anger or celebration was the appropriate response.

Andy King looked around at the rest of his team: Sam, looking pale and in pain, but composed; Derryl, implacable as always; Annie, mouth drawn into a tight, determined line.

"Anybody agree with him?" he said, nodding at the communications console.

Nobody said anything for a moment. "Let's do it," Annie said finally. "Now."

Andy nodded. "Now." And he leaned forward and took manual control of the assault craft. *This is for you, Tahirih*, he thought as he pointed the nose toward the glowing red triangle that marked their fog-shrouded target on the heads-up display. *And for everyone else these bastards murdered on Marseguro.*

Revenge might be a dish best eaten cold, as the old saying went, but he intended to serve it up piping hot.

He took a deep breath. The triangle flashed green: in range. "Commencing attack," he said to no one in particular, and pressed the firing button.

Chapter 21

EMILY, LYING IN THE PRISON tent with her eyes closed, not quite awake but not fully asleep, at first barely registered the approaching roar of an aircraft. As it swelled, she opened her eyes and sat up on her elbows, twitching her head irritably from side to side as she did so: already, her gills itched.

Richard! was her first thought.

Or was it the Kemonomimi?

Or—

Whump! She heard and felt the explosion at the same instant, like someone had pounded her on the back. Shelby jerked upright. "What's—"

WHUMP! Closer this time, the punch of air flapping the tent walls. She could hear shouts from Holy Warriors, running feet.

"An attack. I don't know—"

And then came the third explosion.

The tent ripped apart. Emily felt herself flying through the air in a rush of scorching heat, then hit the ground hard and rolled, mud and rocks and bits of torn grass fluttering down all around her, along with something much heavier. She had a half-second, horrifying glimpse of the legless torso of one of the Holy Warriors who had been guarding the tent, lying not two meters away, then something heavy crashed down on top of her so hard it drove the breath from her body, enveloping her in darkness at the same instant.

For a few seconds she simply struggled to breathe, the continuing thump of missile fire racing to the end of the camp almost fading from her hearing. At last she drew a shuddering, painful breath, and the noise rushed back: aerial cannon fire now, she thought, a deep, earth-shaking chattering. It thundered toward her, then past her.

She pushed desperately against whatever it was that held her down. Heavy canvas pushed back. Part of the tent, then, but something else, too, something lying across her legs. She pulled mightily, but couldn't free them. More explosions, more cannon fire: the attacker making another pass. She remembered the video she'd seen of the attack on Hansen's Harbor. She'd been safe in deep water at the time, but now she knew how terrified those left behind must have felt, helpless to do anything but wait, protected from the rain of death only by luck.

The cannon fire chattered past. It sounded closer this time, and she could hear men screaming even above its noise.

And then, suddenly, she could see. Someone had pulled the tent off her head.

Shelby.

Blood poured down his face from a scalp wound, but he didn't seem to notice. "There's a pole lying across your legs," he panted. "Just a second." He disappeared from her view: a moment later the weight was gone from her legs and she could scramble out from under the piece of tent that had held her captive . . .

. . . just in time to see the assault craft scream overhead once more, cannons chattering.

The missile fire seemed to be over, but she could see fire rippling from the leading edges of the assault craft's wings, and she could see the line of destruction racing through the camp. Tents and bodies burned. Holy

Warriors ran to and fro, trying to pull their wounded to safety. A few stood their ground, firing up at the shuttle as it screamed past again, but they might as well have been using peashooters for all the good it did.

"Let's get out of here," Shelby pleaded, pulling on her arm.

"What?" She looked around. For the first time she realized they were alone. No one had time to bother with them, and the guards that had been put on the tent were dead ... messily dead. The tent hadn't been much protection, but somehow it had been enough that they'd come through relatively unscathed.

The safety of the woods lay just fifty meters away. "Right," Emily said. "Let's run."

They did. But they weren't as unobserved as they'd hoped. As they reached the tree line, a single rifle shot cracked behind them ... and Shelby screamed and fell, clutching his leg, into the tall grass through which they were pushing their way through. Emily threw herself into the weeds on top of him, and peered back at the camp. A Holy Warrior lowered his rifle and started toward them ...

... and disappeared in blood-red mist as cannon fire stitched a fiery line right through him, and through the piece of tent Emily had been lying under not five minutes before.

She rolled off Shelby, and pulled his hand away from the wound in his leg. "Just a graze," she said. "No arteries or bones hit, thank God." But they had nothing to bind it with. She looked back. There was little left of the man who had shot Shelby, but she could see another body lying in the same area that looked reasonably intact—and, more importantly, fully clothed.

The fog had blended with the smoke from the attack to the point that the only other Holy Warriors she could see were indistinct shapes. Several of them seemed to be clustered around one of the few cargobots in the camp.

She thought they were pulling something free from it; then smoke swirled and she couldn't see them at all.

The roar of the assault craft had faded away. It would surely be back any minute, though. Taking her chance, she dashed out into the open.

No one shouted at her, no one shot at her. In a moment she was kneeling by the body she had seen before, pulling off its heavy coat, then its shirt, trying not to look at the bloody mess below the waist. She was struggling to free the corpse's belt when she heard the assault craft coming back.

Abandoning the belt, she took what she had and ran for the woods.

Maybe the crew had been reloading in flight: the assault craft seemed to have missiles again.

She heard them as before, whump! *Whump! WHUMP!*, the final one close enough to knock her to the ground. She thought the cargobot must have been hit, but when she rolled over, it was still there: and the explosions had cleared away the smoke so that she could see the Holy Warriors near it.

The assault craft's roar faded, changed pitched, started to swell again as it came in for another pass.

Two of the Holy Warriors held a long tube on their shoulders, with the one in back peering into a glowing screen. He said something, or probably shouted it, but her ears were ringing and she couldn't understand the words.

Their meaning became clear an instant later, though, as the tube roared and spat fire from one end and something leaped into and out of sight almost before she could register it, leaving behind a pencil-thin trace of white smoke.

An instant later there was a new explosion, sharper, more metallic, from somewhere in the clouds.

The roar of the assault craft changed, becoming ragged,

shrill. The sound rose to a tortured scream, seemed to be rushing straight at her . . .

. . . and suddenly the assault craft burst into sight through the low-hanging cloud, a jagged hole in its wing, red flame and black smoke streaming from it. It rolled from side to side, its nose pitched up as though the pilot were making one final, desperate attempt to pull it out of its dive . . . but then the wing snapped off.

The assault craft swerved sharply, rolled over, and plunged upside down into the forest on the far side of the valley, exploding in a ball of fire.

As bits of hot metal crashed sizzling into the wet ground around her, Emily staggered back into the forest.

"The assault craft has vanished," Claude told Richard quietly. "I think it's down."

Richard closed his eyes. He almost wished he still Believed, so he could say a prayer for Andy King and the three who had ridden to death alongside him . . . belated victims, in a way, of the Body's attack on Marseguro.

He wondered how many Holy Warriors they had taken with them . . . and if it would be enough to halt the Avatar's advance. Somehow, he doubted it.

He sighed. "Let's get airborne ourselves," he said. "But stay away from the Holy Warrior camp. We've got Emily and Shelby to find."

The Avatar stood on an upthrust, lichen-covered rock and surveyed the damage. For fear of an ambush by the Kemonomimi, he'd ordered the men to spread out the camp as thinly as possible when they'd camped. Now the wisdom of that decision was apparent. They'd taken casualties . . . at least a hundred, by last count . . . his Right Hand, Ilias Atnikov, among them . . . and lost a lot of tents, half a dozen horses, and two cargobots, but the bulk of their equipment, and the majority of his men, remained unscathed.

This time the Purification of Earth would be complete. There was nothing the moddies could do to stop it.

At first he'd thought the attack must have come from the Kemonomimi, but enough of the assault craft and its crew had remained intact to prove the truth: the assault craft belonged to *BPS Sanctification*. It was, in fact, one of the very craft that had taken part in the failed attempt to Purify Marseguro.

God has a very black sense of humor, he thought.

Its crew had been Marseguroite, too: three Selkies, one nonmod, if they'd put the pieces together right.

So the attack hadn't come from the Kemonomimi, but from Richard Hansen. *Is that the best you can do, Hansen?* the Avatar thought, looking up into the sky, where the fog, at last, was beginning to thin.

He smiled, then. The enemies of God had taken their best shot. And God, in the person of Its Avatar, had laughed at them.

The Purification could not be halted. The world would be freed from the abominable pollution of genemodded humans, and God would bless it once more, and once more raise the Body Purified to hegemony over it.

The dead were already being buried. The wounded were being treated. The damage was being cleaned up. The fog was lifting.

In the morning, the Body Purified would resume its march on the Kemonomimi.

Nothing could stop it now.

Chris Keating spent the night shivering in his tent, surrounded by the constant dripping of fog-drenched foliage. One of the wounded Kemonomimi had been carrying the camp heater; another had been carrying most of the food. At least he had his sleeping bag, but it wasn't as warm as it looked, and Chris spent part of the night thinking black thoughts about Victor Hansen, who surely knew what he was doing when he had the Kemonomimi pack it.

What Chris had come to realize, as he opened his pack that night, was that although it appeared to contain everything he needed to survive in the wild, it was in fact woefully inadequate—though surprisingly heavy for all of that. Victor, he suspected, had wanted to ensure that he remained dependent on his Kemonomimi escort right up until he reached the Avatar, and that if he did try to make a run for it, he'd have to slink back with his tail between his legs or die a lingering death in the woods.

Well. He couldn't be far from the Avatar now, and the Avatar couldn't be far from the deadly pass that Hansen had booby-trapped with his special bomb. In the morning he would reach the Holy Warriors and warn the Avatar about the trap. The Avatar would either disarm or remove the bomb, and then Victor Hansen would find that the force he intended to destroy was instead marching right down his throat.

Chris sneezed. He couldn't wait.

And then . . . then the Avatar could deal with the *other* Hansen.

A universe without multiple versions of Victor Hansen. If that wouldn't be a sign that God had once again blessed the Body Purified, Chris didn't know what would.

Richard Hansen spent the night in the shuttle, landed in another alpine meadow after a fruitless afternoon in the fog looking for some sign of Emily and Shelby. Reclining as best he could in the pilot seat, while sleep still eluded him, he stared up through the cockpit into the pitch-black sky. Beside him, Claude snored. In the cabin, the rest of the crew slept. A faint green glow from the nearly dimmed control panel readouts provided the only light.

As far as they knew, Andy, Sam, Derryl, and Annie were dead, and Richard . . . Richard couldn't help wondering if he were responsible. Like the refrain of a song that had become stuck in his head after endless repetitions, his bad decisions since coming to Earth paraded through his head, one after the other, in an endless cycle of second-guessing.

He shouldn't have landed on Paradise Island so willingly. But he had. He could have destroyed the contents of the vaccine chest. But he hadn't. He'd done it to save the lives of the crew of *Sawyer's Point* . . . and, to be honest, his own. But he'd also done it because, even then, he'd thought there might be some use in letting the Body have the vaccine, that the best way to get the most vaccine to the largest number of survivors as quickly as possible was to make use of the Body's resources.

It still *felt* like the right decision . . . but it had been, once again, the wrong one. All he had done was enable the Avatar to march on the Kemonomimi, and he had no doubt that after dealing with them, the Avatar, if he discovered they existed, would next destroy the Earth Selkies . . . and eventually, if he could muster the resources, the ones on Marseguro, as well.

In each case, he had made what seemed like the only possible decision.

In each case, disaster had followed.

Story of my life.

Story of my grandclone's *life.*

Victor Hansen had created two races of moddies . . . just because he could. Then he'd made other decisions, to leave clones of himself behind, to implant them with gene-bombs . . .

The results? Death, destruction, misery on a grand scale. The original Victor Hansen had even launched the program that had led to the development of the doomsday plague. Untold millions had died as a result—a fact Richard knew intellectually, though he suspected he'd been sheltered from a full understanding of it so far because all his time had been spent in this remote region of the planet.

He would remedy that, if he got the chance: if whatever decisions he had still to make, in the days ahead, did not finally bring disaster down on his own head, he would make a point of seeing what havoc his actions had helped wreak on Earth.

Of course, if disaster did find him personally, as it very well might, perhaps it would only be just.

He kept staring out into the darkness, searching for any hint of light.

He didn't find it.

Between the fog and the forest, Emily and Shelby were soon thoroughly lost, even at the slow pace Shelby could manage with his wounded leg. And though the saturated air clung to them like a cold, wet blanket, it wasn't saturated enough to halt the slow dehydration of their gills.

They needed water, a body of water large enough to submerge in, and as night was falling, the gray fog lifting a little just as the light began to fade, they literally stumbled into it, slipping down a muddy embankment into a shallow stream.

The thigh-deep water was cold, cold as ice, and Shelby gasped at it bit into his wound, which she had bound tight with strips of cloth from the dead Holy Warrior's shirt. But unpleasant though it was, it wasn't as completely unbearable as Emily suspected it would have been for a nonmod, and she welcomed its wintry embrace a moment later as she stripped down to her skinsuit and threw herself headlong into it. Shelby was close behind her.

With relief she felt her nostrils snap shut and her gills snap open, water at last flowing through them. Her lungs stilled and her heart beat faster to push more blood through her gills for oxygenation and then to the rest of her body.

The maddening itching faded away.

After five or six blissful minutes, though, the cold began to penetrate even through her insulating layer of subcutaneous fat, and she sat up. Shelby saw her motion and rose out of the water too, his gills wriggling like cilia for a moment to shake off the water, then closing tight against his neck. She felt her own do the same, and regretfully started breathing with her lungs again.

"We'll camp in that clearing we went through a few minutes ago," she said. "Then in the morning we'll follow the stream downhill. Eventually, it's bound to lead us to the sea."

Shelby nodded. His teeth were chattering, Emily noticed: she quickly got up and helped him up the embankment. They both pulled on their jumpsuits again, then she wrapped him in the Holy Warrior coat he'd been wearing all day and led him back to the clearing. With no tools and the light almost gone, the best she could manage for shelter was a rough lean-to covered with branches, but it was better than nothing, and would at least capture some of their body heat overnight.

Body heat. She looked at Shelby, huddled in the coat under the lean-to she'd just finished, barely visible now in the gloom. *This is going to make his day,* she thought, and then got down on all fours and crawled into the lean-to with him.

"Cuddle up," she said. She lay down on the damp leaves she'd spread over the muddy ground. She patted the ground next to her. He hesitated, then lay down, not quite touching her. She sighed, rolled over, and pressed her body against his side, pulling the coat over them both. "Body heat," she said into his ear. "It's the only way to keep warm."

"Um," he said. She could feel how tense he was, and

she knew perfectly well *why,* but there wasn't anything she was about to do about *that*, and as the warmth between them gradually warded off the chill of the night and the ground and the stream, she let her own eyes close.

Boys, she thought, and drifted into sleep.

Chapter 22

MORNING.
 The fog had vanished during the night, blown away by a rising wind from sea. Dawn came clear and cold, turning the sky the color of fresh salmon behind the jagged black silhouettes of the inland mountains.

As birds began to sing in the trees, Chris Keating groaned, rolled over, and sat up. *Today*, he thought. *Today I meet the Avatar.*

Richard Hansen opened his eyes and blinked at the improbably pink light beginning to crawl down the mountain he was facing, though the valley was still shrouded in shadow. *Today*, he thought. *Today we'll find Emily . . . and Shelby. We have to.*

The Avatar stood on a rock in the middle of the camp and watched his Holy Warriors dismantle tents and prepare for the day's march. *God has given us good weather at last*, he thought. *The tests have ended, all save the final one. Today or tomorrow, we attack.*

Emily Wood woke but didn't open her eyes at first, instead nuzzling closer to the warm body in her arms. "Richard . . ." she murmured, then suddenly remembered. Her eyes opened wide.

Shelby still slept, face relaxed and childlike in the morning light now finding its way through the many openings in their shelter. She disentangled herself carefully. Shelby stirred, but didn't wake, as she got to her feet and crawled out into the clearing, then stood and stretched, trying to work out the kinks brought on by a night on the ground. *Today,* she thought. *Today we should make it back to the sea.*

All around, the birds chorused with joy as though there had never been a more beautiful morning in the history of the world.

Richard wanted to get back into the air almost as soon as he woke up, but of course it took longer than that, with more than a dozen men and women needing to wake, stretch, relieve themselves, wash, and eat. The pink light was long gone from the mountains on the west side of the valley, replaced by brilliant sunshine on gray rock and dark-green pine, before everyone was settled.

As he had the day before, Richard had routed every exterior camera on the shuttle to the vidscreens in the back: two at the front of the compartment, and one on the back of every seat. What one pair of eyes might miss, he hoped a dozen might find. "Take her up," he said to Claude, and took a deep breath as the lifters roared to life and the shuttle rose into the air, then moved off across the valley floor.

Today, he told himself again. *We'll find her today.*

It took longer for the Holy Warriors to get ready than Karl Rasmusson would have liked, too. You simply couldn't hurry hundreds of men on their way, especially after yesterday's attack. One of the cargobots they'd thought undamaged turned out to have thrown a tread, and they had to shift everything they could from it to another bot, and divvy up everything that wouldn't fit on the second bot among two dozen men and their surviving horses. Grand Deacon von Eschen moved among the men, shouting and cursing, but still, the sun had almost cleared the mountains before the column began to move, climbing up toward the final saddle-backed ridge blocking their access to the town where the Kemono-mimi waited.

They'd been on the road for about an hour, Karl, as usual, walking near the head of the column, when he heard a shout off to the left. He turned, shading his eyes, and saw one of his scouting parties emerging from the forest with someone else, clearly not a Holy Warrior, in tow.

For a moment he thought the Warriors must have stumbled on one of the Selkies who had escaped during the attack, but as they came nearer, he realized that the young man with them was a normal human, and as they came nearer still he frowned. The youth's face seemed strangely familiar.

Karl Rasmusson hadn't become Right Hand without a prodigious memory for names and faces. As the Holy Warriors brought the prisoner to him, and the column continued its steady, trudging march behind him toward the ridge, he said, "Chris Keating, I presume." He motioned to the guards, and they released their grip on the youth. One of them was holding a backpack, presumably Keating's; he dropped it to the ground, then unslung his rifle and stepped back watchfully. The other guard opened the backpack and began looking through it.

The Avatar ignored them and waited to hear what the prisoner would say.

Chris had hoped to walk up to the column freely, but he'd been intercepted by the Holy Warriors well back in the woods: possibly just as well, he had to admit, since they'd taken him in an entirely different direction than he'd thought he needed to go, and yet emerged from the forest right on top of the army. Left to his own devices, he'd still be wandering through the forest, if he hadn't fallen off a cliff by now.

He'd been pleasantly surprised by the size of the Avatar's force. Hundreds of heavily armed Holy Warriors, a few cargobots, even horses. The Kemonomimi didn't stand a chance if the Holy Warriors got through.

Well, it was his mission to see that they did.

He'd known at once that the man the Holy Warriors were leading him to—perhaps a bit more firmly than was really warranted—was the Avatar. Alone of all the men on the field, he wore black, relieved only by a thin braid of gold at the neck and wrists.

At last, Chris thought as he was half-dragged across the muddy field. *At last!*

It wasn't the way he'd always dreamed of it, of course. He used to picture himself being presented to the Avatar in the House of the Body in the City of God Itself, in the main sanctuary, probably with thousands of cheering citizens on hand to see him receive his just reward for having revealed the long-concealed hiding place of Victor Hansen's abominable creatures.

Richard Hansen had screwed up those plans, helping the Selkies survive the Holy Warrior attack, helping them spread their plague not only across the face of Marseguro but back to Earth itself.

And since then, of course, there had been no opportunity for Chris to talk to anyone within the Body and explain just how much he had done in God's service.

But here was the Avatar, at last, and if this muddy valley was not exactly the soaring marble-floored chamber he had dreamed of, it would do.

He'd already opened his mouth to introduce himself when the Avatar took the wind out of his sails by addressing him by name.

"Chris Keating, I presume," the Avatar said.

Chris closed his mouth, stunned—and immensely pleased. "Yes, Your Holiness," he said. "But how . . . ?"

"I was not Avatar before *BPS Retribution* brought you and the rest of its deadly cargo to Earth," the Avatar said. "I was Right Hand. It was my business to know who was aboard that ship when it returned. Unfortunately, we weren't aware of its true passenger list until it was too late." He folded his arms. Karl Rasmusson wasn't a large man, but he held himself with a kind of strength and determination that made Chris feel like an awkward boy. "Before I have you executed, tell me: how did you come to be here?"

Executed? Chris' pleasure of a moment before vanished like a pricked balloon. *No,* he thought, *no, no, no ... he doesn't understand ...*

"Your Holiness," he burst out, "I have been a True Believer all my life! So were my parents! The Selkies on Marseguro *murdered* my father. They let my mother die an early death. But I kept my faith and my determination to serve God. I was the one who activated the distress signal that led the Body to Marseguro. You have no more loyal follower than—"

"My patience is limited," the Avatar said. "Answer my question. The last I heard, you were imprisoned in the Holy Compound. How did you come to be here?"

"I was released from prison during the ... final days," Chris said. "I lived on my own, scavenging, for many weeks. Then the Kemonomimi came. They brought me here. They introduced me to their creator." And *here's* something I'll bet you don't know, Chris thought. "They introduced me to Victor Hansen."

The Avatar's eyes narrowed. "Another clone?"

Sharp, Chris thought with admiration. "Yes," he said. "Although he doesn't believe he's a clone. He thinks he's the real thing."

"Does he?" The Avatar smiled a little at that. "And he leads them?"

"Blasphemous though it might seem, they worship him."

The Avatar shrugged. "It's not blasphemous at all. They're not human, and he is their creator, or at least a reasonable facsimile thereof. Which was precisely why I had him secretly birthed at the same time as Richard Hansen."

"You . . . know about him?"

"Well, he didn't spring out of thin air," the Avatar said. "We hoped that Richard Hansen might be able to lead us to the Selkies, a hope that was fulfilled. It occurred to me that another clone might be able to lead us to the Kemonomimi . . . which he would have, if he hadn't managed to escape his incompetent guards a few years ago and vanish into the wilderness.

"But never mind that. So that's why you're here, in British Columbia. But why are you *here,* standing in front of me?"

"Because Victor Hansen has set a trap for you, Your Holiness," Chris said. He pointed up at the ridge. "Beyond that ridge is one last valley, the only way for your army to approach the town where the Kemonomimi lurk."

"I know that," the Avatar said impatiently. "Why do you think we're marching into it? But this Victor Hansen of yours has already sprung his trap—with the help of his fellow clone, Richard Hansen—and it failed. An assault craft attacked us yesterday. We lost a hundred men, but the craft was shot down. He's got nothing else."

"Yes, Your Holiness, he does," Chris said. He paused, enjoying the moment. How many times had he had information that, if only he could have gotten someone to listen, would have turned the tide in favor of the Body? Now, at last, he stood before the Avatar himself. Now, at last, no one would stop him from receiving the accolades he deserved.

"Well?" the Avatar snapped. There was a ripping sound behind Chris, and the Avatar's eyes flicked past him. Chris turned to see the man with his backpack tearing out its lining. *He won't find anything in there*, Chris thought. *There was barely enough stuff to keep me alive for a single night.*

Chris faced forward again. "There's a bomb," he said. "A massive bomb. A matter/antimatter device, Victor Hansen called it."

The Avatar frowned. "Massive?"

"Yes," Chris said. "They planted it in the valley. They're just waiting for all of you to be in there, and they'll set it off. It will kill you all.

"Victor Hansen's insane," he went on. *That should go without saying.* "He believes the Kemonomimi will inherit the Earth."

To Chris' surprise, the Avatar snorted with derision. "Hansen was lying to you. He might have some sort of bomb planted in the valley—but it certainly isn't a matter/antimatter bomb. They're tiny. You could hide one in a . . ." his eyes slid past Chris again, and his voice trailed off.

Chris turned around. The Holy Warrior, digging deep into the bottom of the backpack, had pulled out something the size and shape of a flattened grapefruit, made of silver metal, featureless except for three red lights on top.

No wonder the damn thing was so heavy, Chris thought. *I wonder what—*

It was his last thought, and it went unfinished.

The Avatar saw the flattened metal ovoid come out of the lining of Chris's backpack, and knew immediately what it was. He would have known even if he hadn't just been explaining it to Chris.

It was, indeed, a matter/antimatter bomb, its explosive force capable of being finely tuned, and designed for remote detonation. They were ideal for putting down insurrections on distant planets, where you might want to destroy a city or two but not poison the biosphere: they produced no fallout. As Right Hand but acting Avatar, Karl Rasmusson had personally signed off on their development and use against the insurrection on New

Mars. He'd seen detailed images of them, read their specifications, studied their schematics. He'd also seen vids of the destruction of Burroughston by just such a device as he now, for the first time, saw close up.

It's another test, he thought, heart suddenly racing. *It must be. We'll have to disarm it, prove once and for all to God Itself that we are worthy to serve it. Perhaps God wants us to use it on the Kemonomimi. And after that—*

But there was no "after that."

Without even time to be astonished or disappointed that the God he had served all his life had utterly abandoned him, Karl Rasmusson, last Avatar of the Body Purified on Earth, vanished with all his remaining Holy Warriors in a fireball of pure energy brighter than the sun.

The flash came first. Fortunately *Creator's Glory* was facing away from the explosion, so Richard wasn't blinded by it, but even the reflection off the snow-covered peaks in front of them made him cry out and throw his arm up over his eyes. Claude, with his more sensitive Selkie eyes, screamed and ducked down behind the control panel. Surprised shouts echoed from the passenger compartment.

The blast wave hit them seconds later.

The shuttle groaned with the impact as it was hurled skyward, the sudden acceleration pressing Richard down into his couch twice as hard as he'd ever been stomped on by G-force at takeoff. Claude, half out of his chair, was smashed to the cockpit floor, his breath whooshing out in an explosive grunt. More shouts of surprise and pain sounded in the passenger compartment.

Then suddenly they were dropping, falling into turbulence that threatened to shake Richard's teeth from his jaw as he forced himself upright and reached for the controls.

"I think my arm is broken," Claude moaned. "What's happened?"

"An explosion. Big one. Nuclear, maybe." Richard's hands flicked over the controls. "Half our systems are down. Claude, I need you. You're the expert."

Claude hauled himself into his chair again, left arm cradled against his chest. His face had gone pale, but he reached out with his right and studied the controls. "Looks like I'm not the only one with a busted wing," he said. "I think something punched a hole in one. Compensating with main thrusters." He moved his hand across the board, and Richard felt himself pushed down into his chair again. Their rate of descent slowed to something that almost looked controlled . . . but it didn't stop.

"We don't have full power. We don't have enough lift to gain altitude," Claude said.

"Can we reorient, head for space?"

"Ground-to-orbit engines are offline. Looks like they took a hit, too." He looked at Richard. "We're going down. The best we can hope for is a controlled crash."

Richard took a deep breath. "All right," he said. "Can we make the sea?"

Claude punched a control, called up a map. "Maybe."

"Go for it."

"Yes, sir." Claude took his own deep breath, one that caught on a moan, then leaned in to the controls.

Richard unsnapped himself and made his unsteady way back to the passenger compartment. Around him, *Creator's Glory* bucked and jumped. Beneath all the sharp, sudden motions, he could feel a deep, shuddering vibration.

Most of his crew seemed to be intact, although Dominique had a nasty cut on her forehead that Chang was tending. "What happened, sir?" she asked.

"I don't know," he said. "Someone set off a bomb. Maybe a nuclear one."

"The Avatar took out the town?" Chang said.

Richard shook his head. "It wasn't the town. It came from behind us, up in the mountains. I think someone just took out the Avatar."

"The Earth Selkies?"

"The Kemonomimi?"

Dominique and Chang spoke at once.

"I don't know," Richard said again. "But whoever it was almost took us out as well." He had to grab the back of one of the chairs as the shuttle lurched. "We're too damaged to keep flying and too damaged to make orbit. We're going down, and we may not have much choice as to where.

"We're going to try to make the sea for a water landing. Failing that, we'll look for somewhere flat. But, whatever happens, it's going to be rough.

"So secure everything that's loose and then secure yourselves. It won't be long."

As if to emphasize that fact, the shuttle lurched again.

Richard made his way back to the cockpit, trying not to think about the one thing he couldn't help but think about: where had Emily and Shelby been when that bomb went off?

If they'd been captured by the Avatar, they might have been in his camp. And if they were . . .

Not for the first time, Richard wished he still had a God to pray to.

Creator's Glory groaned and rolled left, throwing him hard against the wall of the short corridor between the cockpit and passenger compartment. It righted itself reluctantly.

If he had such a God, he just might be offering a prayer for himself, too.

Emily and Shelby were taking a break from their steady downhill trek, soaking in a relatively calm pool in the stream at a place where it wound through a small, flat-bottomed valley. Emily was underwater when the bright blue sky she could see above her through the rippled surface suddenly turned white, the ripples sparking cold and sharp as diamonds for a moment.

The light vanished. Emily surged upward. Shelby had been sitting on a rock on the shore, nursing his bandaged leg, but she found him standing now, staring back the way they had come, toward the high ridge that lay between them and the Avatar's camp. That ridge had been prickly with the tops of distant pine trees: now it was bare, and black smoke and dust boiled up from its far side, climbing high into the air to join a mushroom-shaped column that told Emily more than she wanted to know about what had just happened.

"The bastard did it," she breathed.

"What?" Shelby said.

"Victor Hansen. He blew up the Avatar. All those men . . . they're gone."

The ridge had protected them from the blast. It couldn't protect them for long from any radioactive fallout that—should the weapon have been nuclear, and it sure looked that way—might soon be coming down from those clouds of smoke and dust now stretching up high enough to blot out the bright sunshine of a few moments earlier.

"Let's get moving," she said. "The sooner we're under deep water the better."

Shelby nodded. He looked scared as he glanced over his shoulder one more time at the towering cloud, and Emily couldn't blame him. She was scared, too, and not just because of whatever risk the cloud might pose to the two of them.

If Victor Hansen had weapons like that at his disposal, what hope did the Selkies or nonmod survivors of Earth have against the Kemonomimi?

She splashed over to the shore and joined Shelby, and the two of them begin hurrying downhill. The little flat-bottomed valley petered away oddly at its western end, and as they got there Emily realized why: beyond it, the land fell away sharply down to the sea, which she could see now, calm and beautiful, looking so much like the ocean of Marseguro that she felt her breath catch in her throat and her gills tingled.

And the streambed they were following flowed right into the river that in turn flowed through Newshore, whose roofs and runway she could see not all that far below.

Flowed?

In fact, she suddenly realized, the stream had almost stopped flowing. She looked back up the valley. Water still glimmered in pools, but very little was coming down. *Debris from the blast must have dammed it*, she thought. *Well, we're almost to the sea. Plenty of water there.* She looked back out at it again, its sunlit waves so inviting, especially with the tower of smoke and dust looming to the west. At least the prevailing winds seemed to be pushing that ominous cloud inland.

Shelby joined her. "We're not going through the town, are we?" he said.

"Not if I can help it," Emily said. "We'll stick to the stream till it levels out down there, right where it joins the river." She pointed. "Then we'll head off through the woods. How's your leg?"

"It's . . ." Shelby's head jerked around. "What's that noise?"

Emily heard it, too, then, a growing, screaming roar. She spun around and looked up just in time to see a shuttle, trailing smoke, sky showing through a gaping hole in one wing, burst into view over the valley. It hurtled over their heads so close it almost looked like she should be able to touch it, then plunged onward, shuddering, rolling from side to side so violently she expected it to turn sideways and crash at any second, but somehow remaining under control.

It screamed low over the town, braking rockets thundering, and she thought she could see movement, Kemonomimi running for their lives: and then it hit.

It pancaked down onto the runway, hard, but not fatally hard, she thought, and slid along it in a shrieking shower of sparks, smoke and dust. The runway ended: the shuttle kept going, ripping through fencing, tearing through bushes, finally sliding onto the beach in a geyser of sand and stones and then, almost gracefully, turning sideways, slipping lengthwise into the ocean in a huge explosion of spray and steam, close by the mouth of the river.

"Who . . . ?" Shelby said.

"I don't know," Emily said, but her heart screamed, *Richard!* "Let's get down there."

They lost sight of the town and the crashed shuttle behind the trees almost as soon as they started to descend. Emily would have galloped down the slope, but she could move no faster than Shelby could hobble on his wounded leg.

About fifteen minutes along, she heard a new sound, a new roaring. For a moment she thought it must be another shuttle, but it had a different quality, more organic, somehow, like ocean waves, like—

She spun and stared back up the streambed to the mouth of the valley they'd just left, just in time to see the massive wave of muddy, tree-choked water explode over the edge and begin pouring down the slope toward them.

The impact, when it came, was harder than Richard expected. It drove the breath from his body and made him see stars, tossed him like a rag doll in his restraints until his teeth chattered. He bit his tongue hard, and tasted blood. But the shuttle didn't disintegrate, and the cockpit window, designed to withstand micrometeor impacts in orbit, didn't break, and when the thunderous roar and scream of tortured metal finally ceased, Richard found himself looking up through the cockpit at the rippled underside of waves, shaken, tongue sore—hell, *everything* sore—but essentially undamaged.

Then, of course, the water stared pouring in.

The wall of water hit Emily and Shelby like the proverbial ton of bricks, and there was nothing they could do about it. Emily lost sight of Shelby instantly, as she was plunged beneath the flood. Drowning didn't worry her, though the muddy water felt gritty and unpleasant in her gills. But trees and rocks and other debris rode the water with her, and she had no control. Tumbled end over end, she banged hard against something, felt something else smash her in the side so hard she thought she felt a rib crack, then finally got her head to the surface and was able to see where she was going, though she still wasn't strong enough to fight the current. Then the swollen stream shot her into the much wider river. She found herself more or less in the middle of it, away from the trees that bent, and in some cases broke and uprooted, in the muddy torrent carrying her faster than she could have run down toward the sea.

But before the sea came the town.

The water rose faster than Richard would have believed possible, pooling around his ankles, lapping at his knees, almost reaching his waist before he could even get his restraints unsnapped. It rushed in around the edges of the cockpit window, which had apparently sprung despite being uncracked, and bubbled in from under his feet. One of the last things Claude had done before the impact had been to kill all power systems; earlier, he had dumped the remaining fuel from the main tanks, leaving just enough for braking. If not, Richard suspected he would either now be electrocuting or they all would have gone up in a massive fireball.

Claude! He turned to help the pilot, and congratulate him on getting them down safely, but the words died on his lips. Claude's head hung at an unnatural angle, and blood stained his lips. His sightless eyes stared at Richard.

His neck was broken.

Richard felt a surge of black anger at the universe, or maybe the God he claimed no longer to believe in, but there was no time for grieving or cursing: the water had climbed above his waist and he couldn't breathe it like more than half his crew could.

With difficulty he pulled himself uphill into the passenger compartment. "Anyone hurt?" he said.

"I've felt better," someone said, but everyone was moving, though some were bloodied and bruised.

"Let's get out of here," he said.

"What about Claude?" Dominique called from the rear.

"Dead. Come on. Out the back hatch."

Manually undogging the inner air lock door, and then the outer one, took a good five minutes, but finally Richard pushed open the outside door and let a flood of cool, salt-smelling air into the shuttle's muggy, stale interior.

The first thing Richard saw, framed by the hatch, was the towering cloud of dust and smoke to the east, behind the first ridge of the mountains. Thankfully, it was being pushed away by a strong west wind, the same wind that slapped a steady surge of surf against the beach and the bow of the shuttle. Spray drenched the small portion of him not already wet as he at last emerged into the open.

He brought his gaze down from that vast gray tower to see the Kemonomimi waiting for them.

They ranged along the beach, fifteen men and women, unclothed, furred, armed with long knives and automatic rifles, their slit-pupiled eyes staring at him as he eased himself out, so that he felt rather like a mouse at a cat convention. They looked more inhuman and alien than ever.

But beyond the immediate welcoming committee, he could see other Kemonomimi: unarmed, most of them, among them many children of varying sizes. They'd come rushing down to the water's edge to see the wrecked shuttle, but now they hung back, on the wooden bridge that spanned the river and on either bank, watching.

Richard still remembered clearly the little girl he had seen in her mother's arms in the Holy Warriors' holding pen just off the pier in Hansen's Harbor, when he still imagined he served the Body Purified. Her frightened face had had as much to do with changing his allegiance, he sometimes thought, as anything else that had happened.

These people aren't our enemies, he thought. *They should be our allies. They're moddies, like the Selkies, but they're also still human, like all of us.*

There are no aliens here.

And then, from behind the front rank of cat-people, an ordinary human being stepped to the fore, an ordinary human whose face was as familiar to Richard as his own, because in most respects it *was* his own.

Richard stared. "You're—"

"Victor Hansen," the man said. "Creator and leader of the Kemonomimi. Creator, too, to my vast regret, of those fishy monstrosities I see behind you." He made a gesture with his free hand, and all the rifles in Kemonomimi hands rose and aimed at the air lock: at *him*. "Get everyone out here. Now."

Slowly, Richard climbed down onto the pebbled beach. Behind him, the shuttle hissed and popped as metal cooled. The long muddy gouge they had plowed on their way to the beach stretched away past the Kemonomimi, scattered with debris from smashed fences, bushes, and one unfortunate house. He hoped no one had been in it.

The rest of the crew climbed down as well, though a couple needed help to reach the beach and then had to lean against someone else for support.

"I know who you are," Victor Hansen said. "You are my clone, Richard Hansen."

"I'm not *your* clone," Richard said evenly. "I'm a clone of the original Victor Hansen. As are you."

Victor laughed. "I'm no clone. I remember creating the Selkies, and the Kemonomimi. I sent the Selkies away to safety—my biggest mistake, after creating them, but apparently I was sentimental, then. I rolled back my own aging and, young once more, went to find my *true* children. *Homo sapiens hanseni*. The Kemonomimi. The race that, thanks to the plague I engineered, thanks to my destruction of the last Avatar and his Holy Warriors—" he pointed at the towering black cloud, "—will now rule the world."

Richard looked at the Selkies and nonmods ranged on either side of him. "There are others on this world," he said. He didn't mention the Earth Selkies: didn't know if "Victor" knew they existed. "They deserve to live, too."

"They can live," Victor said dismissively. "If they ultimately survive my plague, which I doubt. But they cannot be allowed to rule: not themselves, and not my people."

Richard didn't speak for a moment. He remembered everything he had read about the real Victor Hansen, the one who had led the Selkies to safety on Marseguro. He'd been utterly dedicated to his new race, willing to do whatever was necessary to save them.

But he'd never even mentioned the Kemonomimi, never told his new race of moddies that they were his second creation. He had apparently utterly repudiated the cat-people, making no effort at all to rescue them from the Body Purified after the Day of Salvation.

This clone, the only one in which the gene-bomb Victor Hansen had designed to implant his memories and personality had apparently functioned as intended, had simply made the mirror-image decision of the original.

But he's not *the original,* Richard said. *No more than I am.*

"Anton," he called. "Will you step forward, please?"

A Selkie roughly the size of a small mountain detached himself from the rest of the crew and came to stand beside Richard. "Are you thinking what I'm thinking?" he growled to Richard. He had the most amazingly deep voice Richard had ever heard.

"Tell them," Richard said.

Anton raised his voice to a pretty good approximation of thunder. "When I was a small boy on Marseguro," he said, "I met Victor Hansen. He was almost ninety Earth years old at the time, frail and liver-spotted, but still alert. He shook my hand and told me to keep studying science. And two weeks later, he died." Anton pointed at the nonmod among the Kemonomimi. "This man is not Victor Hansen. He is a clone of the original."

Richard didn't know what kind of reaction he expected. Howls, maybe, or shaking fists. But the Kemonomimi barely reacted at all . . . although a few heads turned in "Victor's" direction. For his part, Victor only smiled. "You cannot turn my people against me with simple lies," he said. "They know who I am."

"How?" Richard said. "Because you told them?" He raised his own voice. "Look at me! Look at your so-called creator! We could be brothers—because we *are* brothers. Identical twins, separated only by our birth dates. I'm a clone, too. I'm a clone of Victor Hansen, the *real* Victor Hansen. And so is your creator!"

Did Victor's smile slip a little? Richard couldn't be sure. He *was* sure, though, that the Kemonomimi were looking closely from him to their Victor, and though the front rank remained poised, the children and adults farther back along the river were murmuring among themselves.

"You cannot shake my people's faith in their creator," Victor said. "And if you continue to attempt to do so, I—"

"You'll shoot us all?" Richard said. He kept his voice loud, wanting everyone to hear him. "For making your people question their faith? You sound just like the Avatar."

That got through. Victor's face reddened. "The Avatar is dead," he said. He jabbed a finger again at the towering cloud. "His ashes lie beneath that cloud. The Body Purified is finished, thanks to me and my Kemonomimi. And now we will claim the Earth for our own, as is our right."

"The Avatar is dead," Richard said bitterly. "Long live the Avatar."

"I've heard enough," Victor snapped. "Take them to the . . ."

But nobody was listening to him.

A rumble had suddenly made itself felt through the ground, and the air filled with a rushing, roaring sound like a great wind, or a forest fire, or . . .

"Flood!" someone screamed. The Kemonomimi on the bridge, mostly children, started to scatter to either end of it. The Kemonomimi along the riverbank turned to run.

Most of them didn't make it.

A wall of brown water, debris swirling and tossing within it, swept down the riverbank and smashed into the bridge.

The bridge groaned, children screamed, and then the bridge collapsed, dumping everyone on it into the swirling water that had also sucked in dozens of Kemonomimi along its banks.

The Kemonomimi closest to Richard tossed down their weapons and ran toward the river. "Wait!" Victor shouted after them, but they ignored him.

"Come on," Richard shouted to his own crew, and those that could ran toward the flooded river.

Already the surge of water had subsided, but it had done its damage. Here and there heads bobbed in the water. Children screamed as the current carried them farther out into the bay. Some of the Kemonomimi had splashed in after them, but it was obvious few among the cat-people were strong swimmers. Many simply stood on shore, weeping and shouting. Others ran for the boats, but they were a kilometer from the pier.

"Into the water!" he shouted to the Selkies. "Get as many as you can!"

The Selkies in his crew were already shimmying out of landsuits and hurling themselves into the river and the Bay. Almost at once they began hauling victims to the shore. Richard wished, not for the first time, that he had more in common with the Selkies than just the genetic sequence that protected him from the plague, but he was as helpless in the water as any nonmod. Nevertheless, he waded into the surf to help bring the victims up onto the shore as the Selkies retrieved them, and sent one of the nonmods from his crew back to the shuttle to bring all the first-aid and survival equipment they had down to help in the effort.

As the minutes past, the frantic effort slowed, then ceased. The Selkies continued to swim back and forth across the bay, searching for any remaining victims, but it soon became apparent any Kemonomimi who could be found had already been found.

Richard stood panting on the shore. Not far away, Chang ministered to a little Kemonomimi girl with a broken arm. Others from his crew were handing out blankets.

A few other blankets had been laid over bodies.

Richard became aware someone was standing behind him. He turned to find himself face-to-face with Victor.

"This doesn't change anything," Victor snarled. "The Kemonomimi will rule Earth." He held something in his hand; for a moment Richard thought it was a weapon, but it looked too small: it looked like a globe of glass.

Richard heard a strange sound in the Bay, and turned to look. Out between the headlands, something emerged from the water, a long, black, rounded shape: a submarine. And clinging to its sides as it rose were Selkies: twenty at least, maybe more.

"*They* might have something to say about that," Richard said.

Hansen's eyes had widened. "How many of those fishy devils did you bring with you from Marseguro?" he snarled.

"They're not from Marseguro," Richard said. "They're from Earth. The Selkies have been living here right alongside you since the Day of Salvation. And they're not going to hand the planet over to a new dictator just because he's a clone of their creator."

"I'm not a clone," Hansen snapped, then shouted, "Kemonomimi! To arms!"

The Kemonomimi looked out at the submarine. A few of them picked up rifles that were close at hand, but they held them pointed down, and looked at each other uncertainly.

One of Richard's crew had just emerged from the water a few feet away. Richard ran down to her. "Get out there," he said. "Tell them not to do anything aggressive."

She nodded, dove cleanly into the surf, and disappeared from sight.

Hansen was running up and down the beach, grabbing rifles and putting them into his people's hands. "We're being attacked!" he shouted. "What's wrong with you?"

He stopped in front of a white-furred Kemonomimi woman, picked up a rifle from the ground and shoved it into her hands. "Cleopatra, why aren't you armed?"

Cleopatra looked down at the rifle, then looked up

at him. "I don't see any enemies," she said. "None of us do." She looked along the beach; the Kemonomimi stood silent, watching her and Hansen.

"I am ordering you—"

"I think we've had enough orders," Cleo said. "The Avatar is dead. The Body Purified is no more. We've fought and hidden for decades from both. Now that we've won, you want us to start a new war with a new enemy. But the first thing this new enemy of yours has done is help to rescue our friends and our children." She threw the rifle to one side. "I see no enemy."

Rifles clattered to the beach in all directions.

"They're watching us," Hansen growled then. "The Selkies. My worst mistake. They're watching us now for weakness. They've just seen you disarm yourselves. You think they're not your enemies. But that's not how they think about you. They'll try to take the world, now that we've killed the Avatar. They don't want to share it with you."

"We will fight if we must," Cleo said. "We always have. But we won't fight just because you say so. We won't kill just to kill." She looked him up and down, gave Richard a similarly searching look, then looked back at Hansen. "Clone."

Hansen's grip on the strange sphere he carried tightened. He glared at Cleopatra; but then his gaze slid further along the beach, and a strange smile flicked across his face. "We'll see." He strode past her.

Cleo didn't even turn around. But Richard, puzzled, looked past him. Further along the bank, he saw two figures, Selkies, one lying on the ground, one bending over the first. He blinked. That zebra-striped skinsuit looked just like the one that belonged to . . .

"Emily!" he shouted, and ran after Victor.

In the final mad rush through the town Emily twice came close to being crushed between tree trunks whirl-

ing like giant bludgeons through the foam, escaping
only by plunging deep into the turbulent waters. But she
didn't dare stay submerged either, because the water
was so muddy she could see nothing down there, and
didn't know when a rock or broken stump might suddenly appear to smash her.

The swollen river scoured its banks as it thundered
through Newshore, collapsing piers, smashing boats against
the sides of buildings. An entire boathouse collapsed as she
swirled past, and she could see the water breaking against
the sides of houses on either bank, knocking one off its
foundation but not quite carrying it along.

And then ... up ahead, the sea, but before the sea, a
bridge, an ornamental wooden bridge, spanning the river,
crowded with people ... Kemonomimi, she realized ...
looking the other way, at the crashed shuttle ... and
then they were looking her way, and though she couldn't
hear them above the sound of the river, she could see
the round shapes of their mouths as they screamed, and
then they ran, but they were too late.

The river was going to crush her against the side of
the bridge like a bug, she suddenly realized, and she
dove at the last possible moment, sweeping under the
collapsing span. Suddenly she spilled out into the sea,
the water going from fresh to salt in an instant, but she
wasn't alone anymore, she was surrounded by struggling
Kemonomimi, many of them children, screaming, flail-
ing, sinking.

She plunged beneath the waves and found a small
body she had seen disappear into the water an instant
before, turned, and swam strongly toward the shore, ignoring as best she could the jabbing, fiery pain in her side
from the cracked rib. She struggled out of the sea with
the child, his fur soaked and bedraggled, coughing and
choking in her arms, handed him to the waiting arms of
a Kemonomimi on the shore, turned, and plunged back
into the waves.

For a few moments all was chaos. She dove, peering through the water of the bay, muddied by the outflow of the river but still clear enough that she found two more children as they sank, kicking feebly, toward the bottom.

In the end, there were no more Kemonomimi to find. She'd been aware there were other Selkies in the Bay, assumed they must be from the crashed shuttle, but there'd been no time to talk to them, no time to find out what had happened, no time for anything but the frantic effort to save as many lives as she could.

At last she found herself on the beach, sucking air into her lungs as best she could, one hand pressed against her damaged side. She glanced down the beach, saw the crashed shuttle, but then saw something else on the pebbles much closer to it, a young Selkie lying there motionless, and ran to Shelby's side.

For a moment she was certain he was dead, but his eyes fluttered open as her shadow fell across his face. "Made it . . . to the sea," he said. "What a ride, huh?"

She smoothed her hand across his short black hair. "It sure was," she said, with a huge sense of relief. "It sure was."

"My leg . . . hurts . . ." he said, and when she looked she saw why: the same leg that had been shot now lay at an unnatural angle, clearly broken.

"Just a break," she said. "You'll be all right."

"Good," he said. He closed his eyes. "I'd really like to go home," he said faintly.

"Emily!" she heard someone shout, and her heart leaped.

"Richard!" She looked up at the familiar face on the man running toward her . . .

. . . on the *two* men running toward her . . .

She lunged to her feet, then froze, as Victor Hansen stopped not a meter away, pistol in one hand, something else in the other. Keeping the gun aimed at her, he circled up the beach so that he could watch Richard . . . God, it really was Richard! . . . running toward them.

"Stop or I'll shoot her," Victor said, almost conversationally, and Richard skidded to a halt, breathing heavily.

"This won't accomplish anything," Richard panted. "You've already lost the Kemonomimi. They won't follow you now."

"Won't they?" Victor looked out at the sea, where the Selkie sub was now just a hundred or so yards offshore. The Selkies on it were watching the beach. Atop the sail, a man with binoculars seemed focused on them; Emily heard him shout something. "So many Selkies close at hand. Good."

He looked at Richard. "My great flaw, as a young man, was too much compassion. That's why I helped the Selkies escape. But I have regretted it bitterly since. My Kemonomimi are young, they share that flaw. But I will not let it keep them from their destiny."

He held up the globe in his hand. "I pride myself on using the best tool for any task. To remove the Body from power, the plague. To remove the Avatar permanently, a matter/antimatter bomb of the Body's own design. And to remove the Selkies from the equation . . . this."

He held up the globe so that the sun shone on it. Its contents, the color of gold, glinted in the light. "I intended to give this its first test on Emily and the boy in my hidden lab, but the Avatar's scouts interrupted our journey there. No matter: I'm confident in my work." He lowered the sphere, smiled at Richard. "It's the plague," he said. "The same plague that has cleansed the Body from the Earth . . . but with two small alterations.

"One: your vaccine will not work against it. Two: Selkies are not immune to this version. Kemonomimi are." He gestured to Emily and Shelby. "When I smash this vial, the new version of the plague will begin to colonize Earth's biosphere, helped along by a rather clever set of self-replicating nanomachines. The plague will spread from this spot all over the world. These two—" he indicated Shelby and Emily, "—will be Case One and Case Two. But soon enough, every Selkie—and every remaining nonmod—will be dead. And the Kemonomimi will finally have the world they deserve."

Emily stared at him, hating him. How could she hate him so much, she wondered, when just beyond him stood his identical twin, a man she loved more than she had ever loved anyone before?

"You'll die, too," Richard said. "If you've made the immunity specific to something in the Kemonomimi DNA . . ."

"Nonsense," Victor said. "I said *your* vaccine will not work against it. Mine, on the other hand, works just fine." He held up the vial again. "Enough talk. Welcome to your new world." He pulled his arm back to throw the vial—

A single shot rang out, and a neat hole appeared in Victor's chest, a hole that vanished a moment later in a gout of blood.

He dropped to his knees, and as the vial fell from his suddenly nerveless fingers, Emily leaped forward. She caught the glass globe in midair and cradled it to her like a child as she rolled over and over in the sand, the cracked rib stabbing her side like a red-hot knife.

Victor looked down at the sea of red spreading across his chest with a look of utter disbelief, then fell to his knees. He looked down toward the sea, where Cleopatra was just lowering her rifle.

"You . . ." Victor choked out. "You . . . I loved you . . . I created you . . . and you've betrayed me . . . you've betrayed your Creator . . ."

"I hear it's the human thing to do," Cleo whispered, and as Victor Hansen pitched forward onto the pebbles and died, she dropped her rifle, covered her face, and wept.

Emily heard horrific, wrenching sobs from somewhere else, and turned her head to look inland.

Just above the beach, on the road to Newshore, the black-furred Kemonomimi woman Ubasti knelt, mourning her Creator.

Chapter 23

TWO WEEKS LATER, Richard sat in the captain's chair on the bridge of *MSS Victor Hansen*, with Emily standing behind him, hands on his shoulders. The bridge crew were in place, the computer once more firmly under his command, thanks to Simon Goodfellow, and President McLean was on the main communications screen, her son visible behind her.

"It looks like there are more survivors than we'd estimated, scattered around the planet," McLean was saying. "And we're bringing more and more microfactories on line to produce vaccine, every one we can track down and program with Ann and Jerry's help. The South Africans Andy King contacted have been almost evangelical in their zeal to spread the vaccine around the globe. Cleo ... sorry, Prime Minister Cleopatra ... and her Kemonomimi have North America covered. And every time another microfactory goes on line, the supply increases and more people fan out to find still more survivors. We're still losing people, but we're reaching everyone we can."

"Any more trouble with the Body enclaves?" Richard asked. In the first week or so after the Avatar's death, they'd contacted all the Body outposts around the planet from the Avatar's old base at Paradise Island and told them of the new reality. Most had promptly agreed to help with the vaccine distribution, but a few had gone ominously silent, and in Gdansk a few Holy Warriors in pressure suits had raided a vaccine-producing microfactory in a former cheese plant, destroying the factory and taking the vaccine for themselves.

The remaining assault craft, recovered from the bottom of the ocean—the third had been found wrecked in the Himalayas—had been sent into the area with a Kemonomimi pilot at the controls, and when the Holy Warriors emerged for a second raid, they'd found themselves seriously outgunned. A few had tried to fight, and those few had died. The others had surrendered.

"No," McLean said. "Though I'm sure they'll be more trouble in the future. True Believers can go underground for years."

Richard thought of Chris Keating. "I know," he said. "What about Victor's pet bug?"

"We haven't found his laboratory in the mountains yet; the Kemonomimi swear he never told any of them where it was. But the vial he had on the beach went into a plasma torch."

Richard heard Emily's breath catch. "There could be more of that Selkie-killing virus lurking somewhere?" she said.

"We'll find his lab," McLean said. "It's only a matter of time."

That troubled Richard, and he was sure Emily was no happier about it, but there was nothing to be done.

"How are you doing, Shelby?" Emily asked.

Shelby moved forward to come into better focus. "Pretty good," he said. "My leg's getting stronger all the time. I still have that gill rash from the dirty water, but it's clearing up."

"Mine, too," Emily said. "And I can breathe without it hurting now. So it looks like we're both on the mend."

Shelby looked like he was going to say something else, but then he looked at Richard; then at his mother;

and finally cleared his throat and said, "Have a good trip back to Marseguro."

"Your mother is standing by, Emily," President McLean said. She reached out, and the camera panned left, revealing Dr. Christianson-Wood.

"Emily," she said. "Give my regards to Marseguro."

"It's not too late to come home with us," Emily said, with the tone of someone who had already lost an argument but was too stubborn to admit it.

"I'll come home some day, Emily. But not for a while. They need my help. The vaccine works, but it may not be a hundred percent effective—there's been some genetic drift between Earth and Marseguro over the years, you know. And it's taking a terrible toll among nonhuman primates, too." She spread her hands. "I created this monster, Emily. I never meant it to reach Earth, but it has. I let the genie out of the bottle, and now I've got to try to force it back in. I've got all the resources I need to create a countervirus, one even more infectious than the plague, but one that provides immunity rather than causes disease." Her eyes unfocused for a moment. "I can see exactly how to do it," she said. "If I . . ." She blinked, then looked right at the camera again. "Sorry," she said. "Short version: I can do it, but it might take a year or three. Then I'll see about coming home. Or who knows? Maybe you two will decide to live here."

"I daresay we'll be back and forth," Richard said, but he knew in his heart he would never live on Earth again. Marseguro was home now, with Emily. There was still so much to be rebuilt there, not just infrastructure, but trust between nonmods and Selkies. Plus, they had seventy years' worth of Earth's technological knowledge stored in their computers, and holds full of modern microfactories and raw materials with which to manufacture that technology. With it, they could spread humanity across Marseguro, free from the fear of discovery that had hampered their society's development for so long.

Free, at least, from the fear of discovery by Holy Warriors on Earth.

"President McLean," Richard said, and the camera panned back to her. "I know resources are limited, but you've got to get more manned ships into orbit. I don't imagine anyone will approach Earth right away, not with the stories of the deadliness of the plague spreading out among the colonies. But there are still Body Purified ships, and Holy Warriors, out there. And eventually, they're going to try to return."

"We'll be ready," President McLean said. "Will Marseguro?"

"We'll do our best." Among the microfactories aboard *Victor Hansen* were the seed factories for starship manufacture, but it would be months before they could bootstrap their way to full-scale dockyards, even assuming the minebots could find the resources needed on Marseguro's one landmass, deep in its ocean, or among its system's asteroids.

"I am not a Believer in the Body Purified," the president said, "but I believe in a God: a kind and loving God, not the monster created by the First Avatar in his own image. I'll be praying for Marseguro, Richard Hansen, and for Earth. We've both undergone our baptism by fire. I'm confident God has better things in store for us in the future."

Richard didn't know how to respond to that. He had believed in the First Avatar's God, and that belief had been shattered. He couldn't now—he doubted he *ever* could—put that shattered belief back together ... and even if he could, after all the death and pain of the past few months the God he thought he would find would be anything but kind and loving.

So he said nothing.

Emily cleared her throat. "Thank you, Madame President," she said quietly. "I'm sure a great many people on both planets will join you in that prayer."

President McLean nodded, then said briskly, "I have a Provisional Planetary Council meeting with Prime Minister Cleopatra and our respective staffs in ten minutes," she said, "so I'd best cut this short. Have a safe trip home and . . ." She smiled suddenly. "Thank you. For everything."

"Thank you, Madame President," Richard said. "Good-bye, Shelby. Good-bye, Dr. Christianson-Wood."

" 'Bye, Shel," Emily said. " 'Bye, Mom. I love you."

"I love you, too, sweetie," her mother said. "Tell Amy I love her, too, and I'm sorry I missed her wedding. Oh, and tell John Duval that if he doesn't treat her properly, I'll design another plague, just for him, personally." She smiled, blinking back tears. "Good-bye."

The screen went blank.

Richard heard Emily's soft sob, even if no one else did. He reached up and took her hands, warm on his shoulders, and squeezed them, and felt her lean forward and kiss the top of his head. He smiled.

"All right, then," he said. "Let's go home."

Edward Willett

TERRA INSEGURA
978-0-7564-0553-3

MARSEGURO
978-07564-0464-2

LOST IN TRANSLATION
978-0-7564-0340-9

"We have reversals of fortune, reversals of loyalty, and battles to satisfy the most bloodthirsty fan."
—*SF Scope*

"The action and surprises keep coming. Willett sets his scenes, establishes the Selkies as loving, intelligent, almost cute creatures, and then lets loose with nonstop action and plot development."—*Sci Fi Weekly*

"Brisk-paced space opera...Willett delivers a neatly constructed plot, peopled with lots of aliens, i ncluding a ruthless S'sinn warmonger and a chilling human traitor.."—*SF Site*

To Order Call: 1-800-788-6262
www.dawboks.com